WANTON ANGEL

The way he moved his thumb over the back of her hand sent delightful chills along Saxan's arm, but she retained enough wit to say, "You want sons."

Botolf edged closer to her, lightly caressing the side of her neck with his other hand. "What man does not? I also wish to enjoy the making of those sons," he said in a soft, husky voice. "I do not need to tell you that I would enjoy the bedding of you." He smiled gently when she blushed and lightly kissed her cheek. "You know that I desire you."

"Ah, but desire can be a fleeting thing, burning sweet and hot for a time, then turning to ashes."

She found it somewhat difficult to think clearly when he moved even closer. He slipped one strong arm around her shoulders and held her near. It was not necessary, for she was already leaning into him. He slowly covered her face with warm, soft kisses, firing her blood and clouding her thoughts. She clutched at his broad shoulders as she succumbed to the need to touch him and steady herself.

"Desire has never run so hot or so sweet for me," he whispered as he teasingly nibbled at her earlobes.

"If I do not say aye to marrying you, I will still say aye to this," Saxan whispered.

A soft, hungry sound escaped Botolf as he gave Saxan the kiss she craved . . .

* * *

ZEBRA BOOKS
KENSINGTON PUBLISHING CORP.

ZEBRA BOOKS are published by

Kensington Publishing Corp.
850 Third Avenue
New York, NY 10022

First Printing: July, 1995

Printed in the United States of America

Prologue

Northern England—1319

Saxan Honey Todd was startled awake by her own cries. She shivered as she sat up, the cool air in her bedchambers rapidly drying the sweat soaking her chemise. Fear was an acrid burning in the back of her throat. The images that had tormented her into waking up still haunted her. She lay back down, huddling beneath her blankets, and struggled to convince herself that it was only a dream.

It was hard to shake the feeling that she had just foreseen her twin brother Pitney's death. The image of his murderer was so clear it was as if he stood by her bedside, his dark features twisted into a triumphant smile as her brother's blood dripped slowly from his hands. She doubted she would ever forget that face with its dark beauty only faintly marred by a small scar near his left eye, his eyes as dark and cold as a grave.

" 'Tis but a dream," she whispered, burying her face in her pillows as she fought to banish the image of the dark man.

Sighing with resignation after a few moments, Saxan finally accepted that the dream had ended her chances for a good night's sleep. She turned onto her back to stare up at the ceiling. The worst of her fear had passed, but a lingering unease had settled itself firmly in her heart.

"I pray you are safe, Pitney," she said aloud, slowly clenching her hands. "But if this dream proves to be a prophecy and not just some vision born of my concern for you, your spirit can seek its rest without hesitation. I swear upon all the Todds who have gone before us that, if you are murdered, your killer will not live out the year. I myself will cut the villain's black heart from his body."

One

Banners fluttered noisily in the cool spring breeze. Botolf Corwine Lavington muttered a curse as he pushed aside a stray lock of raven hair, but his dark gaze never faltered from the crowd. The knights' shields and colors were well displayed outside each tent. None of them were the ones he sought, but he was not surprised. His enemy had become increasingly secretive. The Earl of Caindale and his guests began to seek the seats from which they would view the tourney. Ladies laughed, flirted, and gifted their chosen champion with some favor to carry into the mock battle. Botolf knew he would have to join them soon. As the Baron of Merewood and the new Earl of Regenford he was expected to take his full part in the tourney.

For a moment longer he stood before his tent watching all the activity with narrowed eyes. On his orders, his vassals and close friends, Sir Roger Vane and Sir Wesley DesRoches, also kept a close vigil upon the milling, cheerful crowd. Somewhere amongst the brightly clothed revelers was a person with murder in his heart. Botolf knew the gay confusion of such an event would aid an assassin.

"Be careful, Botolf."

Turning his head, Botolf smiled briefly at his petite mother, Lady Mary. "I will be. I always am. Go find your seat, Mother. Do not fear for me."

Lady Mary sighed. "Do men never change? Thrice has an attempt been made upon your life, yet you tell me not to worry."

"And thrice the attempt has failed."

"Aye, but once, the last time, success came too near for my liking. This evil from an unknown—"

"We both know who means to see me dead." He fought down his fury when he saw how his mother paled.

"I cannot believe it," she said weakly. "Cecil is your brother."

"My half-brother."

"You share blood, a father's blood."

"We also share the day, the month, the year, the hour, and even the moment of our birth. It matters not. We both know 'tis Cecil who hunts me." He lightly touched his mother's still-smooth cheek. "Go. Enjoy the celebration. I will be safe. We will not talk upon this again. It only brings you pain."

"She does not wish to accept the truth," Sir Roger said quietly after Lady Mary had left, his blue eyes revealing his sympathy for the woman.

"It is too painful a truth to accept. She held Cecil to her breast, treated him as her own son. To her it is much akin to Cain slaying Abel."

"Aye. He had a better life than many another, yet he wants it all."

" 'Tis often the way of it. Now, who is this lad?" Botolf flicked a smile at the boy that another of his vassals, Sir Talbot Yves, led over to them.

"Pitney Todd, m'lord," Talbot replied. "Your squire, Farold, has injured his ankle and cannot serve you. Pitney will do so in his stead."

"How old are you, Pitney?" Botolf asked, finding it difficult to resist the urge to stare at the boy's hair, a silver-blond color that was nearly white.

"Eighteen, m'lord," the boy replied.

"From the North?"

"Aye, m'lord. Sir Chad Brainard, your castellan at Regenford, sent me here last week. He has many boys and thought I would find more to do here, if it pleases you, m'lord. I have been well trained, m'lord."

Amused by the eagerness in the boy's light-blue eyes, Botolf said, "It could be naught else if Sir Chad trained you. How many boys does he have?"

"Seventeen at last count, m'lord."

"S'elp me God! Does the man think to breed an army up there?"

"They are not all his boys, m'lord. You have two of his sons with you. Sir Chad trains four Kipps from Ricadene, three Binks from Upwode, three Jagers—my cousins, m'lord—from Wolfhill, two Kirkleys, two Rowans, two Verges, and one Torans. Sir Brainard is much favored as a trainer."

"So it would seem." Botolf exchanged a laughing glance with Roger over the boy's readiness to chat.

"There is a need for well trained men at the borders. The Scots never know when they are beaten," Pitney added.

The men laughed and Botolf sent the boy to ready his arms for the tourney. He could not recall when he had been as eager, as filled with the joy of life, as the young squire. Although he was but seven and twenty, he often felt twice that age. Deep inside he craved peace but, as soon as Caindale's festivities came to an end, he had to return to Regenford. It was time to take up his duties as a marcher lord. He would find little peace there. Although Botolf knew too long a time of peace could possibly turn sour on him, he did wish for a taste of it.

"Where in God's fine earth did the lad get that hair?" Sir Roger burst out once Pitney was gone.

"Ah, the Todd family is of Saxon descent," replied Sir Talbot. "Their ancestor was one of the few to hold onto his land after the Conquest, though 'tis a small holding and none too rich. He sat secure whilst all about him were set the Conqueror's men. If Baron Alhric were akin to that ancestor, then it was skill in battle and guile that kept him secure."

"Where is Lord Alhric now?" asked Botolf.

"Dead, m'lord. He died in your father's last acre fight at Regenford. The tale goes that the baron was found beneath a dozen dead Scots still clutching his sword."

"The lad looks too delicate to come from such fierce stock."

"Lord Alhric was fair and slight, but I would have thought long and hard before facing him with a sword. Brainard claims the boy is like him."

A page's approach stopped their idle talk. Botolf frowned as the boy held out a delicately embroidered cloth. It was Lady Odella Alanson's kerchief of pleasance. Reluctantly, Botolf accepted it, giving the page the appropriate words of gratitude to take back to the woman. To have done otherwise would have been an insult.

"A fair flower," murmured Sir Roger.

"Aye. Pretty, well-mannered, and one of my mother's favorites."

The cold flat tone of Botolf's voice insured that his men would restrain from making any further remarks concerning the fair Odella. Lady Mary and even the king wished him to remarry. His mother dared not push him too hard, and the king had as yet declined to exert his power. That suited Botolf just fine. For now, the earldom of Regenford existed with no hope of an heir. As he entered his tent to prepare for his turn in the tournament, Botolf hoped he would be allowed to delay the need for remarriage a little while longer.

It did not take Botolf long to see young Pitney's value as a squire. The boy seemed to anticipate each move and command Botolf made. He found himself wishing Pitney were his squire instead of the accident-prone Farold. Then he felt the pinch of guilt. Farold was his cousin's youngest son. The boy had been performing to the best of his ability. It was not Farold's fault that his ability left much to be desired. Sighing with regret as he donned the last of his armor and made his way to the tournament field, Botolf hoped he could accept Farold's eventual return with good grace.

Botolf took his turn upon the tourney field quickly and efficiently, retiring from the field amidst hearty congratulations on his skill. He came very close to beaming at the young Pitney when he found a hot bath readied for him. It was not until he had sunk his aching body into the soothing hot water with a pleasured sigh that he recalled that he had no such amenity as a tub amongst his baggage. Looking around for Pitney, he discovered that the youth knew the game of least-in-sight very well. Laughing softly, Botolf began to scrub himself clean of the sweat and dust from the tourney field.

His laughter increased as he heard one of his recent opponents, Sir Walter Trapp, bellowing, "What rogue has stolen my tub? You there, lad, where are you taking that water?"

"This water, sir?" asked Pitney, his sweet voice heavily ladened with a false innocence.

"Aye, that water."

"To my Lord Botolf so that he may rinse away the dust raised when he felled you earlier."

"Impudent whelp," grumbled Sir Walter. "Let us go and see what he rinses in, eh?"

"Sir," gasped Pitney in dramatic outrage. "Do you accuse the honorable Baron of Merewood, the Earl of Regenford and brave defender of our northern borders, Lord Botolf Lavington, of being a common thief?"

"Of course not," blustered Sir Walter.

Botolf could hear a great deal of laughter. Although quieter in his mirth, he was enjoying the exchange as much as those who watched it. He hesitated in rinsing his soapy hair, not wanting to miss any of the confrontation being enacted before his tent. Botolf suspected that the somewhat dull Walter was easy prey for the clever Pitney.

He grinned as he heard Walter desperately try to extract himself from the insult he now believed he had delivered. Suds slowly trickled down Botolf's face as he listened. Absently, he flicked at them, cursing viciously when they went into his eye, stinging and blinding him. He groped for the drying cloth he had watched Pitney leave within his reach.

A steely arm suddenly curled around his neck. Botolf heartily cursed Providence. Naked, soap blinding him, he knew he was easy prey for the murderer who had managed to slip past his guards and into his tent. His cry for aid was stifled at its birth by a gloved hand clamped firmly over his mouth.

Botolf became a creature of fierce, thrashing muscle, his sole interest throwing off his attacker. The murderer's soft curses reached Botolf's ears as a knife thrust itself into the fleshy part of his shoulder instead of piercing his heart. When his sight began to clear Botolf saw the killer raise his dagger again. The man was trying to strike one more time before Botolf succeeded in throwing off his hold. Botolf was not sure he could stop that thrust either, and he felt the chill of impending death.

"Murder!" Botolf heard his new squire scream, and the assassin's choking grip abruptly lessened.

Struggling to stand, his weakness and the water impeding him, Botolf saw Pitney hurl himself at the startled attacker. The boy revealed no hesitation despite the fact that the man was twice his size. Sir Walter, Sir Roger, and Sir Wesley all stumbled into the tent to gape at the unevenly matched pair thrashing on the ground.

Obeying Botolf's bellowed commands, Sir Roger helped him out of the tub. The other two knights moved to stand near the fighting pair, prepared to strike as soon as they were able to do so without hurting the boy. Botolf rushed to dress and grab his sword in order to lend a hand.

An instant later there was an opening, but Botolf loudly cursed the manner in which it arrived. Knowing he was caught, that death loomed over him, the killer thought only of insuring that he did not die alone. Before Botolf or the other men could stop him, the erstwhile murderer buried his knife in Pitney's chest. When the man rose up to stab at the boy again, Sir Walter found the chance to strike. With one fierce swing of his sword he cleanly removed the man's head from his shoulders.

"I wish you had not done that," Botolf said, sighing with a mixture of frustration and disappointment.

"The man tried to kill you," Walter grumbled. "He did kill the boy."

"Nay!" Botolf cried in denial. "Close the tent flaps," he ordered Roger when he caught sight of the small crowd of curious onlookers outside.

Botolf continued to curse as he listened to the people leave, murmuring the tale that someone had tried to kill Lord Lavington and his brave squire Pitney Todd had given his life to save that of his lord. There was no time to put an end to their gossip. He fleetingly prayed that none of the boy's kin would be caused unnecessary grief as he turned his full attention to Pitney. There would be time enough later to correct what was being said.

Moving quickly, he knelt by the slim youth's side. Even as Botolf searched for a heartbeat, the boy opened his eyes. The soft depths of his eyes were clouded with pain. Botolf found himself thinking rather irrelevantly that the boy had uncommonly pretty eyes.

"Not dead yet, m'lord," the boy whispered in a hoarse voice.

"And you are not going to die," Botolf snapped as, with Roger's help, he worked frantically to staunch the profuse flow of blood from the boy's wound.

" 'Tis comforting to know." Pitney sent Botolf a weak smile. "I mean no insult, m'lord, but, perchance you prove wrong, my body must be returned to Wolfshead Hall. I must lie with my ancestors." His smile became a grimace of pain. "A few herbs and tight wrappings and I ought not to stink too foul."

"Stop talking."

"As you wish, m'lord," Pitney whispered, slipping into unconsciousness with barely a sound.

"What has happened here?" demanded a voice from the front of the tent.

Botolf spared barely a glance for Lord Sealing, the plump Earl of Caindale, as the man strode into his tent. He ordered Walter and Wesley to explain everything to their agitated host.

To Botolf's consternation, Lady Mary rushed into the tent. He watched her sway with blatant relief when she saw that he was still alive. The sight of the decapitated attacker turned her somewhat pale, but she did not leave. She quickly moved to help Botolf tend to Pitney's wounds and then began to tend to Botolf's injuries as well. Botolf was grateful for her calm and skillful aid.

"So this boy caught the man," said their host, Lord Sealing.

"Aye," replied Wesley. "He screamed murder and leapt upon the assassin."

"There is to be rain tonight. The damp that will bring will not aid the boy's healing. I will have a room prepared near yours, Botolf. Young Pitney deserves the best for his selfless bravery."

"Thank you, Edward." Botolf rose to finish dressing. " 'Tis Sir Pitney now."

"Fitting." Lord Sealing nodded even as he strode away.

"And there is my tub," muttered Sir Walter. "The little rogue had me believing I impugned your honor, Botolf."

Roger chuckled. "The lad ran circles round you, Walter."

"He be clever with words, 'tis all. Just like the rest of his cursed family."

"You know the Todds?" asked Botolf as Roger helped him with the tedious chore of tying all his points.

"Aye, and the Jagers and the Healdons. All the same. All look like angels but have the devil's skill with words. There is a tale that once the Baron Alhric sat outside the gates of an enemy's keep and convinced the man that the only reasonable course to take was to surrender the well-stocked keep and one hundred men-at-arms to him and his six pretty knights." Walter shook his head. "I would never doubt it, never doubt it at all."

"How I wish more men would use words ere they pull their swords on each other," Lady Mary said tartly.

"Well, there are few who could better a Todd or his kin in a fight. Even the women are to be reckoned with. Alhric's wife held Wolfshead Hall against the Scots for two months ere he and his men could return to aid her. They are a little odd, though."

"Odd? How so?" Botolf discovered that he was suddenly interested in this particular group of his vassals.

"They go to great lengths to be buried with their kin at Wolfshead Hall. Their grandfather died in the Crusades but was brought all the way home in a vat of wine. They all know Latin and French, but will often speak in English like their serfs. Alhric always said that we speak the language of our ancestors, so he will speak the tongue of his. Says we all will someday."

"All speak English?" Roger laughed. "Did he think we would all become peasants?"

"Nay. He said we would all become Englishmen. Did not really understand the man. Thought we were," Walter muttered. "Done with my tub?" he asked Botolf abruptly.

Realizing Sir Walter had no more to tell him, Botolf nodded, smiling faintly when the burly man dragged his tub away. Roger picked up Pitney, carrying the boy as they started toward Caindale. Botolf paused only to order Wesley to stay behind to see that the tent and arms were taken care of. Lord Edward's wife, finding herself short of rooms, put Lady Mary in a suite of three rooms with Botolf and the wounded boy. Botolf left Lady Mary to soothe the woman with assurances that they all understood that there was a shortage of space. He paused only long enough to tell her ladyship that he considered it the best of all possible arrangements. In spite of his wound and all that had happened, he had to attend the feast.

Despite the hearty amount of food and the merry company, Botolf's thoughts lingered on Pitney throughout the feast. He had seen death in all its forms, seen it take the young and innocent as well as the old and depraved. He had seen death come slow and hard and seen it come swiftly, unexpectedly. Yet, he found that he was anxious, nearly desperate, that Pitney survive.

"How fares the little knight?" asked Lady Odella, interrupting the distracted mood Botolf had fallen into.

It was hard, but Botolf managed a smile for the lady seated on his left at the head table. He knew she was not in love with him but suspected she found him easy to look upon. He also sensed that most of her attraction for him was due to his suitability as a husband. He was rich, powerful, and titled. Botolf also believed she considered it an advantage that he would be forced to spend a great deal of time at Regenford in the barbarous North while she could linger at the safer, more elegant Merewood.

He knew that many men would find a great deal to say in favor of a wife one need not see too often. Odella was nineteen and becoming an object of some less-than-flattering speculation. Twice a marriage had been arranged for her, and each time the groom had managed to die just before the wedding. Botolf knew he would be readily accepted if he asked for her hand in marriage, but he hesitated.

"I think he will live," he finally answered.

"It was very brave of the boy to leap upon your attacker even though he was unarmed and much smaller than the man. Howbeit, the Todds are well known for their valor."

Botolf began to wonder if all the world save him knew of the Todds. "You have met the clan?"

"Only once. It was at a tourney. Lord Alhric looked a troubadour, a poet. He was so fair and slender. So, too, were his two eldest sons, Hunter and Roc. I remember them clearly not for that, however, but for how they behaved in the tourney itself. Their skill and daring, their near savage enjoyment and participation, came as a surprise to most of us. They took nearly all the honors of the day, yet at the feast which followed that eve, they were again the angels with the pale gold hair and lovely eyes, sweet-tongued and charming. 'Tis hard to explain."

"You did very well, m'lady. It is as if two people dwell in the same body. A knight cannot always shed his brutish ways with his armor nor can a poet become a demon with a sword, yet most tell me that these Todds can be both. What else do you know of them?"

"Not very much. They have a large family, many of the children born to them living to reach adulthood. They flaunt their Saxon heritage." Her laughter trilled, a skill she was obviously very proud of. "To be so arrogant about a line traced back to the defeated is a little strange."

By the time Botolf had retired to his quarters, he had begun to think the Todds were an even mixture of charming and mad. Amongst people who proudly traced their lineage, when they could trace it at all, back to William the Conqueror, his intimates, or important families in France, the Todds boldly declared themselves Saxon of a nearly pure strain that ran back to Oswiu, the king of Northumbria and Bernicia in 641 AD. In the mates they chose, they considered a lineage traceable back to the conquered Saxons as important as any dowry. Their banner held the figure of a rearing black stallion, a wolf cringing beneath its hooves. The horse was known to have been the national emblem of the Saxons. Botolf shook his head as he entered his chambers, wondering how the family had survived for so long. It was an oddity that must have caused the Todds trouble at the start, especially in the rebellious North.

"How fares the boy?" he asked as he moved to stand by his mother, who had steadfastly remained at Pitney's bedside.

"There is no sign of a fever." With a smile she accepted the goblet of wine he served her.

"How is it that I have never met these Todds? This evening my ears have rung with tales of the family until my head spins."

"You were never about when they were or were spoken of. Until now, your life has always been Merewood. The Todds do not often leave Wolfshead Hall. They are deeply bound to their lands."

Botolf sipped his wine as he studied the boy who was so nearly a man yet looked a sweet-faced child as he slept. "They sound a strange lot."

"Oh, they are. None will argue that, not even they. 'Tis a harmless thing, however. It rather adds to their enchanting air."

"Enchanting but skillful. Their family has held Wolfshead Hall for nearly seven hundred years."

"Skill and cunning have accomplished that astounding feat. Your father," her face was briefly shadowed with a still-raw grief, "once told me that, in all the troubled times that have passed since the Conquest, there has been at least one of that clan on an opposing side. He said that the Todds drew lots to see who would fight on the side opposing that of their traditional liege lord, the Earl of Regenford. There was a Todd with Stephen and one with Matilda, a Todd with King John and one with the barons, a Todd with the early Saxon rebels and one with the Conqueror."

"And so on. Very clever. No matter who wins, a Todd can still hold Wolfshead Hall."

"They have always proven their worth in holding back the Scots, more times than can be counted."

"Then it could well be they I lean on when I arrive at Regenford."

"It will be. Your father did." Placing her hand upon Pitney's forehead, she checked for the ever-present danger of fever.

"Mother?" Pitney murmured, his clouded gaze fixing on Lady Mary.

"Nay, child," she replied in a gentle voice. "I am Lady Mary."

"An angel, nonetheless, though you sit at my bedside and not in God's kingdom," he said quietly, smiling sweetly.

"Oh, my." Lady Mary laughed, flushing slightly over the effusive flattery.

"We nurse a budding rogue," Botolf drawled.

"Budding?" Pitney murmured. "I see I must practice more."

Botolf laughed softly. "I think you need very little practice."

"Come, son," Lady Mary helped him sit up a little, "you must drink this. It will ease your pain and help you sleep."

"Were it poison, m'lady, I would still drink it willingly for 'tis nectar when served up in such fair hands."

"God's teeth." Botolf laughed again. "Put the boy to sleep ere I do so myself more directly." He playfully shook his fist at Pitney.

Pitney was unable to do more than whisper a few more lavish compliments as Lady Mary checked his wound, reapplying an herbal paste. He failed to keep his eyes open as she gently bathed his face.

When Pitney was asleep again, Lady Mary looked at her son. "You carried Lady Odella's kerchief of pleasance into battle today."

"Aye. She sent it to my tent. It would have been a grave insult to send it back."

"Oh." Lady Mary sighed. "Botolf—"

"I know. I should wed. If I dawdle much longer, King Edward himself will see to it."

"Then why not choose a bride yourself? Why wait until one is chosen for you?"

"I want no bride at all." He cursed softly when he saw his mother's crestfallen face. "I will settle the matter before the year is out. Duty requires that I beget an heir. I know that. I merely wish to ignore it for a while. Go to bed, Mother. I will sit with the boy. I swear, I will see to my duty to produce an heir before this time next year."

It was the early hours of the morning before anything disturbed Botolf's vigil. He heard the movements of the guests toward the great hall, where a morning feast awaited, just as his mother arrived to take his place. Botolf hurried to prepare himself to join the others.

He was just about ready to leave when a man calling himself Sir Edric Healdon urgently requested admittance to his chambers. Botolf paused in the doorway connecting the rooms as Lady Mary answered that summons at the hall door. He smiled faintly as he watched his mother's reaction to the knight standing there. The man's kinship to Pitney was easily seen in his slim elegant build, fair hair, and blue eyes.

Sir Healdon looked confused yet painfully hopeful, and Botolf cursed his forgetfulness. He had intended to make certain that the true tale of the attack was told and that no rumors or speculations were still being whispered which might cause unnecessary distress. He watched as the man hurried to Pitney's bedside.

"By God's sweet mercy, he still lives," Sir Healdon rasped, staring down at a still-sleeping Pitney.

"Aye, sir," replied Lady Mary. "There is no sign of fever, so I feel that his chance of recovery is very good indeed."

He took Lady Mary's small hand in his, bringing it to his lips. "The lad must have thought himself in heaven if he woke to find such an angel tending to his needs."

"I already called her an angel, Uncle," came Pitney's sleepy voice.

Sir Healdon sent his nephew a mock scowl as Lady Mary giggled. "Go back to sleep." He then smiled at Lady Mary. "With such a fair lady to stir one's soul, I am sure I will produce flattery that even you have not yet used."

"Falter away, Uncle. Although, I am thinking 'tis an art best left to us younger men."

"And here I was rejoicing that you were not dead as I had first been told."

"Ah, you came to take me back to Wolfshead."

"We will take you to Regenford in a while," said Botolf as he joined the others by the bed, pausing to shake Sir Healdon's hand. "Do you journey home,

Sir Healdon? If you do, you are most welcome to travel with us."

"I thank you, m'lord. I—" Sir Edric suddenly clapped a hand to his forehead. "God's teeth."

"What ails you, Uncle?" Pitney asked, his voice a little hoarse as Lady Mary helped him sit up.

"Kenelm and Olan are on their way to Wolfshead to tell them of your death," Edric replied.

"You must send someone after them."

Sinking down onto the edge of the bed, Edric buried his face in his hands. "They are beyond catching. They left but moments after the attack. If there is naught else my fool sons can do well, 'tis to ride hard and fast."

"Aye. I must think. Who is at home to receive them? Hunter, Roc, Udolf and Kyne are all in Berwick-upon-Tweed. Denu and Tuesday are with their husbands and far gone with child. That leaves little Thylda and—" he groaned, "Saxan."

"Aye, Saxan."

"They will tell Saxan the right tale, will they not? Even if they have the wrong ending, the tale itself should cause no trouble."

"Who can say? 'Tis that uncertainty which concerns me most. The lads were very reluctant to go, not wishing to be the bearers of such sad news to Wolfshead."

"Then let us hope that they are at least clear upon one point and that is that the assassin is already dead."

"Mayhap if I leave right now—"

"You will arrive too late to stop the tale from being told."

"Or the consequences if there are any."

"It is sad that his family must suffer from the belief that Pitney is dead," Botolf said, wondering what troubled the pair. "Howbeit, when we arrive at Regenford, we will immediately notify them of this understandable error."

"That is if there is anyone there to notify," Pitney muttered, then looked at the frowning Botolf. "M'lord, we are a God-fearing family, but there is one of His rules we have never adhered to well. That is His word that 'vengeance is mine.' If a Todd or one of his kin is murdered, Todds and all their kin will come from every corner of this land to hunt that murderer down. If it is thought that I was murdered and that my killer still lives—" Pitney shrugged faintly, deferring to his wound.

"They will come hunting him," finished Lady Mary in a hushed voice.

"Ah, but they must be gathered first," said Botolf. "There is still time to divert them."

"Only if my cousins are alert, m'lord," replied Pitney.

"A skill I fear my sons have not yet acquired," grumbled Edric.

"If they are not alert, the one at Wolfshead will set out immediately and that, I fear, is Saxan," Pitney said.

"We will leave word that your brother may show up here and that he is to be told the full truth," Botolf assured him.

"Saxan is my sister, m'lord. My twin sister. Ten minutes my elder."

"Surely a young maid will not set out upon an errand of revenge?" Lady Mary said, her shock and disbelief clear to read upon her face.

"Aye, she will, the wretched girl." Edric sighed, shaking his head. "I should have written the tale down for the lads to deliver. Surely they could not alter the truth of the written word."

"Well, there is no sense in worrying on the problem," Pitney said. "We can do naught to stop the delivery of the message, right or wrong. All we can do is hope that Kenelm and Olan get the tale right and that they keep a close eye on her. If that does not work, we must hope that we meet Saxan as she travels here and we travel to Regenford."

"That is a powerful lot of hoping to be done."

"And far too much talking by this boy," Lady Mary said sternly. "Help me sit him up just a little higher, Sir Edric. I have some gruel for him."

Botolf almost laughed at the look that passed over the boy's almost-pretty face. Even Pitney's cheery nature and glib tongue were stilled by the thought of eating gruel. It would be a little while, however, before he could be given more sturdy fare.

Botolf was soon chased from the room, along with the flirtatious Sir Edric. Side by side they made their way down to the great hall. Just as he walked through the hall's large doors, Botolf caught sight of Lady Odella. Before he could make a discreet retreat, she saw him and signaled him to join her at the head table.

"That one has marriage in her pretty eyes," murmured Edric.

"I know. So does my mother."

"Aha, cornered, eh? I faintly recall the feeling. My sweet Nelda died birthing Olan. I was besieged to rewed, but I held firm against all the ploys. There was none that I saw who could replace my Nelda. Of course," he drawled, "I already had two sons."

"And I have none," Botolf said heavily. "Duty calls."

"Aye, I fear it does. 'Tis far more important for a man in your place than for one in mine."

Greeting Lady Odella cordially, Botolf suddenly

and reluctantly found himself thinking of his late wife Alice. He did not know if he had the strength to go through all of that again—the loving, the marriage, the betrayal, and the death. It seemed far too high a price to pay to perform the duty owed to his name and kinsmen.

Pitney gained strength with an enviable speed. In less than a week, Botolf was able to prepare for the journey to Regenford. A cart was arranged so that the boy could ride more comfortably with Lady Mary close by his side. Although Botolf was a little surprised his mother wished to go to Regenford, he decided she was simply eager to continue nursing the endearing boy who had so thoroughly charmed her.

Fleetingly, he wondered if Lady Mary were also trying to stay close to Sir Edric Healdon. Botolf knew Pitney would fare better for her continuous care, but he could manage without it. It was hard to ignore the fact that under Edric's flattering attentions his mother was feeling young again. She might be reluctant to give that up.

Botolf quickly shook away that thought. He had noticed that Sir Edric only played his charming, witty games with Lady Mary. At the moment it was still only flirtatious repartee and pretty flattery, however. All women loved attention and Botolf knew he should not expect his mother to be any different. But she was no foolish girl whose head was easily turned. Botolf decided he was worrying about nothing. He had matters of a great deal more importance to deal with.

For one thing, Edric's sons would have delivered the false news of Pitney's death to Wolfshead by now. Although little mention was made of it, Botolf sensed that Sir Edric and Pitney continued to be concerned about what could result at Wolfshead when the erroneous news reached its halls. He was a little surprised that a man of Sir Edric's years could be so foolish as to believe a young maid would set out upon an errand of vengeance. There was nothing he could do about Edric's delusions, but he did think he could ease the boy's mind. Just as his entourage was prepared to begin the journey to Regenford, Botolf stopped by Pitney's cart.

After a moment of idle conversation, Botolf made what even he thought sounded like a speech, pointing out the impossibility of a young girl traveling so far with murder on her mind and reminding the boy of the delicacy of women. Botolf was not really surprised to see that all of his pontification had done little to change the boy's mind.

"I do not wish to be impertinent, m'lord," Pitney said quietly. "You are correct in most of what you say. The type of maid you describe is indeed the type most often met. They are not, however, my Saxan. Nor are they Todds. Nor, m'lord, are they my twin. Saxan will seek out my murderer if she believes he still lives. I but pray that she is at least certain of who that is."

Two

Kenelm and Olan stared helplessly at their cousin. Saxan could see that she was making them uneasy, but she could not move, could not speak. It was as if she had been turned rigid and could do no more than stand on the stairs, staring down at them. But a moment ago she had been skipping down the stairs, smiling and laughing as she had rushed to greet them. Olan had blurted out the sad tidings they had brought and she had immediately ceased to move.

"Pitney is dead," she said finally, causing her cousins to start in surprise.

"Aye, Saxan," Kenelm replied, his voice little more than a croak. "Stabbed."

"Murdered."

"Aye. That was the way of it."

"Who?"

"Well, the earl—" began Olan.

"The Earl of Regenford?"

"Aye, that is the man. He—"

"I see."

Saxan turned, stiffly making her way back up the stairs and ignoring her cousins' calls to her. She felt cold inside, as if all the blood in her veins had been replaced with icy water. Pitney, her twin, her womb-brother, was dead. It felt as if someone had just torn a large part of her soul away. She was too full of grief to even think of crying. Pain flowed throughout her body with each beat of her shattered heart, but she did not cry out.

A moment after she reached her bedchambers, her sister Thylda rushed in. Saxan was not surprised to hear the younger girl burst into the room, but she did not turn from the chore of carefully, almost reverently, dressing herself in Pitney's clothes. She knew Thylda only wished to try to stop her. She could not allow that. The overwhelming need to seek immediate retribution for Pitney's murder was the only thing that was keeping her from complete collapse.

"If you kill this particular man they will show you no mercy," Thylda warned her.

"He killed Pitney." Saxan methodically braided her waist-length hair.

"At least let me send for our brothers first."

"By the time our brothers can get away from their duties, the earl will be safe behind the high walls of Regenford. 'Twill be impossible to reach him there. I know he travels this way, for it has been well touted that he would do so as soon as the tourney ended. The tourney was over more than a week ago." She wrapped the thick braid of her hair around her head, then pulled a dark wool cap over it. "I mean to catch that murdering bastard while he is still on the road."

"You will be killed," Thylda cried, her voice thick with tears, clearly terrified for her sister.

"Then I shall be killed, but Pitney will be avenged."

Moving to where Thylda stood by the door, Saxan embraced her younger sister. Newly turned thirteen, with honey-gold hair and soft blue-grey eyes, Thylda was full of the promise of a true beauty. The girl also possessed a still-budding, but voluptuous figure, one akin to their sisters', Denu and Tuesday, and far-removed from Saxan's lithe shape. Their elder sisters had been wed a dozen and ten years respectively, so she and Thylda had always had only each other. That closeness had been enhanced by their mother's death only a few months after Thylda's birth. Thylda was almost as important to Saxan as Pitney, but even her dear sister could not sway her; and she knew Thylda was fully aware of her determination.

"You must keep Kenelm and Olan ignorant of my plan for as long as possible," she told Thylda, absently patting the back of the softly weeping girl.

"Why will you not take them with you?"

"They would not let me go at all, and you know it. But even if they would, it is better that they stay behind. I love them, but they are not suited for vengeance. And 'tis best if as few of us are involved in this undertaking as possible. What I must do could ruin the name of Todd unless I do it alone. Then it can be blamed upon the madness of a woman."

"You do not even know what the earl looks like."

"I do. Tall and dark with a scar by his left eye. I saw him in a dream nearly a fortnight ago. I saw him with blood on his hands. Although it troubled my sleep for a few nights, I paid the dream no real heed for I was not completely sure that it was Pitney's blood." She stepped away from Thylda, collecting her dagger and small bow. "Send word to our brothers only if you wish to. Hunter and Roc will return here soon anyway, for their forty days of service to the king will be at an end."

"Then wait. Please, Saxan, wait. At least wait to speak to them about what must be done."

"Nay, I cannot. They will understand." Pinning on her heavy dark cloak, she kissed Thylda's pale cheek. "It is dark. I must go now."

It was not easy to get herself out of Wolfshead

unseen. The men her brothers had left to guard the demanse were vigilant. Nevertheless, they looked outward for danger and that gave Saxan an advantage she made quick use of. She kept her hand on her mount's nose, leading the animal until she was sure she was completely within the shelter of the thick woods just beyond Wolfshead Hall. Only then did she mount. She continued to walk her horse quietly, however, until she felt confident that she was well beyond the hearing of the men upon the walls.

Grief and an intensity of purpose kept her from being afraid. There was simply no room in her for fear. Even though she had never traveled far from Wolfshead Hall, she knew the route the earl would travel to Regenford. It was one that had often been discussed by her kinsmen, and the earl rarely deviated from that path. She was confident she would meet up with the earl's entourage in a few days. Then, with either her light bow or her dagger, she would kill him. She would repay blood with blood. It was not only the custom of her family, but something she felt a searing need to do.

As she wended her way through the dark forest, she wondered how long young Thylda would be able to delay Olan and Kenelm from pursuing her. Such a tactic would require lying and Thylda had little skill in that art. That the girl would have to lie to her own kin, cousins she was fond of, would only make it harder. Saxan doubted she would be ahead of her cousins by many miles, but it did not matter. She would still be ahead of them and, despite Olan's and Kenelm's riding skills, she could probably maintain her advantage long enough to exact justice for Pitney.

Her horse Midnight, a strong, speedy stallion, was one of the best in her father's stables. Her cousins' horses had to be exhausted after their hard ride to bring her the devastating news. The boys would have to choose new mounts from the Wolfshead stables and she was confident that none could match Midnight.

Pitney's image haunted her as she rode. Memories of him kept her grief sharp. Although she loved every member of her large family, none of them was as close to her as Pitney had been. None of them ever could be. She and Pitney had shared a womb. They had often known each other's feelings and thoughts without a word being exchanged. She was surprised that she had not been keenly aware of the very moment Pitney's soul had left his body. Saxan had always believed that her soul was connected to Pitney's in a mystical bond.

The thought of coldly killing a man did not make her falter. Death was no stranger to her. She had even killed before, forced to defend herself in the heat of battle. Now, however, her enemy would not be attacking her. The earl could even be unarmed. It did not matter. He had Pitney's blood on his hands, and his culpability would give her the strength she needed to strike him down. She felt it would be easy to kill him even if he were totally helpless and even though she would be signing her own death warrant when she struck.

Saxan felt she was prepared to die. She knew that readiness was aided by her deep grief. Since the moment her cousins had told her of Pitney's murder, she had thought of nothing except to seek revenge. Her every move was aimed at achieving that result. She rested little, mostly for the sake of her horse. She ate little and gave no thought to the dangers of riding alone, dangers that even her disguise as a boy could not lessen. As she rode, she spent her time deciding on the best place to intercept the earl. Her mind became fixed upon getting to the Boar's Head Inn at Wiggins Knob as soon as she could.

"How is Pitney faring?" Botolf asked his mother as he edged near the cart, briefly peering inside to check on the youth.

"Well enough, Botolf, but it has been a long day," Lady Mary replied.

"The Boar's Head Inn is but a mile or so ahead of us. I was pressing to reach that."

"Aye, that would be nice. Some place dry where he could be kept warm. I think the nights we needed to camp out have, if not harmed him, certainly not aided his healing."

Botolf smiled at Pitney when he caught the boy watching them. "Hang on a little while longer, lad."

"I am fine, m'lord," Pitney replied. "Truly. 'Tis merely the pain that wears me down, and there is little anyone can do to vanquish that."

"A softer bed will help."

" 'Tis not something I will refuse," Pitney said with a tired smile. "I am sorry to be so much trouble."

"Nay, you are no trouble. I owe you my life. What little extra care I have taken in traveling to Regenford is a meager repayment. I have sent a man ahead to tell the innkeeper we are coming, so things should be readied for us."

The Boar's Head Inn was ready for the earl when his entourage finally drew to a halt before its doors. Botolf suspected that the activity in the inn had been frantic from the moment the innkeeper received word of his imminent arrival. The innkeeper, Will Meeks, prided himself on serving the earls of Regenford. Botolf knew he would be the third earl to use the inn as a stopping place on the way to his castle, and the innkeeper clearly had no intention of losing such profitable custom.

The activity around them continued at a frantic rate as Botolf, his mother, Pitney, and the higher ranking members of his entourage were hastily settled into their rooms. The horses were tended to and the carts were pulled beneath some shelter. Hot baths were prepared on request; and from the hearty aromas reaching his nose, Botolf anticipated a great quantity of food.

As he joined Sir Edric in heading to the common room, Botolf caught sight of Will Meeks—who kept a close watch on his two fulsome daughters—and bit back a grin. Once settled, the knights were known to greedily eye any maid. Botolf decided that caution was the reason the man was so quick to catch his eldest daughter as she started to slip upstairs with food for the wounded Pitney.

"But, he is just a lad," the girl protested, "and he looks an angel. Ye worry overmuch, Papa."

"Aye? That lad's name is Todd," growled Will Meeks, causing Botolf and Sir Edric to halt in their descent but steps above the pair. "Half the bastards twixt here and the end of Christendom could be carrying that name by rights."

"Slander!" cried Sir Edric with such an excess of drama that Botolf had to laugh. "Retrieve those words, you dog."

Will Meeks narrowed his eyes for a moment, then gaped slightly as he recognized Edric. "Sir Edric Healdon. Aye, and the rest of the nameless brood could carry the name of Healdon."

"Never. We are no seducers of young maids."

"Humph. Nay? What of young Anne in the next village? Your boy Kenelm had her in her father's hayloft last year. He left a babe with her."

"Nonsense. Kenelm would never bed a girl in a hayloft. The boy likes his comfort. Hay has the habit of stabbing a man in awkward places." Sir Edric smiled sweetly at the young girl, who could not fully repress a giggle.

"Here! Get off with you now. Don't ye be starting on her with your smooth words and guiling smiles."

Struggling to control his laughter, Botolf moved to take the tray from the girl. "I will speak to the boy, Master Meeks."

Watching the man drag his daughter away, railing at her every step of the way, Edric murmured, "That man was misnamed."

"Go and have yourself something to eat, Edric. I will join you in but a moment."

When Botolf entered Pitney's chambers, he chuckled at the fleeting sweet smile that crossed the boy's face, followed quickly by a look of mild disappointment. Farold Moreton, his squire, sat by the bed looking uneasy. Setting the tray down, Botolf fought to look at least mildly stern.

"You are not to seduce the maids here, young man," he ordered Pitney.

"I was not going to seduce her, m'lord," protested Pitney. "Truth tell, I do not think I would be able to. I am not that healthy yet."

"Able or not, there will be no tussling the maids whilst you are in my service. I do not hold with the seduction of virgins."

"She was one of those, was she? I was not sure what with the way she was rolling her eyes and swishing her hips."

"The way Meeks hangs over her, I suspect that she is untouched. My father felt such seductions were naught but an abuse of our position and power. I must agree."

"Ah, you mean they bed us more for our lofty place in life or because they fear the consequences of refusing us than for our looks and charm."

"In your case, I doubt it," Botolf drawled. "Howbeit, you will behave yourself."

After receiving assurances from Pitney that he would behave, Botolf went downstairs to enjoy a hearty meal. He had barely finished his last bite of succulent roast when his mother rose to retire for the night, taking her lady-maid with her. Botolf knew his mother was leaving so that the men would feel free to be less circumspect in word and deed. He had to smile at the way the ale began to flow far more freely the moment she mounted the stairs to her bedchamber. As the page refilled his tankard, Botolf looked forward to an evening of good companionship.

Saxan smiled to herself as she rode up to the Boar's Head Inn. A quick glance around was enough to tell her that the earl had already arrived. Leaving Midnight with a stableboy, she strode inside the inn only to be met immediately by the burly innkeeper. Inwardly she cursed and hoped the man would not prove to be too great an obstacle. Olan and Kenelm were not far behind her. She had even caught a glimpse of them and had had to ride the last few miles at an almost dangerous pace. Either they had proven swifter than she had anticipated or poor Thylda had failed badly in holding them at Wolfshead Hall.

"I have no rooms, lad," the innkeeper told her. "Howbeit, there may be space for you in the stables."

"That will do me." She fought to keep her sultry voice as low and as curt as possible. "Have you any food left?"

"Aye, we can feed you right enough. Go in there and set yourself down," he told her, pointing toward the common room. "I will see that something is brought to you. Just do not trouble the earl and his company."

"I would never be so impudent, sir."

As soon as the innkeeper left her, Saxan slipped into the room where Botolf and his group were gathered. They were too involved in their talk and drink to notice her, but she still kept to the shadows of the room. Inch by inch she drew closer to the earl, her gaze locked upon the man, her hand clutching her dagger.

As she edged along, she carefully studied the man she intended to kill. He was tall and broad of shoulder. She suspected he reached the rare height of six feet, yet there was a lean graceful strength to his large frame. Saxan knew she would be given only one chance to strike.

Pausing, she tucked an errant curl back into the cap she wore. She had rinsed out her hair that morning and, sensing that her cousins were close on her heels, she had not taken the time to braid it and pin it up. Now she wished she had taken that time. Her hair was constantly slipping free of the cap and could interfere with her mission.

Taking a steadying breath, she began to move again. Her gaze was fixed so steadily upon the earl's face her eyes began to sting. He held none of the fair handsomeness she was accustomed to. The man was embued with a heavy, dark somberness. He neither smiled nor laughed as fully as his fellows. His features were sharply cut. An aquiline nose and high-boned cheeks added to the aloofness of his face. He was handsome, but she felt he was also cold. Cold enough to plunge a knife into a youth given into his care, she thought, her fury so intense that her stomach ached. She clung to that thought to cure herself of a sudden hesitation.

Slipping her dagger from her belt, she walked stealthily toward him. Her whole body tensed as she left the concealing shadows at the edge of the room. Just as she was near enough to strike, she heard a heavy footfall behind her and knew someone had entered the room. Cursing softly, Saxan lunged at the earl.

"M'lord! At your side!" the innkeeper bellowed.

Botolf caught his attacker by the wrist even as the knife plunged toward his heart. He bellowed in surprise as he fell backwards, the small bench he sat on crashing to the floor at the same time he and his assailant did. Every man in the room sprang to his feet. Hands gripped the hilts of swords, but none moved to interfere. Botolf felt confident that the small size of his attacker insured his victory.

As he and his assailant hit the hard, wooden, rush-covered floor, Botolf wondered fleetingly why Cecil was sending children after him. Intent upon questioning the boy, he tried not to hurt him too badly. That hesitation made the struggle last far longer than it should have.

He was amazed at the skill and strength displayed by the slim youth who wrestled with him. His amazement turned swiftly to stunned astonishment when, as he flipped his adversary over and attempted to pin the lad down, the boy's cap slipped off and a thick mass of silver blond hair spilled out.

"By Christ's foot, 'tis a maid," gasped Botolf even as he finally won his battle and securely pinned the thrashing girl down.

" 'Tis Saxan," cried Edric, rushing to Botolf's side only to be diverted as his two flushed sons suddenly burst into the room. "You fumbled the telling," he accused as they also rushed to the earl's side.

"We did not mean to," protested Kenelm. "Olan blurted out the news that Pitney was dead, and Saxan just stood there staring at us, not moving, not saying a word. I fear it greatly overset us. We did not even realize that we had, more or less, told her that the earl had done the murder. It was Thylda who made us see our error."

"Aye," continued Olan. "Once we talked to Thylda we saw how Saxan may have misunderstood us, but Saxan was gone by then."

"So we set out after her," finished Kenelm.

"And were very nearly too late," snapped Edric, cuffing each son aside the head.

Although aware of every word Edric and his sons said, all of Botolf's attention was fixed upon the girl he held. She was not watching him, however. Her wide sapphire-blue eyes darted from her cousins to her uncle and back again. In contrast to her fair hair, light brown, delicately arced brows and long thick lashes highlighted her beautiful eyes. A small straight nose led to a full mouth that sorely tempted him. Her tiny oval face was thoroughly enchanting. He almost smiled when he found himself thinking irreverently that he had never known a lovelier assailant.

Botolf felt Saxan's lithe body relax beneath him as she began to understand what her kinsmen were saying. He leaned on one elbow, cupping his chin in his hand as he stared at her. It was hard, but he restrained the urge to smile when she finally looked at him.

A small part of Saxan's now confused mind took note of the fact that beneath the earl's vaguely winged dark brows was a pair of lovely, soft-brown eyes. "You did not kill Pitney?" she asked.

"Nay, mistresse," he replied.

"I see. Who did kill Pitney?"

"Actually, 'twas a man who was sent to kill me, but Pitney intervened." He reluctantly stood up, helping her to her feet.

"Ah. And the fate of the assassin?"

"He died a moment after he stabbed your brother."

"Do you have Pitney's body?"

"In a manner of speaking." He glanced toward Edric and his sons, then realized that they intended to leave the telling of Pitney's survival to him. "You see, Pitney is not dead." Botolf frowned as he watched all the color flood from her face, leaving her a sickly grey.

"M'lord, I do believe that, for the very first time in my life, I am going to faint."

Botolf caught her even as she began to collapse. Seeing that her kinsmen were struck dumb by shock, he picked her up in his arms. He stepped over to his bench as one of his men righted it and sat down with Saxan settled comfortably on his lap. Edric and his sons cautiously edged closer to him.

"Well, God's bones, will you look at that." Edric picked up one limp slim arm and let it drop. "She truly has swooned."

"Plainly she spoke the truth when she said she had never fainted before," Botolf drawled as the Healdons seated themselves.

Before Saxan's kinsmen could reply, a pale, worried Lady Mary hurried into the room. Botolf realized his mother had not yet been asleep and had heard the ruckus. After all that had happened, she had naturally assumed that he was being attacked yet again. He almost laughed as she halted briefly in the doorway to gape at him. Instead of finding him in a life-or-death struggle, wounded or dead, she found him comfortably seated with a maid in lad's attire settled neatly upon his lap.

"Botolf," she cried as she shook free of her shock and hurried to his side.

Looking to heaven only to find no aid there, Botolf faced his mother. He could not really blame her for the accusation that was clear to read in her brown eyes. " 'Tis not what you think, Mother." Glancing at the Healdons he found no help from that quarter, only wide grins of amusement at his dilemma.

"Do you know, she looks very familiar," murmured Lady Mary.

"The hair, is it, m'lady?" Edric inquired with an overdone innocence.

"Why, aye, 'tis the hair. 'Tis just like Pitney's. Oh. Oh, my, 'tis your niece?" she asked Edric.

"Aye. 'Tis Pitney's sister Saxan. Just as I and Pitney feared my lads got the tale all twisted about. I blush to admit it, but Saxan came here to kill his lordship."

"Kill Botolf?"

"Aye, but he caught her as she struck and we were able to explain the misunderstanding," continued Kenelm.

"Did you hurt the child, Botolf?" Lady Mary asked her son.

"Nay, m'lady," answered Olan. "My cousin fainted when his lordship told her that Pitney was not dead."

"Ah. Of course. Why are you holding her, Botolf?"

"Well, he picked her up," Olan pointed out with sweet, uncomplicated reason.

"I see," Lady Mary said very carefully, laughter straining her voice, laughter that matched the amusement in Edric's and Botolf's eyes.

"I think the girl is coming 'round," Wesley said.

"Aye," agreed Botolf. "I believe you are right."

Saxan opened her eyes slowly. She was suffering from a profound sense of disbelief. Never before had she done anything so weak. Then she recalled everything that had been said just before she had swooned. Her eyes widening, warily she lifted her gaze to meet that of the man who held her. Despite her high hopes and rising excitement, she found herself thinking yet again that the earl had rather lovely, soft eyes for a man.

Botolf was immediately captivated. The girl's eyes were rich sapphire pools alive with emotion. Her lashes were even longer than he had first thought, for their light-brown color faded until they were nearly silver at the tips. Shaking free of his distraction, he hoped he did not look as foolishly spellbound as he felt.

"My brother is alive?" Saxan demanded.

He made no effort to recall her to the indelicacy of her position. "Aye, although he is wounded. Fear not, 'tis a wound he is rapidly recovering from. Your brother saved me from being murdered. Unarmed, he threw himself at my attacker. For that I saw him knighted."

For one brief moment Saxan feared she would embarrass herself by swooning a second time. She closed her eyes until she grasped some thread of control over the emotions swelling up inside her. As she grew calmer, she became all too aware of her immodest position upon the earl's lap. What puzzled her was how dangerously content she was to be there. Subduing that feeling, she again opened her eyes. This time she turned her attention on her far-too-amused uncle.

"Did you not happen to notice that I am seated upon a strange man's lap?" she asked with a false idleness.

"Well, he is not really strange, lass. 'Tis the earl, our liege lord."

"I do realize that, Uncle. Do you think that the

next time a message of any importance must be sent to Wolfshead, you could use someone other than these two wooden-headed fools?" The one clear thought which came through all the others thrashing about in her head was that, due to her cousins' ineptitude, she had almost killed an innocent man.

"Saxan!" Olan protested, looking highly outraged.

Slowly, she rose from Botolf's lap, glaring at her two cousins all the while. "Aye, mayhap fools is a poor choice of word. Idiots is a better one, or doffs, or even tomfools." She swung at Olan, who had already nearly fallen from his seat in his frantic attempts to avoid her steady advance. "Mops!"

"Now, Saxan, 'twas only a misunderstanding," Kenelm said in a nervous attempt to soothe his furious cousin. "Surely you can forgive that?"

"I will show you my forgiveness!" She threw Kenelm's tankard at his head, savoring his curses when her aim proved true.

Olan grabbed her even as she reached for something else to throw. He was too slow. She had already grabbed a plate, and the metal made a clear, ringing sound as she slammed it down on his head. Saxan found it a highly gratifying noise, then cursed as she and Olan tumbled to the floor. Her curses increased when Kenelm dashed to his brother's aid only to end up in the scramble himself. Saxan was aware of the laughter of Botolf's men, but she was too furious to worry about being the object of their amusement.

Botolf looked at a heartily laughing Edric. "Do you not think you ought to put a stop to this?"

"Nay. Saxan will not hurt the boys too badly."

"Sir Edric," Lady Mary scolded softly.

"Be at ease, m'lady, I will put an end to it shortly. The lads deserve a bit of abuse, and methinks Saxan needs to give her anger some release. I will step in when the lads forget that their cousin Saxan is a lady and start to really fight back or when she takes to cursing too loudly and too profanely."

Laughing, Botolf realized such an occurrence was common, for Edric was right at hand when the change of circumstances he had mentioned took place. Only a man accustomed to such rows could be so alert and skilled. Just as Kenelm drew back a fist to deliver a very ungallant tap to Saxan, Edric grabbed his son. The other two combatants turned on Edric, glaring at this unwelcome interference. Botolf struggled to control his laughter.

"Just let me hit her the once," protested Kenelm. "The shrew bit me."

"Now, you know you cannot bloody her nose," Edric said calmly. "She is a girl."

"Well, there is naught to stop me from bloodying his," Saxan proclaimed as she leapt to her feet, swinging one small fist at Kenelm.

With remarkable agility, Edric tossed Kenelm aside. The man not only deflected Saxan's blow, but caught her firmly in his arms. It was done so neatly Botolf was confident the move had been developed for just such an incident. Botolf had to bite the inside of his cheek to repress his grin as Edric dragged the still-furious Saxan back to his side.

"Now, my omnipotent niece, allow me to introduce you to your liege. You do recall the man you nearly skewered but a moment ago?"

"Aye, but you need not sound so condemning," Saxan grumbled, embarrassed and a little afraid, but determined to hide her discomfiture. " 'Twas an honest mistake, and I missed."

"This impertinent wench is Saxan Honey Todd, m'lord. Saxan, your near victim is Botolf Corwine Lavington, Baron of Merewood and Earl of Regenford." Edric eased his hold on her. "Make your curtsey. Let him see that you have at least a few manners."

Saxan scowled at her uncle, but smiled sweetly at Botolf. Despite her attire, she managed to pantomime a credible, graceful curtsey, then sat on the edge of the bench next to her uncle. Now that her fury at her cousins had eased, her thoughts centered on one thing. The possibility of punishment for her attack troubled her only briefly. She was beginning to feel confident that there would be none.

"May I see my brother now?" she asked politely.

Botolf suppressed the urge to laugh aloud. The impudent girl revealed neither embarrassment nor repentance despite her attempt to kill him and her undignified brawl with her cousins. He felt sure she did not understand that her behavior was highly unusual amongst young ladies. It was evident she fully expected to be accepted for what she was, oddities and all; and, if she were not, she cared not a fig.

For the first time in a long while, Botolf found himself keenly interested in a female for far more than lust. Covertly appraising the lithe frame revealed so clearly in her black jerkin and hose, he admitted to himself that lust was certainly there as well. He was fascinated by her. Botolf wondered fleetingly if Saxan's oddness was the basis of his attraction for her. If she lacked so many of a lady's delicate airs, did she also lack the faults? Shaking his speculations aside, he set his mind firmly upon the matter of her brother.

"Of course. I will take you there myself." He rose, holding out his hand.

Saxan hesitated. Holding hands was not the usual way a gentleman escorted a lady. Then she shrugged and placed her hand in his. The way his large hand closed so completely around her tiny fingers stirred an unfamiliar feeling within her. She fought to keep her sudden confusion from showing in her face. That chore was made easier when she risked a glance at his cool features. Plainly, he was not feeling a thing.

Botolf suddenly felt strongly inclined to drag Saxan upstairs to his bedchamber. Glancing down at her, he was ashamed of the wave of blind lust that had swept over him as she had placed her delicate hand in his. She was such a tiny woman, fragile. The sensuous plans whirling in his mind would probably break her if not terrify her.

"You say Pitney heals well?" she asked Botolf as he escorted her up the narrow stairs toward the bedchambers.

"Aye," Botolf replied, pleased to hear none of his lustful thoughts reflected in his voice. "My mother has stayed at his side since he was wounded. He was well enough this eve to flirt with the innkeeper's eldest daughter."

"He would flirt with a maid if he were on his deathbed," Saxan remarked with dry sarcasm. "Even Kenelm and Olan, for all they have naught but air between their ears, can turn a pretty phrase and a maid's head. My kin seem to be born with the skill." She tensed when Botolf halted before a door.

Pitney was asleep when she and Botolf entered the room, as was young Farold. Botolf roused Farold and sent him away. He kept a close watch on Saxan as, slowly, she approached Pitney's bedside and decided it would be best if he left the pair alone. He hesitated as he started out the door, pausing to assure himself that the reunion went well. If Saxan swooned again, Pitney was in no condition to help her.

"Pitney," Saxan whispered as she reached out one trembling hand to touch his cheek.

Pitney's eyes fluttered open and he fixed his sleepy gaze on Saxan, smiling weakly. "Greetings, Ugly. The fools told you wrong, did they?"

"Aye," she answered in a voice thick with tears. "Rest easy, I have not slain the earl."

"That is news to ease my fears, although I cannot fathom why you should ever wish to kill the man. Confound you, you are not going to start weeping on me, are you?"

"Aye, I believe I am."

As Pitney wrapped his arms around the weeping Saxan, Botolf slipped quietly from the room. It was moving and somehow reassuring to see that a family could be tied together as closely as the Todds and their kin seemed to be. He wondered briefly if that was one of the things that made them seem odd to so many people. Such familial love was becoming sadly rare. Botolf saw only good in it. He knew it was yet another reason he wanted to keep a close eye on Saxan Honey Todd.

Three

Botolf bit back a smile as he caught his mother watching him. It was a wary, intent observation that had endured throughout the morning meal. She had clearly sensed his distraction, and her motherly instincts told her that his deep thought was inspired by one Saxan Todd. Botolf felt she should be pleased that he was regaining some interest in women other than the harlots and paramours he used to serve his manly needs. The look on his mother's face, however, hinted that she was not sure she liked his choice. Lady Mary probably found Saxan Todd confusing. Botolf sipped his cider calmly, waiting for his mother to garner up the courage to ask the questions so clearly troubling her.

"Saxan does look remarkably like Pitney," she finally said, glancing at Sir Edric, who sat on Botolf's left.

Edric smiled faintly. "And acts much like him, too." He chuckled when she blushed and began to falter for a denial. "Nay, m'lady, do not waste your kind words. I speak the truth, and we both know it. The poor girl's mother died thirteen years back, and mine was already long buried by then. She has two sisters, but they were wed and gone ere she was much more than a bairn."

"Surely there were other women who could have taken her into their care."

"At first Alhric sought a woman who could come to Wolfshead Hall and care for Saxan and the younger Thylda." Edric shrugged. "It did not work. The women who did come were far more interested in trying to secure Alhric for a husband since they were either widowed or spinsters. Alhric finally turned to rearing the lasses himself with occasional assistance from me and our cousin Sir Fridolf Jager."

"Why could the elder sisters not take the girls in?"

"They offered, but Alhric did not wish to part the twins. That is one reason Pitney was trained at Regenford. Also, Denu and Tuesday were busy raising their own families, as well as aiding in training the young girls from their husbands' families. But, in all truth, Alhric was ever loath to see any of his bairns leave the nest."

"I think all parents suffer that, Sir Edric," Lady Mary murmured.

"And, as a result, Saxan and Thylda received an upbringing that few ladies do," said Botolf.

Edric nodded. "They were raised alongside the boys. Mind me, they are not without a lady's skills, but I will concede that they have enjoyed a strange rearing for young ladies. 'Twas often easier, aye and pleasanter, to toss the lasses amongst the lads and treat all alike. Since we men treated the girls in such a manner, the lads did the same. 'Twas not until Saxan and then Thylda began to look more like women than girls that our lads began to treat them any differently."

Recalling the fight that had ensued between Saxan and her cousins, Botolf grinned. "They still forget from time to time."

"Aye." Edric laughed, then sent Lady Mary an

apologetic smile. "We are often alone in these wild lands, m'lady. There is little of the courtly manners and rules about here, and we saw naught wrong with what we did. And, in these past two years or so, her brothers have had the rearing of the girls. The eldest of them is but four and twenty. The fact that all four lads are away leaving their sisters in command of Wolfshead tells you clearly how they think of the girls."

"The girls were left alone in such a troubled area?" Lady Mary asked, her eyes wide with shock.

"Aye, Sir Edric, it does not sound particularly wise," said Botolf. "No castle is always safe, but out here we have our own particular dangers. Rogues like the Black Douglas often raid."

"Very true, m'lord. Howbeit, their mother once held Wolfshead Hall for two full months against the Scots. Saxan and Thylda are very much like her."

Botolf idly placed his hand over his mouth to hide his frown as he thought over all Sir Edric had said, for he did not want Edric to think his look was one of censure. Saxan Todd was much akin to a boy in her manner. He could see how such an attitude would result from such an unusual upbringing. Knowing Sir Edric and Pitney as he now did, Botolf was certain there was no real bad in the girl. He hoped that would make it easier for his mother to accept Saxan as she was, although he was not sure why that acceptance mattered so much to him.

In the back of his mind, a wild plan was being born. Botolf found himself actually considering marriage to the girl, and he intended to observe Saxan carefully. Life would certainly be much easier for him if his mother and Saxan were able to get along. Lady Mary and his late wife Alice had never done so, and there had been continuous strife in his household. Botolf wanted no more of that.

When he saw a look in his mother's eyes that promised a great deal more questioning, he excused himself, claiming a need to see to the preparations for the journey. He was still too uncertain of what he planned to do to give her any satisfactory answers. His mother would undoubtedly find his hesitation and need to step slowly puzzling, but he felt he had to be careful. He dreaded the possibility that he could find himself burdened with another wife like Alice. The very thought made him shudder. Botolf did not think he had the strength to endure another such disastrous marriage.

Although he could not believe Saxan was anything like Alice despite their short, violent acquaintance, he could not let instinct sway him from caution. He warned himself sternly not to allow the ache Saxan stirred in his loins to sway his judgment. When he had helped Pitney undress his sleeping sister last night, Botolf had quickly recognized the danger. The image of her gently curved, half-dressed lithe form was seared into his mind's eye. He grimaced as, despite all his warnings to himself, he found himself watching for Saxan as he oversaw the preparations for leaving the inn.

Saxan found herself caught firmly in the chilling nightmare again despite all her efforts to suppress it. The earl stood before her, his strong, long-fingered hands dripping with blood. Only, it was not the earl. The man spreading terror through her dreams looked like the earl, but her heart told her he was not. She could see that clearly now, now that she had come face to face with Botolf. This time surprise woke her with a start. She sat up abruptly, her eyes wide and her mouth hanging open.

"The earl has no scar," she whispered in sudden realization.

"By the blood of Christ!" cried Pitney, clutching his tray of food as her abrupt movement caused it to bounce. "What ails you?"

She blinked at her annoyed and startled brother then calmly replied, "Lord Botolf has no scar by his left eye." Saxan helped herself to some bread and cheese from Pitney's tray. "I had this dream over a fortnight ago. In it I saw the earl standing before me with blood on his hands. That dream was what made it so easy for me to believe the earl had murdered you, that he would coldly kill a lad put into his care. Well, I have just had that dream again, only this time, I noticed something beside the blood. Although the man I see looks much akin to the earl, he is not the earl. The man in my dreams has a scar over his left eye. I wonder who he is?"

"Bad beef most likely," Pitney grumbled. "Did you really try to kill the earl?"

"Aye. I truly thought he had murdered you. Those fools Kenelm and Olan got the tale all wrong. I rode here on Midnight. I nearly succeeded, too. Howbeit, Master Meeks saw me and gave the alarm. Once the earl and I ceased to tussle, I learned the truth. Then I fainted." She giggled. "That surprised our uncle and cousins."

"I do not doubt it." Pitney shook his head, watching her as she rose from the bed to begin dressing. "Did the earl say anything to you after all this excitement?"

"Nay. I believe he understood that it was all a mistake. If there were to be any punishment meted out, it would have been done by now."

"Aye, it would have."

"Um, Pitney? How is it that I am only half-dressed?"

"You fell asleep after you soaked me to the skin with all your weeping, so the earl helped me get you comfortably settled."

"Oh." Saxan bent over to tug on her soft black boots, letting her hair fall forward to conceal her blushes.

"Who else was at home at Wolfshead when our cousins brought you the news?"

As Saxan turned to look at her brother, she frowned. Although he was talking to her, his dark frown indicated that he was deep in thought. Then she felt a pang of guilt. Having saved the earl's life and been knighted for his bravery, Pitney now had a real chance to become an important member of the earl's household. He could find many opportunities for advancement often denied to a younger son. Pitney would never fault her for what she had tried to do, but he was only human. He had to fear that her rash actions might have destroyed his opportunities even before he had a chance to grasp them. She did not believe the earl was going to seek any retribution, but she was not sure how she could convince Pitney of that.

"Thylda was with me," she answered finally, moving to sit on the edge of the bed and securely tie her hair with a leather thong. "I must get word to her or she will be worried beyond enduring. She knew I sought the wrong man shortly after I left. Kenelm and Olan told her just before they raced after me. Those two fools," she muttered, shaking her head and wishing her cousins were near enough to slap.

"Do not beleager them too much, Saxan." He exchanged a brief grin with her, then grew solemn. "I feel some evil stalks our liege lord."

"So do I, Pitney. There is my dream to consider. I have had it again; yet if it were a warning about you as I thought it was, I should not have. 'Tis a warning, but now I believe it concerns the earl."

"Someone certainly wishes the man dead."

"We must watch carefully."

"Aye." He set his tray aside and rested against his pillows. "I had so many questions, yet now I feel that all is clear."

"Good." She kissed his cheek, stood up, and strode to the door. "I will see you later, brother."

"See me later? What are you going to do? Saxan!" he called, but she hurried out of the room. "I hope our uncle is vigilant!" he yelled as she shut the door behind her.

Saxan laughed softly, hurrying down to the common room. Peeking inside, she discovered that her uncle was far from vigilant. If she were any judge, Edric was so interested in Lady Mary the man would not notice much else. Lady Mary sat near Edric, blushing faintly and struggling to make conversation. Since the topic was the threat to Botolf, Saxan decided to listen for a while.

"It troubles me," Lady Mary said. "I fear I have erred toward Cecil in some way, that 'tis my fault he has caused such trouble for his brother. I cannot believe 'tis Cecil who is trying to kill him, however."

The fact that Botolf was being threatened by his own brother deeply shocked Saxan.

Edric covered Lady Mary's small, fretful hands with his. "That it may be your fault is something I can never believe. He was a bad seed, m'lady. Fated to do evil. They appear without warning in families hitherto unblemished. No blame can be laid at anyone's feet for such a child."

"Do you truly believe that, Sir Edric?" She leaned

toward him in her eagerness to have some reasons for the family's tragedy.

"Aye, I believe it." Edric brought his face even closer to hers, his voice lowering in a way Saxan easily recognized. "M'lady, forgive me, but I intend to kiss you."

"You do?"

"Aye, without doubt."

"Be quick about it then, for I fear that I may soon come to my senses and flee the room."

Saxan nearly gasped when the couple began to kiss. Here could be trouble. Shrugging, she slipped by the doorway and headed for the stables. She wondered if Lady Mary had had other reasons for staying so close to Pitney's side. Saxan knew her uncle had charm and an allure many a lady found compelled to respond to, just like all the rest of her male kin. The problem this time was that the lady her uncle wooed was the mother of their liege lord. Her musings were brought to an abrupt halt when, just as she drew near the stable door, her path was blocked by the earl himself.

"Just where are you going, Mistress Todd?" he asked.

"To the stables, m'lord. You see, my horse is in there and I shall need him to reach Wolfshead Hall," she replied in a tone one might use to explain something to a very small child.

"You will travel with us, you impudent wench."

"I do not wish to trouble you, m'lord."

" 'Tis no trouble at all." He took her hand in his. "Come, I wish some ale before we leave for Regenford."

Thinking of the scene she had just witnessed in the common room, Saxan advised, "I should not go in there if I were you."

"Why not?"

"My uncle is kissing your mother." She was not surprised when he came to an abrupt halt, dropped her hand, and gaped at her. "I should close your mouth, m'lord. We are near the stables, and the flies are thick about here."

"Are you sure?" he demanded.

"Quite sure. I saw them with my own two eyes."

"My God."

"You do not approve?" she asked, feeling the tickle of insult and prepared to defend her uncle.

"My shocked mind has not reached the point where it can consider the weighty matter of approval or disapproval."

"Oh. Just where is your mind then?" She tried not to giggle, but her laughter could not be fully suppressed and it trembled in her voice. "Sorry."

"So you should be, wench."

"Wench, is it?" She easily caught an apple tossed her way by her cousin Olan as he ambled by. "What happened to Mistress Todd?"

Disgruntled, for he had not caught the apple tossed his way as smoothly as she had, he drawled, "I begin to think she does not exist."

"I wonder what not existing feels like."

"I doubt it is very painful." As he bit into the apple, which was surprisingly crisp despite having been stored through the winter, he wondered at the absurdity of their conversation.

"That is something that eases my mind, although I suspect that, if I do not exist, neither does my mind."

"Quite true." He watched her even white teeth bite into her apple with more interest than such a mundane act merited. "You realize that, if you do not exist, nor does your mind, than neither does your mouth."

"I shall remind it of that, m'lord, as soon as it is done with this apple." She watched Sir Roger and Sir Wesley walk past on their way into the inn. "Ah, ah, ah. I should not go if I were you."

"Why not?" asked Sir Wesley. "I must have an ale before we journey on."

Botolf frowned at his apple, wondering what to say, only to turn his stare on Saxan as she replied, "There has been a horrible accident. Master Meeks' leg was crushed beneath an ale barrel. They have the poor man stretched out on top of the largest table in the common room. When I left, they were preparing him."

"Preparing him for what?" Sir Roger cast a nervous glance toward the inn.

"To cut the poor mangled limb off, Sir Roger," she answered, her tone of voice as solemn as her expression.

At that moment Master Meeks himself appeared in the doorway and hailed them. "Ah, m'lord. I have just breached a new keg of ale. I thought you might be wanting a tankard or two ere ye leave."

Struggling to reply over the laughter clogging his throat, something made all the harder by the way Roger and Wesley were staring at Meeks' legs and Saxan was looking as innocent as a newborn, Botolf finally said, "Thank you, Meeks. We were all just longing for some."

"I will set out the tankards, m'lord," he called and disappeared back inside.

Sir Wesley eyed Saxan with a mixture of annoyance and amazement, clearly wondering how she could have the audacity to look so sweet after telling such a huge lie. "He lost his leg, did he?"

"It grew back," she replied.

Before anyone could stop her, she dashed past the

men. She intended to put a stop to her uncle's wooing of Lady Mary before anyone else caught him at it. Surprise brought her to an abrupt halt in the doorway of the common room. The couple who had looked so loving only a few moments ago was now split apart, each person seated at the far opposite ends of the long table. Saxan was immediately aware of Botolf as he stepped up beside her even though he had approached without a sound.

"Are you sure of what you saw?" Botolf asked softly, noting with an odd sense of tenderness that Saxan barely reached his chest.

"I am quite, quite sure of what I saw," Saxan replied, scowling at the couple. "Either they are playing at being innocent or something has gone sadly amiss."

"What could go amiss?"

"How should I know? Romance and the meanderings of the heart are not things I have had a great deal to do with." She fell silent when Wesley and Roger arrived.

Botolf took her gently by the arm, directing her to sit by his side at the table. As he signaled to Wesley and Roger to take their seats, he, too, wondered what could have gone wrong. One look at his mother's and Edric's faces told him that they were not playing innocent. They looked too tense and unhappy.

"Will we be leaving soon, Botolf?" Lady Mary asked.

"Aye, Mother," he replied. "As soon as I have quenched my thirst."

"Then I shall go and assure myself that my maid Elizabeth has collected all my things." She hurried out of the room.

Sir Edric stood up an instant later. "And, if you will excuse me, m'lord, I will see if Pitney needs any assistance." As soon as Botolf nodded, he also hurried from the room.

Seeing that Wesley and Roger were deep in conversation, Botolf met Saxan's inquiring gaze and shrugged. "I have no idea what could be troubling them."

"Do you wish to know?" she asked, keeping her voice low so she could not be overheard. "After all, your mother is Lady Mary, the widow and mother of earls, and my uncle is only a knight, a man with a somewhat meager holding and two sons he must provide for."

"Do not be an idiot. Thank you, Meeks," he murmured as the innkeeper served the ale.

" 'Tis not idiocy," she said as soon as Meeks left.

"Mayhap not. Your uncle's position and wealth matters little to me. The people who may be concerned have naught to say, for my mother is past the age to bear a child. I just do not believe such matters should be interfered with," he said in a stern voice.

"I never suggested such a thing."

"Hah! You were thinking on it."

"Well, mayhap just a bit," she admitted reluctantly. "I will merely watch."

"Watch for what?"

"For signs, m'lord. Sometimes one can see a great deal in the manner a person adopts."

"Ah, of course. You are right. And what if your uncle merely flirts, dallies a little?"

"Uncle Edric would never dally with a lady who can sit higher at the table than he can. Nay, and not with any wellborn lady of your good mother's ilk."

"You may watch them if it pleases you, but no more than that."

"Aye, m'lord. As you wish," she murmured with an overplayed meekness.

"Your father did not beat you enough," he drawled, smiling slowly.

"My father never beat me."

"Nay?" He looked at her in unconcealed disbelief.

"Nay. I was ever quicker of foot." She grinned.

As they drank the ale and idly talked, Botolf realized with a start of surprise that he felt remarkably comfortable with Saxan. So, too, did he easily indulge in a type of light nonsense he had never participated in before. He caught the look of speculation on his friends' faces, but ignored them.

Roger and Wesley were as close to him as brothers. Usually he was able to tell them everything. If he had had too much to drink, he even told them things they did not particularly wish to hear. This time, however, he felt a strong desire to remain private. He was heartily enjoying the ease with which he could talk to Saxan, the strange yet strong feelings she stirred within him when she laughed or smiled; and, selfishly, he had no wish to share that with anyone. If nothing else, he wanted to consider the implications of these experiences before putting them into words.

Words came easily to him when, as they prepared to leave, Saxan led a large ebony stallion out of the stables. It was clear that she intended to ride the beast to Regenford. Botolf moved quickly to stop her as she started to mount. As he tightened his grip on her arm, he mused that even her anger was more like a man's, lacking the pouting attitude too many women employed. It was an anger he felt more capable of dealing with. There was nothing he had to pander to.

"You cannot be thinking of riding this horse," Botolf said.

"And why not?" she demanded.

"A slight girl like you upon such a strong beast? 'Tis absurd."

"I rode him here," she snapped.

"Then you are fortunate you did not break your fool neck."

"Hah! I have been riding Midnight for years."

"She has that, m'lord," said Olan as he meandered up to them.

"Well, she will not ride him in my company," Botolf declared with what even he recognized was a great deal of arrogance.

Saxan glared at him. "I will not, hmmm?"

"Nay, you will not."

He caught her firmly around her tiny waist when she made a lunge for her horse, but she proved to be a difficult little bundle to hold. He was heartily glad that the cart was near. Saxan derided his character every step of the way. In retribution, Botolf tossed her into the conveyance with her brother Pitney and Lady Mary with a distinct lack of gentleness. He felt an even mixture of surprise and amusement at her volatility.

"Here is where you will ride, Mistress Todd," he said. "A massive black stallion is no proper mount for a lady."

"And just who calls me a lady?" she snapped, then cursed for that was not what she had meant to say.

"Very few, I suspect, but there is always hope." He hid his grin by turning sharply, striding back to his horse.

Saxan had a great many things she wished to say; but, in deference to a shocked Lady Mary, she could only glare at Lord Botolf's broad back. Her reticence brought a stifled laugh from her brother. Saxan ignored him, watching as Midnight was tied to the back of the cart. Assuming an air of docility, she sat back and began to plot her escape.

It was not until after their brief midday stop that

Saxan saw her chance. Lady Mary was sleeping and none of the men riding near the cart were paying her any heed. Trying to be as quiet as possible, she urged Midnight to draw closer to her.

"You are going to break your stupid neck."

She gave a start of surprise when her brother spoke, then flashed him a frown of annoyance. "Never." She turned her attention back to Midnight. "I know what I am doing. You just go back to sleep, Pitney."

"Oh, nay, not until I have watched this."

Ignoring him, she continued to coax her horse. Once the stallion reached a speed that kept its head nearly inside the cart, she untied his reins. She stood up as straight as she was able in the cramped space, took a deep breath, and leapt. Her landing on Midnight was far from perfect, but she managed to keep from hitting the ground. After a brief struggle, she was seated firmly on Midnight's strong back. She quickly veered around the cart and spurred her mount into a gallop even as a cry went up.

Hoping to get out of sight of her pursuers, she raced down the road. She intended to slip into the wood lining the road. In its shadowy depths she felt she could successfully hide until Botolf and his men grew weary of searching for her. To her delight, a chance arrived after but a few moments of hard running as she went around a curve in the road. Veering sharply to the left, she hugged the neck of her horse as he galloped into the wood. She slowed his pace only a little so that Midnight could navigate the paths through the trees safely. Once she was sure she was far enough from the road to remain unseen, she reined her horse to a halt, dismounted, and secured his reins to a low branch. Silently, she made her way back to the edge of the road. The wide smile which curved her mouth as she watched her pursuers race by faded slightly when she failed to discern the figure of the earl amongst the riders.

Finally, shrugging, she wended her way back to her horse. She was deep in thought about when she should begin the long ride back to Wolfshead Hall, her gaze fixed upon the ground, when she realized her escape had not been successful. A pair of fine black boots planted firmly between her and Midnight entered her line of vision, telling her she had not been as clever as she had thought. Slowly raising her gaze to meet his, she swallowed hard. The earl looked far angrier than she had anticipated or than he deserved to be. A quick glance around the looming Botolf revealed an intensely curious Wesley standing next to Midnight.

One more look at Botolf made Saxan decide that the cart with Lady Mary and Pitney was exactly where she wanted to be. It definitely looked safer, she mused, as she began to edge backwards. "Ah, well, I believe I will go back to the cart now." She spun around and raced back through the wood.

"Watch the horses, Wesley," Botolf ordered as he charged after Saxan.

Botolf was angry. He did not like his commands to be ignored, especially by some tiny silver-haired girl. He had suffered a deep concern for her safety and did not like the feeling. Although it was clear she could ride well, her method of mounting the horse had been recklessly dangerous as had been traveling alone through the woods. Beneath his anger swelled a growing admiration for her fleetness of foot. She just might have been telling the truth when she told him her father had never beaten her because she was too difficult to catch.

Just as Botolf began to think she could outrun him all the way back to the cart, she stumbled slightly as she ran out onto the road. He caught her, grabbing her around the waist. Their unchecked speed sent them crashing down onto the dusty byway. After a brief, furious tussle, Botolf pinned her firmly beneath him.

"I should beat you," he said, struggling to ignore how her disheveled clothes revealed the gentle swells of high firm breasts and how they pressed against her jerkin as she fought to catch her breath.

"I should not bother, m'lord. I feel thoroughly beaten now. This ground is not soft."

His anger began to ease, another more basic emotion replacing it as he became all too aware of the lithe frame sprawled beneath him in a highly suggestive position. "Oh? Strange, for I am quite comfortable."

When he shifted his body slightly, Saxan swiftly realized what had replaced the anger in his dark eyes. "Methinks you may be a bit too comfortable, m'lord," she whispered, wondering why the knowledge of his arousal should make her feel so warm, so strangely tense.

"And mayhap beating you is too harsh a punishment, but you should pay some forfeit for your disobedience." He fixed his gaze upon her full mouth.

Saxan felt her blood quicken alarmingly as she realized what he intended to do. "A forfeit?"

"Just a small one," he murmured as he gave in to the overwhelming urge to kiss her.

Warmth flooded Saxan's body at the mere thought of Botolf giving her her first kiss. It was a warmth which rapidly, almost frighteningly, increased when his well-shaped mouth covered hers. The feel of his lips, so soft and so gentle, belied the hardness often shown by his finely chiseled, thin-lipped mouth.

When he released her wrists to comb his fingers through her tousled hair, she curled her arms around his neck. Her whole body ached to attach itself to his. As he caressed her hair, his kiss grew more intense. Despite her total lack of experience, she welcomed that intensity.

Brushing feverish kisses over her cheeks, Botolf hoarsely commanded, "Part your lips, sweeting."

"Like so?" she whispered as she obeyed.

"Aye, little one. Just like that."

The first gentle proddings of his tongue made her shudder. Saxan heard a soft moan and realized it came from her. It blended perfectly with the deep, muted growl of pleasure that escaped Botolf. He slipped his mouth off hers, moving his kisses to her throat and the tender skin exposed by the open neck of her jerkin. She threaded her fingers in his thick black hair, tilting her head back in unconscious supplication.

Botolf thought it strange that her eloquent act of acquiescence was what helped him gain some semblance of composure. Gritting his teeth, he moved so that he was only half-sprawled on top of her. He dredged up every ounce of his willpower in an attempt to regain full control of his body. It was not easy when she kept looking at him, her rich, sapphire eyes afire with passion.

Even knowledge of her total innocence did not make reining in his rampant desire easy. Saxan had a fire within her, a flame that responded to his touch. He was consumed with a desire to taste its depth. Now was not the time, however, and the middle of the road to Regenford was certainly not the place.

"The kiss is over?" she whispered, her voice thick and husky.

"That was more kiss than I had meant to take." He gently brushed strands of her brilliant hair from her flushed face, noting how his hand shook. "Child, do you know how near I am to taking you right here upon this road?"

"Someone would come," was all she said.

"No doubt. That thought was not our salvation, however," he commented as he stood, helping her to her feet.

He said no more and, to her disgust, Saxan could think of nothing else to say either. He took her back to the horses in silence. He sent Wesley to tell the others that Saxan had been found so they could start on their way again. Botolf mounted his horse, set her before him, and took up Midnight's reins to lead the animal. She cursed a wordless oath when, once they rejoined the entourage, he had Midnight tethered behind the supply wagon and set her back in the cart. She realized she had used up her only chance to escape.

When they camped for the night, Saxan retired early. Her mind was full of what had occurred between her and Botolf. She found it difficult to sit amongst him and his people while memories of the kiss they had shared tormented her. Ignoring the bedding laid out for her, she stripped to her underclothes and slid in next to Pitney. She wanted to tell her brother about her first kiss, but she also wanted to keep it to herself. Feeling his warm, breathing body next to her eased the last of her fears that he was lost to her. Despite the disturbing experiences of the day, that was enough to help her go to sleep.

Botolf noticed the deep frown on his mother's face as she joined him by the fire. "Is something wrong?"

" 'Tis probably silly of me," Lady Mary mumbled even as she led her son to the cart she shared with Pitney and Saxan. "After all, they are brother and sister."

Looking at the sleeping pair, Botolf smiled crookedly. He recognized the twinge of jealousy that struck him as he saw the way Saxan was so comfortably curled up in Pitney's arms. "They are twins, Mother. They shared a womb. I do not believe any two people can be closer."

"Of course, you are right." She smiled. "They look like sweet babes."

They did, but Botolf said, "One of those babes saved my life at the risk of his own."

"And the other tried to take your life. I still find that hard to believe."

"Your surprise could be no greater than mine, but they are tightly bound and her grief ran too deep for mere weeping. I can understand that. 'Tis why I take no action against her for what she tried to do. And none of my people expect me to. Nay, for all those two look like the sweetest of babes while they sleep, they are not children. Pitney is now a knight I know will serve me well. Saxan, well, in her still lurks the child, but she is a woman ripe for marriage." He turned to walk back to the fire, adding quietly, "More than ripe. I will send for Lord Todd, her brother, as soon as we reach Regenford. He is the one I must speak to," he mused aloud, flashing a quick smile toward his gaping mother.

Four

"If you are set in your mind about my teaching the girl a few courtly ways, mayhap you should speak to her," Lady Mary said to her son as he directed the breaking of camp. "We will reach Regenford on the morrow, and she still thinks she will be traveling on to Wolfshead Hall."

"You are right, Mother. 'Tis past time to speak to her. Where has the wench disappeared to?"

"Mistress Todd walked toward the river with her cousins a few moments ago."

Before his mother had finished, Botolf strode toward the river. Despite knowing about Saxan's eccentricities and those of her large family, he was still shocked by the sight that met his eyes at the water's edge. Even if she, Olan, and Kenelm were cousins, it did not seem right for her to romp in the water with them in such a state of dishabille. She wore a boy's braies and a shirt; her cousins wore only their braies. Trying not to be too judgmental, Botolf crossed his arms over his chest, leaned against a thick, old oak, and waited for the three to finish their play.

He lost most of his carefully contrived control the moment the three stepped out of the water. The cousins were totally unaware of the immodesty of Saxan's drenched attire. He wished he could be as unmoved by the sight of her small, perfectly formed breasts clearly outlined by the thin, wet cloth. Botolf needed to take several deep breaths before he could regain enough composure to step closer to them.

"Is it time to leave, m'lord?" Kenelm asked, startled by his liege's sudden appearance.

"Aye, nearly. With your permission, I would like to have a word with Mistress Todd—alone," he added firmly.

"Oh, aye, of course," replied Kenelm as he hurried to tug on his clothes. "Come along, Olan."

Botolf wondered if it were blind trust or just plain stupidity that caused the two youths to walk away, still tugging on their clothes, and leave him alone with their lovely, half-dressed cousin. There were no black rumors about him, but he felt Saxan's kinsmen should have been more cautious. It was evident that they simply did not see the danger, that they did not see their cousin and childhood playmate as a desirable woman.

Looking at Saxan, Botolf fervently wished that he did not either. Saxan stood only steps away, brushing out her wet hair and cursing every tangle. She eyed him with a hint of curiosity, unconscious of her attire and how it might affect a man. Botolf found it impossible not to look at her lovely breasts or to try and measure her tiny waist with his eyes. He could not stop himself from thinking about how it would feel to stroke her gently rounded hips and have her slender, well-formed legs wrapped around him as they sought their pleasure.

"Will you put your clothes on?" he demanded suddenly, his voice hoarse and strained.

Saxan was startled and a little frightened by his harsh, angry tone. She glanced down at herself and nearly groaned at how inadequately she was covered. She was almost naked. For the first time in her life, she tasted shame and found it painful. A deep blush burned her cheeks as she stumbled to her clothes. When she reached for her tunic, Botolf covered her hand with his. Saxan was unable to look at him and crouched by her clothes.

"Look at me, Saxan," he ordered as he knelt by her side.

Not trusting herself to speak, she shook her head.

He cupped her chin in his hand, gently but firmly forcing her to face him. "I apologize. I did not mean to make you feel so ashamed."

"There is no need to ask my pardon. Shamed is exactly what I should feel." She sighed, shaking her head. "I have no sense of what is right."

"You judge yourself much too harshly. I think you have a deep sense of what is right in all that truly matters." Although it sorely tried his hard-won control, he helped her get dressed. " 'Tis but the refinements you lack. I have known this from the moment I met you, and I was wrong to speak as I did."

"Then why did you?" she asked with a hint of annoyance.

"My dear, wide-eyed child, I am neither your brother nor your cousin." He smiled faintly at her look of confusion. "I do not see you as a mere kinswoman or an old playmate, but as a woman."

"Oh." She blushed again, obeying his silent command to stay seated at his side on the riverbank once she was completely dressed.

"Aye—oh. I am certain that, considering the kinsmen you live with, you know how matters can be betwixt a man and a woman."

"But, you are the earl, my liege lord."

"I am first and foremost a man, Saxan. You may give me as many titles and honors as you wish, but I am still just a man. If that is not enough, I am also a man who has been without a woman for a very long time."

"Oh," she whispered, making the short sound into two syllables.

Botolf chuckled. "I have never heard that small sound given such a depth of meaning before." He was pleased to see her bright, easy smile.

"Since I was with my cousins I fear I gave my attire little thought," she murmured. "I have had few dealings with men other than my kinsmen."

"And that is one of the matters I wish to discuss with you."

"Are you going to tell me about men?"

When he saw her impish look, he gave her a mock scowl. "Be silent, wench. S'truth, you no doubt know more about men than 'tis wise for any woman to know. Nay, I wish to speak about your lack of training in the ways and manners expected of a lady of your breeding. Nay, do not look at me so."

"And how was I looking at you?"

"As if you were deciding whether or not I had just insulted you. 'Tis not my intention to cause any insult."

She shrugged, uncomfortable with the ease with which he had guessed her thoughts. "I am well aware that I am not what most people would consider a lady."

"That is nothing to feel ashamed of."

Saxan heard the bite of bitterness in his deep voice and fought to hide her knowledge. He had clearly had some dealings with one or more of those ladies who hid a mean-spirited whore beneath silks and fine manners. Someone had hurt him. She wondered how deeply that hurt went.

"Then I need not change," she said, meeting his frown with a sweet smile.

"Saxan, you are eighteen, a woman grown. In truth, you should be wed. Has nothing been arranged for you?" he asked, tensing for her reply.

"There was a choice or two discussed, but the men died ere anything was decided. My father did not believe in marriage bonds arranged at cradleside. Do you intend to introduce me to some suitable gentlemen?"

"I mean to see that you become acquainted with life outside your tight circle of kin."

"Outside?" she asked with growing suspicion.

"It will need your brother's approval, but I plan for you to come under my mother's gentle guidance. For that you must stay at Regenford."

"It will take you time to gain Hunter's permission, so I will return to Wolfshead Hall until then."

"Nay, you will come to Regenford. Your uncle has assured me that your brothers will agree to my plans."

"Has he? If I need leave Wolfshead Hall to become a lady, then I will stay a heathen brat."

"Do not be so foolish. You cannot mean to spend all your days at Wolfshead Hall."

"Aye, I do, until a better place comes along and brings a good reason for me to go there."

"You cannot continue to run wild." He tried but failed to keep his rising annoyance out of his voice.

"Far better to do that than to prance about on embroidered slippers, smiling as I lie and flirting heartlessly with all and sundry simply to stroke my vanity."

"My mother would never teach you such things. That is the type of foolishness you can teach yourself if you choose to."

"Well, I do not choose to learn any of those useless skills. I have no need of them. What is the purpose of them?"

"To make you a woman."

"You find it easy enough to see me as a woman now."

"I can see any as such if they possess breasts," he said, surprised at the nasty tone of his voice and at how quickly she could stir his usually even temper.

Just as Saxan took a breath to spit out a scathing retort, she heard a sound that pushed all thought of their quarrel from her mind. "Shush," she ordered him.

"I will not shush. This matter must be resolved. I—mmppff." He was stunned when she abruptly put her hand over his mouth and wondered if there were no limit to the girl's impertinence.

"Will you be silent? Just listen. Someone draws near," she added in a whisper, taking her hand away from his mouth and smiling at him as if they were not in any danger, but still talking, blissfully unaware. "You have enemies, my liege?"

"Mayhap it is the Scots," he replied in an equally soft voice.

" 'Tis a wee bit far south for them, but, aye, it could be they."

Their confusion was ended a moment later as two burly men charged from the concealing bushes to their left. Saxan cried out as both men raced toward Botolf, their swords drawn. She quickly rolled out of the way, allowing Botolf to meet the attack armed and ready to fight. Saxan leapt to her feet; but, before she could call for help or run back to the camp, a third man stumbled out of the thick bush and grabbed her.

Botolf saw the third man wrap his thick arms around a cursing Saxan. Suddenly, he was fighting as fiercely as ever he had before, desperately trying to break free of his assailants so that he could rush to her aid. The sight of her being so roughly handled enraged him.

He knew he was risking a misstep, which could easily prove fatal, but he kept glancing toward Saxan. When she managed to turn in her captor's arms enough to drive her knee into his groin, Botolf winced as the man screamed. The men he fought with were also diverted, which insured that his own inattention did not cost him too dearly. They also suffered from the overconfidence that comes from outnumbering one's opponent. Botolf knew, however, that he was losing a perfect opportunity to cull the number of his adversaries when, an instant later, he joined them in gaping at Saxan. She pulled a knife from inside her soft boot and plunged it into her captor's unprotected back. He saw the brief look of horror that crossed her pale face as she retrieved her knife and turned toward him.

The effect on his attackers of losing one of their number was immediate. Botolf found himself hard pressed by their united, fierce offensive. He cursed, realizing he was using up all his strength simply to hold them back. He was contemplating a rash move to end the stalemate when Saxan leapt onto the back of one of his opponents.

Howling and swearing, the man frantically tried to shake Saxan off even as she fought to plunge her dagger into a suitably vulnerable spot. Botolf pressed the man facing him while he still reeled from his surprise over Saxan's entry into the fight. One on one at last, Botolf quickly went from defense to offense. Just as he plunged his sword into his foe's chest, Botolf heard a chillingly familiar gurgling sound. It did not come from the man he had just cut down. Suddenly terrified for Saxan, he yanked his sword free and spun around only to find himself gaping in astonishment yet again.

The man Saxan had been fighting was slowly collapsing to the ground, his throat slashed. A white-faced Saxan leapt clear of him even as he fell. The girl certainly knew how to use her knife, Botolf thought dazedly as she flung herself into his arms. He held her close, burying his face in her tousled hair. It was a moment before he realized that her whole body was trembling.

As he tightened his hold on her, he wondered where her people were. They should have come looking for them simply because he and Saxan should not have been alone, not for this long. Edric should certainly have the sense to notice. The man had been keeping a close eye on his niece since her abrupt arrival at the Boar's Head Inn.

Botolf pressed a kiss to the top of Saxan's head as he asked with concern, "Are you hurt? I can see no wound."

"Nay, I am not injured." Saxan continued to cling to him, finding that the pleasant feelings his nearness invoked helped to ease the horrors of the last few moments.

It had been frighteningly easy to take a man's life while caught up in the heat of battle. As soon as the threat to Botolf and herself had passed, she was too painfully aware of what she had been forced to do. She could not stop thinking about how her hands had cut short the lives of two men. It was a memory she desperately wished to banish.

"You tremble," Botolf whispered.

"I have just killed a man," she replied.

"Two."

"Aye." She shuddered, bile stinging the back of her throat.

"I could grow very weary of being rescued by Todds."

"Are you going to knight me?" she jested in a weak voice.

"I cannot knight a female." Cupping her face in his hand, he turned it up toward his own. "Howbeit, some reward is certainly due."

Saxan knew he intended to kiss her again and she smiled faintly. "A reward? Last time you called it a forfeit."

"You talk too much." He brushed his lips over hers and watched her slowly close her eyes.

"So I have oft been told, but ne'er so sweetly," she whispered against his mouth. "Silence me, m'lord, if you dare."

He ended any further pertness from her with a kiss. She tightened her slender arms around his neck as they both reveled in the simple pleasure of being alive. Botolf pressed her so close to his body he was surprised she did not cry out in pain. Instead it was a deep, rich voice that jerked him back to his senses.

"I had expected at least some of this," drawled Edric.

Botolf hastily ended the kiss and fruitlessly tried to appear calm and unaffected as he turned to face Sir Edric. "Which some do you refer to?" He noticed with relief that Saxan's cousins were paying little attention to the confrontation.

"Not the dead bodies."

"This one still lives," Kenelm announced as he crouched by the man Saxan had stabbed in the back.

Gently setting Saxan aside, Botolf hurried to kneel by the dying man and demanded, "Who sent you here to murder me?"

"I do not know," the man replied, his voice a hoarse, thready whisper. "I never ask questions."

"What did he look like?"

"You. He looked like you. Odd," the man said even as he breathed his last.

Hissing a curse, Botolf rose from the dead man's side. "Cecil, curse his eyes. He still hunts me."

"Cecil?" Saxan stared intently at Botolf as she recalled her dream. "Does this Cecil look like you?"

"Aye. We share not only looks, but the year, month, day, and hour of our birth. In a small way he is my twin."

"Except that Cecil has a scar above his left eye."

"How do you know that?" Botolf demanded.

"I saw it in a dream but a few nights before I received word that Pitney was dead. I fear it was easy for me to believe you had killed him, for I thought I had seen you in my dream holding out your hands, which were soaked with blood. I believed it was Pitney's blood. Later, the morning after I tried to kill you, I recalled that the man in my dream had a scar above his left eye. You see, I had the dream again and it confused me. Then I realized that it was not a warning about Pitney, but about you. 'Twas your blood on his hands," she whispered, chilled by the thought.

"He certainly craves the spilling of my blood. Howbeit, I do not intend to give him the chance to dabble in it."

"You do not question my dream?"

"Nay. My mother has had one or two herself."

"And," interrupted Edric, "we have all had a feeling that has led us in some way. We can see no clear reason to heed that sensation, yet it usually proves to be right."

"I get such feelings quite often, Uncle," Saxan said with a faint smile. "They are most unsettling."

Botolf suddenly noticed that Saxan was trying desperately not to look at the bodies of their attackers. She was also still too pale, and he quickly suggested, "Kenelm, Olan, take your cousin back to camp. Your father and I will search the bodies, although I do not really expect to discover anything useful." As the youths led Saxan away, he added, "And do not speak of this to Lady Mary. There is no need to upset her with such ill tidings." He frowned at the look which briefly crossed Saxan's wan face. As soon as she was gone, he asked Edric, "Why did Saxan look at me so strangely?"

"Mayhap because you asked her to keep something secret from Lady Mary," Edric replied as he began to help Botolf search the bodies.

"My mother does not need to hear about yet another attack upon me."

"Saxan will understand that once she pauses to consider the matter." Edric scowled down at the last body he had searched. "There is nothing here."

"Nor here. There is no armor save for a padded jupon. They were poor assassins."

"That may explain why there were so many of them. An unrelenting attack could be your enemy's plan."

"True. Even the poorest of swordsmen can eventually score a hit if he lunges often enough."

Edric nodded. "The question one must ask is, does he have the funds to hire the best when and if he chooses to?"

"He can get them if pressed to it."

"And these attacks have increased?"

"Aye. Since the day I left Merewood to wend my way here, there seems to have been an attack at every corner I turn." Botolf dragged his fingers through his hair in a gesture of frustration.

"He hopes to kill you ere you reach the safety of

Regenford. To try and attack you there will require men who ask more than he can afford to pay. I know this man is your blood kin; but would it not be wise to try and grab him ere he attacks again? Mayhap 'twould even be best to kill him ere he kills you."

"It took a long time for me to seek him out, but I have recently done so. The man is very elusive."

"He also leaves you no proof so that you may bring what laws there are to bear against him."

"I fear not. This man's statement is the closest I have come to grasping the proof I need that 'tis Cecil who hunts me. Howbeit, 'tis not enough." Botolf sighed and shook his head. "And I must consider my mother with each step I take. It would cause her untold pain to have it heralded far and wide that Cecil tries to murder me."

"Let us return to camp then or she may guess that he has been at it again."

As they started back, Botolf realized that Edric had made no reference to his discovering him and Saxan in a heated embrace. Botolf knew the man could not often have found Saxan in such a compromising position. Concerned that the man restrained himself because he feared insulting or angering his liege lord, Botolf decided to speak up. He needed to clear away any misconceptions.

"I mean your niece no dishonor, Sir Edric," he said.

Edric's tone was cool as he replied, "A kiss is a long step from dishonor, m'lord."

"It could lead there quickly enough."

"I am not so old that I do not recall that. Howbeit, you are an honorable man, m'lord. If you trespassed, you would atone for the insult. I rushed to the stream when I realized my dimwitted sons had left her alone with you in a state of undress not to stop what might pass between you and her, but because of the consequences of it."

"The consequences?"

"The shame Saxan might feel. The marriage that might be forced upon her by such an incident. Even the outrage of her kinsmen."

"And there would be a vast amount of outrage," Botolf murmured.

Edric nodded. "I fear so. It would not be just her brothers, either."

"I assumed not. It has been clear to see that your clan is tightly bound."

"Aye. Some of that is bred of the land we live in. It would badly weaken our family if we fought amongst ourselves, and the weak do not long survive out here. The fighting never really stops near the border."

"Nay. My father often remarked upon that. Is there never any peace?" Botolf asked as he stepped over a fallen branch.

"Oh, aye, but the watching ne'er stops. Not on either side," Edric added somberly.

"It does not seem to. Well, you may put your army of kin at ease concerning Saxan. I truly mean your niece no dishonor."

"May I be so bold as to ask what you do intend for her?"

"I cannot answer that yet. I will say only that I have already sent word to her eldest brother, who stands as her guardian. I have requested a meeting with him." Botolf frowned as he entered the camp and saw his mother immediately hurrying toward him. "My mother looks displeased."

"Saxan would not have disobeyed your request to be silent, but I cannot promise that she did not stir up mischief," Edric said, smiling faintly as he shrugged.

"Botolf," Lady Mary said, nodding briefly at Sir

Edric, who made a hasty retreat. "I wish to speak to you, son."

"Here I stand. I would guess that you are displeased," Botolf said.

"Displeased? Botolf, that poor child Saxan returned to camp wan and clearly shaken in spirit. I pressed her for the cause, and she finally told me that the two of you had fought."

"She did, did she?"

"Now, I realize 'tis not my business to know all that passed between you, but it cannot be wise to put the girl in such a troubled state."

"You are, as always, quite correct. It is not. I will speak to her," Botolf said and bowed to his mother as he added to himself, "aye, I will speak to the brat—right after I strangle her." He strode toward the cart Saxan shared with Pitney.

"Here he comes," Saxan murmured, looking at Pitney.

Pitney shook his head. "I think you forget that he is our liege lord."

"Some of that is his fault. 'Tis not easy to recall he is my liege lord when he calls me *wench* or *little one* or by my given name." She smiled briefly at her brother's surprise, then turned to greet Botolf as he stopped in front of her.

"Could you not have thought of something to tell my mother that would soothe her instead of enraging her?" Botolf demanded.

Saxan fought to look sublimely innocent as she met his scowl. "I fear I did not have the time to be clever."

"I think you were very clever. And I have already

heard you spin a tale with great skill in the blink of an eye."

Sighing, Saxan stared down at her feet. "I did not want to lie to Lady Mary."

"I do not like to lie to her either, dearling," he said in a soft, gentle voice as he placed a finger beneath her chin and tilted her face up toward his. "This constant threat to my life greatly upsets her. I simply wished to avoid adding to that." He glanced briefly at an intensely curious Pitney, including him in the conversation as he said, "I wish this trouble to remain a private matter."

"A Todd can be as silent as the grave when it is required," Saxan vowed dramatically.

"The Cecil who tries to murder me is my half-brother, my father's bastard."

"But you said the two of you share a birth date—the hour, year, and all," Saxan blurted out, then flushed for the sins of his parents were none of her concern.

Botolf smiled, caressed the color that touched her high-boned cheeks, and savored the feel of her silken skin beneath his fingertips. "Cecil was born late, and I was early. My parents were betrothed as children. My father knew whom he was to marry, but did not know his bride. Cecil's mother was my father's leman at Merewood for many years. She died birthing Cecil, and my mother took him to her breast. We were reared as brothers."

"Ah, and that gave Cecil ideas far above his station," Saxan murmured.

He leaned against the wagon and crossed his arms in an attempt to resist the urge to keep touching her. "Exactly. Cecil was not without opportunity and funds, but he hungered for it all. I am not quite sure when he began to try to murder me, for I was slow to see the truth. Howbeit, even though he knows I am now aware of the deadly game he plays and must spend his life in hiding, he continues his attempts against my life. My mother does not wish to see the truth. Cecil was as her own babe."

"And by stabbing at you, he stabs at her. The painful curse of an ungrateful child." Saxan studied Botolf for a moment. "He looks much akin to you."

"As close as a twin save for that scar above his eye." Botolf sighed. "I gave him that."

"So, you have already come to sword point."

"God's beard, aye." Botolf quickly thrust away the painful memory of Cecil making love to Alice. "So, now you must see why I try to keep as much of this trouble as possible hidden from Lady Mary."

Saxan nodded. "It can be no small distress to you as well. Cecil is forcing you to kill him or be killed. He presses you to spill his blood, blood gained from the same father. It would be best if a sword other than your own were the one to put an end to his treachery."

Botolf tensed at her tone. He noticed that Pitney reacted as well. For a moment, Botolf scoffed at the idea of a woman tracking Cecil and ending the assassin's machinations, but only for a moment. Saxan had hunted Botolf when she had believed he had killed Pitney. Just moments ago, she had fought and killed with an indisputable skill. She might think she owed him something because he had cared for her brother or even because she had tried to kill him. Saxan could also see it as a wonderful adventure.

"Do not even think upon it," he ordered.

Saxan did not try to deny that she had considered ridding him of the problem of Cecil. "I could do it. Well, mayhap I could. It would take very careful planning."

Botolf glanced at Pitney, who rolled his eyes then scowled at Saxan. "I begin to fear that madness lurks in your family." He grasped her by her slim shoulders and gave her a slight shake. "I will have your word."

"My word?" Saxan asked sweetly as she pushed her tousled hair off her face.

"Aye, your solemn word that you will not act against Cecil."

"Oh, all right. My word, then. I did have a very good idea," Saxan murmured.

"You may now forget it."

"M'lord? There is one thing. Does it not seem strange that Cecil so often knows exactly where to strike?"

"We were raised together," Botolf answered, even as he frowned in thought. "Cecil knows my habits well."

"True, but I think you should not ignore the possibility that someone within your entourage is aiding Cecil."

"You are right, Saxan. There have been times when I was most surprised to be set upon. It does bear some study," he said, then muttered a farewell and strode away.

Saxan watched Botolf rejoin his friends, then looked at Pitney. "I sincerely hope the earl does more than simply ponder the matter."

"He is not without sense," Pitney replied.

"Of course not, but, in this matter, he does have a weakness."

"Which is?"

"Unlike Cecil, our liege lord does not wish to spill the blood of a kinsmen, of the man who shared a mother's milk with him. We must try and insure that such a weakness does not kill him." Saxan spoke quietly, then smiled sweetly at Lady Mary when the woman joined them in the cart.

Botolf could not set aside Saxan's warning. It rang in his mind with each step his mount took toward Regenford. Arrogance and pride had made him dismiss any thought of a traitor in his ranks, but that could now cost him his life. Many of the men who rode with him remembered Cecil; some had known him throughout the years Cecil had lived with the family. Despite Cecil's evil ways and his cruelty, the man had a way of gaining strong and often intensely loyal allies.

"Do you worry o'er what you may find at Regenford?" Wesley asked as he and Roger rode up to flank Botolf.

Botolf shook his head, then, without preamble, said, "Cecil knows my every move."

"It would seem so," Roger agreed slowly. "Why do you think on that now?"

"It has been hinted that Cecil may have eyes and ears amongst those who travel with me," replied Botolf. "It is most strange that even a man who knows my habits well could guess my every move as accurately as he does."

"God's teeth," hissed Wesley. "Habit certainly did not take you to the tournament. You attend few. Not all of those who favored Cecil's company left with him." He looked at Botolf, his eyes widening. "Then Regenford—"

"May not be safe," Botolf finished and sighed, shaking his head at the enormity of the problem he faced. "I must be wary. I need to look for a traitor, yet not cause offense to those loyal to me. Some who befriended Cecil are now true to me, and I must not affront them with hasty, false accusations. If I blunder too badly, I could make enemies where none existed before."

"Which man warned you of this?" asked Roger. "If he is not a knight, mayhap he should be so honored for his keen insight."

"That would be difficult, Roger," Botolf said with a smile as he started to move away. "My advisor was Mistress Saxan Todd. I think, for now, I have gifted that clan with enough accolades."

"Does something trouble you, Saxan?" Pitney asked as, that night, she slipped into bed beside him.

"Tell me of kisses, Pitney," she demanded, staring at the roof of the cart.

Pitney tensed. "You know of such things, or should, considering whom you call kin."

Saxan ignored the hint of dismay and suspicion she heard in his voice. "True, but I wish to know about the feelings a kiss can rouse in a person. Are there many kinds? Is there a way to know if 'tis only lust?"

"I am not sure. As yet, lust is all I delight in."

"And does lust heat your blood until all thought is seared away?"

"I have never grown that warm. Although thought does not hinder me, 'tis not completely banished."

"I see." Saxan was disappointed; she needed more knowledge than Pitney seemed able to give.

"It is said that lust can be blinding, can shield a man's eyes until it is too late," Pitney added. "Men have wed or made complete fools of themselves because of lust or because they mistake it for love. Later, when the lust burns away, they are left with naught but regrets and shame."

"Is there no way to tell lust from love?"

"I would think it would come when the couple is not entwined or captivated by passion. 'Tis love if you can still care about and like the one you lust after even when your passion wanes."

"Ah, aye. Therein lies the answer." She took her brother's hand in hers even as her eyes were weighted closed with the force of encroaching sleep. "Thank you, Pitney. Thank you for simply answering my questions and not pressing for the reason behind my interest."

He gently squeezed her hand. "I hope you will tell me when you deem the time is right."

"I will. Do not worry o'er me."

She smiled crookedly when she heard him mutter, "There is advice I shall never heed."

Five

As they crested a small hill, Regenford loomed ahead of them. Saxan could not fully quell a sense of awe, the same sense of wonder she had had since she was a child. Lord Botolf's ancestors had planned well when they had built Regenford as a bulwark against the Scots. The large multi-towered keep was encircled by two thick walls and a moat. It sat on a small cleared rise. No one could approach its walls unseen. To get a better look, she wriggled forward in the cart and climbed onto the seat next to the stocky, grey-haired driver.

Botolf trotted up alongside, and she felt a return of her uncertainty. Her talk with Pitney last night had eased only a few of her qualms. It was not as easy to understand her feelings for the man as she thought it ought to be.

" 'Tis a fine castle, is it not, mistress?" Botolf asked, his pride clear in his voice.

"Very fine. One would think the Scots would run back to Scotland the moment they set eyes on it."

"That would be a blessing, but I fear they see Regenford as a challenge," Botolf replied, smiling.

She returned his smile shyly, but her expression swiftly faded when she finally noticed the mount he was astride. "You are riding my horse."

Although she spoke quietly, her words carried the

force of an accusatory shout. Saxan looked as angry as Botolf had expected her to be. He smiled, benignly patting her horse's strong neck as if oblivious to her fury.

"He is a fine beast," he said.

"Aye, and he is mine," she snapped.

"Have I ever questioned that? I need to ride him if I am to fairly decide the question of his suitability as a lady's mount."

"He is a suitable mount for me. I have ridden him since my father gave him to me as a gift."

"Your father gave you a stallion to ride, a mount fit for a knight's destrier?" Botolf could not keep his surprise out of his voice.

"A fit mount for a Todd."

He grinned at her haughty pride. "We will see. Have you been to Regenford before?"

"I have seen it a few times," she muttered, deciding the argument about her horse would have to wait. "I have been within its walls only once—when I was a very small child."

So Botolf described his home, and she felt her anger about Midnight ebbing as he piqued her curiosity. She struggled to hide her keen interest without appearing rude. She did not want Botolf to think she was prepared to agree to his plans for her to make a lengthy stay.

Once within the thick high walls of Regenford, Saxan lost sight of Botolf as he was caught up in the bustle of greetings and unpacking. She began to feel uneasy beneath the stares of his people. It was clear they had never seen a woman in a lad's attire. When Lady Mary requested that she accompany her, Saxan accepted the invitation with a relief she found difficult to hide.

It proved to be a short respite from confusion, however. Lady Mary led her up the narrow stone steps, around corners, and down halls until she was hopelessly lost. She was then left alone in the bedchamber allotted her. Saxan sat gingerly on the large, ornately carved bed; the quarters were much too large for her needs. She replied eagerly to a soft rap on the door only to suffer a sharp pang of disappointment when three young maids entered. Saxan heartily welcomed the bath they readied for her, however. A dainty brunette lingered after the other two maids left.

"I am called Jane, m'lady," the girl said and curtsied. "His lordship said I am to tend to all your needs while you stay at Regenford."

Saxan cast a rueful glance at her travel-stained clothing, "I hope you can find me some clean and more suitable clothes," she said.

"They will soon arrive," Jane replied as she helped Saxan undress. "Lady Mary herself is tending to it, m'lady."

Saxan sank into the hot bath with a delighted sigh. "I am but the fourth sister of a baron, Jane. There is no title for me. I am simply Mistress Todd."

Jane touched Saxan's long, pale hair. " 'Tis easy to mark you as a Todd. Some of your kinsmen are at Regenford. They have already gone to visit with your brother, Sir Pitney." Jane began to wash Saxan's hair.

"Sir Pitney Todd," Saxan murmured, making no effort to hide her pride in her brother. "That has a very nice sound to it, does it not?"

"A very fine sound," agreed Jane. "It was well earned. Your brother was very brave."

"God's beard, has the story winged its way through Regenford already?"

"The herald brought it when he arrived two days past to tell us that his lordship was soon to arrive."

"Of course. This is a very large household."

"Aye. You will see that even more clearly when you go to the great hall to dine. It is necessary to keep Regenford well manned. You will find many friends here."

"I am not sure there will be time for that. I must return to Wolfshead Hall."

"But—" Jane frowned. "I was told you would be staying with us for a long time."

"So his lordship says. We shall see." Saxan almost laughed at the look of surprise on Jane's face and knew the girl was unaccustomed to anyone's questioning her lord's orders.

Jane's words prompted Saxan to consider her situation more seriously. It was clearly accepted at Regenford that she was to be staying for a long time. That determination probably came from Botolf himself, and that could mean trouble. Her eldest brothers' impending arrival might not make any difference. Botolf was also their liege lord. They might not feel they could resist the man's wishes. It was quite possible that she would have to make a long stay at Regenford, and it might be wise to start to accept that.

She grimaced as she climbed out of the tub. Regenford was a fine keep, but it was not her home. Most of the multitude of people rushing about its halls were strangers to her. She was not too pleased about the idea of taking lessons in manners either, even if her teacher were to be the sweet, kind Lady Mary. Saxan could see no practical purpose in such affectations.

Perhaps, she mused as she donned the gown a maid had brought in while she bathed, what she needed to do was to show the earl that she did not need lessons. She had not been raised totally ignorant of courtly ways. If she made the effort, she could present her prettiest manners. Then Botolf would have to allow her to go home.

For one brief moment Saxan wondered why she was so eager to leave. New places and people were usually exactly what she sought out. The opportunity for both was right in her hand, and yet she could only think of running back to Wolfshead Hall. A small voice in her head whispered that the earl himself was the reason. His kisses and the fire they ignited within her were constantly in her thoughts. That passion was both frightening and intriguing. She hated to admit it, but she could well be running from her desire for him as well as her inability to guess exactly what the man's intentions were. Saxan could not shake the feeling that it was not particularly safe for her to stay too close to the Earl of Regenford.

Saxan straightened her shoulders and told herself not to be such a coward. There was nothing to fear from the earl or from what he made her feel. If his intentions proved to be dishonorable, she had plenty of kinsmen to turn to for aid and guidance. Pride of family alone would make every one of them willing to stand firm against the earl if it were revealed that Botolf sought no more than a pleasant tussle. The earl would have to look elsewhere if he thought to make her his leman. Saxan felt confident, however, that her own common sense and strength would prove armor enough against any dishonorable intentions.

Feeling more at ease, she smoothed her skirts and allowed Jane to lead her down to the great hall.

Botolf sat at the head table in the great hall and watched his guests and retainers drift in. When he realized that he was watching for Saxan, he scowled. That was a habit he would have to put a quick stop to.

Then Botolf became aware of the attentions of Saxan's kinsmen. Evidently, they had noticed his interest in Saxan and had decided to keep a close watch on him. Botolf was amused, but also irritated. Edric's surveillance was almost unnoticeable. His sons and the three young Jagers, Saxon's cousins, did not possess Edric's subtlety, however.

At first, Botolf was insulted, but he easily shrugged that aside. The Todds and the many branches of the family were closely tied. Botolf knew that if he had a sister or any young, pretty, female relative, he would act as they did. He had not made his intentions clear. They were right to wonder what game he played.

He grimaced as he admitted that he was not exactly sure what his intentions were. He needed a wife because, if he did not find one on his own soon, one would be chosen for him. That was a fate he dearly wished to avoid. Saxan intrigued him and aroused him. He could talk to her openly, plainly. Nevertheless, he was glad that it would be a few days before her eldest brother, Lord Hunter Todd, would arrive. He had made his decision, but he needed time to adjust to it. Botolf also felt that time would help insure that Saxan would at least be amenable to the plan.

"God's teeth," Wesley whispered.

His friend's oath interrupted Botolf's thoughts. Botolf followed his sergeant-at-arms' gaze and echoed his curse. Saxan dressed as a lad had been tempting, but Saxan dressed as a lady proved sweet torture. The soft, blue gown she wore enhanced the rich color of her eyes and flattered her slim figure. Her bright hair was neatly braided, the thick braid draped over her shoulder. He was astonished that such a difference could be wrought by a mere change of clothing.

Saxan blushed beneath all the gazes turned her way as she entered the great hall. Gathered there were all the men she had traveled with and who had seen her dressed as a boy. She readily accepted Lady Mary's proffered arm, needing the support, and allowed the woman to lead her to Botolf. Saxan wondered if she should be insulted by the men's looks of near-amazement, then shrugged the pinch of hurt aside. They had simply become accustomed to seeing her as a headstrong girl in boy's clothing and now had to struggle to adjust to the change. It was quite possible that some of them had not really seen her as a woman. A smile curved her lips as she realized that many of them were probably trying frantically to recall if they had said or done anything that could be offensive to a lady. They would soon come to understand that her sensibilities were not so delicate and again be at ease with her.

She hesitated when she was urged to a seat on Botolf's right. "Is this not rather high up the table for me?"

Her nervous query broke the spell which held Botolf and he motioned to her. "Nay. Come, sit down."

"But—"

"Saxan—sit."

Although his imperious tone irritated her, she obeyed. Glancing over her shoulder, she saw her three cousins, the Jagers. She smiled broadly and waved. They cheerfully waved back. Whatever confusion she suffered concerning a stay at Regenford did not dim the pleasure she felt over a chance to visit with them. It had been far too long since she had seen them.

"Saxan, child," Lady Mary called, laughter tinting her voice.

"You wish something, m'lady?" Saxan asked as she turned to face the woman seated opposite her.

"Simply to tell you that we are now being served."

Botolf bit back a smile, for he knew his mother had intended to scold Saxan for her small, amiable lapse in decorum, but then had lacked the heart to do so. "I think you will enjoy the fare set before you, Saxan."

Saxan enjoyed the hearty, delicious meal. The conversation swirling around her consisted mostly of Botolf relating even more information about Regenford. Since the lords of Regenford had been the liege lords of her family for many generations, she had heard most of what he told her, yet the way he told the stories cast them in a new, even more interesting light. He did not always see things as others did. She did not hesitate to tell him when she believed he was mistaken, either.

"I am certain that Sir Tarkington's forces entered that particular battle from the right," she argued at one point, pushing aside her empty plate and sipping her wine. " 'Twas my uncle, Sir Jager, who rode in on the left."

"You may be right," murmured Botolf as he hastily rethought the battle in question.

"Of course I am," she replied with haughty assurance only to destroy her pose by giggling at his raised eyebrow.

"Cousin?"

Saxan turned to face the three Jagers and the Healdon brothers. "You wish to speak with me?"

"If m'lord permits," Addis, the eldest of the Jager brothers, said with a small bow toward Botolf. "Would you care to join us for a walk ere you retire for the night, Saxan? It has been a long time since we have seen or spoken with each other."

"May I, m'lord?" she asked Botolf, unable to hide her eagerness.

"Of course," Botolf agreed with a hint of reluctance. "Mayhap I will join you in a while."

"You would be most welcome," she said even as she left her seat and strode away with her cousins.

"They mean no insult, m'lord," murmured Sir Edric, a ripple of laughter in his voice as he moved to sit closer to Botolf.

"And I take none. As soon as I finish my wine, I, too, will walk outside. I mean to let them know that I am not so easily diverted."

"Diverted from what, m'lord?" Sir Edric asked sweetly.

Botolf merely smiled and turned to speak to his mother. He noticed how hard she worked to keep her attention away from Sir Edric. Yet again he found himself wondering what had passed between her and Edric at the inn. Unfortunately, unless his mother or Edric chose to speak to him, he would never know. He knew his mother was no light, fickle female, yet she had kissed the man and now avoided him. It was puzzling. When he glimpsed a sadness in his mother's eyes, he almost wished he had not ordered Saxan not to meddle.

"Ah, 'tis indeed a fine night," Saxan murmured, gazing up at the full moon and bright stars with appreciation.

"Why, the moon is so bright you could roll the dice by its light," said Addis.

"You may be right, Addis," she replied and grinned, knowing he wished for a game.

"We should test the truth of it," said Kyne, the youngest Jager. "All we need is a flat place."

"If I recall, there is a good spot just around that

corner," said Kenelm. "A toss or two of the dice would be enough to prove Addis's speculation."

Within moments, Saxan was kneeling on the ground with her five cousins deep into a game of dice. She only briefly worried that it was not a suitable occupation for a lady. There was no one around to see her but her cousins, and they did not care.

Botolf rose finally to seek out Saxan, and Edric quickly got to his feet. "If m'lord allows, I should like to join you in your walk."

"Of course," drawled Botolf as he strode out of the hall. "Nearly all the rest of your clan is out there."

"Far from nearly all, m'lord," murmured Edric. "We are a very large family."

"Of which the Todds are the head?"

"Aye, even though there are a few of us who hold higher titles. 'Tis recognized that the Todds are the trunk of a many-branched tree."

Botolf shook his head. "Your family sounds a strong, full-branched oak whilst mine is but a thin sapling."

"There have been years where it seemed there were but a few of us. The yearly gatherings grew small and it was worrisome. No man likes to see his family wane, to realize that, mayhap, its time draws near an end. 'Tis sad to see any name fade from the rolls. Howbeit, it breaks a man's heart to look about him and find few, then fewer, of his blood, to see that all trace of him and his is fading."

"When each union produces but a few children, such an end becomes fated." Botolf swiftly reviewed his own dwindling family and murmured, "Few of my scarce kin have born more than one or two children. There are not many bastards, either. It does appear as if the Lavington line is dying. Even my father saw it." He shrugged. "Mayhap God wills that our time is over."

"M'lord, I speak now with no motive but to do what little I can to raise your hopes. Aye, and to help save a family that has been naught but good to and for my family."

"Ah, you are about to say something which could be seen as a ploy to make me choose a particular wife."

"I fear so, m'lord."

"Speak freely, Sir Edric. I know that such trickery is not your way."

"Mayhap what afflicts your family is the choice of wives. When a man holds a high title and a rich lineage, he is more apt to make a marriage for reasons of politics, alliances, land, or coin. That is all he looks at." Edric nodded absently at one of the men-at-arms as he and Botolf walked through the inner bailey. "True, there is a careful look at the bloodlines, but only to provide a proper purity. Often there are marriages within the clan. Has this been the way of your family?"

"Mother was cousin to my father, and my late wife was cousin to me." Botolf frowned as he tried to recall the lineage of other Lavington brides. "Do you believe it is wrong to marry cousins? I realize the church frowns on it, but 'tis still done."

"Nay, not wrong, but, if one's family is waning, if their broods are growing smaller, is it wise to continue to choose a mate from that line? Whether the weakness is God's will or no, 'tis there and should not be ignored. If one can look at wealth, land, and lineage, why can he not look at the ability to breed? Is it really wise to choose a bride who is the only child of an only child? True, that bride might well bear many healthy babes, but we all carry the mark of our fathers and 'tis not wise to ignore that. We wed to produce heirs. 'Tis our duty. So, why do we so often ignore signs that tell us the woman's family has not done well in that endeavor?"

"This is how your clan chooses its mates?"

"We try." Edric smiled. "Ah, but the heart oft rules the head. My wife came from dying stock. She gave me two sons, but, e'en had she survived, there would have been no more. They were all the fruit her body could bear, but I was well pleased."

"It seems unkind to wed a woman only to keep her with child at every turning."

"That is not what I suggest for, aye, 'tis unkind and it robs the woman of her health and beauty. Aye, I know God wishes us to be fruitful; but, no matter what the priests say, I cannot believe He means for us to slaughter our women in obedience to His command. A woman is fruitful for many years. She can rest and regain her strength between each child yet still give a man a large brood. She can have three babes or twenty. 'Tis for her to decide."

"Her? Surely you mean to say that it is her husband's decision."

"Who knows the strength of her body better than the woman herself?"

Botolf's eyes widened as he realized the wisdom of that, a wisdom that should have been obvious to him. "Of course. And of what use is making a woman so weak she bears weak babes who will not live out their first year?"

"Your family fades, m'lord. Your people see it and worry o'er it. I will not flatter you by saying 'tis all for love of you. The Lavingtons have been good liege lords. We want no change which could easily be for the worst. All I suggest is that you look to your bride's family. Are they forced to put all of their hopes into but one child for no other was born to them? Death lurks at every turn, and not all can elude it long enough to become a man. A large family is not only a joy, but a surety against all that can rob a poor child of a full life. Mayhap all your family needs to halt its slow death is some new blood, strong blood."

"Fruitful blood," Botolf murmured. "Wise words, Sir Edric. It is but prudent, when my own line wanes, to examine a bride's family's history of procreation. God's beard," he whispered as he and Edric rounded a corner and found Saxan and her cousins.

His shock at finding Saxan down on her knees indulging in a boisterous game of dice with five young men faded quickly. Amusement swiftly replaced it as six handsome faces turned his way, their expressions ones of identical consternation. He had to force down a laugh as he took Saxan by the arm and helped her to her feet.

"Who was winning?" he asked as, briskly, she brushed off her skirts.

"She was," replied Addis with a heavy sigh. " 'Twas foolish to think her twice-cursed luck would fail at last and allow me to win back all I lost to her the last time we played. 'Tis good that we keep our wagers small or I would have naught but rags to wear."

"Enough moaning, Addis," Saxan said. "Where are my winnings? Mayhap you need help to gather it all up for me."

"Braggart," scolded Kenelm with a laugh as he and his cousins gathered up the coins scattered on the ground and put them into her outstretched hands. "Ah, well, the pain of loss is lessened by the knowledge of how you will spend your winnings."

"Do you not have somewhere to go?" Saxan spoke in a near purr, glaring at her talkative cousin.

Edric chuckled as all five youths made a hasty, somewhat undignified retreat. "Child, if you could do that to the Scots, our armor would soon rust away."

"What do you spend your winnings on?" Botolf asked Saxan.

"Oh, nothing." Saxan found it impossible to look at Botolf and be evasive, so she concentrated on filling her pockets with her winnings. "Have you come to escort me back into the keep?"

A quick glance at Edric's impassive expression told Botolf that Saxan's evasiveness was no surprise to the man. He decided he would allow the subject to rest for now, but that he would get an answer soon.

"I came to beg your company for a walk through my mother's garden," Botolf said to Saxan.

He took her by the arm and led her along the well-laid-out paths which wended through his mother's ever-increasing gardens. It nettled him when Edric fell into step beside them. He knew some form of chaperonage was to be expected, but he did not want it. Although he had no intention of doing anything dishonorable, he did wish to be alone with Saxan. Botolf felt he could gain a better knowledge of the girl and of his own mind if they were left alone to speak and act without restriction.

"Uncle," cried Orick Jager as he stumbled up to them, "I think you had best come with me."

"Why? What is wrong?" Edric frowned when Orick grabbed his arm and started to pull him away from Saxan and Botolf.

"Kenelm has set about thrashing Addis." Orick glanced at Botolf. "You will excuse us, m'lord?"

"Of course," Botolf said, meeting Edric's scowl with a wide grin.

"I will be but a moment," Edric said firmly as he hurried away with Orick.

"Do not hurry on our account," he called after Edric, then held on to Saxan as she attempted to follow her uncle and cousin. "And where are you off to?"

"To watch the fight," she replied.

"I begin to think that you see a great many of them. Let this one pass and walk with me."

"As you wish." She fell into step beside him as he began to walk amongst his mother's plantings. "You are quite right. Addis and Kenelm fight often. Addis is clever, you see, and often loses patience with Kenelm, who is not. I think Kenelm must learn to think more and Addis must learn to control his temper. Did your mother plan this garden herself?"

It took Botolf a moment to adjust to her abrupt change of subject, a habit she employed frequently. "She did," he replied. "At first my father and I thought it foolish, but we soon appreciated the peace and beauty of it. 'Tis a good place to do one's thinking." He smiled down at her, noting how the moonlight added a glow to her hair. "Is there a garden at Wolfshead?"

"A small one, for we do not have as much room within our walls as you do. 'Tis difficult for my sister Thylda and me to agree on how it should look. I like simple paths through plants allowed to grow as they wish, but she likes more order to it. Thylda also favors reds and whites whilst I like blues and yellows. Then my sisters Denu and Tuesday are apt to plant something and not tell us."

Botolf shook his head. "Why should they do that? Is it not presumptuous?"

"Very," she replied with a quick grin. "Howbeit, I fear they have no choice. They would bring us seedlings for the garden, lovely flowers and vines, and Thylda and I would argue so much over where to plant them and how they should grow that the poor things died. Now my elder sisters just creep off to the garden and plant their gifts where they please. Thylda and I always hurry to see what they have done after they leave. I think my uncle returns."

"Aye, I think he does."

To Saxan's astonishment, Botolf abruptly tugged her into a cluster of tall shrubs. Despite her confusion, she obeyed his signal for silence, but nearly gasped aloud when he sat down, pulling her after him until they were hidden on all sides by the greenery. Saxan began to wonder about the earl's sanity, but said nothing, even when her uncle and his son Olan stopped directly in front of them.

"They must have gone inside, Father," Olan said.

"I suppose, although I somehow doubt that," Edric muttered as he started toward the keep.

"Well, they are not in the gardens and they would not hide from us." Olan hurried after his father.

"Nay? I would not lay any wager on that."

"Why did you hide from my uncle?" Saxan asked as soon as Edric and Olan had left.

Botolf did not move from where they sat as he looked at her and shrugged. "To be contrary." He laughed softly when she eyed him warily, her expression hinting that she had a question or two concerning his sanity. "You are very well guarded, little one."

"Nay. Why should they guard me?"

"They have caught us in an embrace."

"True, but 'twas only that one time by the stream and we have only kissed twice."

He slipped his arm around her shoulders and pulled her close. "Shall we make it three times?"

Saxan did not resist and curled her arms around his neck. "I should call for my uncle," she murmured.

Botolf was pleased at this sign of favor and smiled as he lowered his mouth to hers. "Call him then."

"Uncle," she whispered and met his mouth with an open eagerness.

He wrapped his arms around her slim body, holding her very close. A growl of pleasure escaped him when she parted her lips in welcoming at the first prod of his tongue. Slowly, he urged her pliant body to the ground and reached for her laces.

When Saxan felt his fingers on her laces she only briefly thought of resisting. She felt no fear or shame over the heat he was stirring in her. It all seemed right, as if it were the reason she had been born a woman. She also trusted Botolf implicitly. A murmur of pleasure escaped her as she tilted her head back and allowed Botolf the freedom to cover her throat with heated kisses. She shivered faintly when the cool night air touched her newly bared breasts, then cried out her delight when he chased the chill away with soft, warm kisses. What little coherent thought she clung to fled completely when he lathed her hardened nipples with his tongue.

What little control Botolf had maintained fled the moment he felt the hard tip of her breast against his tongue. The feel of her lithe body arching beneath him and the sweet taste of her as he drew her nipple deep into his mouth drove all sense of caution from his passion-clouded mind. He edged his hand beneath her skirts to stroke her slender legs.

It was not until he slid his hand over her thigh and touched the braies she wore that his control began to return. Touching cloth instead of the warm unfettered femininity he sought checked his passion enough for him to regain his senses. That thin barrier, one he would not have found beneath another woman's skirts, recalled him to other barriers he had allowed desire to wipe from his mind. He groaned as he let his full weight rest on her and pressed his face against her breasts as he fought to douse the fire in his veins.

Although physical disappointment was a sharp pain in her midriff, Saxan realized that Botolf's abrupt ending to their lovemaking was for the best. She felt him tremble against her, his breath hot and uneven, and sought to relieve that. She recalled what she sometimes did to ease the soreness of muscles in the backs of her kinsmen, muscles strained by swordplay or labor. Moving her hands to his back, she began to gently knead the broad, taut expanse of his back with her fingers. It was not long before she felt the tension there begin to lessen.

Botolf was surprised that those long slender fingers, which could so arouse him, could also smooth away the knots in his muscles caused by reining in his passion. She made no reprimands; nor could he sense any blame in her. As he gently put her clothing back in order, he carefully measured the words he would say. Once she was dressed, he sat up, tugged her up, and kissed her.

"That was ill done of me," he said quietly as he stood up and helped her to her feet. "I am your liege lord. 'Tis my place to protect you, not tussle you in the bushes." He smiled faintly and brushed her lightly flushed cheek with his knuckles. "You are as heady as the finest wine. I believe it would be wise if I ceased being so contrary and allowed your kin to guard you."

"I am capable of guarding myself if I wish to," she said softly. "I had no wish to."

"There is no need to feed my vanity with such words. That was done well enough by the warmth of your kisses." He took her by the arm and led her back toward the keep. "I fear that warmth robs me of all sense of responsibility. You are innocent and, although I am not a man of vast experience, I am not. No matter who we are, 'tis still my place to see that we do not sin. Well, mayhap sin is too harsh a word, but I can think of no other. 'Tis evident that I am unable to behave as I should, so," he winked at her, "there will be no more walks in moonlit gardens."

"As you wish. M'lord, exactly what do you plan for me?"

"You will know soon enough. Here comes your uncle. He has been looking for us again."

Saxan frowned. She recognized that an answer to her question, a query she thought to be an eminently reasonable one, had been neatly avoided. Although she did not believe that Botolf would plan anything bad for her, she sorely wished to have some idea of what lay ahead. Saxan cursed as her uncle fell into step at her side. She was not sure she had the patience to wait, but one quick glance at Botolf told her she would have to acquire it.

Six

"Where is Saxan?"

Botolf struggled to make his question reflect only an idle curiosity. Two days had passed since the kiss in the garden and he had seen little of Saxan. He had hoped that a trip to the town midway between Wolfshead and Regenford would allow him some time to be with her. Instead she had disappeared moments after they had entered the town, leaving him standing before the stables with Kenelm. Although there were few places that could be safer for Saxan, her disappearance made Botolf anxious. That was not something he wished to reveal, however, for he suspected he would look foolish since her own kinsmen appeared unconcerned.

"I think she went to the church, m'lord," Kenelm replied after a brief consultation with Olan.

As soon as he felt few people would notice, Botolf made his way to the small stone church near the northern edge of town. He could not be as sanguine as Saxan's relatives concerning her roaming about unattended. Even though it was obvious by the many hearty greetings sent their way that the Todd clan was not only well known, but well liked in the town, Botolf could not dismiss the feeling that it was unsafe for any young woman to move about as freely as a man.

He entered the small church. It took a moment or two before his eyes adjusted to the gloom. Saxan was easy to find, for even the dim light of the tallow candles glowed in her hair. She and the priest were clearly well acquainted. There was an ease between them which only came from familiarity and friendship. When Botolf saw her place a weighty purse in the priest's hands, he knew instinctively that it was her winnings from the dice game in the garden.

"How fares little Elizabeth, Father?" she asked the plump priest.

"Well, very well," Father Chesney replied. "We were right, my child. She will make a fine nun. She truly has the calling."

"I am so glad that she is finally happy."

"God has found an excellent servant. And this," he hefted the purse in his hand, "this will certainly aid the Blacks."

"Will it allow them to finally hold one of their babes in their arms for longer than a year?" she asked, sadness weighing her voice.

"That is in God's hands, my child. A little food and a home will aid Him in that work, I think," he added with a smile.

"I hope so." She turned to leave and immediately saw Botolf. "My liege!"

"Lord Botolf," Father Chesney murmured, bowing as the earl walked toward him. "We rarely see you in our little church."

"I would like to say 'tis piety which brings me here now; but, I fear, 'tis Mistress Todd I seek," said Botolf.

"It cannot be time to return to Regenford already," said Saxan.

"Nay. I realize that I hold an opinion of one in

this matter, but it does not please me to see you wandering about alone."

Saxan tensed, frowning. "I can fend for myself."

"Aye, you can, but your lack of size and strength means that you can be overcome in many a confrontation. If you can put aside your pride, you will see the truth of that." He held out his hand. "If your visit here is done, we can leave."

She put her hand in his with an audible sigh of resignation. "Aye. I am done here. Until next time, Father," she said to the priest.

"God be with you," Father Chesney said as the couple began to leave.

The moment they stepped outside the church, Saxan said, "This is really not necessary. I have no enemies here."

"That is easily seen, but enemies can come from afar. Do you try to tell me that your family has none at all?"

"Nay. There are a few. But—"

"Saxan, there is no argument you can muster which will alter how I feel in this. I know you are capable of protecting yourself, that you have courage and skill. Howbeit, I can also see that you are small and womanly soft. I cannot be at ease allowing you to move about unattended. 'Tis not my way and I do not believe it can ever be."

For a moment Saxan said nothing. She realized she was not dealing with simple male arrogance. Botolf did not see her as weak and helpless. He was acting as he had been reared to act. She was a woman and must be watched over. If an attack came, he would see nothing wrong in her fighting at his side, but he would feel he had failed in some way if she had to face some trouble alone.

"Where shall we go then, m'lord?" she asked.

Botolf gave her a courtly bow. "Wherever you wish, m'lady. I am but your humble servant."

She curtsied. "How soothing to my vanity and how prettily false." She took his hand. "I would like some mead, I think."

He led her toward an inn to buy some mead and murmured, "False, am I?"

"Nay, not you; your words of flattery are false. You, m'lord, are no one's servant, save mayhap God's and the king's. And you are certainly not humble."

"Do you believe that I am arrogant?" He was not sure if he should feel insulted or not.

"All men are in one manner or another. I think it is a humor they are born to. 'Tis because they are most often larger and stronger than the rest of us. They are also taught from cradleside that they are the ones to rule, that 'tis they who direct the ways of the world be it by word or by sword. When one holds power of any sort, one will be at least a little arrogant."

"I should like to disagree, but your words hold too much truth. Here is where we will find our mead," he said as he stopped before the inn.

Botolf went inside and got them both a tankard of mead. As he searched for a place where they could sit comfortably, he bought a few meat pasties as well. A large tree drew him and he sat down, handing Saxan her mead and a pastie as she sat beside him. They had a clear view of the bustling market day in the town, yet were comfortably separated from its noise and crowds. That suited Botolf perfectly. Although the night in the garden had shown him the danger of being alone with Saxan, he felt a need for some privacy so that he could come to know her better.

"You are not very close to your married sisters?" he asked her after a few moments of idle talk.

"Not as close as I should like to be," Saxan admitted. "They were wed and gone whilst I was still very young. Once they had begun their own families, the time they spent at Wolfshead Hall grew less and less."

"How many children do they have?"

"Well, let me think." She frowned slightly and brushed away a fly that was eager to drown itself in her mead. "Denu has three and now carries her fourth. Tuesday has two and will soon bear her third." She sent Botolf an impish look. "Her husband was often away for the first few years of their marriage."

Botolf laughed, but his thoughts were on what Sir Edric had said about the fruitfulness of a family. Saxan's sisters had certainly proven they were of good, strong breeding stock. He grimaced. He did not like to look at marriage as if he searched for a good cow or ewe, but forced himself to do so. He could no longer ignore the fact that his family was dying out.

He reached out to stroke her thick braid. "Are they all so fair?"

"Nay. Tuesday's husband is a dark man. Her two sons are also dark. She hopes for a daughter now."

"And Denu?"

"Ah, well, her man has red hair. One of her sons and her daughter do also, but her younger son is fair."

To hide how he felt, Botolf took a long, calming drink of mead. In his mind he made a swift tally. Her two sisters had produced four sons from five births. Her mother had borne five sons out of nine children. Those were numbers he could not shrug aside. He craved a son to insure that his lands continued to belong to the Lavingtons. Botolf did not want Saxan to see his interest, however, for he knew he would never marry her for that reason alone and he did not want her to think that was his sole consideration. His delight over her promise of fruitfulness was something he would strive to keep to himself.

"Where did your sister's husband go so often during the first years of their marriage?" he asked.

"To battle. There is always one somewhere." She frowned. "I believe their union was sorely troubled at the start, but I have ne'er heard why. I have been reluctant to ask. After all, if there were trouble, it would be painful for her to remember it."

"But all is well now."

"Very well, if the number of times you catch them kissing is any sign." She rolled her eyes in mock disgust and Botolf guffawed.

"None of your brothers has yet married?"

"Nay. Hunter was betrothed two years past, but she proved to be a faithless bitch. It sorely hurt him," Saxan added in a slow hiss, curling her small hands into tight fists as she recalled the incident.

Botolf quickly covered one of her fists with his hand and said quietly, "Mayhap she loved another."

"I think Hunter would have understood that and accepted it. Well, in time. But, nay, this woman loved no one but herself and—" She sighed and shook her head. "Nay, I must not say it. A true lady would not, and your mother works very hard to make me one."

"I believe I can guess what you have left unsaid. My wife was such a woman," he admitted, startled by his candor.

Saxan stared at him in astonishment. Her mind became crowded with the memories of the heated kisses they had shared. She could not stop herself from looking him over. It was easy, and a little heady, to recall the length, breadth, and hardness of his manhood as he had pressed against her during those embraces. When she lifted her gaze, she caught the gleam of amusement in his eyes and blushed vividly over her errant thoughts.

She turned away and muttered, "She must have been very greedy indeed."

Although flattered and seized by an urge to kiss her, Botolf let his amusement rule and laughed. "Saxan, you are a delight."

A crooked smile curved her lips as she looked at him, but then she grew serious. "Did she speak of love to you?"

He stared down at their entwined hands as he murmured, "Nay, although I allowed myself to believe that she did."

" 'Tis very easy to hear what you wish to in the words a person says. In a way, she was kinder to you than Elaine was to Hunter. She swore undying love to my poor besotted brother, filled his ears with sweet promises, flattery, and love words. She wished him blinded, and he was for a while. Howbeit, she grew too brazen, too confident of her hold on his heart and mind. The whispers of others who were not as blind soon grew too loud to ignore. She had played her part well enough, however, to keep him doubting until he caught her with the smith's son. Elaine tried to cry rape and was willing to toss away the lad's life just to save her own. Hunter turned away from her then.

"Hunter was satisfied just to drive her from his sight, but I fear I was not." Saxan shook her head. "She had hurt him badly and caused a rift within our family. That rift has been healed, thank God, but it was still fresh then. I intended to see that she would not be able to do that to any other man, but Hunter discovered my plan and stopped me."

"What had you planned to do?"

"Scar her. I wished to take away that beauty she used so evilly."

Botolf nodded, squeezing her hand in a gesture of understanding. "I often thought of dealing thus with my wife Alice."

" 'Tis a dark tale to linger on," she muttered. "Do you think my brother will soon arrive?"

"Aye," Botolf replied and deftly turned the subject to the constant fighting between Scotland and England over the border town of Berwick.

It was late afternoon before they returned to Regenford and found that Lord Hunter Todd and his twin brother Roc had arrived. Botolf wondered if Hunter had been conjured up by talking about him. He watched Saxan fling herself into Hunter's arms with a squeal of delight and then do the same to Roc a moment later. Botolf recognized that he was faintly jealous.

Several hours passed before he was able to be alone with Hunter in his chamber of office. It did not surprise Botolf when Hunter asked if Roc could be privy to their discussion. By watching Pitney and Saxan, he had come to understand the deep bond between twins. It was unsettling, however, to face two golden-haired, silver-eyed men whose handsomeness had even affected his mother.

"Our service to the king is completed, m'lord," Hunter said as he sat on a stool facing Botolf's writing table. "We are now at your service."

Botolf leaned forward, resting his arms on the highly polished table. " 'Tis not your service I wish. I called you here so that we may speak of Saxan."

"M'lord, what occurred at the Boar's Head Inn—"

"Is forgotten. Truly. I wish to take your sister as my wife." He smiled at their identical looks of astonishment which they quickly strove to hide. "You are surprised."

Hunter nodded. "We have always been vassals to the lords of Regenford."

"The king has but yesterday sent me his approval of this match," Botolf said quietly.

"I see. And what does my sister have to say?"

"I have not discussed this with her yet. 'Twas my belief that you, her guardian, would have the say in this matter."

" 'Tis not the way of the Todds to say too much concerning the marriage choices of our kin. I realize some people feel we must be quite mad, but we like to give our women the freedom of choice."

"So I have heard, but I am a man of my breeding and I was taught to speak first to the king and the woman's kinsmen. I would be a good husband," he added bluntly.

"But will you be a good lover?" Roc asked in a quiet voice, shrugging when Botolf glanced at him in surprise.

"M'lord, why have you chosen our sister?" asked Hunter. "Forgive my impertinence, but I feel a need to ask. I think you do not propose out of love."

"Not that I have recognized," Botolf admitted with honesty. " 'Tis hard for me to explain what I do feel. I admire Saxan, her spirit and her honesty. She fascinates me."

"And yet you have your lady mother work to change Saxan," accused Roc.

"Nay," replied Botolf. "My mother does not try to change her, just educate her. My position as a marcher lord requires certain things of me and of my wife. I but seek to protect her from scorn."

"Aye, I can understand that. Howbeit, do you not

think you could begin to scorn her for her lack of courtly ways?"

"Nay. They matter not at all to me. I often find them troublesome. Believe me when I say that I only try to protect her."

"I believe you," Hunter murmured and Roc nodded. "Saxan could benefit from a few lessons."

Botolf realized that the brothers waited for far more than words of admiration and he confessed abruptly, "I want sons. I need sons."

"M'lord, what happens if Saxan gives you none? There have been a few of our number who have failed to beget children or bear only daughters."

"Then I shall see it as God's will that my line die out for none could hold the promise of fruitfulness as your sister does."

Hunter grinned. "There is the truth."

"I have not decided this without thought although I do need to find a wife. Soon the king himself will be seeking one for me." His face showed his displeasure at the prospect. "My thoughts were clear earlier, but I seem to stumble over the words I need to explain them now." He cleared his throat nervously. "Now that my father has died, I must reside here more often. Saxan understands this life, loves it, and thrives in it. She holds the strength to survive here. She is honest and, after the hell of my first marriage, I crave that honesty." He dragged a hand through his hair and smiled sheepishly. "Saxan gives me laughter and I find I can talk with her easily. These things may sound foolish, but they weigh heavily in her favor." Botolf met Hunter's gaze and admitted with direct sincerity, "I want her."

"I see. And does Saxan desire you?"

"Aye, she does, but you need not fear for her chastity. If I had not seen the danger of being too private with her, your kin would have been protection enough. At every turn I find a Jager, a Healdon, or a Todd." He grinned when the twins laughed. He quickly grew serious again and continued, "I am a man who believes in the marriage vows. Saxan will not face faithlessness. True, I am no saint, but what man is? Howbeit, a wife who does not turn me from her bed will be woman enough."

" 'Tis good of you to tell us all of this, m'lord. You could wed her whether we agreed or not."

"Aye, I could since I have the king's hearty agreement, but I wish all concerned to be agreed."

"This is a marriage many would pray for, but I must speak to Saxan." Hunter stood up and sighed. "I will not command her to be your bride, m'lord, but I will speak strongly in your favor. Saxan is a young girl and she may think on love, but I know the value of what you have offered. I believe she will, too. There is but one question I must ask."

"Which is?" Botolf prompted when Hunter hesitated.

"Is your first wife fully dead to you, m'lord?"

"She was dead to me months before she went to her grave. There will be no ghosts in my marriage bed."

Saxan eyed her brothers warily as they entered her bedchamber and dismissed Jane. She knew they intended to have a serious discussion with her; she could see it in their faces. If they only wanted to tell her they agreed with the earl's wish that she train with his mother, they would not require privacy nor look so solemn.

"What sin are you about to lecture me on?" she

asked with a stab at levity as Roc and Hunter sat on her bed and looked at her.

"None, loving, although 'twas madness to try and kill the earl," Hunter replied.

"I believe I was in the grip of madness at the time. When I thought Pitney was dead, my grief turned my mind."

"That I can understand." Hunter took a deep breath then blurted out, "The earl has asked for your hand in marriage."

Although she opened her mouth, Saxan could not utter a word. She was too stunned. Botolf wanting to wed her was not a possibility she had considered. For one brief instant, her heart soared, but then it jerked back into place. Now she began to understand his actions since their violent meeting at the Boar's Head Inn. She wondered exactly when he had begun to plan it.

"Why?" she asked hoarsely.

Hunter took her hand between his. "The earl did not speak of love, but what he did say makes me believe he will be a good husband. The match is to be envied."

Suddenly, Saxan recalled the conversation she and Botolf had had earlier beneath the tree in town and sighed. "He wants sons."

"Aye," Hunter admitted reluctantly. "The Lavington line is dying out."

"Are you certain?"

"Very certain. Botolf will not hold it to be your fault if you bear him no sons. If that happens, he says it will be the will of God. Howbeit, he recognizes that few other women hold the promise of bearing him a fine brood as you do."

"You cannot fault the man for thinking of children,

Saxan," Roc said. " 'Tis most often the reason a man marries."

"I know that," she said. " 'Tis just hard when it is yourself who is being viewed as the brood mare."

"Would it be hard for you to bed down with him?" Hunter asked.

Color flooded Saxan's cheeks as she shook her head. "Nay. In truth, 'tis Botolf who has restraint. I have none."

Hunter laughed, pulling a reluctant grin from Saxan. "Restraint in such a matter has never come easily to a Todd." He grew serious again. "What are your feelings for the man, dearling?"

"I fear I cannot say for certain. From the moment I ceased to wish him dead, he has been a great puzzle to me. He can make me angry, yet—" She blushed. "—when he holds me, I have no wish to push him away. Strangely, it seems right to allow him to have his way."

"But you do not love him?" Roc asked.

"I dare not say that I do," Saxan replied, nervously twisting her braid in her hands. "I am not sure. I desire him; I trust him; I fear for his safety, and I enjoy his company."

"It sounds much akin to love to me."

"Mayhap, Roc, but those are words one should be very sure of before one utters them."

"Saxan, the king has heartily approved this match," Hunter said.

"Heartily, is it? Then 'tis set." She was angry that she was clearly the last one to be consulted.

"It could be, but the earl wishes everyone to be in agreement, as do we."

"I am not in disagreement. Do I have time to think about this?"

"Aye, loving." Hunter stood up and kissed her cheek, and Roc followed suit. "I will not press you."

"But?" she murmured, hearing his hesitation.

Sighing, Hunter added, "Aye—but. I think you can guess the reasons for that *but.* The earl will be a faithful husband."

"Did he say that?" That was a promise Saxan knew was rarely given, for many men felt it was their right to bed any woman, where and when they pleased, despite their marital status.

"Aye, he believes in the vows exchanged. Think on that as well," he urged her, then left to find the earl, Roc at his heels.

Botolf led his mother to the front hall, growing more perturbed each step of the way. He wondered what imp of misfortune had decided he needed the complication of Lady Odella and her entourage now. Since Hunter had told him that Saxan had said she would consider his proposal, Botolf had planned to spend the afternoon preparing for her answer. Instead, there was Lady Odella acting as if she had a reason to expect a warm welcome. He was in no mood to give her one, although, as he reached the bottom of the stairs and Odella rushed into his arms, he tried to keep a firm hold on his good manners. Offending the woman would only cause a trouble he did not need.

"We had not expected you, Lady Odella," Botolf said politely as he extracted himself from her hold.

"Oh, but I was certain all was settled with your lady mother when we last spoke," Odella said.

Lady Mary flushed when Botolf looked at her. He knew his mother had not made any definite invitation, but that courtesy prevented her from saying so. With a forced smile, Lady Mary deftly eluded Botolf as she conveyed Lady Odella and her father to their chambers. Botolf was determined that it would prove only a temporary reprieve for his mother.

When Hunter and Roc walked up to him, Botolf tensed. The very last thing he needed now was Saxan's protective kinsmen thinking he was playing some game with her. He turned to explain Odella then saw the humor lighting their eyes.

"I envy you not, m'lord," drawled Hunter. " 'Tis dangerous to be caught between two women—one pondering an answer and the other pressing hard for the question."

"I can see how deeply you sympathize," Botolf murmured then joined the brothers in laughter. He could see the humor in his situation despite the trouble it could cause him, a trouble that would undoubtedly begin as soon as everyone gathered in the great hall.

Saxan studied her appearance one more time before making her way to the great hall. She prayed no one would press her for an answer to Botolf's proposal for, despite having considered it for several hours, she was still uncertain. Her own feelings remained a puzzle to her, Botolf's even more so. A large part of her was more than willing to become his wife, but her doubts stopped her from immediately agreeing to the marriage. She wished she did not have the knowledge that her decision was not really necessary in the end. It ended the delusion that she had some choice in the matter.

She slipped into Pitney's room. It delighted her to see him on his feet although his walking was confined to a small area and he needed someone to help him. The page assisted him back into his bed and left discreetly.

"You will soon join us in the great hall," she said as soon as they were alone.

"I mean to be on my feet for your wedding," he said, watching her closely as he got more comfortable in his bed.

"Ah, so Hunter has spoken to you. I had thought to surprise you."

"I am glad that he did tell me, for I had begun to fear that the earl sought no more than a tussle in the grass."

"He always pulls away before that can happen."

Pitney chuckled. "You sound disappointed, even offended."

" 'Tis shameless, I know. Still, I cannot deny that the earl could have me if he but crooked his elegant finger."

"Then, mayhap, dear sister, you had best marry the man. Then he may crook his elegant finger all he wishes and you need not sin to answer the call," Pitney suggested baldly.

"There is that to consider." She exchanged a sly grin with him, but then sighed, somber once again. " 'Twould be nice if love were involved. In truth, I can foresee that I could love him, may do so e'en now but simply do not know it. Howbeit, I have no idea of his feelings for me."

"And you may never get one. Not all men can speak their heart. You must consider the fact that he has chosen you. Consider all he has to choose from. That he has asked for your hand is the highest flattery."

"True, but," she sighed, "he wants sons and ours is a fruitful lot." She moved to the door. "You are right, though, I will think on how easy it would be for him to possess me and what a high honor he does me by asking for my hand in marriage. Neither should be shrugged aside. Keep walking, Pitney, for I believe there will be a wedding soon." She paused in the doorway and sighed again. "The more I consider it, the more I realize that saying nay will trouble me far more than saying aye—despite all my doubts."

Now that the lovely Lady Odella had arrived, Botolf feared he was about to hear a resounding no from Saxan. Odella's pursuit had been tolerable when he had still been in the market for a wife. Now her pursuit would only cause problems. He walked into his mother's bedchamber and glared at her, knowing it was not truly her fault, but needing to blame someone.

Lady Mary took one look at her son's dark expression and said, "I did not invite that woman. Truly, I did not. I was most vague when she pressed me."

"Clearly you were not vague enough." He paced the room, animated by frustration. " 'Tis my fault as well. I did not turn her aside, but allowed her to ply her wiles. I knew I must soon find a wife and she was not an intolerable choice."

"Then 'tis not such a dire matter that she has arrived."

" 'Tis a disaster. Mother, I have chosen a wife. I but await her acceptance."

"Saxan Todd," she guessed in an instant, her eyes wide.

"Aye, Saxan Todd." He sighed with relief when he saw no sign of distress or distaste on her face.

"What do you mean you await her acceptance? Her brother cannot disapprove of the match, can he?"

"Nay. He has agreed. E'en the king agrees, most

heartily. I cannot help but wonder if he would have made the same choice had I left it to him."

"Then we must begin to plan the wedding."

"It might be wise to begin, but quietly." He eyed her sheepishly. "I could force the marriage, but I want Saxan to accept my offer on her own. I want to know that she wants me as her husband."

"That is not foolish, dear. Do you fear that Lady Odella's presence will cause some difficulty?"

"Aye. As Hunter said, I am now caught between a woman who ponders her answer and one who presses me for the question."

Lady Mary made a face. "A precarious place to be."

"Aye. I cannot say I am betrothed to divert Lady Odella, yet cannot honestly tell Saxan that I gave Odella no hope. After all, I let her play her games and now I cannot be rude to the woman. I wish her pursuit of me to end, but I have no wish to offend her."

The urge to offend took shape, however, but moments after he led his mother into the great hall. Odella took her place at his side and would not be dislodged when Saxan arrived. Botolf had never noticed before how tenacious the woman could be. He did not know how it could have happened, but he got the strong impression that Odella knew of his decision to marry Saxan. The way Saxan's small face grew tighter, her expression more closed, told him that Odella was waging a game and scoring points.

Saxan told herself sternly not to be foolish. She could see with her own eyes that Botolf was being no more than courteous to Lady Odella, but her emotions were not as reasonable as her observations. Her feelings saw only the way Lady Odella clung to Botolf, kept her shapely body between her and Botolf, and flirted outrageously with the man. She had a strong urge to break every one of the woman's dainty fingers, which kept touching Botolf. She grew tired of the way the woman talked to Botolf as if she and the earl were close and had been so for a very long time.

When Saxan went to bed, she tried to review her feelings clearly and with no bias. She began to think that she was suffering from a severe bout of jealousy. That hinted that her feelings for Botolf ran far deeper than she had guessed. A person had to care about someone to succumb to jealousy. Saxan had never been overpowered by possessiveness before.

Sighing heavily, she admitted that the desire to be Botolf's wife was too strong to ignore. Neither doubts nor uncertainty nor jealousy could make her say a firm no. On the morrow she would tell Botolf that she accepted his proposal of marriage.

As she settled down to sleep, she mused crossly that she might encounter some difficulty finding a moment alone with the man.

Seven

Saxan grumbled to herself as she sat down on a low crumbling wall in Lady Mary's gardens. For two long days she had not been able to get any time alone with Botolf. She could not help but wonder if she had been wrong to believe he was simply being courteous to Lady Odella. The shapely blond was extremely lovely. Botolf could easily be enjoying all the attention the woman was lavishing on him.

She stiffened as she heard voices drawing nearer to her. The urge to scream nearly overwhelmed her when she recognized the voices as Botolf's and the tenacious Odella's. Worse, she had no way to escape. If the pair carried on in a manner they wished to be kept private only to discover her, they could easily think she had been spying on them. Saxan hated the thought of that as much as she did the idea of the two of them behaving like lovers in the moonlit gardens. She was intensely relieved when they kept walking until they reached her.

"So, here you are, Saxan," Botolf said. "I wondered where you had fled."

The look that flitted over Lady Odella's face almost made Saxan laugh. She knew Botolf had not intended it to sound as if he had taken a walk in the gardens just to look for her, but Odella clearly felt that he meant that. It was easy to see that the woman's vanity was badly stung.

"I often take a walk here," Saxan replied, frowning when she heard other voices drawing near. "It has ne'er been this crowded."

Hunter and Roc smiled in greeting as they ambled over. Saxan saw the way they glanced at Lady Odella, who was firmly attached to Botolf's side. She had tried to look unaffected by the woman's constant presence, but would not be surprised to discover her brothers had guessed that she was upset. She hoped they would devise some way to loosen the woman's grip on Botolf. It was past time she had a moment with the earl without Odella intruding.

Glancing at the three Todds, Odella murmured, " 'Tis far colder than I had realized, Botolf. Shall we walk back to the great hall?" She turned, tugging on Botolf's arm.

"I find it to be quite a pleasant night." Botolf stood firm, neatly extricating himself from her grip.

"Ah, then allow us to escort you, m'lady," said Hunter as he took Odella by the arm while Roc quickly put himself between Botolf and the woman. "My brother and I have also enjoyed as much of the night air as we care to and plan to return to the hall. Your beautiful presence will lighten our way."

"Are you remaining here, Botolf?" Odella asked even as her escorts began to lead her away.

"Aye, for a while," he replied.

Hunter glanced back over his shoulder and said pointedly, "We will see you soon, though."

Botolf laughed softly and sat down next to Saxan. He could sense her reticence, but felt certain he could cure her of that. Only part of his attention and a great deal of his time had been stolen away by the determined Odella. That could be easily atoned for.

"It has been a long while since we have talked," he said.

"I have been near at hand, m'lord," she murmured.

"Aye and so has Lady Odella."

Saxan looked at him and said carefully, "She seems to believe she has a right."

"I fear I cannot say that I gave her no reason to think that. Before now there was no cause to push her away or stop her games."

"And 'tis only her game?"

"Only hers. As I said, there was no reason to rebuff her." He took Saxan's hand, pressed a soft kiss to her palm, and said, "Now, if I were betrothed, I could simply tell Odella so and end this foolishness without causing offense."

Saxan stared at their joined hands. "Are you certain that is what you wish to do?" she asked.

"Very certain. I have thought about little else since I first set eyes on you."

The way he moved his thumb over the back of her hand sent delightful chills along her arm, but she retained enough wit to say, "You want sons."

He edged closer to her, lightly caressing the side of her neck with his other hand. "What man does not? I also wish to enjoy the making of those sons," he said, his words husky with longing. "I do not need to tell you that I would enjoy the bedding of you." He smiled when she blushed and lightly kissed her cheek. "You know that I desire you."

"Ah, but desire can be a fleeting thing, burning sweet and hot for a time, then turning to ashes."

She found it difficult to think clearly when he moved even closer. He slipped one strong arm around her shoulders and held her near. It was not necessary, for she was already leaning into him. Slowly, he covered her face with warm, soft kisses, firing her blood and clouding her thoughts. She clutched at his broad shoulders as she succumbed to the need to touch him and steady herself.

"Desire has never run so hot or so sweet for me," he whispered, nibbling at her earlobes. "If the fire wanes, and it may, a little or a lot, there is trust and a liking for the person you are. Are you of a mind to say nay?"

"I have no say. You are my liege lord. The king has approved. My family would think me mad."

"I wish for you to be agreeable."

She slid her arms around his neck and tried to urge his wandering kisses from her neck to her mouth. "I must be agreeable."

"I do not wish to force it upon you."

"Oh, but 'tis still something I must do, for, if I do not say aye to marrying you, I will still say aye to this."

A hungry sound escaped Botolf as he gave her the kiss she craved. The implication that she did not have the will to refuse him his pleasure of her set his blood to racing through his veins. Her passion was his, he thought with a thrill of triumph. He ruthlessly quelled the sudden traitorous thought that her passion might be given to any man possessed of the right skills.

It required all his willpower to pull away from her. He held her tightly and pressed his cheek against her hair as they both fought for control. The wedding must be soon, he determined, for his self-restraint grew more elusive each time he held her.

"I will ascertain how much time it will take your family to travel here, and we will be wed as soon after that as is possible," he said. "Tomorrow eve, when everyone gathers in the great hall, we will announce our betrothal."

Saxan pulled away to look at him and mused aloud,

"My family could be gathered more speedily than you wish, m'lord."

He kissed the tip of her nose, stood up, and pulled her to her feet. "Considering what flares between us, little one, the sooner the better."

"My kinsmen will no doubt agree," she murmured as she fell into step at his side.

Botolf's steps faltered slightly. "Your kinsmen know?"

"They have eyes, m'lord."

"Too many, I begin to think." He smiled ruefully when she laughed.

"I spoke about it to my brother Pitney," she confessed.

"That comes as no surprise."

"And Hunter and Roc," she added in a muted voice.

"You are so close to them that you can speak openly of such private matters?"

"Well, aye, we are close, but I spoke out because it was asked of me. My admission also eased their minds. They wished me to accept this marriage, but the tradition of choice is an old one within our clan. My brothers wished to know if I hesitated to answer your proposal because of the bedding."

Botolf nodded. "A reasonable concern. Were you as honest with them as you were with me just now?"

"Aye, m'lord."

"Then I am most surprised that they have left us alone."

"If there is aught my kin understand, 'tis a fever of the blood. I have also assured them of how honorable you are."

He bit back a smile when he heard the hint of irritation in her voice. "And so I shall remain until we are wed. I wish no questions raised on the morning after our wedding." He lightly traced the blush that touched her cheek with his fingertips. "All will be as it should be."

"I should be well accustomed to hearing such blunt speech."

"I am not your kin."

"True. That must be what causes the color to rush to my cheeks so often and causes me to stumble o'er the words." When they entered the great hall, she was surprised to be steered to a relatively private corner of the room. "I had thought to seek my chambers, m'lord."

Botolf sat down, tugged her down beside him, and retained his hold upon her hand. "You may do so in a moment or two. 'Twill ease the way of our announcement on the morrow if we are seen to sit alone and mayhap flirt as lovers are apt to do."

"I fear I have done little flirting, my lord. I may not be too convincing."

"Call me Botolf."

"If it pleases you, I should like to save such familiarity until we are wed."

"Is there a reason for that?"

Saxan smiled crookedly. "Not one that I can easily explain. I feel it will ease the change from maid to wife. 'Tis something my sisters did and, although they often claim a benefit from the practice, they were unable to put it into words clearly. I find I suffer from the same inability."

"As you wish then."

For a while they spoke of inconsequential things. Saxan quickly forgot the attention they drew from the others in the great hall and began to relax. It was nearly an hour before she rose, bid Botolf a good night, and left to seek her bed. On her way, she took a moment to see Pitney.

When Saxan entered the room, Pitney looked up from the game of chess he played with Edric. "So, you have decided about his lordship."

"Aye," she replied, not surprised by Pitney's insight. " 'Twould be a much finer thing if love were involved. Howbeit, I cannot believe such emotion is beyond our reach. My jealousy of the fulsome Lady Odella had me thinking that such an emotion is nearer to my heart than I may think." She smiled when her kinsmen laughed softly. "Well, I am to bed. I believe I shall need a good rest if I am to face the morrow with any calm. Good sleep."

"Wait," Pitney called to her, then looked at Edric and asked, "What do you think of all of this?"

"She could make no better match," Edric replied.

"That does not need to be said. Since I am tied to my bed, I have been unable to view the pair together. It would greatly ease my mind if I could be certain that more exists between them than a fever of the blood."

Even though she was interested in her uncle's reply, Saxan scowled at her brother. "What does that matter? I have said aye."

Pitney ignored her. "Uncle?"

"There is more," Edric replied. "There is an ease between Saxan and the earl, a companionship. One can almost see the earl relax when he draws near to her. That gives me more hope for a good marriage than this fever they share."

"I hope you are right. If he hurts her, it may well be I who next tries to skewer him."

"I have no wish to be a widow," Saxan grumbled, annoyed at the way they discussed her as if she were not there.

Edric grinned then grew serious. "I do not think the earl will ever intentionally hurt her, but a danger does exist." He curtly reminded Pitney of Cecil and the man's attempts to kill the earl, one of which had resulted in Pitney's injury. "Cecil wishes to inherit all Botolf holds."

"And, if Botolf begets a son, the chance that he will do so lessens greatly," said Pitney. "The moment the betrothal is announced, Saxan will become a target for that madman. The earl puts my sister's life at risk."

"Do not fault the man for that," Saxan said. "The earl is a powerful man and such a man will always have an enemy somewhere. He cannot allow that to stop him from doing his duty to his family. Sons must be born or this family will die out. Such is the urgency that Botolf cannot wait, not even to clear away the trouble Cecil causes. That could take years."

"It could also take his life," Pitney snapped.

"Aye," Edric agreed, but added soberly, "and unless a son is left behind, his death could bring the abrupt end to his house."

"There would be Cecil."

"Not for long. Even if Cecil gained what he seeks, his murder of the earl would set our clan against him. I cannot believe Cecil has given that much thought. Nay, if he survives the murder of the earl, he is still a dead man." Edric sighed. "We are all sworn to avenge the earl's murder."

"There will be no murder save for Cecil's own," Saxan vowed. "Good sleep." She hurried from the room, determined to hear no more about danger and revenge.

When Saxan strode into her room, Jane was waiting for her. She forced herself to calm down as Jane helped her prepare for bed. It was as Jane brushed out her hair that Saxan began to think of Thylda. Since Thylda's birth, she and her sister had never been separated. Her leave-taking had been abrupt, and now she would not be returning to Wolfshead Hall except for the occasional visit. She could not help but wonder how that would affect Thylda.

They had both known that she must marry soon. Each man who had passed through Wolfshead Hall had been viewed as a possible husband. Even Thylda had begun to look for a mate. There had been no one suitable, however, and no expectation of a marriage in the near future. This was all going to be a great shock to Thylda.

"Are you troubled, mistress?" Jane asked. "You frown so."

"I was but thinking of my younger sister Thylda. We have never been apart before," Saxan answered.

"She has no other sisters to turn to?"

"Nay. Thylda and I were the last ones still living at Wolfshead Hall. The others are married. Now poor Thylda will be all alone."

"You are a grown woman. She must have expected you to marry soon."

"Oh, aye, but when I left Wolfshead Hall there was no man in my heart or my future. Nay, not e'en one in my past. Suddenly Thylda shall find herself alone, and I worry that she is not really ready for that."

"Mayhap she should come to Regenford and stay here for a time," suggested Jane.

"Linger on after the wedding?"

Jane nodded. "Then she will see you with your husband and grow accustomed to it."

Saxan leapt to her feet, excitement filling her. "And Thylda can also learn from Lady Mary. After all, she will now be the lady of Wolfshead Hall until Hunter is married. True, Thylda is more the lady than I am, but she has had no proper training either."

"Where are you going?" Jane asked in surprise when Saxan threw on her robe over her thin night rail and opened the door.

"To speak to his lordship," Saxan replied.

"Mistress, you cannot go to his lordship's chambers dressed so and alone. If someone sees you—"

"Of course. Well, then you must come with me."

"Can this not wait until the morning?" Jane asked as Saxan dragged her through the door and down the hall to Botolf's room.

"Botolf will be sending word of our wedding to my kin in the morning. If he agrees that Thylda may stay, her invitation should go out to her then." As Saxan raised her hand to rap upon Botolf's thick door, she heard voices in his room and felt her heart contract painfully.

"What is wrong, mistress?" Jane whispered with concern as Saxan paled and stepped back from the door.

"He has a woman in there," Saxan hissed, fury bubbling up through her hurt. "Lady Odella is entertaining him tonight."

Saxan strode back to her room, only faintly aware of a worried Jane hurrying along behind her. The young maid stood near the door, wringing her hands, as Saxan furiously paced her room, occasionally hitting out at the wall or a table with one small tightly clenched fist. It took several minutes before Saxan's anger began to wane and she was able to think more clearly on what she had heard. She suddenly swung around to face a nervous Jane, her hands on her hips.

"Something does not feel right about this," Saxan said.

"Mistress?" Jane asked, her voice barely more than a squeak.

"This matter of Lady Odella in Botolf's bedchamber. 'Tis all wrong. Although it has not been formally announced, the earl and I are betrothed. I cannot believe his lordship would treat such a bond so lightly.

So, too, is the fact that Odella is a lady born. For the earl to lie with her now, before our betrothal is announced, could bring a loud cry of outrage from her kin. Botolf could easily find himself bound to wed her. Does that make any sense at all?"

"Nay, mistress," replied Jane. "For a man to bed a lady as highborn as Lady Odella is a grave matter."

Saxan's eyes widened as an idea formed in her head. "It could be a plot. Such a trick has been played on my kin before. She intends to halt his marriage to me. Come along, Jane. We must go back."

Jane cried out as Saxan grabbed her hand and dragged her back to the earl's room. "What if there is no trick being played?"

"Ah, you mean what if the earl is only having himself a lusty tussle? Then I mean to know that for certain. I must know if the words he spoke are empty promises."

Botolf sent away his squire, donned his robe, and poured himself some wine. He had sought his room out of a need for privacy. A soft rap at his door made him curse with exasperation. He curtly bade the person enter and gaped when Lady Odella slipped in wearing only a thin night rail. She shut the door behind her with a distinct snap.

"Odella, are you mad?" he demanded, tensing as she moved toward him.

"Oh, Botolf," she cried and flung herself against him. "You are always so cool toward me. I can no longer bear it."

Despite his best efforts, Botolf was keenly aware of the full curves she pressed tightly against his body. He quickly and easily shrugged that spark of interest aside. His body was knotted with frustration, but

Lady Odella was not the cure he needed. All he could think of was how it could become known that she had come to his bedchamber and word of it could reach Saxan.

"M'lady, this is foolishness." He struggled to detach her. "Someone may have seen you."

Odella clung to him even more tightly and moved her body against his. "I do not care. I do this out of love."

For a moment Botolf listened to her amorous vows. They tickled his vanity. He was only a man, and no man could help but be flattered when a woman as lovely as Odella claimed to be sick with want for him. He then decided that it was unkind to allow her to express her feelings so openly when he was no longer free and not interested. Once again he tried to pull her off him without being too abrupt.

"Please, say no more, m'lady," he urged when he finally managed to force a few inches of space between their bodies. "I cannot—"

"I know," she said, tears glistening in her eyes as she pressed her palms against his chest and subtly slipped them beneath his robe. "You are unable to return my feelings. That is what has driven me to this. I understand. Truly I do. The heart cannot be forced. Oh, Botolf, if you can give me no more, at least do not deny me this night. Let me know but once how it feels to be held in your arms."

"I would be a man of very little honor if I took such base advantage of you, m'lady." He tried to wriggle free of her again only to freeze when another soft rap sounded at the door. "Nay, wait," he cried out even as the door opened. He stared in horror as Saxan entered his room, dragging her maid Jane in with her.

"Saxan," he groaned, foreseeing only disaster ahead.

Even as she shut the door firmly behind her, Saxan closely studied Botolf and Odella. She was not quite sure how to interpret the look of horror on Botolf's face, but the fleeting expression of gloating triumph which passed over Lady Odella's features was very easy to understand. She also saw how Botolf's whole body was arched away from Lady Odella, how he held the woman's hand at a distance, and how Lady Odella was pressing toward him. There had not been enough time for him to assume such a position simply as a ploy to fool her. Whatever Odella had planned, she was not finding it easy to accomplish. Saxan felt only anger now, an anger she aimed solely at Lady Odella.

Botolf practically tossed Lady Odella aside and tentatively edged toward Saxan. "What are you doing here, little one?"

"I wished to speak with you, m'lord," Saxan replied as she sat down on his bed, struggling to keep her anger at Odella out of her voice.

"Does it concern your maid? Jane, is it not?" He glanced at the maid, then looked back at Saxan.

"Aye, 'tis Jane, but I brought her along to insure that this visit does not appear improper to any who may hear of it. I may not be well taught in the manners of a lady," she continued, "but I do know what is thought if a lady goes to a man's bedchamber in the night. I have no wish to be thought of as the basest of whores."

Jane gasped and clapped a hand over her mouth. Out of the corner of her eye, Saxan saw Lady Odella move toward her and was prepared for the attack. When the woman swung at her in fury, Saxan caught her by the wrist. She gave the woman's arm a sharp twist, and Odella sprawled at her feet.

She stared into Lady Odella's flushed face, murmuring between gritted teeth, "Checkmate," and released her.

Odella scrambled to her feet and hissed, "This is but part of the game. Do not savor victory so soon."

Before Saxan had time to consider the meaning behind the woman's words, there was a loud insistent rapping at the door. Botolf opened it and frowned when he found Lord Alanson standing there, but the older man paid little heed to him. Lord Alanson gaped then glared at Saxan and Jane, who was trying desperately to hide in the shadows at the far edge of the room. Odella snarled, grasped her father by the arm, and towed him off down the hall.

Botolf checked the corridor for more intruders, secured the latch, and walked to his bed. Jane scurried to the door in order to give Botolf and Saxan some privacy. Unsure of Saxan's mood, Botolf sat down cautiously next to her.

"I was almost ensnared," he murmured, torn between disbelief and a growing anger.

"Aye, m'lord. She played an old game." Saxan tried very hard to ignore that he was obviously naked beneath his robe.

"Is that why you came to my chambers?" He began to relax, for she clearly understood the game which had been played.

"Nay." She sighed. "I did wish to speak to you on a certain matter before you sent your messengers out. I was at your door a few moments earlier, heard Lady Odella's voice, and returned to my room."

Unable to resist any longer, he reached out to stroke her hair. "Why did you return?"

"Well, my temper cooled somewhat and I began to think on the matter. I could not believe you would ask her to your bed after you had asked me to marry you. That is when I began to wonder if she played some game. 'Tis one which has been tried on some of my kinsmen. 'Tis their good fortune that it has always failed." She looked directly at him. "I also decided that, if it were no game, I should know that, too. I needed to know if I were a fool to trust your bond."

He nodded, understanding her reasoning. "I was trying to make her leave." He groaned. "I should have seen the trick."

"I suppose one's vanity wishes to believe other things," she murmured.

"Painfully true. What did you wish to speak to me about?"

"My sister Thylda."

"I intend to send word of our marriage to her at Wolfshead Hall."

"Aye, but I was wondering if she could stay on after the wedding."

"Do you feel you will have a need of her?"

"Oh, I shall certainly enjoy her visit, but 'tis not that. Thylda and I have ne'er been apart before. I left in the dead of night on a mission of vengeance. Now I am to be wed. Without warning, she is now alone, the only sister still living at Wolfshead Hall. Thylda has the skill to be chatelaine, but I am not sure she is prepared for it in her heart and mind."

"And you feel that, if she stays here to see you wed and settled, she may accept it with more ease," he concluded.

"Aye, m'lord. She could also learn from Lady Mary. Thylda is not as rough as I am, but she is also without training."

"I do not mind if she lingers here." He brushed a kiss over her cheek. "And you are not rough." He smiled when she blushed. "I will include an invitation for her to stay with us when I send out my messenger.

Is there a woman to take her place as chatelaine while your sister is here?"

"Old Marta. She is all things, yet not any one thing. Her whole life has been spent at Wolfshead Hall."

"We have a woman like that named Elizabeth. There is no place she has not held at one time or another." He watched her pulse and breath quicken when he smoothed his hand over her throat. "She, too, has spent every day of her life in this one place."

Saxan covered his hand with hers, took a deep breath to steady herself, and said quietly, "I believe it comes time for me to leave." She frowned as she mused aloud. "I think it is for the best that you did not wed the Lady Odella."

"A woman capable of such deception is certainly not one I wish for as a wife," he agreed, unable to believe that he had been so wrong in his judgment of Lady Odella's character. It made him fear that he had learned nothing from his disastrous marriage to Alice.

"I was not thinking of that, but, aye, it is a consideration. May God forgive me if I slander Lady Odella, but I think that, if you had married her, you would not have found all, er," she blushed, "as it should be on the wedding night."

"Mayhap, although her father did make a timely arrival."

"True, but, if you were not so honorable or if you were weaker of flesh, where do you think the two of you would have been found?" She glanced at his robe even as understanding widened his eyes, their dark depths sparkling with anger. "Time would not have been wasted in the shedding of your clothes," she drawled. "To my way of thinking, a maiden would find it very difficult to come to a man's bedchamber with the plan of dragging him into bed. Maidens need the heat of the moment to banish a natural reticence. Cold plotting is not their way."

"Nay, and until I set eyes upon you, it was in my mind to offer for her." He slipped his arms around her, but held her lightly and winked. "On the one hand you have rescued me, but on the other, you have sorely abused my vanity."

"How so, m'lord?" She smiled faintly, recognizing that he was teasing her.

"I was quite flattered by her avowals of burning love and need." He sighed with an overdone mournfulness. " 'Twas all air."

Saxan laughed. "You must feed your vanity with the knowledge of the great trouble she went to in an attempt to gain you." She suddenly became far too aware of how close they were and how little they wore. "I think it is time I returned to my own chambers," she declared unsteadily as she quickly stood up, breaking free of his light hold. When she saw his knowing grin, she scowled. "Good sleep, m'lord."

Botolf followed her to the door. With each hint of her passion he grew more eager to marry her. He fixed his gaze upon the long waves of silver that rippled down her slim back. He ached to wrap himself in its silken depths.

Saxan paused as she stepped from the chamber and flushed beneath the warmth of his gaze, then smiled pertly. "I should bar my door, m'lord."

He grinned and tugged her against him, gave her a brief hard kiss, and gently pushed her toward a wide-eyed Jane, who waited in the hall. "Good sleep."

Saxan grumbled about men in general all the way back to her bedchamber. It had been difficult enough in his presence when he wore nothing but a robe.

Now she had that brief but hungry kiss to think about. She tempered her annoyance just enough to bid Jane a pleasant good night. The girl had been more than helpful, and she did not want to take her frustrations out on her maid.

"I ought to march back to his chambers and give him a little something to ruin his sleep," she groused as she tried to settle her restless body comfortably in her bed, but then laughed ruefully over her threat.

There was no doubt in her mind that, if she went back to Botolf's room, she would not leave it until the morning. She could not heat his blood to the point of discomfort without doing the same to herself. The fire burned both ways. Such heat could not be so carefully controlled.

The strength of her desire for the man puzzled her. Despite all the times they had talked, she could not honestly say that she knew him well. Saxan could not help but wonder how much of her desire was for Botolf the man and how much was simply her lusty Todd blood reacting to the caress of a young, handsome, strong male.

Her heart ached for it to be more than that, so much more. She wanted a marriage like so many of her own kin had, one where both love and friendship were intertwined with a happiness and a satisfaction that would last. She did not want to find herself alone in her later years with a man who was still a stranger to her and stuck in a bed that had grown cold. Her fears were real and ran deep, but she realized that even those were not enough to make her turn away from Botolf.

Eight

"You are such a lovely bride," Thylda murmured, sitting on Saxan's bed and watching the preparations for the wedding.

Saxan grinned at her sister, who had been at Regenford for a fortnight, having arrived within a week of Botolf's sending out his messenger. "Loyalty prompts your flattery, Thylda."

"Not fully, Saxan," said Lady Mary as she wove another bright ribbon through Saxan's hair. "You are lovely, and this hair will draw all eyes to you. It will not be the bright ribbons, either. The gown fits perfectly and, now that you wear it, I realize that the blue is truer than I had thought. 'Tis nearly a perfect match for your eyes. Stop worrying your hands, child."

"I cannot help it." Saxan's nerves grew tauter with each passing moment.

"Ah, well, most brides become nervous."

" 'Tis not becoming a wife which makes me tremble, but the ceremony itself, m'lady."

"What is there about the ceremony that could frighten you?"

"That I shall do it all wrong. That I shall trip and fall on my face. That I shall make an utter fool out of myself." Saxan clapped a hand to her forehead and wailed. "That, when it is time to stand after kneeling before the priest, I shall discover that my legs no longer work."

Lady Mary firmly repressed a laugh, made all the more difficult by Thylda's giggling, and said sternly, "Do not be so fretful. As Botolf's wife you had best become accustomed to ceremony and being before many people. Now," Lady Mary fought against the color that tinted her cheeks, but her voice remained calm. "I know I am late in asking, but is there anything you wish to ask me?"

"Ask you? Nay, I do not believe so."

"I think she means any questions concerning the night to come, Saxan," Thylda said.

"Oh. Nay, I know all about that." Saxan smiled at Lady Mary's shocked expression. "M'lady, with kinsmen such as mine, I would need to be deaf, blind, and a simpleton not to know all about that. The wedding night does not worry me."

"Not even a little?" Lady Mary asked in surprise.

"Well, I do wish there were no need to endure the bedding ceremony. 'Tis well that I need not be naked as was required in my father's time. I should swoon. The rest? Ah, well, that is but nature and God's will. I can see no reason to worry on it."

"Would that I could have gone to my marriage bed so calmly."

"You were raised a fine lady. I cannot help but feel that the lessons taught to fine ladies are not the wisest ones. No bride should go to her wedding bed all atremble with fear. 'Tis not a good way to begin."

"I think 'tis not only the bride who goes to the marriage bed with fear," Lady Mary quipped, and they all laughed.

* * *

Sir Wesley eyed Botolf with friendly annoyance, his green eyes expressing both anger and amusement. "Will you stand still, Botolf? I cannot tie these points."

"I am standing still," Botolf grumbled.

"Ha! You tremble and fidget as if you were the virgin to be bedded tonight."

"Have patience, Wesley," Sir Roger said with a laugh. " 'Tis a grave deed the man performs this day."

"Aye," agreed Sir Talbot as he served them all wine. "He will soon claim all those Todds, Healdons, and Jagers as his kin."

"A handsome lot though," Roger murmured.

"That they are, Roger." Wesley grinned. "That young Thylda holds great promise." He straightened up. "There. Your lacings are done, but do not hold me to blame if any of them come undone, m'lord. 'Tis hard to do it right when you are squirming about so. What ails you?"

Botolf smiled crookedly. "I am not sure. 'Tis not as if I have never done this before."

"Then, since there is nothing new to face, you should be far easier of mind than you are."

"Ah, but there is something new, my friend. I have never bedded a virgin."

"But, Lady Alice," Sir Talbot began, then flushed at touching upon a long-forbidden subject.

"When one is half-mad with love, the lack of a maidenhead seems a small fault," Botolf drawled. "Now, with what occurred with Lady Odella to consider, I begin to wonder how many of these self-proclaimed ladies go to their marriage beds as chaste as they claim to be." He smiled when Wesley frowned yet clearly hesitated to voice his thoughts. "Saxan is chaste," he said, laughing briefly when Wesley blushed. "God's beard, the girl was innocent of even kisses ere I gained hold of her. When one sees the beauties that infernal clan produces, it seems almost a miracle. Their kinsmen guard them very well indeed."

"Yet there is something in your voice that makes one think you wish Saxan were not so chaste," Roger said.

"There is a part of me that does wish that, Roger," Botolf replied. "Consider all I could do wrong tonight."

"Have you ever seen any fear in her before this?" asked Wesley.

"Nay," Botolf answered, "but I have restrained myself and, of late, I have made sure that we are rarely left alone."

"You have restrained yourself? The girl does not pull away?" Wesley asked with an assumed idleness.

"Nay." Botolf thought of the night in the garden when they had been hiding from Edric and nearly allowed passion to steal away their good sense. "Do you think I worry for no reason? Well, mayhap I do. Still, she is such a small woman. I have no wish to hurt her and, if I hurt her too badly, I could kill all the promise of passion she now holds. I have heard of promising unions that died on the wedding night."

"We all have, but I cannot foresee that happening to you. The girl is no gently reared maid despite her innocence. She does not quail from a fight or the need to use a weapon. A little pain and bloodletting on her marriage bed will not turn her craven. Thinking on the lusty family she comes from, I believe she fully knows what is to come." Wesley clapped the earl on the back. "Come. Let us get you wedded and bedded so that you may finally set all this worry aside," he said as, with Roger's and Talbot's assistance, he urged Botolf out of his bedchamber.

When Botolf reached the great hall where his guests had gathered, he had to smile. Saxan's kin had turned out in large numbers, and there seemed to be a veritable sea of fair hair. He was noting how many of his bride's family were male when he found himself alone with Hunter and Roc. They were tall for Todds, but still several inches shorter than he was.

"Relax, m'lord," Hunter teased. "My sister is not so fearsome."

"You must call me Botolf," the earl said. "We will be family soon."

"That would be easier, for we could m'lord ourselves to death otherwise." Hunter grinned when Botolf laughed, but then grew serious. "You are tense. Do you regret your choice now that the vows are about to be said?"

"Nay. I do not believe I shall ever regret my choice."

"Ah, then 'tis the bedding that troubles you." Hunter laughed when a light color touched Botolf's cheeks. "You wed no swooning child. Saxan is as chaste as any maid can be, but she is not ignorant. She holds no fear of what happens between a man and wife. Aye, she is small of build, but most of our women are and there has not yet been one who has broken beneath a man's passion or fled from loving. Indeed, when I think of the blood that runs in Saxan's veins, I begin to fear for you."

In a few moments, the lusty jests of the twins eased Botolf's fears. If they were not worried for their sister, then he felt his own concerns must be foolish. Those worries flickered to life again, however, when Saxan entered the great hall and moved to his side. She looked beautiful in her wedding finery, but she also looked delicate and very young. When he took her hand, he felt her tremble and wondered if she suffered from some of the same fears he did.

Saxan was unable to relax throughout the entire wedding ceremony. It was not until Botolf kissed her, marking the end of the ceremony as clearly as the loud chaos of the crowd, that her tension left her. She smiled widely at Botolf and saw passion darken his eyes. For once she did not immediately respond to that show of desire. All she could think of was that she had accomplished the difficult part of the ceremony without a fault and now she could enjoy her own wedding.

As the servants and pages hurried to set the tables with the wedding feast, Saxan tugged her new husband over to meet Denu's and Tuesday's husbands, Thomas and Godric respectively. "I had not expected to see either of you, Godric," she exclaimed as she hugged and kissed Tuesday's husband. "Are you fathers again yet?" she asked even as she greeted Thomas in the same manner.

"I have that honor," Godric replied. "A daughter." He smiled at Saxan's obvious and vocal delight. "We called her Honey Pipere Soames. She has flaxen hair, but she was only days old when I left so I cannot tell you what color her eyes are. Tuesday would have been here, but I swore I would tie her to her bed if she tried to move," he growled, but a smile continued to curl his lips. "She sends her love, many wishes for happiness, and a hearty prayer for the man daring enough to take you as his wife."

After scowling at the three laughing men, Saxan asked, "How fares Denu, Thomas?"

"Our babe will soon be here. I should not be surprised to find the birthing over when I return. Denu sends her good wishes and love as well."

When she and Botolf were finally seated at the

table, Saxan could not resist a glance toward Odella and her father. Due to their high position and relatively favorable place in Edward's court, Botolf had not felt he could refuse them if they wished to stay for the wedding. To her dismay, they had decided to remain. Although she was no longer concerned that the woman would try any more tricks with Botolf, Saxan found Odella's constant venom unsettling. Saxan could not shake the feeling that there was more trouble coming from that direction, but did not know what form that trouble might take. She prayed that the Alansons would leave immediately after the wedding.

The gaiety of the guests soon diverted her from her concerns. People came and went from the head table, including her husband. At one point, she found herself alone and glanced toward the door leading to the garden. She was just about to give into the temptation of some fresh air when she saw Lady Mary leave, quickly followed by Edric. Saxan grabbed Thylda by the hand and hurried after the couple. She signaled Thylda to be quiet as she crept along until they were hidden by some greenery yet could still see and hear Lady Mary and Edric.

Botolf frowned as he watched his wife and her sister leave. "And where are they going?" he wondered aloud.

Hunter shrugged. "They did appear to be a little furtive. Ah, well, no harm can come to them. Uncle Edric is out there. Aye, and your lady mother. They both wandered out there a moment before my sisters left."

"Is that so," Botolf drawled and, knowing exactly

what his wife was doing, waited only another moment before going after her.

Lady Mary stiffened when Sir Edric approached her. "It began to get very warm in the great hall."

"Too many people. Your musicians play very well." Edric took a deep breath. "I wondered if you would dance with me."

"I think it would be best if I declined," she replied in a soft voice.

Saxan knew her uncle had been pushed to the point of desperation when he grasped Lady Mary by the shoulders. Edric would never normally handle a woman so roughly. It was all the proof she needed that something very strong flared between the couple, something Lady Mary fought to deny. She hoped that they would soon reveal exactly what that something was. There could be a simple solution they had failed to see.

"Would you have me toss aside my given oath?" Edric demanded in a hoarse voice. "Is that what you demand of me?"

"Nay," Lady Mary replied, her voice thick with tears. "To do so would be to destroy the man you are."

"Are you saying you would not wish the man dead if he succeeds in killing the son of your body?"

"Nay," she cried, breaking free of his hold. "Oh, sweet lord, I do not know. I cannot say I will do as I fear, but I cannot chance it. It would pain me as much as it would you if I held all that could be between us only to watch it die because your vow forced you to cut down Cecil. Please, have the kindness to cease tormenting me."

Saxan hurried away, dragging a stunned Thylda after her. She winced as they came face to face with Botolf just outside of the door to the great hall. Hastily motioning him to be silent, she linked her arm with his. Thylda quickly did the same. When Edric suddenly rounded the corner and saw them, it appeared as if they had just stepped out for a breath of fresh air.

"M'lord," Edric said with a forced cheerfulness, "is it not enough for you to have such a lovely bride? Must you lay claim to the prettiest maiden at your wedding as well? Soon we shall be marrying you off, Thylda."

"There is time yet, Uncle," Thylda said.

"At least a few more years, I pray." He kissed Saxan's cheek and briefly hugged her, murmuring, "Be happy, child."

"I will, Uncle," she said quietly and frowned after him when he walked away only to have her attention quickly drawn by Lady Mary's approach.

Lady Mary gave Saxan a forced smile. "At last I have a daughter."

"And soon babes to spoil, if God wills it," Botolf said, his voice soft as he sensed his mother's unhappiness. In an attempt to allow her to cut short her time with their company, he added, "The hour grows late. Mayhap, when we return, you could begin the bedding ceremony. We will be only a few moments."

"All right, Botolf." She smiled at Saxan. "I will try to slip you away as quietly as possible."

As soon as his mother was gone, Botolf turned a stern gaze on his new bride. "You promised not to meddle."

"I did not meddle. I simply listened," Saxan replied.

"You eavesdropped."

She shrugged, then asked pertly, "Do you want to know what their trouble is?"

He laughed and shook his head. "All right, what is their trouble?"

"Cecil."

"I do not understand. What has Cecil to do with all this?"

"Cecil is trying to kill you. I think your mother finally begins to believe that. To her, 'tis as if her sons battle each other. She cannot help but see Cecil as her own child."

"I know all that, but how does it affect Edric and my mother?"

"If Cecil succeeds in murdering you," continued Thylda, "then our uncle is affected."

"Aye," agreed Saxan, fighting the discomfort she felt over even considering the possibility of Botolf's death. "My uncle's vow to you will extend beyond your death unless it is from illness or nature or any death that carries no blame to it. Any hint of murder, and my kin are still bound to you by a vow—a vow of vengeance. So, if Cecil murders you, my uncle must join our kin in hunting him down and making him pay with his own blood."

Botolf cursed. "And even though Cecil had my blood on his hands, my mother might find it difficult to accept that Edric now had Cecil's blood on his hands."

"Exactly. My poor uncle cannot break his vow, and 'tis that vow which now stands between him and your mother. She fears allowing them to follow their feelings, for whatever they may build between them will be destroyed if my uncle must take up his sword against Cecil. Lady Mary does not dare chance love for fear it could turn to ashes later."

"There is nothing that can be done then." Botolf sighed and dragged his fingers through his hair.

"Not unless someone can rid the world of Cecil, someone outside this small, highly concerned circle," Thylda mused aloud.

"She is as mad as you are, Saxan," Botolf muttered as he guessed what plot whirled in Thylda's mind.

"I prefer to think of it as reasonable and courageous," Saxan drawled, sending Botolf a look filled with impish laughter.

"Of course." He firmly repressed a smile then looked at Thylda. "You will not do anything, young lady."

"I will not?" Thylda asked sweetly.

"Nay, and I will now have your word on that."

"Oh, all right."

"She is as amiable as you are as well," Botolf murmured to a giggling Saxan. "Come along, you two. We must return to the great hall." He tugged them gently in that direction. "I can foresee no solution to this problem, but I will think on the matter."

"Cecil must be stopped," Thylda said. "And if his blood is to be spilled, Uncle Edric must not be the man to do it. That is the only solution I see." She sighed. "There is no knowing how long that could take to come about. Uncle may be so old he is no longer interested."

"If I know our uncle, he will still be interested when he is on his deathbed," Saxan grumbled. " 'Twill be the same with all the men in our clan."

As she stepped into the great hall, Thylda crossly eyed her male relatives scattered about the huge room. "Lecherous dogs."

Unable to hold back any longer, Botolf burst out laughing. The sisters' identical looks of feminine disgust only amused him more. He was just calming down when their brother Udolf, a silver-haired, blue-eyed man of twenty, strolled over and draped an arm around the shoulders of each of his sisters.

Thylda leaned toward Botolf and whispered, "You think we jest. Heed this, m'lord." She turned her attention back to her brother. "Udolf?"

"Aye, sweet Thylda, what does the babe wish?"

Standing straighter, Thylda said, "I am no longer a babe."

His eyes brimming with laughter, Udolf carefully looked over her rounding form and drawled, "Aye, I can see that."

She rolled her eyes, making Saxan giggle, and asked, "What are your favorite things on God's good earth?"

"Ah, an easy question to answer." Udolf hugged them. "Women."

"There," Thylda muttered, looking at Botolf. "You see how it is, m'lord?"

Before Botolf could make any reply, his mother approached them and said quietly, " 'Tis a good time to slip away now. Most everyone watches the jongleurs."

Udolf kissed Saxan on the cheek, then released his sisters. He lightly slapped Thylda's backside as the three women began to walk away. Her angry glare only made him laugh.

"I fear it will not be long ere Thylda is wed as well," he said to Botolf. "We shall then have no sisters left at Wolfshead Hall."

"She is a fair lass with both wit and spirit," Botolf agreed.

"It was kind of you to ask her to make a long visit, m'lord."

"The pleasure will be all mine . You must call me Botolf, at least at such gatherings as this. You are, after all, my wife's brother."

"Then allow me, as a brother, to boast that you have chosen well."

Botolf grinned. "I certainly think so."

Abruptly, Udolf grew serious. "Saxan was raised to stand at her man's side . . . ." He winked, ". . . even if he is being a total fool. Ah, here come your men and Hunter to attend to your bedding."

Three knights and his brother-in-law ushered Botolf out the door of the great hall. The ribald remarks came thick and fast. It surprised Botolf to hear so much coarse revelry from Saxan's own kinsmen. Just outside the door, he was caught hold of by a somber-faced Godric. Botolf's attendants moved away to allow them the privacy the man so clearly wanted.

"You could choose no better mate than a Todd woman, Lord Botolf," Godric said. "Do not err as I did and thus lose precious time with such a jewel. I know you little, but what I do know tells me that you may share some of the foolish notions I once held. Those notions nearly cost me my marriage. These Todd lasses are unusual."

"How so?" Botolf asked with unfeigned interest.

"They are as hot of blood as their men yet would never willingly be faithless. They also think much like a man. That is something you should try to remember. It will lessen the times when your bride may confuse you." He grimaced and shook his head. " 'Tis not easy to put it into words."

Botolf clapped him lightly on the shoulder. "I thank you for trying and I believe I understand. I have seen the truth of it already."

Even as Botolf turned to rejoin his companions and continue on to his chambers, Pitney approached. The youth had spent most of the celebration with his cousins. Botolf noticed that the boy was pale and feared he had dangerously worn himself out.

"Do you seek your bed now, Pitney?" he asked.

Pitney passed by the earl on the stairs and did little more than grunt, "Aye."

"Pitney," Hunter growled, angered at this snub of their liege lord.

Stopping, Pitney leaned against the cool, greystone wall. He closed his eyes with a sigh then suddenly laughed. Still chuckling, he opened his eyes, smiled at Botolf, and bowed slightly.

"Forgive me, m'lord," Pitney said.

Perplexed by the boy's strange mood, Botolf murmured, "It has been a long day. You are tired."

"Aye, I am, m'lord, but 'tis not that which makes me act the sullen churl. This day you laid claim to what has always been mine. You have taken away part of me. I am but jealous. It steals both my manners and my humor."

"I do not think I could ever fully take her away from you," Botolf reassured him.

"Nay," Pitney replied, grinning impudently. "Howbeit, 'twill take a while for me to settle to this. Ah, good evening, sweet ladies," he said as the two young daughters of one of Botolf's vassals moved hesitantly past the men on the stairs.

Botolf and his companions watched in growing amusement as the girls inquired after Pitney's health. In but a few moments the youth was being escorted up the stairs by the two young women, his arms around their waists. The murmured words and soft laughter made Botolf wonder just how soon Pitney would actually get his rest.

"That boy grows to be a danger," Hunter jested. "Come, Botolf, or my sister will think that you have forgotten her."

When Botolf entered his room, he found that Farold had not failed him. A hot bath and warmed drying-cloths were waiting for him. He wasted no time in shedding his clothes, aided by Sir Wesley and Sir Roger.

"It pleases me to see that Saxan will get all that is needed," observed Hunter, lazily surveying Botolf's naked form as he poured them all some wine. "I could be jealous myself as I think on what you shall be doing whilst I must lie alone."

"I cannot see you lying alone," said Botolf, then he grinned. "Why, the Lady Odella looked much interested."

"Ah, her. Nay, I will not take that. Once was enough."

Botolf was so shocked he faltered and nearly fell headlong into the bath. "You have bedded Lady Odella?" he asked as he eased his body into the steaming water.

"Aye, I believe it was a year ago. 'Twas at court. You have not enjoyed the lady's favors? I had thought, when I saw her arrive that day, that you were her new lover. Ah, of course not," Hunter continued when he saw Botolf scowl. "She was looking to pull a proposal from you and so played the chaste maid."

"It would appear so. Er, just why was once enough?"

"Lady Odella is one of those women who must be forever flattered."

"I have not noticed that that came hard to you Todds or to your kinsmen."

"Nay. Some say we are born with the skill. Howbeit, 'tis always best when given freely. Lady Odella constantly begs a man for the words—often at times when he does not feel inclined toward clever, pretty phrases." Hunter grinned when his companions laughed. "Aye, there is delight to be found there, but it requires more work than I wish to give."

"She is also looking for a husband," Botolf warned.

"She was then as well, but I need not fear that. Odella's gaze is set higher than a baron with one small holding in the North."

"That may have changed. She could easily discover that you are far from poor, as attested by Saxan's handsome dowry."

"That was mostly set aside by my mother. And, Botolf, do not forget that we carry the taint of merchants. Trade with the East and all of that."

"There is money to be had there?" Sir Wesley asked, too often the victim of an empty purse.

Talk of trade occupied the men until Botolf stepped out of his tub. Their attention was quickly brought back to the night ahead of him. Botolf smiled at their jests, returning a few of his own. His heart was not fully in the teasing and levity, however.

Slowly all of his fears began to return. The jests about his well-endowed form and readiness only made him think on the delicacy of his bride. By the time he donned his robe and he and his companions moved toward Saxan's bedchamber, all of his tension had returned and no amount of common sense and knowledge would banish it.

Saxan sighed with pleasure as she breathed deeply of the scented bath awaiting her in her bedchamber. "Ah, but this is lovely."

Thylda laughed as she helped Saxan get out of her wedding finery. " 'Tis to bathe in, not smell like some rich stew."

"I shall smell very sweet. A scented bath, scented sheets, scented night rail. 'Tis almost too much scent." She giggled as she sank into the hot water while Lady Mary hastily pinned up her hair, which had been freshly washed before the wedding.

"You are so tiny," Lady Mary murmured, a hint of concern in her voice.

"My sister's husbands are all large men, and my sisters are not much bigger than I. Rounder, aye, but still small."

"I should not speak so. They were unwise words before a new bride."

"M'lady, you worry more for me than I do for myself." Saxan chided, then looked at her maid. "Jane? Could you scrub my back, please? Thank you kindly." She returned her attention to Lady Mary, who poured out a tankard of wine and set it by the bed. "I told you, I know all that is about to happen. So, too, do I know it could pain me some, but that pain does not last and it can be dimmed if the fever runs hot."

"And does the fever run hot?" asked Lady Mary.

"I blush to admit it, but, aye, it runs very hot indeed. 'Tis said that the first time for a woman may not be a great pleasure, but I do not fret o'er that. There will be a next time and all the times after that to gain what my wedded sisters sigh over."

"Your sisters have spoken to you about what happens in their marriage beds?" Lady Mary could not hide her shocked surprise.

"Only my sister Tuesday was old enough to have the pleasure of our mother's advice on such matters. The men in our clan feel no need to keep their women blind to what is nature's way despite how well they guard our chastity. Howbeit, they speak of it from a man's point of view. Tuesday, and then Denu, felt no harm could come of it if we knew a woman's thoughts on it all. Cold duty can produce children, but it will not hold a man faithful to his marriage bed. Neither will it hold a woman. Our sisters wanted us to know that it is no sin to find pleasure in our marriage beds. True, many priests try to say it is. Not our Father Chesney, though."

"Our Father Chesney is an unusual man." Lady Mary held out a drying-cloth for Saxan.

"I have amused you?" Saxan stepped from the tub and began to dry herself.

"Nay. I was just thinking that my son will soon believe himself a very fortunate man."

" 'Tis my hope to make him think so," Saxan quipped, her smile sweetly lecherous, and she laughed softly when Lady Mary's eyes widened.

Saxan's humor dimmed and she blushed as the woman helped her into her night rail. It was scandalously thin, tied at the shoulders and down the front, blatantly designed to be easily removed by her new husband. That did not trouble her, but she wished it covered and hid more of her body. When she let her hair down, it provided her with a greater modesty and she relaxed a little only to tense again when a knock resounded at her door. A moment later, Botolf was led in by her brother Hunter, Roger, Wesley, and Talbot.

Even as she flushed beneath the stares of Botolf's friends, Saxan was all too aware that her husband wore nothing beneath his robe. She wished everyone gone so that when he shed that robe, she could freely look her fill. As she slipped beneath the covers and Thylda carefully fluffed the pillows behind her back, Saxan confessed to herself that she wished Jane and Thylda in particular would go away. She did not want them to have even the most fleeting glimpse of Botolf's form, the glimpse they got an instant later when Botolf dropped his robe and climbed into bed at her side. That hint of possessiveness in herself surprised Saxan.

"You have yourself a man and a half there," whispered Thylda as she handed Saxan a tankard of wine.

Hunter appeared suddenly, nudging Thylda aside. He looked too serious for Saxan's liking. It was far too late to stop the marriage now, she thought with a mixture of relief and irritation. She then admitted to herself that she did not want Hunter to even try.

But he grinned as he bent to kiss her cheek and whispered, "Go easy on the poor man, Saxan."

She burst out laughing and playfully tugged at his hair. "Wretch."

"Be happy, little one."

"I intend to be."

Nine

Saxan could not tear her eyes from the tankard of wine she held so tightly now that she and Botolf were finally alone. She was not afraid, but felt nearly choked with shyness. It was a feeling she heartily prayed would prove fleeting.

Botolf leaned forward to peer at her face, its features partially obscured by her thick hair. He was glad that the bedding ceremony was over. Even though Roger, Wesley, and Talbot were as close to him as brothers, he had resented the view they had had of Saxan. Their obvious appreciation of that sight had only annoyed him more.

"Saxan?" He spoke softly. "Do not be afraid of me."

"I am not afraid," she said.

"Nay?" He smiled when she shook her head, but still refused to look directly at him. "Come, touch your tankard to mine, and we will drink to our marriage."

The clink of their tankards echoed in the room. Saxan gulped her wine hoping it would bring back her lost courage. The way Botolf ran his fingers through her hair and sidled closer until the lengths of their bodies brushed together slowly burned away her shyness and brought the warmth back to her blood. When he set his tankard on the table by the bed, she tossed her empty tankard aside and fell into his arms.

He laughed as he caught her up against him. "Nay, I guess you are not afraid. Why would you not look at me then?" he asked as he began to loosen the ties of her night rail.

" 'Tis not an easy question to answer." Lightly, she traced the lines of his face with her fingertips. "To be set in a bed with you so coldly left me feeling awkward and shy." She shrugged. "I could not think of what to say or do." She pressed a kiss to his cheek and smiled against his freshly shaven skin. "Then you touched my hair and moved closer and the fever started."

When he tugged her night rail off and discarded it, she gasped and pressed her face against his shoulder. The feel of his warm skin touching hers sent her senses reeling. His lightly haired chest teased at her breasts. She pressed closer.

Botolf turned her face up to his and kissed her. She swiftly matched his hunger with her own. He groaned, held her tight, and rolled until she was sprawled beneath him. A muted moan of pleasure escaped her when the full length of his lean, hard body was pressed to hers.

He cupped her breasts in his large, callused hands, kneading them as he trailed feverish kisses over her throat. Saxan threaded her hands in his thick hair and arched toward him when he touched his lips to the sensitive skin of her breasts. She moaned and shuddered, moving against him restlessly when he drew the hard tip of her breast slowly into his mouth. Each hungry pull raised the heat gathering in her loins. He smoothed his palm over her legs, and when he inched his hand in between her thighs, she was in such a fever of need she offered no resistance to his intimate touch. She opened to his stroking fingers as he edged his stirring kisses back toward her mouth.

"You are already damp with welcome," he rasped as he teased her lips with his and settled his body between her slim thighs. "I do not wish to hurt you."

Saxan forced her eyes open to study his passion-taut features. She clasped her hands at the back of his head, urging him to give her the fuller kiss she craved, and moved her body against his in a heated plea to be possessed. When she breathed his name against his lips, calling him Botolf at last, she felt him tremble. Even as he plunged his tongue into her mouth, he began to unite their trembling bodies.

Despite the gentleness of his entry and the blinding strength of the passion gripping her, Saxan was not able to ignore the pain caused by the breaching of her maidenhead. She tried to smother her cry against his broad shoulder, but it was still clear and sharp and she clenched her hands on his back so tightly she scored his skin with her long nails. It proved to be a fleeting pain, however. Botolf had abruptly ceased to move, and she had a moment to adjust. Slowly, his caresses revived the passion that had been cooled by the pain. She relaxed her grip on him and rested against the pillows.

Closing her eyes again, Saxan concentrated on the joining of their bodies. The sensation made her lagging desire soar as she became more fully aware of how they were united. She also realized that something was not quite right. Saxan strongly suspected that Botolf had not yet fully possessed her, may well have even drawn back a little. Now that her pain had eased and her passion had returned in its full demanding glory, she had no wish to be so pampered. She wrapped her limbs around him as she reopened her eyes.

She almost smiled when she saw Botolf's face, strained from fighting to deny his body what it craved. But another emotion that she could read in his eyes stirred her sympathetic amusement. The pain of losing her innocence had affected him far more than it had her.

"Saxan, the pain—" he began hoarsely.

"Is done, but, I think, you are not," she murmured as, simultaneously, she pulled him closer with her legs and arched her hips. "Ah, Botolf." She spoke his name in a tremulous whisper as her movement drove him deeper within her.

Botolf groaned and kissed her hungrily as he began to move. He tried to go carefully; but his need, as well as the way she so eagerly met his every thrust, strained what little control he had. The soft sounds of pleasure which escaped her kiss-swollen mouth and the way she stroked and clutched at him with her soft, delicate hands severed it completely. His thrusts grew fiercer, but she met them without hesitation.

When he sensed that her passion was about to crest, shock cut through the heat of his desire and he faltered. Saxan cried out and clung to him, nearly frantic in her need. She urged him on, and it proved easy to answer her demand. As desire's apogee beckoned to him, he heard her cry of release. She clung to him as he shuddered, then collapsed in her arms.

He stayed wrapped in her slender, warm body for a long time, savoring the feel of her and the complete satisfaction of their lovemaking. When he finally eased free of her body, he stayed enclosed in her arms and trailed his hand down her side to rest it possessively on her shapely hip.

Her passion was a treasure he had not expected to unearth. He understood what Godric had meant. It would be easy to think she was flawed simply because she met his passion with equal ardor. It was a common assumption that a proper lady did not feel or express such desire. Botolf was glad he had the good sense to see her warmth as the benefit to their marriage that it was.

Reluctantly, he rose from the bed and cleaned them both off. A smile curled his lips as he bathed her womanhood and she blushed deeply, for he easily recalled how thoroughly desire could burn away that shyness. The sweet youthfulness of her face served as a perfect disguise for the passionate woman she was.

Saxan watched Botolf from beneath her lowered lashes as he returned the wash basin and cloth to the table near the window. She enjoyed the way he moved, and found his lean muscular form exciting. He was dark all over with only a modest amount of body hair. That suited her fine; she liked the feel of his warm skin stretched tautly over firm muscles. When he climbed back into their bed, she greeted him with open arms, eager to touch all she had just admired.

As she moved her hands over his chest, Botolf eased the coverlet down to her waist. He watched as the tips of her small breasts hardened with invitation. That indication that she could be aroused simply by touching him renewed his passion.

"Are you sore, Saxan?" he asked as he kissed the hollow by her ear.

"Nay," she whispered and slid her hand over his thigh.

"Good." He began to kiss her with a barely controlled hunger.

Even though her eyelids protested almost painfully, Saxan opened her eyes, wondering crossly why she was awake. Dawn's meager light was only just creeping into the room. It was that eerily uncertain time of not-quite-night and not-yet-day. Her body ached, but, oddly, she rather enjoyed the feeling. There was a soreness between her thighs, but she felt no inclination to complain, for it meant that she was now truly Botolf's wife. It was not enough to wake her up yet she still felt a need to be awake. It made no sense.

As she was about to force her eyes closed again, she caught the shadow of a movement out of the corner of her eye. She gaped at the man who now stood on Botolf's side of the bed. When he raised his arm, she saw the glinting blade of a knife in his hand. Saxan screamed and scrambled to her knees. She grabbed the attacker by his wrist with both hands, halting his deadly strike when the knife's point was a mere inches from Botolf's broad chest.

Botolf was jerked awake by a piercing scream. His ears ringing and a lingering haze of sleep still clouding his eyes, he saw Saxan struggling to push away a knife blade aimed at his heart. All traces of sleep and confusion were immediately shoved aside. As his attacker prepared to strike Saxan, Botolf drove one hard fist into the man's belly.

His erstwhile murderer sprawled backward from the force of the blow, gasping loudly for air. Botolf caught Saxan before she could follow the man she still had a tight grip on. Pushing her to safety, he flung himself at his assailant before he could fully recover. A small part of Botolf's mind noted that his tiny wife had a lot of voice as she continued to scream for help.

Saxan hastily wrapped herself in the bed coverlet as the door to the room was kicked open and men in various stages of dress and alertness stumbled inside in response to her cries. When she saw the crowd gathering in the hall behind them, she grabbed Botolf's robe. The moment the attacker was subdued, she tossed the robe to Botolf.

Even as Botolf wondered why Saxan was concerned about his nakedness at such a time, he slipped on his robe. But as he tied it closed, he noticed the crowd in the hallway, many of them female. He realized that Saxan was as loath to have others see too much of him as he was to having even his closest friends see her in dishabille. For a moment that negated all his other concerns, and he turned to smile at her. His smile vanished with a curse when he saw the blood on her arm. He strode to her. She knelt on the bed clutching the coverlet.

"You are hurt," he said in a near growl as he grasped her by the wrist.

Saxan stared at her arm, surprised to see that at some time during her struggle with Botolf's attacker she had been badly scored by the knife. Suddenly, she became aware of how much the freely bleeding wound stung. Despite the vast amount of blood, however, she was sure that it was not a severe wound.

"It looks far worse than it is," she assured a scowling Botolf.

Lady Mary—Thylda and Jane right behind her—quickly reached Saxan's side and said, "We will tend to this, Botolf." She led Saxan to the washbowl, adding, "You must find out what this is all about, son."

Botolf moved to where Hunter stood over the man who minutes before had tried to kill him. "Does he still live?" he asked.

Hunter nodded. "Aye, though it will be awhile ere he wakes up."

"This came too close." Botolf glanced briefly toward Saxan, who sat quietly as Lady Mary bandaged her arm. As soon as Udolf had shut the door, giving them privacy, he added, "I think it was not particularly wise for me to marry now."

Hunter walked to the large bed and flung back the linen to reveal the proof that Saxan had been a maid and that Botolf had dutifully consummated the marriage. "It is far too late to change that, m'lord." He tossed the covers back over the bed. "This is not how the wedding ceremony should be conducted, but I think we can declare it done now." There was a murmur of agreement from Udolf, Pitney, Roc, Wesley, Roger, and Talbot. "What you must think about now, m'lord, is the killing of the man who wishes you dead."

"To strike on a man's wedding night shows a foolish boldness or rash desperation," grumbled Wesley.

"Mayhap it was clever planning," murmured Hunter with a shake of his head.

"True," Botolf agreed. "After such a celebration many of the people gathered are nearly senseless. The guard would be at its weakest."

"And a man does not take his weapons to his marriage bed," Udolf drawled then grinned faintly. "Not at first, leastwise."

Even Botolf smiled briefly as a ripple of laughter went through the gathered men, but he quickly grew serious again. "He is not one of Regenford's people."

"Nay," agreed Pitney. "He could have come with one of the wedding guests."

"Aye, or someone in Regenford aided in letting him inside the walls." Botolf cursed and ran a hand through his hair. "We can only guess until we are able to question the man. Talbot, Roger, see that the man is well secured for now."

"The guard on you and Saxan must be strengthened," advised Hunter as Talbot and Roger carried out the prisoner. He lowered his voice so that the women could not overhear him as he added, "Each time you bed with Saxan, you could be seeding your heir."

"And if it is Cecil who strikes at me, and I feel certain it is, Saxan is now a target as well." Botolf sighed. "I had thought about that. Howbeit, I had also believed she would be safe within these walls. Now I am shown that, even here, there is no safety to be found."

"You must hunt the man down," pressed Wesley. " 'Tis not only your own life you play with now."

"I fear that is the only way to put an end to this," agreed Hunter.

When Botolf frowned blackly, Wesley clapped him on the back in a gesture of sympathy. "We can talk on this later. Our fast will be broken in a few hours. By then the blackguard should be able to talk with us and we should be better able to discuss the matter. We will leave you now."

As soon as the others had left, Saxan sat in the middle of the bed, her gaze fixed upon a deeply thoughtful Botolf. She wished Cecil dead and as soon as possible, but she understood Botolf's hesitation. Even if he no longer felt any bond to the brother he had grown to manhood with, his mother did. He could not do what was needed without causing Lady Mary great pain, and he could not easily overlook that he and Cecil shared a father's blood.

"He forces me to kill him," Botolf said with a sigh as he joined her on the bed.

Ignoring the coverlet, which had slipped down to gather in a swirl around her hips, she wrapped her arms around him and pressed herself against his back. She could feel the tension in him but did not know how to ease his troubled mind. There was no alternative to offer him. The only way to put an end to the murderous feud with Cecil was for one of them to die. Saxan prayed that one would be Cecil.

"You have no choice," she murmured. "You either kill him or he kills you."

"And you. He has added you to his death list." He touched the bandage covering her forearm. "How is your injury?"

"It but stings. It was a shallow cut." She took a deep breath and said quietly, "If it is Cecil, and I fear all points to him as the culprit, then it is also whatever children we may be blessed with who are in danger. They, too, could stand between him and all he tries to steal."

"I know." Botolf ground the admission out between clenched teeth.

To distract Botolf, Saxan untied his robe and slid her hands slowly over his chest, teasing his nipples until they hardened beneath her fingertips. He gave a murmur of enjoyment and leaned back against her. She touched her lips to the lobe of his ear; when she traced its shape with her tongue, she felt him tremble slightly.

Botolf clenched his teeth as he resisted the urge to turn and take her into his arms. He watched her smooth her delicate hands over his skin, his desire growing with each caress. When she curled her long, slim fingers around his erection he groaned, but still did not move. He wanted to enjoy the feelings her touch and the sight of her caressing him invoked for as long as he could. His control broke when she began to stroke his manhood with a slow, sensuous rhythm as she slipped her other hand down to cup the weighted softness beneath.

With a soft growl, he reached for her and dragged her across his lap. He yanked the coverlet off her and drank in the sight of her slender form as he ran his hand down the length of her side.

Saxan met his heated gaze with a sweetly lecherous smile. Touching him and feeling desire flood him beneath her hands had her own desire running hot and fast. His gaze burned over her, stripping her of all of modesty's restrictions. While the fire of passion flowed through her, she was willing to let him look his fill if that was what pleasured him. She found that watching him take such delight in her body only increased her own pleasure.

He gave her a slow, hungry kiss, a low growl deep in his throat signaling his approval when she battled his tongue with hers. As he pulled his mouth away to seek out the taut inviting crowns of her breasts, he eased his hand between her thighs. He drew the tip of her breast deep into his mouth at the same time he slipped his finger inside her.

A shudder tore through Saxan. She pondered dazedly that such feelings could race through her body yet not do her any harm. It seemed to her that they were so strong, so overpowering, they should leave her marked in some way. By the time he lifted his mouth from her breasts, she was desperate in her need for him.

"Botolf," she called in a whisper of a plea.

"You are beautiful," he murmured and, still seated on the bed, moved her so that she straddled him.

Saxan gasped as he eased their bodies together. She was not shocked by the position, for she had known there were many ways to make love even though she had never experienced them. She clasped his broad shoulders tightly as she shivered with delight. The last clear thought she had was to wonder briefly just how many ways Botolf knew.

* * *

"Greedy wench," Botolf murmured as he arranged their lax bodies comfortably beneath the covers.

"I think the accusation of greed can be laid at your feet, too, my fine lord," she replied with a sleepy smile as she curled in his arms. Her smile grew when he chuckled.

" 'S'truth, and I think it will be a long time ere that greed lessens." He hugged her tightly. "Rest, dearling. It will soon be time to break our fast."

"Aye." She yawned. "Time, too, to face all our guests again." She groaned and Botolf laughed.

Stretching languorously, Saxan met her husband's gaze and smiled even as she blushed. She decided it was nice to wake up next to him. As she snuggled up to his warm, hard body, she decided it was far more than nice.

"That is quite enough of that, sweetings," Botolf scolded as, reluctantly, he extracted himself from her hold. "Time to rise," he said as he got out of bed.

Glancing at the stout proof of his arousal, she murmured, "I can see that." She collapsed into giggles when he gave her a stern look which was belied by the twitching of his lips.

"You are impertinent."

"Aye, I fear so, m'lord."

"Out of bed, wench. I need help tying my points," he said as he pulled on his braies.

She slipped out of bed and donned her robe. As she helped Botolf into his clothes, she decided it was a good thing that she had had a great deal of practice in helping her predominantly male kin get dressed. If she had not, she and Botolf would have ended in a sorry tangle.

When he began to help her dress, she feared they

would end up back in bed. She was feeling strongly inclined to snuggle and make love again, and a quick glance at Botolf's face told her that he was, too. Almost simultaneously they forced their minds to the guests and retainers who would be waiting for them. She was intrigued that they both had become serious at the same moment.

She knew instinctively that Botolf shared her musings. "We shall have to get a room for dressing so that we may have our maid and squire tend to us," he suggested slyly. "Otherwise, we may never leave this chamber."

She draped her arms around his neck and murmured, "Would that be so very bad, m'lord?"

"Things would get into such a wretched state, we would soon have the Scots sharing our bed." He kissed her, then took her by the arm and started out of the room. "So behave yourself and let us go and join our guests."

"The Scots would never dare to enter a Todd's sleeping quarters."

"And why not?"

"If it were a male Todd, they might well chance upon their own wife."

He shook his head when she grinned impishly. It was going to be very hard to maintain any sort of distance from her. She seemed to pull at him to share in her love of life and easy emotion. When she made him laugh or smile, he felt something soften inside him. That would have to be stopped, but he was not sure how.

Although he trusted Saxan and wanted to have a strong marriage, he also wanted to avoid the softer, sometimes illogical emotions such as love. He would give Saxan fidelity, passion, security, and prosperity;

but he would be the master of his own heart. Once he had loved, and once was more than enough.

Saxan fought against a powerful urge to blush as she entered the great hall on Botolf's arm. She felt no shame, but did wish it was not so well known how she had spent the night. To her relief, the jests were gentle and few. The attack upon Botolf had grabbed everyone's interest. It was of far more importance than Botolf's bedding his wife. Saxan concentrated on her meal as Botolf deftly turned aside all inquiries, doing his best to avoid openly accusing his half-brother.

"I think it grows too widely known that my own blood kin tries to kill me," he grumbled when the hall began to clear of guests.

"You cannot halt suspicion," Saxan replied in a quiet voice so that they might not be overheard. " 'Tis clear that many people know there was little love between you."

"That is not always reason enough for murder."

"True, but when one hears of such a crime, one first thinks of who would gain the most by your death. Most people feel there must be some driving reason for murder."

"And the one who gains the most is Cecil."

"No other. Why do you try to conceal the truth? Would it not be better if everyone knew? Cecil would find it hard to hide from you then."

"I wish to save my mother the pain of any public accusation."

"Of course. Everyone would speak openly of it then."

"M'lord!"

Botolf, Saxan, and the few others still lingering in the hall stared wide-eyed at the man who raced into the hall. His agitation was quickly picked up by the others. There were many reasons for a man-at-arms to be alarmed, but none of them were good ones. Saxan knew that, for a brief moment, the fear that the Scots were attacking again rippled through the hall.

"Do the Scots ride our way, Charles?" Botolf inquired calmly as the young man raced up to the head table.

"Nay, m'lord. This concerns the prisoner."

"He has died?"

"He has escaped."

"Escaped? How so?"

"We know not, m'lord. The guard is dead. His throat was cut."

"Has he been long dead?"

"I would say no more than a few hours, m'lord. The body is cold, and the blood is drying on the floor."

"Search the grounds, the castle, and for three miles outward all around."

"Do you think he will be found?" Saxan asked after the soldier left.

"Nay," replied Botolf, his voice taut with anger. "Howbeit, I cannot simply sit back and do nothing. There is always a chance."

She sighed. "Someone was very eager that the man did not have a chance to say anything."

"M'lord," ventured Sir Edric, who was seated across the table from Saxan. "I do not like to make accusations, but it should be noted that the Alansons left ere dawn fully lighted the sky."

"And none of the other guests have left?" Botolf asked.

"Not as yet, m'lord."

"Do you think Lady Odella is behind this attack and not Cecil?" For no reason she could pinpoint,

Saxan found that very hard to believe and yet she could not shake a sudden conviction that the Alansons were guilty in some manner.

"I know not, Saxan," replied Edric. "I but point to a fact that, mayhap, should not be ignored. Another is the fact that the assassin slipped in unseen and has left the same way."

"Which would mean it was all done by someone who knows Regenford well," Botolf said.

"Would Odella know the keep so well?" asked Saxan.

"I cannot say," he replied. "She has been here several times. The information was there if she sought it hard enough."

"But surely Cecil would have such information as well."

"He would." Botolf cursed. "I should have thought about that. Cecil would know all Regenford's secrets."

"Yet he was not here himself to put them to use."

"We cannot be sure of that, little one. He could find many holes to hide in nearby, holes from which he could send his men. Cecil was always good at finding hidey-holes and the secret ways of a place."

For a moment Saxan said nothing. She fought the suspicion growing in her mind, for she feared it stemmed from her own jealousy of Lady Odella. That acknowledgment was not enough to fully dispel it, however. Finally, she decided to speak out anyway. There was a good cause for suspicion. She was sure of it.

"Botolf, there is something else that should be considered," she said.

"You sound so timid," he murmured with a smile. "What is it?"

" 'Tis not a pleasant possibility to present to you. Mayhap Lady Odella allies herself with Cecil. Her father as well." She sighed when he looked at her, saying nothing, his expression revealing little. "Mayhap I just allow jealousy to rule my thoughts, but although I scolded myself about that, I was not able to stop puzzling over it. Why did she stay for our marriage ceremony and celebration? Why did she and her father leave at such a strangely early hour?"

"Questions worth pondering, m'lord," said Edric.

"Aye," Botolf agreed. "They are. In truth, I now recall several times that she or her father was near at hand when I was set upon by Cecil's hired killers. Yet," he frowned and ran a hand through his hair, "why should she try so hard to become my wife?"

"What closer ally could Cecil have than your own wife?" Saxan asked in a soft voice.

"And it is a game he has tried before, but Alice died ere he could finish." Botolf clenched his hands.

Before Saxan could ask what he meant, their brief discussion of the problem was ended. Botolf was drawn into the business of Regenford and the leave-taking of their guests. He was kept busy seeing to the securing of the secret ways in and out of Regenford. They no longer provided a way to elude the enemy, but supplied a means for their enemy to draw dangerously close to the lord of the manse. Saxan did not see Botolf alone again until they met in their bedchamber, preparing for bed. Discussion was delayed even longer as they both gave into their passions.

Botolf nuzzled Saxan's breasts lazily as the sexual satisfaction weighting his body drew him closer to sleep and teased her, "This morning you were most eager to get me modestly covered. Jealous, were you?"

"Aye," she admitted with calm honesty. "I find that

I no longer feel Christian enough to share, not when it means I must share you."

Thinking of Cecil and how the man seemed to get close to every woman he softened toward, Botolf growled, "Neither do I."

"Well then, being equally selfish, we should travel along quite smoothly."

He laughed, but the flash of humor did not fully dispel his sudden fear. He would have to keep Saxan well protected, so well protected that Cecil could never draw near her. Instinct told Botolf that Cecil would try to reach Saxan just as it told him that, if Cecil succeeded in becoming Saxan's lover, it would cut him far deeper than anything else Cecil had done. Almost afraid of knowing why he should feel so, Botolf fought to clear his mind of all thought and heartily welcomed the sleep which enfolded him.

Ten

Humming softly to herself, Saxan idly collected flowers in the fields just beyond Regenford's high walls. It was pleasant to feel free even if that freedom was tenuous. It was impossible to see the armed men who were ever around, but she knew they were still close at hand. She also knew that they were a necessity, but they often made her feel more of a prisoner than safe. It would be foolish, however, to think that Cecil had given up simply because there had been no attack in over three months. Cecil could well be waiting for them to relax their guard before he struck again.

Suddenly, she stopped and stared at the flowers she held. It seemed impossible that she had been married for over three months. The time had passed too quickly. She mentally counted the days since her wedding. It was, in truth, closer to four months.

They had been good months, she decided as she began to pick flowers again. Botolf was a most satisfactory husband. He did not treat her as chattel as so many other men did their wives. After the freedom her family had always allowed her, a strict, domineering husband would have proven a severe trial. She was certain that such attitudes had been the cause of so much trouble in Denu's marriage at first.

She frowned, reluctantly contemplating Botolf's

feelings and her own. She knew now, almost without doubt, that she loved the man, yet she had no idea of his feelings for her. For all his sweet words when they made love, he never revealed how he felt. His words were all born of passion. She had hoped to have gained a great deal more by now.

"Foolishness, Saxan," she scolded herself. "Do not mourn for what is elusive. Be grateful for what you have."

Fine words, she concluded, but difficult to heed. She ached for her love to be returned, and no amount of common sense would change that. Although she would never belittle what she did have, she knew she would continually strive for Botolf's love. If nothing else, it would allow her to release the words that constantly burned on the tip of her tongue, words of love that her pride kept choked back because Botolf gave her no sign that he returned her feelings.

She leaned against the trunk of a tree, her gaze fixed blindly upon the flowers she held. Love, she decided, was a troublesome thing. Hidden within its beauty were snares for the unwary and problems too numerous to count. Passion was easier, for it was hard to hide and needed no words to confirm its existence. It was also something men felt no qualms about revealing. Botolf made no effort to hide his. He had even given her warm looks in front of his men.

In an attempt to shake off her bout of self-pity, she reminded herself that Botolf both liked and trusted her. Those had been his own words. It was no small thing for a man to feel like that about a woman. He had also sworn to abide by his marriage vows and to do his utmost to maintain fidelity. Few men even tried.

Suddenly, even as she was aware of a noise and a shadow blocking out the warmth of the sun, Saxan found herself pulled into an embrace. The brief glimpse she got of her assailant told her that he was Botolf, but the kiss told her otherwise. Fighting the man was useless for he had her neatly pinned against a tree, but she remained unmoved by the act, standing still until it was over. Her blood ran cold when she finally got a good, clear look at her attacker. The likeness to her husband was chilling. Except for the small scar and the strangeness of the kiss, she would have thought that Botolf confronted her.

"So cool to your husband?"

The moment the man's grip eased, Saxan twisted free of his hold and drew her dagger. "You are not Botolf."

"Do I not look as he does?"

"Some," she lied, for she found the likeness unsettling. "Botolf has no scar, Cecil."

"Ah, so he has told you about me." Cecil's look twisted her heart with fear.

"It would be strange indeed if a man did not make mention of the one who tries to murder him."

"I? I try to murder Botolf? We share a father's blood."

"Which you do not hesitate to try to spill. You will not be able to beguile me with smooth words."

"The man is powerful and wealthy. He could have many enemies."

"Aye, but 'tis you who sends men creeping through the shadows to strike at his back."

Saxan frowned. Cecil was edging closer to her. She knew he was going to attempt to disarm her, and she feared he could succeed. Despite what she had been forced to do in the past to protect herself, the instinct to kill did not run in her veins. Even though he was a threat to the man she loved as well as to her, she knew she would hesitate. He looked too much like

Botolf. Saxan feared that could steal the deadliness from any strike she made. It would feel too much like striking at Botolf. She opened her mouth to call for help, but Cecil lunged at her.

A soft cry of surprise and frustration escaped her as he caught hold of her, wrestling her to the ground. Just as she had feared, his resemblance to Botolf made her hesitate. Her blade struck flesh, but only the meaty part of his arm. The wound did not even weaken him. An instant later he had stolen the knife from her hold, pinning her firmly beneath him.

"Slut," he hissed. "You have drawn blood."

"Not the heart's blood I sought." She knew it was hopeless, but she still struggled to twist out from beneath him.

He slapped her. When she gasped in pain and shock, he stuffed a cloth into her mouth. "That should silence you. I cannot have you summoning those bungling fools my half-brother surrounds you with," he muttered as he dragged her to her feet and back to the tree. "So, Botolf has wed himself a woman with a sting."

So many angry words crowded into Saxan's gagged mouth she nearly choked on them. Her fury kept her fear in control, although it was a struggle when he began to tie her to the tree. She tried not to think of what he could do to her while she was so helpless. Such thoughts would make her fear gain control of her. She glared at him, her expression holding every ounce of the helpless fury she felt. Saxan was chilled to the bone when he simply smiled. Her whole body tensed with disgust when he caressed her cheek.

"Botolf has chosen well this time. Oh, his last wife was a beauty, but not as lovely as you, Saxan Todd." He began to unlace her gown. "Do not fight your bonds. You will only harm yourself. I was not invited to the wedding and have had no chance to judge the beauty of my brother's bride."

Saxan shuddered with revulsion when he touched her breast. She could see that her reaction enraged him; his face darkened and hardened. That look lessened his resemblance to Botolf. Cecil looked cold. There was a darkness reflected in his eyes that she was sure invaded his very soul. Increasingly, his touch felt unclean.

"Mayhap Botolf did not gain the prize it appears he did. Do you revile his touch, too?"

She knew her expression reflected her hatred as she shook her head. It did not surprise her when he struck her. Disappointment was a bitter taste in her mouth when his blow did not send her tumbling into unconsciousness. She was not certain that he would cease his assault if she were unconscious, but at least she would not have to be a witness to her own degradation.

"Foolish wench. You bring yourself only more pain." Cecil grasped her breasts cruelly to underscore his threat, his anger growing when she made no sound, but continued to regard him coldly. "You are far too proud, I think." He cut open her gown with his knife. "How proud will you be when your husband turns away from you?"

The very thought turned Saxan's blood to ice in her veins, and her heart raced with a fear she struggled to keep hidden.

"He will you know," Cecil continued. "Once he discovers that I have possessed his little wife, he will not warm your bed again. That is how he treated Alice. Our Botolf is most particular. And so unChristian. He is never willing to share. He tried to keep Alice from me, but she was too much the whore. He feared I would leave my seed growing within her and gain all I crave in that way. I tried yet again with the woman he courted, but the slut lost the game to you. Mayhap," he lowered his gaze to her slim abdomen, " 'tis still the way to win this game." He touched the cool tip of his dagger to her skin. "Unless he has seeded you himself already."

Saxan felt her stomach quiver beneath the sharp steel. The struggle to hide her fear grew harder. As she faced possible disembowelment, she calculated when she had endured her last flux. Three months, she realized, two weeks after her wedding! She did not want to know that, did not want to realize that it would be more than her own life spilling out if Cecil used the dagger pricking at her skin.

"Mayhap a good swiving is not the right course to take." He drew his knife across her skin, leaving a stinging cut that oozed blood. "Mayhap I should forestall Botolf's attempts to clutter my path with heirs. One cut, Lady Saxan, and we can both see if Botolf's seed has rooted here."

Bile rose in her throat, gagging her, as she listened in horror to his cruel words. Her mind refused to let her deny the possibility that two lives teetered on the point of Cecil's knife. What she had been blissfully unaware of before was now a certainty in her mind. Beneath that deadly, gleaming point lay Botolf's unborn child. Even more horrifying was that Cecil could well be right when he said they would both see the truth. There was a chance she would live long enough to see him cut the child from her body.

"Lady Saxan?"

For an instant, Saxan was frozen with fear as the welcome voice of her bodyguard echoed through the wood. Cecil's face twisted with fury. She was terrified that he would still slash her and slumped in a near swoon as he chose flight even as the guard stepped into view.

"M'lady!" The young guard rushed to her side and cut the ropes which bound her.

Even as she sank to her knees and yanked the gag from her mouth, the rest of her guardsmen appeared. She pointed in the direction Cecil had fled, crying out hoarsely, " 'Twas Cecil. After him!"

The men obeyed her immediately. Robert, the one who had found her, stayed at her side. He hastily wrapped her in his cloak. She gave him a grateful smile and struggled to her feet only to find that she was still too shaken by her ordeal. Only Robert's strong support kept her on her feet.

"I wish to return to Regenford," she said to the young, handsome man-at-arms.

"Of course, m'lady," he replied.

"I fear you will have to carry me." She smiled weakly at his look of consternation. "My legs are too unsteady to support me. You either carry me or I fear you must drag me or toss me over the saddle like a sack of grain."

"I will carry you, m'lady."

"Aye, I thought mayhap you would." It was almost amusing to see the look on his face as he picked her up in his arms and started toward the keep. "Why do you look as if you march to your doom, Robert?"

" 'Tis naught, m'lady."

"I may have gone wobbly in the knees, but my head is clear enough. What ails you? If this is such a trouble for you, I will walk."

"Nay, m'lady. Then I shall truly get into trouble."

"And what trouble could you get into by carrying me when I am too unsteady of gait to walk?"

"M'lady, you have many kinsmen with short tempers, and it is strongly believed that your husband looks blackly upon any man who pays you attentions of any sort," Robert explained.

"And you fear they will misinterpret this?" she asked.

"Well, you are not a lady who grows faint."

"Nay, and neither am I so foolish as to be toted into my husband's presence in my lover's arms. I would walk if I could. I hate this weakness that has come over me, but I have not faced a man like Cecil before. You can put me down now, Robert," she commanded gently. "I think I can walk with just a little help now."

"I should not wish you to fall, m'lady," he said worriedly even as he set her down on her feet.

She gripped his strong arm and took a few deep breaths to further steady herself. She still felt nauseatingly afraid, but not really for herself, although the helplessness she had endured was something that still terrified her. She also had a fear of facing Botolf. Saxan felt unclean and could still hear Cecil's taunting words about how Botolf had turned from his first wife because she had been touched by Cecil.

Forcing aside those thoughts, she found the strength to walk with a greater confidence and even gained speed. It was important that Botolf be told that his enemy was near at hand as soon as possible. She doubted Cecil would be found, but a more careful watch had to be set up. Cecil had shown her all too clearly just how dangerous he was.

Botolf looked up from the papers his steward had spread before him and tensed as Robert escorted his wife into the great hall. An instant later he was on his feet, moving quickly to Saxan's side. He heard several others join him, but did not bother to see who they were.

"Saxan, are you hurt?" he queried tensely as he touched her arm.

"It was Cecil," she replied.

"Did he do this?" Botolf touched the bruise forming on her face, his voice hard and demanding.

"Aye." She turned so that the men with Botolf, only some of whom were her kinsmen, could not see what she would reveal when she opened the cloak she wore. She signaled to Botolf to turn as well. "And this." She winced as he gripped her tightly by the arms and hurriedly closed the cloak. "The rest of the men who were with me are searching for him. Robert can tell you where they are."

"And mayhap he can tell me how you came to be alone," Botolf said in a tone that caused Robert to pale. "I should stay with you—" he began.

"There is no need. I have ladies to tend to me. Go on, although I fear he has slipped away again."

"If he has not, then he is a dead man."

Even as he strode out of the hall, all the men there hurrying after him, Lady Mary and Jane rushed into the room. Saxan barely uttered a word as she was ushered to her bedchamber. She was suffering the bitter taste of shame. It was a feeling growing so large it was threatening to choke her. Nothing she told herself, no assurances she gave herself, stopped the guilt from flooding her.

She told herself that she had absolutely nothing to be ashamed of. Tied to a tree, she had been helpless to stop any of Cecil's foul advances. She had not succumbed to sweet words or seduction. Even though there had been no penetration, she had been raped. The promise of that final indignity had been easy to read in his eyes, however. She wondered if it could have made her feel any worse.

"Child, would you like to bathe?" Lady Mary asked gently.

Aye," Saxan replied. "A hot bath and lots of soap."

Saxan sat on the bed and watched as her bath was prepared. The two women seemed nervous around her, and Saxan wished she could do or say something to put them at ease. She was too sunk in her own thoughts, however, too involved in her own feelings, to concern herself about theirs. Shame, she concluded, was an extremely selfish emotion.

"Your bath is ready, Saxan," Lady Mary called. "Jane has gone to fetch a compress for your bruised face. Come, I will help you undress." She reached for the cloak Saxan still clung to.

Reluctantly, Saxan allowed Lady Mary to help her shed her tattered clothes. She watched the woman closely. Lady Mary grew consistently pale until, as Saxan stood naked before her, the woman looked as if she were about to swoon.

"Were you raped, child?" Lady Mary asked in a hoarse, unsteady voice.

Glancing down at the bruises on her breasts, Saxan shook her head. "Not fully."

"Not fully?"

"He did not penetrate my body, but is this not rape of a kind? He certainly planned to rape me. He spoke of it, and I could read it in his eyes," she whispered. "It was so hard to see that, for Cecil looks so much like Botolf."

"Nay, not Cecil. It could not have been Cecil."

"You think I do not know the truth of my own eyes?"

"Nay, child, but I cannot believe that Cecil would treat a woman so." She wet a cloth and dabbed at the wound on Saxan's abdomen. "He was always fond of women. To a fault, I fear. Nay, Cecil could not have done this."

Saxan was suddenly and intensely furious and could do nothing to quell the feeling. Cecil had abused her. The man had threatened her honor and her life. Although Lady Mary could not know it, Cecil had held the life of Botolf's heir on the tip of his knife. The man consistently tried to murder Botolf. Despite all that, Lady Mary persisted in her blind belief in the man's innocence. Even though a small rational voice in her head urged calm, told her that it was not really Lady Mary she was angry at, Saxan felt a cold, blind rage seize hold of her.

"The reason the man who touched me still lives is because he looked just like Botolf. Are there three such men then? I simply could not bury my knife in the heart of this man who looks just like Botolf, but is not Cecil."

"It cannot be," Lady Mary protested in a weak voice. "I just cannot believe he would do this."

"Ah, I see." A part of Saxan was astonished at the furious sneer in her voice, but she pressed on. "It was this not-Cecil who nearly killed my brother. It is this not-Cecil who sends assassins after Botolf, even into the bridal chamber. These bruises I bear are the marks of this not-Cecil, too, are they? And this cut upon my belly was done by the knife of this not-Cecil. He is a very busy man."

"Child, you are upset—"

"Aye, I am upset. 'Tis upsetting for a woman to be bound fast to a tree and told that she will be raped by a man who looks like her husband, but who is, of a certain, not Cecil. Most women would be upset to have a knife held to their belly, a belly that has not bled in over three months," she hissed and watched Lady Mary's tear-stained face pale even further.

"Strange, is it not, m'lady, that a man who is not Cecil would be so concerned about what Botolf's wife holds in her womb. He talked of seeding me himself and gaining all he craves that way. Such is the game he played with Alice. Then he puzzled over whether or not Botolf had seeded me already, whether he should simply cut me open and see.

"When will you believe, m'lady?" she continued, a hint of pleading behind her fury. "When your son and his family lie dead at your feet and Cecil comes here to rule, his hands soaked in our blood? Mayhap you need more proof than that of mine own eyes. After today I feel well able to give it to you. I will deliver it to you on a silver salver as John the Baptist was delivered to Salome."

Lady Mary choked out a cry and fled the room. Saxan sighed and shook her head. That tirade had gained her nothing. She had deeply hurt Lady Mary because she had felt a need to strike out at someone. Feeling even worse than she had before, she climbed into her bath, gritting her teeth against the sting from the cut on her stomach.

"Where is Lady Mary?" Jane asked as she entered the bedchamber carrying a compress and an herbal drink.

"My tongue has driven her from the room." Saxan smiled weakly at Jane's confusion. "I was unkind, I fear."

"Nay, not you."

"Aye, me. Come, help me wash my back. I wish to be scrubbed nearly raw. The unwanted touch of a man can make one feel unclean."

"Were you raped, m'lady?" Jane asked tentatively as she complied with Saxan's request.

"Nay. It was but threatened and I was manhandled. Jane? How long have I been wed?"

"Four months next week, m'lady."

"Aye, so I thought. Now, Jane, if the last time I bled was about a fortnight after my wedding night, what would you say ails me?"

Jane stared at her in wonder for a moment. "You are with child."

"So I would think."

"Have you been ill?"

"Nay, though it has become difficult to rise in the morning. I wish to stay abed more."

" 'Tis one of the signs. You are fortunate, m'lady. Many a woman empties her belly every morn or takes to swooning a lot." She shook her head. "I should have noticed. I am your woman and tend you daily. It is something I should have seen. Aye, something I should have been watching for."

"And I, yet I took no notice. Neither has Botolf, even though he was once kept from my arms because of my woman's time."

"Men often fail to notice until the babe begins to round a woman's belly and he can feel it move within. Who knows?"

"I did not realize it until Cecil's knife touched my belly."

Jane's gaze dropped to that part of Saxan's anatomy and she gasped. "You have been cut."

"Not badly, but the threat of a far deeper one was there; and, fate being the cruel mistress she is, that is when I knew I was with child. I have also told Lady Mary, but I think she will say naught. S'truth, I think the woman will not be speaking to anyone for a while."

"So you wish me to be silent until you can tell his lordship."

"Aye, please. Is he still out hunting for Cecil?"

"Aye, m'lady. It has been said that he will be doing so 'til nightfall."

By the time Saxan was bathed to her satisfaction and dressed in her robe, Thylda had arrived. Saxan took the drink Jane urged upon her, then lay down. As soon as Jane had left and the bath was cleared away, Thylda sat on the side of the bed and took Saxan's hand in hers.

"Were you raped, Saxan?" she asked.

"Nay. Does everyone think so?"

" 'Tis whispered that you may have been."

"Jane will correct that. Cecil but put his hands upon me and talked of the deed."

Thylda shivered. "I think I should feel raped nonetheless."

Saxan tightened her grip on Thylda's hand for a brief moment. "That is how I feel, Thylda. I feel defiled. God's teeth, I shudder to think how I would feel had he done as he threatened. Shame eats at me, and I cannot talk it away."

"You have naught to be ashamed of, Saxan."

"A part of me knows that. He tied me to a tree and gagged me. I could do and say naught. How could I stop him from doing as he pleased? I could not. Yet, I feel shamed as if I had asked to be touched so and now regret it."

"That feeling will pass, Saxan. You are clever, and to feel as if this were your fault, as if you have aught to be ashamed of, is not very clever at all. You are still overset and, mayhap, cannot think clearly."

"I hope you are right. This feeling is hard to bear. 'Tis like a sickness. Mayhap there is a potion for it," she jested weakly.

"There is a potion—Botolf. When he returns and holds you, all this will pass."

"Aye," Saxan murmured. "When he returns."

"Come, Saxan, you cannot think he will blame you for this."

"I do not know about that, but 'tis not what I fear."

"Yet something is troubling you."

"Aye. Cecil said that Botolf turned away from his first wife after he had touched her."

"He raped Alice?" Thylda asked in shock.

"Nay, I do not think it was rape. He spoke of her as a whore. Nay," Saxan said firmly after a moment's thought. "It was not rape."

"Then that is why Botolf turned away from her. She went to Cecil willingly. She cuckolded the earl."

"But will he believe I was unwilling?"

"I heard you are marked."

Opening her robe, Saxan briefly displayed her injuries, then tightly closed her wrap again. "Aye, marked."

"A man cannot look upon such as that and think you were willing," Thylda said, her voice revealing how shaken she was. "There is yet another thing to consider about Botolf and his first wife."

"And what is that?"

"Cecil called her a whore. She is little mentioned around here, but I have heard a whisper or two. He is not the only one who thought her one. Mayhap Cecil takes credit for what was not his doing. It is said that Botolf discovered what his wife was. That is why he turned from her. Mayhap finding out about Cecil was the, well, the final stroke that cut the ties. I have not cured your fear much, have I?" Thylda murmured.

"Not yet, but your words are certainly good ones to think on."

"He cut you."

"Aye, but 'tis a shallow cut."

"Why?" Thylda asked.

"He wanted to see if I were with child."

"God's beard." Thylda's eyes widened as she looked at Saxan. "And you are."

"Aye, and 'twas my fate to know it just as he put the knife to my belly."

"How frightening."

"Aye, it was, Thylda. I think it was my helplessness that was most frightening. There was nothing I could do but stand there as he played his horrible games. Even now I can taste the bitterness of that fear, for myself and the child that he threatened. I never wish to feel like that again."

"Hush," Thylda said, smoothing her hand over Saxan's forehead. "You fret yourself, and there is no need. The ordeal is over."

"Is it? I think this ordeal cannot be over until Cecil is dead. He threatens us all. I wonder if I fully understood that. Until now, it was between him and Botolf, man against man, attacks that Botolf could and did fight off."

"But now you see that it is anyone who stands between Cecil and all that is rightfully Botolf's."

"Aye, all—even an unborn babe."

"Mayhap Cecil just meant to frighten you."

"Nay, he meant it. He was going to cut me open. The only doubt was as to when and whether or not he would take me first. I could read the truth of his threat in his eyes. Eyes so like Botolf's," she whispered.

"I think that has made all of this much worse for you," Thylda said.

"That he looks like Botolf?"

"Aye. You knew it was not Botolf, yet your eyes told you that it could be, that this man who so abused you looked exactly like the man who holds you in the night. I am certain that added to your horror. You know they are not the same man, yet they look so much alike. 'Tis so troubling for a mind and heart already infested with fear."

"Sometimes, Thylda, you can sound very old and wise." Saxan managed a weak smile.

"Well, this old and wise woman now orders you to rest."

"Odd, but I do feel weary."

" 'Tis not odd at all. Such an ordeal can easily rob one of her strength. You have had a hot bath, which soothes, and the drink Jane gave you was meant to do the same. Come, close your eyes and rest. Remember that the child you carry shared your ordeal."

"Aye. I must not forget that. I shall have to take care now."

"I am certain Botolf will see that you do after you tell him. Do not fear that I will say anything until the proud father-to-be has cried out his success." Thylda smiled faintly.

" 'Tis what he has waited for. 'Tis what he wed me for."

"That and a few other reasons. The product of your womb was not his only consideration. He wanted you."

Saxan smiled fleetingly. "Aye, he did."

"And he still will," Thylda said firmly as she removed the compress Jane had placed on Saxan's bruised face. "This is no longer useful. Did he hit you hard?"

"Aye, because I would not warm to his touch."

"Which should tell you how foolish it is to feel any shame or guilt. Now, rest."

"You will stay?" Saxan asked, her lingering fear echoing in her voice.

"As long as you wish me to or until Botolf arrives to take my place," Thylda vowed.

Saxan closed her eyes, but frowned as she remembered something Cecil had said. "Have you heard much about Botolf's search for a wife? Whom he may have courted or which ones people may have thought were his choice ere I arrived?"

"Not truly," Thylda replied. "I do not think he looked very hard. Lady Odella is the only woman I have ever heard mentioned. She was not the only one who thought that Botolf would soon ask for her hand."

"So I thought. I believe the Alansons side with Cecil, most certainly Odella does."

Thylda frowned. "We-ell. 'Tis suspicious that they should creep away on the very morning that assassin escapes."

"Very, and now I think Cecil spoke of her. He told me he had tried to seed Alice and gain all he desires through the child, then said that he had tried again with the woman Botolf courted, that he came close that time, but the game was lost to me."

"Odella."

"Aye, I think so." Saxan yawned. "I must not forget to tell Botolf."

"I will be sure to remind you. I think he now mistrusts the Alansons, but 'tis best to make sure he does."

"It all grows so tangled."

"And dangerous."

"Aye, and dangerous." Saxan moved her hand to her stomach and felt Thylda cover it with hers. "For all of us."

"I will speak to our kin."

"Mayhap—"

"Nay, no mayhap," Thylda said, her voice firm. "It

will be done. There is no doubt now. You saw your assailant. 'Twas Cecil who threatens you."

"Aye, 'twas Cecil." Saxan winced as she thought of Lady Mary.

"The word shall be put about. The eyes of all of our kinsmen will be turned his way."

"So many eyes," Saxan jested weakly.

"Let us pray that there are enough to find him."

"Poor Uncle Edric."

"Lady Mary still refuses to believe it is Cecil?"

"I think *not,*" murmured Saxan.

" 'Tis sad, but there is naught which can be done about that. As you say, it is not just men against men now. You are threatened and so is the life of an innocent, helpless babe. This must be stopped. Cecil must die. 'Tis the only answer."

Saxan made no reply, but clung to Thylda's hand. It was the only answer. It was the only way to dispel the danger that loomed over Botolf, herself, and now their child. Saxan knew that only Cecil's death would fully cure her of the fear he had bred inside her.

Eleven

"There is no sign of the man, m'lord," Pitney said as he rode up beside Botolf.

Botolf looked into the distance and swore. It was already dusk, and there was no point in continuing the search for Cecil. The man had disappeared as completely as if he had never existed. The only thing they had seen to prove that Cecil had been on Regenford land was the blood on the ground near the spot where he had accosted Saxan.

Closing his eyes, Botolf fought to quell the helpless rage churning inside him. Not even when Cecil had seduced Alice had he been so eager to kill the man. He could not dispel the image of the bruises on Saxan's fair skin. Those images kept his anger hot and fierce.

"There is no point in continuing, m'lord," Pitney said, interrupting Botolf's thoughts.

Looking at the youth who was swiftly becoming one of his closest men-at-arms, Botolf nodded. "He has slithered off into the deep grass."

"Aye, and though I should like to look beneath each blade, I know it will gain us nothing to do so."

"Let us return to Regenford then. I should like to see how my wife fares," Botolf said as he turned his mount back toward his keep.

"At least Cecil was not able to accomplish what

he so clearly planned to do," Pitney said as he rode alongside."

"So young Robert assures me. Mayhap I should have stayed behind to be certain."

"Nay, m'lord. Saxan expected you to lead this search. If she had felt a need for you to stay with her, one greater than the need to find Cecil, she would have said so. My sister has e'er spoken her mind."

"Aye, she has. If she told me to go, it is exactly what she meant me to do," he murmured, speaking mostly to himself.

His worry was not fully eased, however. After such an ordeal a woman would expect some comforting, but he had not even held her for a moment before dashing off to join in a fruitless search for Cecil. It was possible that she would think he cared little about her hurts.

A harsh laugh echoed in his head, and he pressed his lips together tightly to keep it from escaping. Nothing could be further from the truth. He cared more than he wished to, but the first thought in his head when he had seen her bruises had not been to soothe her hurt. It had been a craving to hack to pieces the man who had inflicted them. That was undoubtedly the usual way for a man to react, but he was not sure Saxan would understand, not if she were in great need of comfort, a comfort only he could give her.

When they reached Regenford, Botolf headed straight for Saxan's bedchamber only to have Pitney halt him on the stairs. "I must see how Saxan fares."

"Aye, m'lord, but I am asking for only a moment of your time," Pitney said.

" 'Tis important?"

"Very, m'lord. Cecil must be stopped, do you not agree?"

"Completely."

" 'Tis a fear for and a love of my sister which prompts me to speak so boldly. The attempts to end Cecil's deadly game have thus far been weak, m'lord. You fight off his assassins and look about some whenever he strikes, but I see little else being done."

Botolf sighed and gave a reluctant nod. " 'Tis a family squabble. I did not wish it to become too widely known."

"I think you must now ask yourself if the cost of saving your lady mother's feelings grows too high."

"You do speak boldly, lad."

"I am driven to it. I am not sure you can understand what Saxan is to me. The bond runs deep and strong, m'lord."

"Aye, I know. I have seen it. So, continue."

"I believe it is past time to set aside consideration for Lady Mary's feelings, although it pains me to say so as I am fond of her. Still, she remains blind to the evil that is Cecil. In order to serve that blindness, you must court death at Cecil's hands. And, now, so must Saxan. Allow me to speak to my kinsmen."

"And what will that gain?" he asked.

"Their numbers are many and they are spread far and wide. You would have many people searching for Cecil and, mayhap, it could still be kept somewhat private. At least there would be many more sword points poking about in the rushes to flush out this adder. That is all I ask, m'lord. Just allow me to spread the word amongst my kin."

"I am surprised that has not been done already."

"Nay, m'lord. I cannot promise that the privacy you crave in this matter will continue, however."

Botolf briefly clasped Pitney's shoulder. "I can see the value in what you say, but I must think on it. I do not wish to say aye or nay when anger still rules me. I will have an answer for you on the morrow."

As he watched Pitney descend the stairs, Botolf cursed softly then turned and strode toward his chamber. The boy was right. It was past time to stop proceeding quietly, to try and keep it as private a matter as possible in an attempt to protect the feelings of his mother. That was going to be a hard step to take, however, and he needed some time to think about it.

"M'lord," Thylda said in surprise when Botolf entered the room, keeping her voice only slightly above a whisper. "She is asleep."

"I will stay with her now. Have some water for washing sent up and some food as well, please," he requested.

"Aye, m'lord," she said and slipped out of the room.

Once Thylda was gone, Botolf took her place on the side of the bed, his gaze fixed upon a sleeping Saxan. He was barely aware of the delivery of the food and water except that it forced him to move from Saxan's side. He did so reluctantly and hurried through his meal and toilette. He wanted to be able to give her his full attention when she woke up.

When he returned to her side, he sat down and held her hand as he watched her sleep. She looked so delicate, so young, and he felt swamped with guilt over the danger he had pulled her into. He had dragged her from the safety of Wolfshead Hall into the midst of a battle for the rule of Regenford. He had turned the point of a madman's sword in her direction. Despite all his vows not to, he had let his feelings conquer his good sense yet again. Marriage should have waited until he had settled the matter of Cecil and his deadly plans.

He brushed a lock of hair from her face and sighed.

Waiting to marry had not been a luxury he had been able to enjoy. However, there had been some time left before he would have been forced into a decision. He could have put that time to better use. Instead, he had allowed his loins to lead him along. For all he had looked at the reasons for wanting her for his wife and his careful inspection of her suitability, it had been his lust for her that had lurked behind his every step.

Nay, not just lust, he thought. Lust was too empty a word for what he felt. Lust was what you spent on the whore in town or on that adulterous wife who smiled so invitingly. Lust was not what you gave a slim girl who could set your blood afire with a smile.

He frowned down at her. She was pulling him into her hold. If he was not careful, she would be in full possession of all he had tried to lock away—his heart, his soul, his love. He had to fight harder, but it was not going to be easy. It was impossible to be cold to her and, without that wall between them, he was vulnerable. Somehow he was going to have to find some compromise in which he kept his heart safe, yet did not wound Saxan with indifference. If he failed in that, if his heart were still delivered into her small hands, then silence would be his protection. She might win his love, but he would never let her know it. Never again would he put that power into a woman's hands. He had learned his lessons well and would not allow Saxan to make him forget.

Saxan slowly opened her eyes. She had sensed her husband's presence even before sleep had fully released her from its grip. She knew it was Botolf who held her hand. When she saw the dark frown on his face, she wished she had stayed asleep.

"Did you find him?" she asked with a touch of hesitation.

"Nay," Botolf replied. "Not a sign. The worm has slithered back into the ooze. I am sorry I left without even asking how you had fared."

" 'Tis more important to find Cecil, and he was so close this time. And, you did inquire about me. You even offered to stay. I said go. There were plenty of women here to tend to me."

"Saxan," he began carefully. "I spoke to Robert—"

"You have not punished my guards, I hope. It was not really their fault."

"They were supposed to guard you."

"Aye, and they did." She shrugged. "But the day was hot and lazy and I wandered away without a word to them."

"Well, they have been punished, but not harshly. The chores they despise and consider beneath them have all been assigned to them for one week's time. They failed in the duty assigned to them, Saxan. I could not allow that to pass unpunished."

"Nay, of course not," she agreed.

"Now, as I was about to say, I spoke to Robert and he told me that he felt certain you were not raped. Is he correct?"

"Aye, he arrived in time. I . . . I was just touched." She dreaded admitting that to him, but felt she had to tell him the full ugly truth.

She tensed as he reached to undo her robe, gently prying her fingers loose when she tried to clutch the garment shut. Such a dark look came over his face as he viewed her bruises that she shivered. She could not stop herself from wondering how much of that fury was directed at her.

"What is this?" he asked in a tight voice as he

touched the cut upon her stomach with the tips of his long fingers. "Why did he cut you like this?"

" 'Tis not a bad cut."

"Cecil had a reason for doing this, Saxan, and I think you know what it was."

"Aye, I do. Cecil spoke of seeding me to gain what he wants through a child." Her voice began to shake as the look of fury on Botolf's face hardened. "Then he wondered if you had already accomplished that. He did this as he spoke of seeing for himself."

Suddenly, Botolf yanked her into his arms. Saxan could feel him shake with the anger that pulsed through his body. It was frightening, for he was a man who was almost always in control. She wondered fleetingly just how much emotion he did keep reined in and why.

"And he meant the threat?" Botolf asked in a hoarse voice.

"Oh, aye, he meant it. I feared he would carry it through when Robert called out for me, but Cecil chose to run instead."

"So close," he whispered.

"Closer than you think," she said with an equal softness.

Botolf grasped her by her shoulders and held her a little away from him. "What do you mean?"

"I mean that, if he had cut me to find out if you had seeded me, he would have discovered that you had." She almost cried out when his grip on her shoulders tightened painfully.

"Are you sure?"

"As sure as I can be."

"You have not been sick." He moved his hand to her stomach, and the cut there chilled him even more than it had before. "I have watched for that sickness in the morning. They say it is the first sign."

"The first sign is that a woman ceases to bleed," she said quietly and blushed.

"But you have bled."

"Once. A fortnight after we were married. I have not bled once since then, and we will be four months married next week."

He stared at her as his mind worked to accept what she was saying. "Aye, not once since then and I would know. I have never left your bed. That means the child will come—"

"In late March or early April," she finished and clutched her robe together when he abruptly left her.

Botolf strode to the door and flung it open. He took one step out into the hall and bellowed, "Pitney! Pitney Todd, come here now." He began to pace outside the door, then grabbed a servant's arm as the woman timidly walked past. "Find Pitney Todd."

A moment later Pitney hurried up to him. "What is it, m'lord?"

"You may send word to each and every one of your kinsmen. I want Cecil found, and I want him dead."

Pitney's eyes widened. "M'lord, you said you wished that decision to wait until your blood had cooled. Excuse my boldness, but I feel that your anger is far greater now than it was then."

Grabbing the youth by the arm, Botolf dragged him over to where a wide-eyed Saxan sat on the bed. "Show him," he ordered her.

Nervously, Saxan obeyed, opening her robe so that Pitney could see her injuries. When her brother paled, she said, " 'Tis only a few bruises and a shallow cut." She hastily closed her robe.

"Beneath the knife point that drew that line lies my child," Botolf said, his voice hoarse as he battled to control his rage.

"God's beard," Pitney breathed, staring wide-eyed at Saxan for a full moment before a weak smile curled his mouth. "So quick."

"Now you must see why, angry or not, I have made my decision," said Botolf.

"Aye, m'lord," agreed Pitney.

"As you told me, the cost of saving my mother's feelings grows too high. When it was but myself in danger, I felt it enough to just meet his attacks and keep a close watch for him. Even Saxan is not helpless, although this incident has shown me, more clearly than the attack on our wedding night, that she is not safe either. But this, this goes beyond all excuse and reason." He took a deep breath as he continued to fight for calm. "Tell your kin that, too, if you wish."

"I will do so immediately, m'lord. Have I your permission to order your runners and dispatch messages?"

"You are free to use whatever means you deem necessary to carry out the plan."

"Pitney," Saxan called as her brother started to leave. "You had best tell Thylda what you plan, for the same thought occurred to her." She glanced warily at Botolf. "I am not certain that Thylda would ask permission first."

Pitney nodded. "I will speak to the brat. She may wish to send her own message to Denu or Tuesday."

As soon as Pitney left, Botolf brought Saxan the food and drink sent up for her along with his own meal. He then moved to gaze out the window. He stared blindly at the waning activity in the darkening bailey as he fought to calm the turmoil inside him. Anger and fear warred with the joy and wonder he felt at the promise of becoming a father. Before he faced Saxan again he had to be rid of the former and show her only the latter. She had had enough of an ordeal today. He had to put himself into a mood that allowed him to be calm and soothing.

Saxan warily eyed Botolf's stiff back as she tried to eat, knowing that it would be best for the child, but the food stuck in her throat. Each bite she forced down made her stomach churn anew. With a soft groan, she pushed the food aside and dove for the chamberpot under the bed. She barely reached it in time before the little she had managed to get down forced its way back up.

Weak and shaking, she was faintly aware of Botolf rushing to her side. He grasped her in his strong hands and held her steady while she was ill. Once her illness had passed, he bathed her face. Numbly, she rinsed her mouth clean and let him help her back into bed.

"I thought you said you did not get sick," he teased a little weakly, her abrupt illness worrying him.

"I have not. Not once."

She took several deep breaths, but it did nothing to quell her sudden urge to cry. Ever since Botolf had entered the room, she had waited for some sign that he was not going to turn from her. She had not seen enough to still the fear Cecil had planted in her heart. Botolf did not appear to view her with disgust, but, except for that one brief hug, neither did he hold her close. Saxan was not sure what she wanted, but there had to be something he could do to ease her fear and he was not doing it. He is being so controlled, so calm, so distant, she thought wildly and burst into tears.

"Saxan," Botolf breathed her name in shock and confusion as she began to weep into her hands.

"I am so sorry. I should have killed that bastard when I had the chance."

"It was Cecil's blood on the ground then."

Continuing to hide behind her hands, she continued brokenly. "Aye, I stabbed him, but I hesitated. He looked so much like you that I lacked the strength to plunge my knife into his heart. That allowed him to get me, and that is my shame."

Botolf sat on the edge of the bed and took her into his arms. "Saxan, there is no shame in this for you."

"I let him touch me."

"He forced you to bear his touch. Did you think I would blame you for that?"

"He said you turned away from Alice." She struggled to control her weeping as he stuffed a cloth into her hands for her to dry her tears.

"Alice was not tied and gagged, her gown cut open, and her chastity threatened at knifepoint. Alice lay down for sweet words and smiles. She always did. She was a whore, but I fought not to see that. When I caught her with Cecil, I could no longer ignore the truth. That is when I turned from her."

Saxan stared at him, but she found it hard to read his expression. The tears in her eyes blurred her vision. "Are you certain?"

"Aye, I am certain." He stood up. " 'Tis clear you are not." He started to take off his clothes.

"What are you doing?"

"I intend to prove to you, in a way words cannot, that I am not going to turn from you because of this."

He smiled crookedly as she watched him with wide, unsure eyes. The first thing he had wanted to do when he had seen Cecil's mark upon her was to obliterate it by making love to her, but he had reined in that urge. She had been badly shaken by the accident with Cecil, and he had felt that that was not the way to comfort her. She did not look certain that it was what she wanted now, but he could think of no other way to erase the doubt and fear in her eyes.

When he slid into bed beside her, Saxan warily let him tug off her robe and pull her into his arms. There was such a soft look in his eyes that she began to lose her doubts. As he made slow, gentle love to her, she was freed of them completely.

For a long time after their lovemaking, Saxan held Botolf close, resisting the inevitable ending of their embrace. It was like a healing balm to have him so close. She was certain no man could make love to a woman so sweetly if he were filled with distaste.

"Convinced?" Botolf asked as he eased the intimacy of their embrace and turned onto his side to look at her.

"Aye. You are very persuasive." She slipped an arm around his waist and cuddled up to him.

"Can you feel our child yet?" He slid his hand down to her stomach, but was careful not to touch the cut there.

"A little. There is a quickening." She smiled. "I thought it was bad beef."

He laughed softly then grew serious. "You have learned a hard lesson today, but I wonder if you will heed it."

"You mean I must not elude the men you set to guard me."

"Aye. 'Tis not just your life you put at risk now."

"I know." She shivered and huddled closer to him.

"When did you know that you were carrying our child?"

"God saw fit to have me see the truth just as Cecil's knife touched me." She heard him curse, and his arms tightened around her. "I thought it a harsh punishment for my folly of being caught out alone. So strong was that sudden truth that I could not question it and thus ease my added fears. Do you know what I feared most? That I would not die the moment he cut me, that I would live long enough to see the murder of our child. I think there could not be a worse death."

The images her words evoked horrified Botolf. He could only guess at how deeply it had affected her. Unknowingly, Cecil had inflicted a bruise that would take far longer to heal than all of the others. Botolf could hear the lingering fear in her voice.

"You must always be on your guard, Saxan, or, by Christ's foot, I shall lock you in these chambers until Cecil is dead."

"I will go nowhere without my guards," she vowed.

For a while they simply held each other. Botolf knew instinctively that Saxan sought to absorb his strength, to refortify her own lagging courage. He relished the fact that she was alive and thought hard on all the things he could do to insure that she stayed that way until Cecil was no longer a threat.

Saxan reluctantly eased out of his hold. She sat up, clutching the coverlet to her bruised breasts, and looked at him. It was time to tell him about how badly she had treated his mother. It was very tempting to leave it until he found out on his own, but she could not practice that sort of deception. If nothing else, he might be able to mend at least some of the damage she had done. She could only pray that she had not committed a sin beyond forgiving.

"Botolf, your mother came to tend me," she said.

"Aye, she would." He grimaced. "I suppose she would not heed any talk that it was Cecil who had committed these crimes."

"Nay." She sighed. "I was so angry, Botolf."

"What are you trying to tell me, Saxan?"

"I was cruel to Lady Mary."

"You? Nay."

" 'Tis comforting that no one can believe I would act so badly, but, aye, me. When your mother insisted that Cecil could not have done this to me, I fear rage seized me by the throat. I could still feel his hands, the point of his dagger, and there she stood, saying that it was not Cecil."

He took her hand in his and asked gently, "So what did you say, little one?"

"Far too much." She took a deep breath and related her tirade. "Then I asked if she would finally believe it when her son and his family lay dead at her feet and Cecil came here to rule, his hands soaked in our blood. Then I asked if she would believe it if I delivered the proof to her on a silver salver as John the Baptist was delivered to Salome."

"And what did my mother do?" he asked quietly.

"She burst into tears and fled the room. I am so sorry, Botolf. She had done me no wrong. I knew that even as I lashed her with my cruel words. She had come to help me, soothe my hurts, and I treated her wretchedly."

He pulled her into his arms, turning onto his back and holding her close. He felt bad for his mother's hurt, but he could not blame Saxan for inflicting it. Fresh from her ordeal at Cecil's hands, it must have been more than she could have borne to hear his mother denying Cecil's guilt. If he had been there at that moment, he felt sure he would have acted much the same.

"My mother's hurt in this matter is mostly self-inflicted. She will not see the truth," he said.

"That was no reason to be so unkind to her," Saxan replied.

"You were speaking only the truth, sweeting. 'Tis her own folly if she cannot heed it. Can you blame your uncle for her pain because they are apart when they should be together?"

"Nay, but 'tis not quite the same."

"Nearly. He will not turn from the truth. He has vowed to end the life of anyone who tries to end mine, and that is Cecil. She cannot accept that, for she will not believe that Cecil is the one. Thus she denies herself a chance of companionship and affection in her latter years, something I know she deeply needs and wants. I, too, have raged at her and made her weep, but the guilt of that fades quickly. 'Tis Cecil who brings her pain, not us. 'Tis her refusal to see the truth that hurts her. If I had been here, I would have been no kinder. I swear it."

"You will not go to her now?"

"Nay. I cannot soothe her in this. God's beard, the time for coddling her in this is far past. If I go to her now, she may again try to deny that Cecil did anything and I shall think on this," he touched the wound on her stomach, "and your words will probably seem kind next to the ones that would spew from my mouth. Nay, not this time. She must seek her own comfort, if there is any to be found for her."

"There is something else I must speak on," she murmured after a few moments of silence. "It is something that could be important."

"Am I to find the maids cowering in the corners?" he teased, languidly moving his fingers through her thick, bright hair.

"Nay." She laughed, then grew serious. "How intensely did you look for a wife, Botolf? Was it halfheartedly or did you court many ladies?"

"An odd query."

"Please, I ask for a good reason, not out of jealous curiosity. In truth, I do not really wish to know whom you held before me."

"Few and only briefly. None as I hold you," he murmured and kissed her even as he cursed the weakness that prompted such words. They were impossible to restrain, however, as he held the woman who now nurtured his child within her body.

When the kiss ended, Saxan had to take several deep breaths to still the desire he had stirred inside her. "Please, I cannot think clearly when you kiss me, and my mind must not be foggy now. Botolf, please answer my question."

He shrugged and replied, "Everyone knew I had to take a wife. Many ladies were presented to me as possible choices; but, aye, my courting was half-hearted. In truth, only Odella could be considered a possible pick, but I do not believe I truly courted her. Mostly, I did not avoid her attempts to gain my interest. That made her appear to everyone and herself as my most possible choice."

"Then it is she," Saxan muttered, growing angry as she began to see, all too clearly, the game Odella had played.

"What is *she?*"

"When Cecil spoke of seeding your first wife and gaining everything that way, he said it was a game that could still work. He said he had tried again with the woman you had courted; but although it was a near thing, the game was lost to me."

"Odella."

"It has to be she he was talking about."

"She and her father disappeared along with the assassin that morning. They are in league with Cecil."

"It would appear so."

"More than appear. They sought to wed her to me and thus make it easier for Cecil to be rid of me."

Saxan said nothing, simply pressed closer to him, trying to soothe the sting of such treachery. He was such a proud man. This attempt to play him for a fool had to cut him deeply, especially since it had almost succeeded. There was little she could think of to say to ease the sting. She was sorry she had had to tell him of the game, but knew she had had no choice. It was always best to recognize one's enemies. Now Odella and her father could not sneak up on Botolf, hiding murderous treachery behind smiles and friendship.

"Is there no one I can trust?" he finally muttered.

She looked up at him and brushed her lips over his. "There are many you can trust. You can trust me, husband."

Botolf could read the clear honesty in her eyes and held her close. "Aye, I can. I do."

As she smiled against his chest, she felt her heart skip with pleasure. Those were not the words of love she ached to hear, but she was not fool enough to ignore their importance. Instinct told her that Botolf was a man who no longer trusted easily. She would treasure the gift of his trust and vowed to do nothing that would abuse it.

Twelve

"A week, Saxan. A full week. Mayhap I should just break down the door to her chamber." Botolf grumbled as he paced the garden path in front of her.

"Sit down, Botolf." Saxan tugged Botolf down onto the garden bench at her side.

Saxan was torn between guilt and worry over Lady Mary, but now she had to calm Botolf. It was hard for Lady Mary had shut herself away, refusing to see anyone. Only her maid was allowed into her bedchamber.

"She eats regular meals and bathes, Botolf. That is a good sign. She needs time," Saxan reassured him.

"For what?" Botolf demanded.

"Mayhap she is in there truly looking at the trouble you suffer. Mayhap she finally fights to come to a decision about Cecil, to heed our words and the evidence right before her eyes. It would take time for her to accept and adjust to the truth."

"And mayhap she hides from the truth by closing out the world. Her woman Elizabeth will tell me naught."

"You must not keep testing the woman's loyalties," she scolded. "She has told you that your mother's health is good."

"Her body fares well, but what of her heart and mind?" Botolf asked.

"We can only wait and see. Lady Mary is a grown woman. If she wishes to see no one, surely that is her right."

He sighed, put his arm around her, and held her close. As his worry over his mother's strange behavior increased, he turned to Saxan more and more. That was not in keeping with his plan to maintain a distance from her, but he could not help himself. Everything about his wife pulled at him, drew him closer and closer to her despite his plans.

In the night, as he lost himself in the sweet passion he and Saxan shared, he heard himself speak words that might have been better left unsaid. Nevertheless, he could not stop himself from repaying her for the delight she gave him with sweet words. It was only afterwards that he feared he might have said too much, revealed too much of his confused emotions.

He looked down at the fair head upon his shoulder and decided that, if he had revealed too much, she had either not noticed or was not going to put it to use. Her manner toward him had not changed at all. She asked little but gave a lot. At times he thought he was being unfair to her, but within him lurked a wariness he could not ignore. In all honesty, it was fear, a fear of giving too much. He knew that if Saxan abused what he gave, it would cut him far more deeply than Alice's games ever had.

His thoughts swung back to his mother, and he frowned. Saxan was right, Lady Mary was a full-grown woman and, if she wished to play the hermit, it was her right. It did not ease his worry, however. His mother had never acted this way.

"I will give her another week, and then I shall break down her door if I must," he said.

"If you feel you must," Saxan murmured.

"I do. She has never behaved like this before, and

that alone is cause for worry, whether she eats well or not. There is one other thing we will do. I will wait no longer to announce that you are carrying my child. Tomorrow eve I shall speak out. Who knows? If she hears that, she may come out. I will tell Elizabeth to let my mother know what my plans are."

"Aye. 'Tis an occasion your mother may feel it is her duty to attend."

By the following day, Saxan saw little change in Lady Mary's self-imposed exile, although she kept a close watch out for the woman. At midday two new arrivals stole all thought of Lady Mary from her mind. Her uncle returned to Regenford and brought Tuesday and her family with him.

"Let the women ready your chambers," Botolf suggested with a grin as he viewed the confusion caused by Thylda, Saxan, and Tuesday greeting each other in the hall.

"You tend to your sons, Godric," Tuesday called as she started away with her new daughter in her arms. "And no more talk of heads rolling. You know that it gives poor little Alhric bad dreams."

"Nay, it does not," the small boy cried out, but his mother had already left.

Edric sat at the head table and gratefully accepted the ale a page served him. "I had forgotten how much Tuesday loves to talk," he said mournfully.

"Papa, might Sennet and I look for Uncle Pitney?" Alhric asked his father.

"Aye, there is a good idea," Godric replied.

"I last saw him with the armorer," Botolf called as the two small boys hurried away.

"Tuesday shall have a word or two to say about that," Edric murmured.

"Or four or five," Godric said with a grin, "but, mayhap, she shall tire her tongue chattering with her sisters."

"Aye, they shall wear themselves out talking about you husbands." Edric laughed heartily at the identical scowls Godric and Botolf wore.

"Oh, she is lovely, just lovely," Saxan said as she sat on Tuesday's bed and held her new niece. "I am sorry I was not able to be at her christening."

"If you traveled to all of the christenings in our clan, you would never be home," Tuesday quipped.

" 'Tis such a surprise to see you."

"Ah, I see that he did not tell you."

"He?"

"Your husband, Lord Botolf. He wrote to Denu and me after you were attacked. You appear to be all right."

"Aye. If that is why you hastened here, there was no need," Saxan said.

"Nay, 'tis not the only reason I came. I missed your wedding and wished to see how you fared. Denu and I tossed the dice to see which one of us would come. I won."

"As always," said Thylda.

"And you met Uncle Edric on your way here?" asked Saxan.

"Nay," replied Tuesday. "He stopped to tell us that he was traveling here and to ask if we wished to send anything with him." She laughed. "I think he was taken aback when I told him it would be all of us."

Saxan joined her sisters in laughing, but her attention was quickly diverted by the lively baby she held. She knew Botolf wanted sons, but surely one of the children she would give him would be a daughter.

Her musings were ended by Tuesday putting a hand on her shoulder.

"When is your child due?" Tuesday asked.

"How could you know?" Saxan could not believe her sister had any special insight.

"It was the look that settled upon your face as you watched little Honey Pipere. It did not say *when* will I have a child, but *will* mine be as healthy as this one."

"Botolf is to announce that I am with child tonight."

"To brag of his prowess to his men, you mean. When is the child due?"

"In late March or early April."

"Ah, the spring. 'Tis fitting. How do you feel? Any illness?" Tuesday asked as she sat on the bed next to Saxan.

"I feel quite well. No illness, no fainting," Saxan replied. "I think that is why I was so slow to realize that I was with child."

"Aye. I was ne'er sick. Not truly. A few foods could set my innards to swimming. And I could not let myself become too emotional or I emptied my belly in a trice. Godric could not argue with me for near to six months at a time." She grinned. "He said it was no fun when it ended with my head in a bucket retching fit to die."

"That is when I got ill. Shortly after the attack and when I was still in a sad confusion of emotion. I was afraid and angry and worried that Botolf would set me aside. 'Tis the only time I was ill. Although," she grimaced, "I find I cannot go near the stables for very long. The smell, I suppose."

"It was the pigs with me. But, tell me, Botolf has not set you aside, has he? You do not have the look of a woman set aside."

"Nay, he did not."

"Ah, Saxan, only you could gain yourself a highborn husband by trying to plunge a knife into his heart."

Saxan sighed and shook her head. "I see that the tale has traveled far and wide."

"Hunter and Roc told me. Such a match." Tuesday patted Saxan on the back. "I would never have thought it. Nor would I have guessed that the king himself would approve it so swiftly and heartily. Howbeit, all of that matters not. What I wish to know is what were your reasons? Are you happy? Is he good to you?"

"I fear my reasons were not very clear, not even to me, Tuesday," Saxan admitted. "All that I was certain of was that it would trouble me far more to say nay than to face a little uncertainty and marry him. There was also the fact that, wed or not, I would have let him bed me."

"Aye, the fever can run very hot in her," Thylda agreed as she sprawled on the bed to play with the baby.

"You are too young to know," scolded Tuesday.

"A Todd learns of such things in the cradle, Sister," Thylda drawled.

"Enough impertinence, brat. Now, tell me, Saxan, does Botolf accept that you can feel a fire as hot as the one burning in him?"

"Aye, Tuesday. Why should he not?" Saxan asked.

Tuesday gave her a sad smile. "Not all men do. That was the trouble in my marriage at the beginning. I wanted Godric and enjoyed the bedding, but he was shocked by that. 'Twas not the way of a lady or so he had been taught. He said nothing, just stayed away. Each time he returned, I thought to try and hold him with me with my passion, to draw from him all the love I needed. All unknowingly, I just kept pushing him further and further away. This painful game was played out for two long years."

"What happened to change his mind, Tuesday?" Thylda asked.

"It was a long while before I learned what troubled him," Tuesday said. "It seems he stayed with an old friend who bemoaned the coldness of his wife. When Godric told the man what he thought his own burden was—a fault he kept coming back to, let us not forget—the man called him a fool, and soon convinced Godric that, indeed, he was a fool. As I said, it was a long time before I learned of all this. He finally told me the whole truth when he realized how much he had hurt me, how I had begun to withdraw from him."

"You had withdrawn from Godric?" Saxan asked.

"Aye. One can only be hurt and rebuffed so many times before one grows very wary indeed. There were a lot of hurts that needed to be healed and that, too, took awhile. For example, I spoke of love on our wedding night, but Godric and I were married for over three years before I ever mentioned it again."

"Botolf has never mentioned it," Saxan felt compelled to confess.

"Men." Tuesday shook her head. "I do not believe they have any idea of how deeply they can hurt us, for you love him, do you not?"

"Aye, although it was awhile before I was certain of that. It is such a confusing thing. There can be so many other reasons for each feeling assailing you."

Tuesday nodded and smiled. "And men will find more of them than any woman could. The men see love as a weakness, I fear, and we all know how much they loathe having a weakness."

"But Godric loves you," Thylda said.

"Aye, little sister, but it is many a long month between each speaking of it, and often it takes many a tankard of ale to properly loosen his tongue."

"Botolf could drink a river of the finest and strongest wine in the kingdom, and the words would never leave his mouth," Saxan grumbled.

"Do you think he cares?" Tuesday asked.

"Cares, aye, but how much?" Saxan shrugged.

"Have you told him how you feel?" Thylda caught the baby as she rolled toward the edge of the bed.

"Nay, Thylda," replied Saxan. "Some pride ties my tongue, true enough, but I also fear to speak of something Botolf does not really want. I could push him away from me, make him uncomfortable, by giving him what he has not asked for."

"She is right, Thylda," agreed Tuesday. "Men are such puzzling creatures. You would think they would be mightily pleased to be loved, but 'tis not always so. It is best to hold silent until you are certain. Aside from that, Saxan, are you happy?"

"Aye. Very happy. Botolf is very good to me, Tuesday. He never leaves my bed, not even when it is my woman's time. He has sworn to be faithful and, although it is only four months or so since we were married, I can see the truth of that promise. Why even his gaze wanders little! I well know what a blessing that can be to a wife."

"A great blessing indeed."

"Sometimes I lie awake in the night, watching him sleep, and wonder what lack there is in me that I cannot merit his love."

"There is naught lacking in you, Saxan," Thylda cried.

"Such loyalty," Saxan murmured, exchanging a grin with Tuesday. "Mayhap not a lacking, Thylda, but something that stops Botolf from loving me as I love him. Then I wonder how he can hold me close in the night and hunger for me as he does, yet never speak of love, mayhap not even feel it. Howbeit, that is the only trouble I allow myself concerning the matter. 'Tis foolish to fret over what I do not have when I have so much. Many a woman would envy me such a husband."

"Aye, and they do," agreed Tuesday. "I have heard the murmurs of envy already. Now, when am I to meet the Lady Mary?"

Sighing heavily, Saxan explained why Tuesday should not hope to meet the woman. Her sister's understanding and assurances eased her guilt, but not her concerns. When Tuesday began to feed her daughter, Thylda and Saxan moved to leave her alone.

"Here, what do you play at?" Saxan demanded when Thylda stopped in the doorway then stepped back a bit so that she was only peering out into the hall. "You nearly knocked me over."

"Uncle Edric is at Lady Mary's door and speaks with her woman Elizabeth," Thylda hissed.

Saxan tried to look around Thylda, but was unable to see anything. "What is happening?"

"I am not sure, but Elizabeth has just let him into the room. Should we go and listen at the door?"

It was tempting, but Saxan shook her head. "Nay. We will know how matters fare if Lady Mary comes down to the great hall."

"What are you two talking about?" demanded Tuesday.

Saxan quickly explained about Edric and Lady Mary. Tuesday's soft heart was deeply touched by the story. Despite the joy of their reunion, Saxan noticed that it was a somewhat subdued group which made its way down to the hall to spend some time visiting with each other.

* * *

"So, how does m'lord like the married life?" Godric asked jovially after Edric excused himself and left the hall.

" 'Tis a very easy thing to grow accustomed to," Botolf replied.

"Aye, it is that. Did my words help at all, m'lord?"

When he recalled the passion he had found on his wedding night, Botolf smiled with a sweet lechery. "Aye. There was a moment when I was, well, surprised. I thought of all I had heard about how a lady-wife should behave, and they became laughable."

"I regret to admit that it took me two years to see the lie and a year to mend the harm my ignorance had caused."

"You need not answer, for it is a private matter, I know, but what was it that changed your mind?"

"True, it is a private matter, but we are wedded to sisters, m'lord. 'Tis for our own good if we be open with each other. Ah, God's beard, women can be such puzzling creatures; 'tis for the best if we men find aid where we can." He laughed along with Botolf. "And Edric spoke true when he said they are huddled together talking about us. I hope you have no habits you dearly wish kept secret," he teased.

"I fear I shall begin to think of a lot now." Botolf grinned then chuckled along with Godric, finding the quick yet firm camaraderie he had developed with the man enjoyable.

"Now, about what happened to change my foolish and stubborn mind. On one of the many times I ran from Tuesday, I met with an old friend. As we drank our ale, he bemoaned his cold wife. He thought I suffered from the same affliction. I think you can guess how he reacted when I told him what I thought my curse was. I but thank God that, whilst I stumbled about in confusion and ignorance, I never took another woman. To deliver such an insult to Tuesday when she was willing to give me all a man needs—" He faltered and shook his head.

"But everything worked out all right. You have two fine sons and now a daughter."

"Aye, my little Honey. She will turn my hair grey in the years to come."

"And have you selected a husband for her yet?"

"Nay, m'lord. I follow the Todd tradition. She will be allowed her heart's choice. Being a chosen mate, I know it is the better way. I have seen it in all of the clan's marriages. If there is some preference, even if love is not truly born yet but comes later, it is best."

"I gave Saxan little alternative," Botolf said quietly.

"A man of your position has few options himself. The ease with which Saxan accepted tells me it was choice enough. If that little wench had not wanted to marry you, she would have gone to the king himself to argue the match. Never doubt that. The girl who came after you, dagger in hand, is not the sort of woman to kneel to the command of mere earls and kings unless she is of a mind to."

Botolf felt a warmth seep through him that had nothing to do with good drink and enjoyable company. He suddenly realized that he had held a few doubts despite Saxan's words on the night she had said that she would marry him and despite her passion. Godric's comments had swept the last of those doubts away. Saxan had married him because she had wanted to. If she had suffered any dislike for the match, if she had had any defiance in her, she would have fought tooth and nail every inch of the way. Her kinsmen would likely have aided her in that fight.

"I have always wondered why you never did anything about Saxan's attack on you," Godric said, abruptly ending Botolf's musings before he could determine why it was so important to him that he really was Saxan's choice of husband.

"Aside from the fact that she failed, I felt no need to punish a person for acting whilst caught in the blind grip of grief. If I had been in her place, I would have acted the same way. The looks upon the faces of my men told me that they saw no weakness in my decision to let the matter pass. That was, of course, aided by the fact that she is a tiny female." He smiled slowly. "They just think that she is admirably spirited."

Godric chuckled. "Aye, those Todd women are certainly spirited. Out here, where the troubles never really end, it is for the best that they are."

"And even in the years you have been married to Tuesday, you have never tried to tame her?"

"I should not really wish her tamed. Would you?"

"There are times," Botolf drawled. "Such as when Saxan stands there poking me in the chest and calling me a horse's rump." He grinned when Godric laughed and nodded in understanding. " 'Tis not the way I am accustomed to being treated."

"And how do you reply to such a scandalous slur?"

"It would be beneath my dignity to reply to such nonsense."

"Ah, of a certain. So what action does dignity demand?"

"Well, the last time I poured water over her head."

As Saxan entered the great hall with her sisters she looked at the two laughing men and smiled crookedly. "Botolf and Godric are getting along very well."

Tuesday grimaced as she looked at her husband. "That most certainly means trouble for us. They have probably been consoling each other. Saxan?"

When she saw how intensely Tuesday studied Botolf, she asked, "What is wrong?"

"Nothing really. I think your man is one of those who keeps a lot inside him."

"How can you tell?"

" 'Tis nothing I can explain easily. It is something in the way he laughs, mayhap. What feelings he may have, he will fight against; and if the fight is lost, he will not tell you. Nay, you will have to have a great deal of patience to love that man."

"Aye, I have seen that already."

"He may never speak of love, Saxan. Can you bear that?"

"I must. He is my husband and I love him. I will have to find my happiness in what he does give me."

As they moved toward the men, Saxan hoped that she had the strength to do that. She continually hoped to gain a return for her love, but she worried about how it would affect her if year after year passed and there were none. It was the sort of thing that could turn a person bitter and unhappy. She dreaded the possibility of such a future. It would destroy whatever happiness she had gained, slowly poisoning her family life at Regenford.

"Such solemn faces," Godric said as his wife sat down next to him.

With her sisters' help Saxan quickly turned the conversation to what news there was of the family. She did not get a moment alone with Botolf until they were ready to dine. Even then she had to wait until just before they were to go down to the great hall for the evening meal for, in the new chambers Botolf had arranged for them a month ago, there was an added room where he went to have Farold aid him in dressing while Jane helped her. The moment they were alone, Saxan kissed Botolf.

"Mmmm. What was that for?" he asked as he held her close.

"Thank you for writing to my sisters as you did," she replied.

"Ah, well, I think I worried them for naught. Is Denu to come?"

"Nay," she answered as they started down to the hall. "Denu and Tuesday live near each other, and it is a bad time of the year for both demanses to be emptied of their masters."

"How did they decide who was to come then?"

"They played dice for the chance."

"Your family is most fond of gambling," he said.

"Most fond," she agreed. "It is why we have learned to keep the stakes low."

As he passed by his mother's bedchamber, Botolf sighed at the sight of the closed door. "Will nothing draw her out?"

"Have patience, Botolf. She may yet show." Saxan knew her uncle was still within Lady Mary's chamber and wondered on it.

Although she was soon to be the center of attention, however briefly, Saxan had to smile. The meal served was just lavish enough, just different enough, to warn everyone in the great hall that something was afoot. The curiosity was almost tangible. Only once was that curiosity diverted from her, and that was when Lady Mary, looking lovely and slightly flushed, arrived on the arm of Sir Edric Healdon.

"Did you know he had gone to see her?" Botolf hissed in Saxan's ear as his mother approached.

"Well, he did not tell me. Thylda and I happened to see him talking to Elizabeth," Saxan replied.

"And Elizabeth let him in?" Botolf weakly returned his mother's bright smile as she sat down, keeping Sir Edric at her side.

"Uncle can be most persuasive."

"Obviously."

"Are you cross?"

"Curious. How did he succeed when all else failed?"

Saxan had no answer for Botolf. As the meal progressed, no mention was made of Lady Mary's lengthy seclusion. She was accepted back without question. All thought of Lady Mary left Saxan's mind, however, as the time drew near for Botolf to make his announcement.

"Come, dearling, why do you look so fretful?" Botolf asked in a quiet voice as he took her hand in his. "The news I have will please everyone."

"Aye, but it will have all eyes on me for a time," she muttered.

"With looks of pride and hope. They cannot hurt you. In you rests the future of my family, and that is nearly as important to my people as it is to me."

"I hope I do not disappoint them or you, Botolf."

The worry he could never fully put aside made Botolf frown. "Elizabeth told me you had passed the most dangerous time."

"Aye, and the life within me makes itself more and more known. The quickening grows stronger each day. 'Tis just that," she smiled faintly, "I could bear you a girl-child."

He smiled and kissed her cheek. "I ask only for a healthy child."

"What if I bear only girl children?"

Biting back a laugh over the scowl on her face, he answered honestly, "I will not say I would not be a little disappointed, but I will not blame you, Saxan. 'Tis in God's hands. Howbeit, I do not really fear that happening. Do you?"

"Nay, not truly, but such worries are not always put aside by good sense."

"Very true," he murmured, but his thoughts were not on the sex of the child she carried. They centered on all the danger she would face in carrying and birthing his child. "Prepare yourself," he warned as he stood and clinked his spoon against his tankard, bringing a quick silence in the great hall. "I have an announcement to make which I hope will please all of you as much as it does me." He held his hand out and, when Saxan put her hand in his, he urged her to her feet. "In the early spring, my lady-wife will present me with a new Lavington."

Saxan blushed when everyone's gaze turned her way, many people looking hard at her still-slim middle. Cheers erupted in the hall, and she could see that people were honestly pleased by the news. When she saw Lady Mary and several other women dab at tears in their eyes, Saxan realized that the fear of the Lavington line's dying out was far greater than she had realized.

"A toast," cried Wesley as he leapt to his feet. "To a fine healthy son and heir."

"Aye, Wesley, a toast." Botolf winked at Saxan. "To a fine healthy child."

In the time that ensued, so many toasts were offered Saxan was sure many a celebrant would be spending the night upon the floor of the great hall. She found herself looking for something, but it was awhile before she knew what that something was. When she began to covertly but steadily watch one man, she knew. She was watching for an informant. Instinct had told her that Odella could not have been Cecil's only spy. He had to have one within Botolf's retinue. Saxan was suddenly sure that she had found him.

"Botolf," she called.

Mellowed by drink, joviality, and the lateness of the hour, Botolf lifted her up in his arms and set her on his lap. "What, dearling?"

"This is very undignified," she scolded, but grinned at him.

"Aye. Do not recall me to it come the morning."

"I promise. Um, Botolf? Do you recall our speaking about the chance of a spy within your household?"

The clouding fumes of drink rapidly cleared his mind, and Botolf tensed. "Aye. I remember that very well. A close watch has been kept for a traitor, but none has been found."

"We-ell, I cannot be sure, but I think I may have found him."

"What makes you think so?"

"Not much, I fear. I found myself watching everyone in the great hall and wondered why. Then I knew when one particular man caught my eye and held it. The news of a child is news Cecil would be interested in, would he not?"

"Very interested. He told you as much when he attacked you."

"Aye, he did. His lackey will be very eager to get this news to him, and when do you think the best time would be to do that?"

His angry scowl was disguised by Saxan, who idly fed him grapes, and his expression was impossible to maintain. "When everyone here is besotted by drink and celebration."

"Exactly what I thought. That man seated near the wall—the one with the red hair and a blue jupon—drinks little, yet pretends that he drinks a lot. He watches everyone around him, yet pretends that he is soddened with drink and can barely stay awake."

" 'Tis James, James Pipp. Aye, he was close to Cecil." Botolf covertly watched the man for a while and saw the same things Saxan had. "He may not be the traitor, but he plays a curious game and bears close watching. Ah, here comes Wesley. Let us pray that he is sober."

Sir Wesley was not drunk, although Saxan guessed that he had been working hard to reach that condition. He sobered quickly when he heard what Saxan and Botolf had noticed about James. Saxan soon saw that Wesley could play James' game far better than the man himself. When Pipp finally slipped away, Wesley was a steady shadow at his heels.

"And now all I can do is wait," Botolf muttered, then smiled faintly when he saw Saxan try to smother a yawn. "We will retire soon."

"You need not come to bed with me, Botolf," Saxan said as she straightened up, regretfully leaving the comfortable resting place against his broad chest. "You may linger here if you wish."

"I do not wish. I lingered only to see if Pipp left and Wesley followed."

Just as they stood up, Lady Mary and Edric hurried to their side. Saxan could sense a tense excitement in the pair. She guessed that Cecil was not all the couple had discussed while secluded in Lady Mary's bedchamber for so long.

"I have a request, m'lord," Sir Edric began with gravity although the glance he sent Lady Mary was one of laughter and happiness.

Botolf began to suspect what the question would be. "And what is that, Sir Edric?"

"You are your mother's only male kin, so I turn to you to request her hand in marriage. I realize that I reach high, m'lord—"

"Oh, Edric," Lady Mary protested, but she was ignored.

"Howbeit," continued Edric. "I must ask. I may not be able to keep her in such luxury as this, but she will want for nothing as my wife."

"All I want is you, Edric," Lady Mary whispered. "That is enough for me."

Saxan held her breath as Botolf hesitated in answering. Although Botolf wished for his mother's happiness and liked Edric, that did not mean he would approve of his mother's marrying a mere knight and vassal. He did have a great deal of pride in his name and could easily have felt that this union could seriously hurt that good name. Although he had no control over his mother, his disapproval could be enough to stop her from reaching for happiness with Edric.

Saxan let her breath out slowly and beamed as widely as Lady Mary when Botolf smiled and said, "My mother has just given you your answer, Sir Edric. When is the wedding to be?"

Saxan stretched sleepily as she heard someone come into the room. She opened one eye and saw a disheveled Wesley leaning over Botolf. When she heard Wesley say that he had found Pipp with his throat cut, she shivered and huddled closer to a tense Botolf. The man's death did not trouble her, for he had been a traitor who was helping Cecil try to kill Botolf, but it did frighten her. Each time they drew a little closer to Cecil, the man slipped out of their reach again. She could not help but wonder if they would ever be able to end the threat to their lives before it could be carried out.

Thirteen

"Stop squirming." Botolf kissed Saxan's ear and held her closer.

"I feel I ought to visit with Denu, who has traveled so far to be here, and I am not really tired, Botolf." Saxan sighed with a mixture of annoyance and resignation.

"Nevertheless, you will rest before attending my mother's wedding. It will be a long, tiring evening. It is the middle of November, and the dullness of winter has already set heavily on Regenford. This chance to celebrate is much looked forward to and will go on for a long time. It could even grow wild."

"You were not really surprised when the king approved the match, were you?"

"Nay. My mother is a distant cousin of the king and past childbearing age. What land she holds is poor and small. She is of little use to him."

"So she may wed where she wishes to."

"Aye. Asking the king's approval was just courtesy. Have you spoken with my mother yet?"

Saxan grimaced. "Nay. I am a coward. Everything goes along so smoothly that I do not wish to bring up a time that was painful to both of us. Mayhap it is best forgotten."

"If you are certain that it has been forgotten."

"Aye. Your mother acts as she always did before I flayed her with harsh words."

"Then let it lie, if you wish."

She propped herself on one elbow and smiled crookedly at her husband. "You think I should speak to her about it. Has she said anything to you? Has she hinted about why she finally left her room? Or why she now accepts my uncle?"

Botolf gently urged her head back down onto his chest and sighed. "Nay, not a word."

" 'Tis a shame Wesley lost Pipp. The trouble with Cecil could well be over now, and we could stop fretting over these things."

"Aye, but now we have to wonder how Cecil found out that Wesley was following his lackey and so killed the man. He could have tried again."

"To cut the throat of a man who was loyal to you," she whispered and shuddered.

"Cecil cares for no life but his own. I saw that in him years ago. He was a cruel child and that viciousness deepened with age." He smoothed his hand over her hair. "We will find Cecil and end this game, do not fear, little one." A soft knock sounded at the door and Botolf frowned, for he had made it clear that he and Saxan were to be left alone. "Who is it?"

" 'Tis your mother, Botolf."

As he sat up, Botolf gently restrained Saxan from doing the same and called, "Come in." When his mother entered, there was a look on her face that prompted him to ask, "Is there anything wrong?"

"Nay, my son." She shut the door and moved purposefully toward the bed. "I but need to talk—to both of you. Nay, Saxan, lie down," she said as Saxan tried again to sit up. " 'Tis good for a woman with child to lie abed now and again."

"Is something wrong with the preparations for the wedding?"

"Nay, Botolf. I wish to talk of Cecil, of my foolish hiding away in my room."

" 'Twas my fault, m'lady," Saxan said. "There was no need for me to spew my rage at you in so cruel a manner."

"Nay, Saxan," Lady Mary said. "Even if I never faced up to the truth of your words, I would never condemn you for them. You had a right to your anger. That much I understood even then. You have naught to apologize for."

"You need not speak on it, Mother. 'Tis forgotten," Botolf assured her.

"I think not. Just this once I wish to talk about it, then I want to hear no more of Cecil. Well, as little as possible."

"As you wish."

"When I think of how stubbornly blind I have been, I feel a terrible fool."

"Nay, m'lady," Saxan protested.

" 'Tis a fool who closes her eyes to the truth, Saxan, and that is what I did," said Lady Mary. "Cecil could be so sweet. He was the second child I was never able to give my husband. It was also hard for me to understand how he could turn against us so when he had been taken into our home, recognized, and trusted. How could he strike out at Botolf when he knew it would be as if he struck at me, too?

"Ah, the excuses I made for him. Even as a child. Aye, Botolf, I was not blind to his games and faults. I thought, mayhap, that he felt the sting of bastardy too keenly. What little I saw was not too bad; but, then, as he became a man, he grew worse.

"When the attacks began on you, Botolf, a part of me did believe, but I struggled to repress that. 'Twas

Cain and Abel, and I could not bear to think that such a sin could emerge within my own family."

"I always understood that, Mother."

"I know, Botolf. You were most forbearing. But, then, when he attacked Saxan," Lady Mary shuddered. "I could hear the tale even as I went to her aid, but I closed my ears to it. Howbeit, here was an evil I could not fully ignore. Here was no shadowy figure that Botolf could fight off and who could have been bought by anyone.

"The reason your words cut me so, Saxan, was because they were the same ones that echoed in my own heart and mind. I was trying so hard to silence those voices, and you strengthened them. They became a deafening roar, and I simply could not bear it."

"I am so sorry, m'lady," Saxan said.

"You have nothing to be sorry for, child," Lady Mary assured her. "Truly. I would have acted the same in your place." She smiled faintly. "Nay, I would have collapsed and mayhap have lost the child because of shock and fear. We can only thank God that you are made of stronger stuff."

Lady Mary took a deep, steadying breath and continued. "I hid away in my room so that I could think, to come face to face with the truth. Even though I knew I was worrying you, I had no alternative. I needed to be alone, to hear no words but those that came from my own mind and heart. It was a time for me to face my own demons, fears, and follies. 'Twas also time to grieve for that pretty dark-eyed babe I had nursed.

"I looked back to the very beginning and made note of all that had been said about Cecil and all that I had known he had done, even when it seemed to be simply naughty, a child's mischief. I included all you had told me, Saxan, for I know you do not lie. Oh, I know Botolf does not lie either, but he had never seen Cecil try to kill him face to face. The murder attempts were all made by others. When I was done, the image before me was chilling. My excuses no longer worked to dispel this view of Cecil, and I knew it was the true Cecil that I saw.

"Then I had to battle my guilt. Nay," she said when both Botolf and Saxan began to protest. "I felt it was my fault, as any mother does when a child goes wrong, when bad blood appears in her brood. That battle was a hard one, but I won it. The evil that is Cecil is none of my doing. Mayhap God felt it was time that the Lavingtons were put through a trial. I know not save that it is not my fault.

"It was as I wondered which way to step that Edric arrived. When I saw him, my first thought was that here, too, Cecil had hurt me, for 'twas Cecil who had made me turn from all Edric offered. I was asking an honorable man to turn from his duty or turn from me, for I would not be able to forgive his ending the evil that is Cecil."

"I was most surprised that Elizabeth had allowed him in," Botolf said quietly.

"Ah, well, Edric used what I call his coaxing voice, and it is a potent tool. Even Elizabeth says she had opened the door to him e'er she knew what she was doing. He then used it on me, for shame held me in my room. 'Tis hard to face the world when you know you have been a fool and all have pandered to that. Do not deny that they did, Botolf, for I know otherwise."

"No one wished to hurt you," he explained.

Lady Mary nodded. "I know, but I saw that, by soothing my feelings, you did not protect yourself as you should have or could have. Edric convinced me that mothers, aye, even fathers, are allowed to be fools for their children, that everyone understands that and would ne'er fault me for it. He talked to me most sternly for a time."

Botolf felt compelled to return his mother's smile and noticed that Saxan did as well. He could see the glow of happiness on his mother's face and hear the love she held for Edric in her voice. For one brief moment he tasted anger. How could she love another man after his father? Was it not rather soon after his father's death for her heart to be captured by another?

Inwardly, he laughed away those thoughts. His mother needed love—and that of a man not only that of a child. She could not gain the warmth she needed from a memory. He was honestly happy for her, pleased that in her later years she would have the love of a good man.

"Well, Edric showed me that I need not hide away, that everyone understood," Lady Mary continued. "He showed me that I need not lend a hand nor even listen much to what must be done about Cecil. I must simply accept it. That is what I will do. I know what must be done and I accept it. In my heart and mind, Cecil is dead. The child I nurtured at my breast is no more. I but await the time when his body is brought home for burial. I do ask that that be done, Botolf."

"I will see to it. I swear it," Botolf vowed.

"Thank you. Well, I had best go and ready myself. 'Twould never do for me to be late to my own wedding."

After Lady Mary left, Saxan sighed. "It must still be very hard for her."

"Of a certain," Botolf agreed. "But she has accepted the situation, and that is a heavy burden lifted from my shoulders."

"Aye, now your hands are free and you need not

fear that each strike you take at your enemy is one that might cut your mother."

He nodded. "I know Cecil was to blame for all her pain. I never asked for this fight, but I have twinges of guilt." He sighed. "There is still a large part of me that wishes no part of this."

"Of course you want no part of this. Cecil forces you to shed a brother's blood to survive. I think that must be the unkindest thing he has ever done."

"We could argue o'er that until a new day dawns, but you are supposed to rest now."

After a long moment of silence, Saxan began to feel drowsy and closed her eyes, but she asked, "Do you truly accept this marriage between Edric and your mother?"

"Aye. Mother needs a husband. That is where her happiness truly lies. So, too, is Edric a man I like and respect. I know he will cherish her." He smiled when he felt Saxan grow lax against him, her breathing slowing as sleep conquered her. "Mother needs more than to live for her son and his family."

"Uncle will make her happy. You will see."

"I already have."

Saxan was groggy when she was awakened by Botolf, but she struggled out of bed to prepare for the wedding. She grew more alert as she bathed and dressed with Jane's help. Soon the joy and excitement of the event began to infect her. By the time Botolf escorted her to the small chapel, the last vestiges of her weariness had faded and she gaily looked forward to the celebration.

The wedding ceremony itself was brief, but Saxan thought it was beautiful. She dabbed at the tears in her eyes and ignored Botolf's grin as they left the chapel and returned to the great hall for the festivities. As she sat with Botolf at the head table, the mood of the guests told her that the celebration would be long and hearty. She decided to take things very carefully so that she could enjoy as much of it as possible before tiring.

She smiled at her sister Denu as the woman sat down next to her. " 'Tis wonderful that you were able to come, Denu. I am sorry that the children could not join you."

"The weather is too uncertain at this time of the year," Denu said. "I dared not let them travel in it."

"Of course. Do you know, I was most surprised that you and Thomas came. I was almost certain that Tuesday would. She almost always wins the toss of the dice."

"Aye, she does, the slattern," Denu agreed with a grin. "She had no chance of winning this time."

"No chance? How so?"

"The dice were weighted in my favor."

Botolf destroyed his pretense of not listening to their conversation by joining in their laughter. Every one of the Todds had that spirit he realized. Despite years of marriage and a growing brood of children, the impish light still shone in Denu's fine eyes. He mused that, with such relatives, his life would never again be dull.

" 'Tis good of you to take Pitney in as you have, m'lord," said Denu.

"A man would have to be a complete fool to ignore one who has so completely proven his valor and loyalty, Mistress Denu," Botolf replied.

"Pitney does have a lot of that," Denu said with obvious pride, then smiled at Saxan. "I may use my dice to insure that I am the first to see your child. 'Tis so hard to believe. You show very little."

"Did your belly round quickly then?" asked Saxan.

Denu giggled. "We-ell, not my belly, but nearly all the rest of me."

"Ah, my dearling, have you missed your man?" Thomas murmured as he came up beside Denu and kissed the back of her neck.

"You have swilled too much ale," Denu scolded as she disentangled herself from his hold. "Have you greeted his lordship, our host?"

Thomas sat next to his wife, his back to the table, and leaned on his elbows. He smiled at Botolf. "Greetings, your lordship."

Botolf grinned and nodded a return to the lazy salutation. A great deal of nonsensical banter ensued, and Botolf enjoyed every minute of it. He realized suddenly that he had enlarged his family tenfold when he married Saxan. There was no lessening of the respect due to a man of his high position, but there was an open friendliness easily extended to him. He was considered one of the family now, a member of the large affectionate clan, and he liked it.

He sensed that a subtle change had been wrought in him since his marriage. Some of the somberness that had settled into his heart had left him. He was not sure if it were for the best, as it softened him, but he simply could not resist it. It felt too good.

Edric and Lady Mary, hand in hand, joined the merry group around Botolf. After smiling at everyone, Edric said to Botolf, "We are going to attempt to slip away unnoticed."

Saxan smiled as she looked at the celebrants. "It can probably be done rather easily."

"If the weather holds, we shall soon leave for my modest demanse," Edric said.

Saxan restrained a frown. She had not really given any thought to that aspect of Edric's marrying Lady

Mary. Although she was honestly fond of Lady Mary, Saxan felt no real pang at the thought of the woman leaving Regenford. Lady Mary could visit whenever she wished to. She did wonder about Botolf's feelings, however, for Lady Mary had always been a part of his household. Although small and much more restrained than her own kinsmen, Botolf's family had been close.

"We will return in the spring, child," Lady Mary said as she kissed Saxan's cheek. "I am eager to see the birth of my first grandchild."

It was not long before Lady Mary and Sir Edric crept away. What few people did notice their leave-taking remained quiet out of respect for Lady Mary. Barely fifteen minutes had passed, however, before Edric was striding back into the hall.

As curious as everyone else, Saxan was disappointed when, after a brief whispered exchange she could not hear, Botolf and Edric left. She tried to quell her inquisitiveness with the knowledge that she would be told what was happening in due time. It was hard to do, however, when the two men returned and began to hand pick the most sober men in the room. She was nearly squirming with curiosity by the time Botolf was back at her side.

"Go to my mother, Saxan," he ordered her. "Mayhap your sisters will go with you."

"What has happened?" she asked.

"I cannot take the time to explain. Mother will have to tell you," he answered and left her, pausing only long enough to assure the remaining guests that there was no need for them to disrupt their celebration, that he and the others would soon return.

Saxan dragged Denu and Thylda up to Lady Mary's bedchamber and found a teary-eyed Lady Mary sitting on her bed holding a small piece of paper. A lovely set of silver tankards rested in her lap. Denu quietly poured the woman some wine and urged her to have a drink. Thylda took away the tankards as Saxan sat down next to her mother-in-law and took her cold hand.

"What has happened to upset you?" she asked the distraught woman.

"Cecil was here," Lady Mary replied.

"Are you certain?"

"Aye. The tankards and the missive are from him."

"Some messenger could have brought them," suggested Denu.

Lady Mary shook her head. "Nay. This was written while Cecil was here. 'Tis my own paper and I recognize his hand."

When Saxan shivered, Lady Mary put an arm around her shoulders, and she managed a weak smile. "I was sent to comfort you."

"My life is not in danger. 'Tis not fear for myself which has upset me. I saw this and all I could think of was how close the threat to you and Botolf had come yet again. The ease with which Cecil comes and goes is most frightening."

"Botolf sealed off the secret ways into Regenford," Thylda said in a quiet voice, her sudden uncertainty clear to hear.

"So we thought, but he and I spent more time at Merewood than we did here. Botolf does not like it, but he can play the courtier better than his father ever could, and so he served his father by holding our place in court, keeping in favor with the king. I helped in that before and after Botolf's first marriage. There may be ways into the keep that we have no knowledge of, ways that Cecil had ferreted out and may even have made himself."

"Or, knowing the guard would be weak and where

it might be the weakest, he but slipped in unseen," Denu mused aloud.

"That could be the way of it," Lady Mary agreed. "Cecil just came near to see if there were a chance of slipping past the guards and took it when he found it." Lady Mary relaxed just a little. "That is something we can guard against." She glanced at the letter she held. "He can still turn a pretty phrase."

When Lady Mary urged her to read the note, Saxan reluctantly did so. It was a sweetly written wish for her happiness. Saxan could not help but wonder how much of the love expressed was prompted by a need to keep his foster-mother tied to him. Cecil knew so much about the comings and goings of Regenford that he could also know he was beginning to lose his hold over Lady Mary.

"He tries to keep me tied to him," Lady Mary said, concurring with Saxan's thoughts in a soft, sad voice. "Somehow he has heard of my newly gained feelings about him."

"Mayhap, Lady Mary, he knows you well enough that he guessed how you would feel about his attack upon Saxan and hopes to soften that sin in your eyes," said Thylda.

"He could fill this chamber with prettily written declarations of adoration and he could never change my feelings on that," said Lady Mary. "That was a crime I can find no forgiveness for. I must be rid of those tankards."

"Nay, m'lady," Saxan said. "Keep them as a gift from the dark-eyed babe you held and loved. When this has ended, you may wish for them to remember what Cecil was long ago when he was too young to give you such a present."

"I will consider that."

It was growing late when the men ended their

search for Cecil. Saxan quickly gave up her place next to Lady Mary when Edric strode in with Botolf. Her husband quietly ushered Saxan and her sisters from the room, but Saxan hesitated when he started to escort them back down to the great hall.

"I think I have had my fill of celebrating, Botolf," she said.

"Do you feel ill?" he asked, brushing his hand over her forehead.

"Nay, just weary. I only wish to seek my bed and lie down."

"I will come with you."

"Nay, return to the hall so that the guests can be assured that all is well. I will be fine."

He left her reluctantly, escorting Thylda and Denu back to the hall. Saxan had looked no more than a little tired, but he could not fully suppress his concern about her. She was right in saying that he needed to ease whatever qualms he had caused his guests, but he soon found himself seeking out Denu, hoping to glean some of her knowledge about pregnancy.

"Saxan did not look ill to you, did she?" he asked Denu as he sat down next to her.

"Nay, m'lord, only tired as she claimed," Denu assured him "I believe that the thought of Cecil being so near to her, gaining access to Regenford, frightened her some. Such emotion is wearying for a woman with child. She simply shows good sense by responding to her body's needs."

"Ah, I see. But, 'tis her first child."

"And yours, and I know well how important that child is. M'lord, if a woman is to suffer difficulty in carrying a child, she most often shows that in the first few months. Saxan was so untroubled she did not even know she was carrying a child. All she needs to do is get a lot of rest and eat well. Why, she may do all she did before, even ride a horse, although a good hard gallop may be unwise." Denu winked and Botolf smiled at her. "From what Saxan tells me and from what I have seen, methinks she will have the easiest time of us all."

Botolf was not sure he believed that, but the rest of what Denu had said did soothe most of his concerns. The assurance behind her words gave them the ring of truth. Denu was Saxan's sister and had borne several children herself. Despite all that, Botolf grew eager to leave the celebration so that he could join Saxan in their chambers and see for himself. In order to relieve his distraction and reflect the appropriate joviality, he drank somewhat heavily all the time he was forced to linger in the hall. As a result, he was not sure what time it was when he sought his bedchamber, dismissed an inebriated Farold's fumbling assistance, and finally sought his bed.

Saxan awoke with a start when she heard a loud thump. She slipped her knife out from beneath her pillow and peeped out of the bed hangings. A sigh of relief escaped her when she saw Botolf. Then she smiled and put away her weapon. Botolf was having a great deal of difficulty in removing his clothes. She climbed out of bed and moved toward him.

"You should be abed," he muttered as Saxan took him by the arm and urged him toward the bed.

"Aye, and I will be again in just a few moments," she said. "Lie down and I will get these things off you."

Although he did as he was told, he protested, "I can manage."

"Aye, and so well, too."

"I stumbled a little, is all."

"So I saw. To let you continue on so seemed most unkind," she said as she began to tug his clothes off. "You were doing a mighty poor job of it. I have ne'er seen you so cupshotten."

"I was trying to remain in a festive mood for the benefit of our guests."

"And it took so much drink to do so?"

"Aye. Are you certain you are feeling well?" he asked.

"Very well. I told you, I was but a little weary."

"And Cecil had drawn close again."

"Aye, that was some of it," she agreed. "When I saw that he had come right inside these walls again, I was deeply afraid for a while. I find such fear very tiring." She neatly folded his clothes after tucking the covers around him. "You found no sign of him?"

"None. He came in o'er the walls. The guard was slack tonight. It is no longer."

"Well, at least you know there is not some other secret way in that you must search out and close."

Saxan got into bed and smiled faintly when he drew her close. It was her opinion that he was far too gone with drink to make love to her. After a few kisses and caresses, he sighed heavily and just held her near.

"Too drunk, I fear," he mumbled.

"I had wondered on it," she said, laughing softly.

"I should not be thinking on it anyway."

"And why not?"

"I might hurt the babe."

"I think not. Denu and Tuesday say they have ne'er found that to be so. They both say they only ceased when they found it more uncomfortable than enjoyable."

"I had not realized that women talked of such things."

"And what did you think women spoke of when they were alone, out of the company and hearing of men?"

"Their stitchery, gossip, fashion. Such as that. Things they are most involved in."

His body was growing heavier against her, his words slurred, but she felt it would be awhile yet before he gave in to sleep. "Are not our husbands, their beds, and the bearing of children also things we are involved in?"

"Quite true. And do you learn much from each other?"

"In some things. Some women are not as free to share their secrets, though. Denu, Tuesday, Thylda, and I find it easier, for we are sisters."

"Such a large family you bring with you."

"Does that trouble you?" she asked, frowning at him.

"Nay. 'Tis just something I must grow accustomed to."

He rested his hand on her rounding stomach and felt the quickening within. For a moment fierce emotion cut through the drunken fog encircling his mind and he held her closer. It was hard for him to accept that he would soon be a father, for the outward signs that she carried his child were still slight. The strengthening movement within her womb was his only real proof, and it always filled him with a wild mix of exultation and fear when he felt it. A birth held an equal promise of great joy and painful tragedy.

And there was still Cecil to consider, he thought in frustration. The man tainted the future. His threat hung in the air and was still too close. Tonight Cecil had shown yet again just how close he could come.

"I will not let him have you," Botolf said.

The words were a softly hissed snarl, and Saxan shivered. "What say you?"

"Cecil." Botolf kissed the top of her head and nuzzled his face in the thick softness of her hair. "He will not have you."

"Nay. I mean to see him thwarted in that aim as well. 'Tis you I fear for."

"I can care for myself."

"Aye, but it may need to be your sword that cuts him down and I fear that that could hurt you."

"Aye, it will hurt. For all he has tormented, slighted, and threatened me, he is still my brother. Howbeit, now he threatens all that is dearest to me—my wife and my child. We could have been brothers as close as Hunter and Roc, sharing the work and the pleasure of the estate my father left, but Cecil chose to turn against me. He now backs me into a corner, leaves me with no choices."

He sighed and kissed the hollow by her ear. "Aye, I wish for another man's sword to end his life; but if mine is all there is at hand, then mine shall do the deed. That will pain me greatly, but it will be regret which I suffer most from. A regret that things could not have been different and anger that he forced me to commit his murder. Such feelings will fade in time. I do not worry that they will scar my mind or my heart."

She held him tightly, praying that what he claimed was true. What Cecil was pushing Botolf to do was horrible. Saxan also prayed that it would be any sword but Botolf's that finally ended Cecil's life. Then they would never have to find out if what Botolf believed were the truth.

"Come, he is no longer in the keep or upon the grounds hereabout," Botolf said. "There are guards below our window and at our door. You will be safe."

Since she did not want to tell him what fear had

made her cling so tightly to him, she nodded. "And my dagger rests beneath my pillow."

He laughed sleepily. "My fierce little Saxan."

"He shall never find me helpless again."

"That troubled you."

"Aye. I think that being so helpless caused as great a fear as all the things he threatened to do."

"He will not gain such a hold on you again."

She had to bite back a laugh, for Botolf's sleepy vow was punctuated by a loud snore. The drink he had consumed had finally drawn him into a deep sleep. It took a lot of tugging and pushing, which he was blissfully oblivious to, but she turned him onto his side so that his snoring stopped. She cuddled up to him spoon fashion, draping his limp arm around her waist.

Gazing at the strong hand she covered with her own, she smiled crookedly. There was so much she wished to place in those graceful, long-fingered hands, but Botolf was not interested in such things. Those hands which caressed her in the night could also wield a sword in her defense at the first hint of danger. She found it astounding that they could be skilled in two such opposing activities. When she thought of how they could also be forced to take the life of a half-brother, her hatred for Cecil grew. She kissed Botolf's palm as if to place some talisman there which would ward off the stain of a kinsman's blood.

The child within her did a strange series of flip-flops and she sighed, closing her eyes as sleep fought hard to claim her. She found the waiting difficult and knew that Botolf did as well. Although she was now about five months along, half of her waiting over, spring still seemed a long way off.

Fourteen

Thylda looked up from the tapestry she labored over. "Pacing will not make m'lord's steed cover ground any faster."

Saxan nodded at the truth of that although the truth did nothing to still the worry gnawing at her. She had been worried since the report had come that Cecil was near. It had been a month since Cecil's presence had briefly darkened the joy of Lady Mary's wedding, and Botolf had eagerly grasped the chance to take up the hunt again.

With a sigh, Saxan stopped pacing the weaving room and sat down next to Thylda. She carefully studied her sister's work. When the baby began what she referred to as a raging battle to get out, she hurriedly grasped Thylda's hands and placed them on her abdomen.

"Oh, my, such an active child," Thylda murmured, her eyes wide with wonder. "How can you rest with all that going on inside you?"

"Not well, in truth. I have taken to lying down whene'er there is quiet within me, no matter what time it is. Howbeit, that is not why I placed your hands there. Do you not find it, well, odd?"

"What do you mean—odd? There is life in there and that can be only for the good."

"Aye, praise God, but does it seem to you that there is a great deal of life in there?"

For a moment Thylda frowned in confusion, then her eyes widened again. "Do you think you may be carrying twins?"

"Aye, the thought has occurred to me. Such activity." Saxan shook her head. "It does feel as if I am being prodded in too many places at one time."

"Have you mentioned such a possibility to Botolf?" Thylda returned to her tapestry work.

"Nay. There is no reason to afright the poor man."

"Botolf frightened? I cannot believe it."

"I think all men are frightened by this wonder. They see the woman's body change and feel the life within, and it is all past their understanding. They also know of all the dangers of childbirth, dangers no man's strength or sword can fight."

"Oh, Saxan, do not speak of such things." Thylda briefly and tightly hugged her sister.

"And why not? Oh, I do not think upon them for very long or often, but only a fool would ignore them completely. I should like to say that they do not afright me, but they do at times, as they must do all women. I prepare my small bag of birthing potions, but somehow I cannot believe that my end will come upon a childbirth bed."

"Do you truly feel certain of that?"

"As certain as one can feel when such a thing rests in God's hands." She studied Thylda's work again. " 'Tis good. It is Papa's story?"

"Aye. I but guess at what he looked like in his younger years."

"It will be lovely, as is all your work."

Thylda noticed Saxan's distraction and smiled. "Your thoughts wing Botolf's way again."

"I cannot seem to help myself. Mayhap it is the

child who makes me foolish, but I have a bad feeling about the search they have gone on."

"Surely you must have faith in a messenger sent by Hunter himself?"

"What has Hunter himself done?" asked a familiar voice.

Saxan echoed Thylda's squeal of delight when she saw her brothers standing in the door of the weaving room. She raced right behind Thylda to greet Hunter, Roc, Udolf, and Kyne. Jane, who had shown the men to the room, smiled as the siblings hugged, kissed, and playfully insulted each other. At a subtle sign from Saxan, she hurried away to be sure there was adequate refreshment for the guests.

As Saxan ushered her family into the great hall, she blushed and laughed over her brothers' teasing. She knew that, when Pitney returned from helping Botolf search for Cecil, he would be heartily pleased to find his four elder brothers at Regenford. They would all be able to spend Yuletide together. It was a treat Saxan had not expected.

"I am surprised that you have arrived so close upon the heels of your own messenger, Hunter," Saxan said after they had exchanged news about the family and enjoyed some light refreshment.

Hunter frowned. "I sent no man here, Saxan, not even a page to forewarn of our arrival."

Saxan felt her blood run cold as she stared at her confused brothers. The bad feeling she had had about Botolf's foray now broke all the restraints she had put on it, threatening to choke her with fear. When she began to shake, her brothers leapt to her side, concern on their handsome faces. A pale Thylda raced to fetch Jane.

" 'Tis a trap," Saxan managed to say after Hunter urged her to drink some mead.

"What is a trap, Saxan?" Hunter pressed. "Come, we cannot help you unless you tell us something more than that."

"Botolf rides into a trap set by Cecil," she said, her voice gaining strength as Jane arrived and tried to warm her mistress's icy hands between her own. All the while, the maid urged calm for the sake of the child. "A man arrived saying that he had been sent here by you. Since he knew so much that was private about this trouble we have, we believed him."

"And he sent Botolf in search of Cecil?" Udolf asked.

"Aye, to a place just off the road ten miles east of the village."

"Is the man still here?" demanded Hunter.

"He did not ride with Botolf for he seemed most weary," Saxan replied.

"I will ask after him, mistress," Jane said.

"Have him brought here if he still lingers within reach," Udolf called after the maid as she hurried away.

It did not surprise Saxan or, she noticed, any of her brothers when a man-at-arms returned with Jane to report that the false messenger was no longer at Regenford. Saxan felt the composure she had only just gained rapidly slip away. Botolf and his men were good fighters, but a well-executed trap put the odds of victory strongly on the side of the one who sprang that trap. Saxan was deeply afraid for Botolf and Pitney, who rode at his side.

"Somehow Cecil discovered that our clan had joined in the hunt for him and used that," Udolf said, sharply banging his fist on the thick table.

"That would not be such a hard thing to do, Udolf," Thylda said.

"Should we hie after his lordship?" asked Botolf's man-at-arms.

"We will go," Hunter told the soldier. "We will take our men. We will need fresh horses, however. It would not be wise to leave Regenford too lightly guarded. There is no way of knowing if Cecil watches for just such a happenstance. There is a lot to protect right here, and I feel sure his lordship would not wish their protection lessened even for his sake."

"Aye, m'lord. I will ready the horses." The guardsman hurried away.

"Do you have enough men, Hunter?" asked Saxan.

"There are only a dozen of us, but we are going to be unexpected and that will add greatly to our strength. Pitney is with the earl?"

"Aye, and I sensed a wariness in him before he left. You see, none of us recognized the man as yours, but he claimed that he had joined your service in Berwick. Since we have had little time to come to know your men since then, we could not call him a liar."

"Aye, and I did add a few men to my entourage. It was a clever ploy."

"I grow weary of clever ploys."

"Come, ease your fears, Saxan. We shall bring our lord home to you. This fretting is no good for the child you carry." Hunter kissed her cheek. "Have faith in us and in your husband. 'Twill take more than clever ploys to bring him down."

"Your horses are ready," an attendant called from the doorway.

Saxan watched her brothers rush off. Their reassurances rang in her ears, but did little to ease her fears. Until Botolf was returned hale and unhurt she would worry. Even concern for her child could not dim her worry.

"Please, m'lady, you must lie down," urged Jane.

"Lie down? Nay, I will wait here," Saxan snapped.

"You may fret as well upon your back, but at least it would be better for the child you carry."

"You grow most bold, Jane."

"Aye, but his lordship gave me leave to be so."

"I will not leave this hall."

"Then I shall fetch a pallet and you may lie down here."

"That may be for the best, Jane," said Thylda. "If she is here, she will not fret that she is missing some news and she will not run down those stairs at the first sign of the men returning."

"I cannot lie down here where all can see me," protested Saxan.

" 'Tis either that or your chambers," Jane said stoutly although she blushed deeply at her boldness.

"Then fetch a pallet, for I will not leave here until Botolf is back."

Botolf scowled at the wood they rode through, the trees still lightly frosted from the last snow. He had felt uneasy about the foray from the beginning. Now that they had found nothing and were returning empty-handed, his uneasiness grew stronger. A glance at young Pitney's face told him that the youth felt the same. That gave him little comfort.

His fears centered on Saxan. This search had left the guard at Regenford light. He did not really think anyone could slip by his men, but he admitted that his fears for Saxan's safety did not often respond well to common sense. Even when he was at her side and a full force of men was within the walls of Regenford, he worried about her safety. He knew that some of his concern was because Cecil was no longer the only danger shadowing her. Despite his best efforts not to, he saw the child she carried as a threat to her. He could not block out of his mind all the horror that could visit the childbed.

"M'lord?" Pitney called.

"Aye?" Botolf answered.

"I fear I may sound an old woman, but I have an ill feeling about this."

Wesley nodded as he rode up to flank Botolf. "As do I, and I am not given to such whims. Mayhap it is just because we found nothing."

"That added to my own unease," Pitney admitted. "I cannot believe that Hunter would have us ride out unless he was sure of the sighting."

"Yet there was no sign that anyone had been there for a long time," murmured Botolf.

"But would we not have met with an attack there if this were just a trick to pull us away from the protection of Regenford?" asked Sir Wesley.

"We were fresh and readied for such a ploy," said Pitney. "It is not where I would plan an ambush."

"Where would you plan one, Pitney?" Botolf asked.

"Ambush!" screamed a man, his warning ending in a high note of fear and pain as a dagger buried itself in his chest.

"Just about here, m'lord," Pitney said dryly as he drew his sword to meet the men swarming from the wood around them and to protect his liege lord from this obvious attempt upon his life.

A melee ensued, and Botolf's men were soon unhorsed by the frightened actions of their mounts or pulled down by their attackers. In the confusion, the warhorses proved useless and the surprise of the attack made them vulnerable. Botolf dismounted voluntarily as his horse became too restive to control well and allow him to battle skillfully at the same time. He noticed that Pitney, Wesley, Roger, and Talbot soon did the same, Talbot fighting to move the animals out of the way.

Although the Regenford men recovered quickly from the disadvantage of the ambush, Botolf could not see much hope for a victory. They simply held their own against Cecil's forces which far outnumbered them. Soon, Botolf knew, his men would begin to tire and the defensive square they had formed would weaken. Then, Botolf found himself face to face with Cecil at last.

Hatred and fury swelled up in Botolf, but he fought those feelings. They could make him act rashly, thus handing Cecil the victory he sought. There was also a strong sense of regret that two men who shared a father should be facing each other sword to sword.

"You no longer hide behind assassins in the night?" he asked Cecil in a cold voice.

"No need to this time, Brother," Cecil replied. "When they find you and your men, most of your people will believe it was robbers or the Scots who felled you. There will be no man left alive to tell them differently. Nay, this one is mine," Cecil cried when several of his men moved to aid him.

"Then we shall end this here," said Botolf.

"Aye, Brother," Cecil sneered, "but do not fear. I shall take good care of your little widow."

It was not easy, but Botolf ignored that remark as he did all the other taunts Cecil flung at him. He knew that game well enough to avoid its trap. Cecil and he were so well matched that only exhaustion or a foolish lunge in anger could give either of them an advantage. Botolf was determined not to give that advantage to Cecil. He closed his mind to Cecil's goading, although it cut painfully close to the bone. As he began to tire, he tried one last time to end the battle to the death that Cecil had imposed upon him.

"Give this up, Cecil," he urged his half-brother. "You can gain naught."

"I can gain what is mine by birthright," Cecil said.

"You have no birthright. You are not even the elder. Father did as well as he could by you."

"Not well enough."

"So you would let your greed kill us both?"

"I do not intend to die, Brother."

"Mayhap you will not be the first of us to die, but die you will. Too many people know about your game. They will know whose hands are stained with my blood, and they will hunt you down. You will not enjoy your gains for long."

"That is yet to be seen."

"M'lord, someone comes," cried one of Cecil's men. " 'Tis a force from Regenford."

Although Cecil was visibly startled by this news, Botolf lost the chance to deliver the killing stroke Cecil's distraction allowed him. By the time he regained his senses, Cecil was beyond his reach. One of Cecil's men brought him a horse and Cecil was ready to flee while Botolf and his men were still too hard pressed by their attackers to stop him.

Botolf looked toward the force of men now charging down the road. The four men in front lacked helmets, and the fair locks whipped by the wind told him who rode to his rescue. He glanced back toward Cecil, but was too late to save himself. Even as Botolf cursed his error in taking his gaze from his treacherous brother, Cecil's dagger was buried in his chest.

"A Yuletide gift for your pretty bride," Cecil called as he spurred his mount into a gallop.

"Chase down those dogs," bellowed Hunter as he reined in by Botolf who, as he started to collapse, was caught by Pitney and Wesley. "M'lord," he cried in concern as he dismounted.

The next few moments proved to be torture for Botolf. His body took a full moment to fully realize the pain caused by the knife buried deep in his flesh. Just as it did so, he was forced to endure its removal. It was awhile before the pain cleared enough so that he was fully aware of lying on a blanket on the ground encircled by concerned faces. He did not need to look to know that they were having difficulty stopping the flow of blood from his wound.

"You have come from Regenford?" he asked in a raspy whisper.

"Aye, m'lord," answered Hunter. "We came to share this festive time with our sisters. Saxan asked about the man I had sent. Since I had sent no one to Regenford, she knew this was a trap."

"Are those your own men?"

"All mine, m'lord. We took none from Regenford in case your brother watched for such a weakness."

Botolf nodded weakly in approval.

"Cecil no longer tries to hide his villainy," Wesley said.

"He felt certain of his victory, Wesley." Botolf grimaced with pain. "He may yet win."

"But there will be the witnesses he sought to eliminate."

"We shall get you back to Regenford, m'lord," Pitney said. "There you will get the nursing you need."

"And a priest," Botolf whispered.

"You will have no need of a friar."

Closing his eyes for a moment, Botolf prayed that Pitney was right. There was too much he desperately wished to live for now. He knew the wound was bad, however, and fought to find the strength to face his own mortality. Although he could sense everyone still watching him, none of them spoke to him. He knew they sought to aid him in maintaining his strength, something he would badly need to endure the ride back to Regenford. When he opened his eyes again, Hunter's men were returning.

"Did you get Cecil?" he struggled to ask, his voice a hoarse thread of sound.

"Nay, m'lord," answered Hunter's sergeant-at-arms, "but we did cut down many a fleeing cur."

"We must get the earl back to Regenford," Pitney urged.

"We have no cart for him," Sir Wesley said.

"Then let us choose the burliest man amongst us, Sir Wesley," Hunter suggested. "He can hold the earl before him upon a sturdy horse."

The man chosen had Botolf staring in groggy wonder. Little Peter, Hunter's squire, had to be five inches or more taller than Botolf and far broader of shoulder. He mused that Hunter and his squire had to make for a strange-looking pair, as Little Peter was also very dark, rough of feature, and extremely hirsute. No greater opposite to the fair, slender Hunter could have been found.

"You mount, Little Peter, and we shall hand the earl up to you," ordered Hunter.

"Do we have a horse willing to take the weight?" Wesley asked, eyeing Little Peter in amazement.

"My horse can bear it for the few miles to Regenford," Little Peter replied, his voice a deep rumble.

By the time he was set before Little Peter, Botolf was awash in sweat and shaking. He could not fully suppress a groan as he was wrapped in a blanket to stave off the afternoon chill. The slightest movement brought a shaft of pain from his wound.

"Lie back against me, m'lord," Little Peter said.

" 'Tis not good to use up what strength is left you just to sit straight."

Casting aside his pride, Botolf did as the man suggested. Each movement of the horse caused him pain, and that pain began to rob him of consciousness. He could hear snatches of conversation around him, but was too lost in a sea of agony to make out many of the words. Enough penetrated his fog, however, to tell him that he was not alone in fearing that Cecil had dealt him a mortal wound and his thoughts went to Saxan, to how badly he wanted to stay with her.

Saxan cried out softly and sat up. She clutched at her chest as she felt a brief searing pain. Botolf's name sprang to her lips and she trembled with fear for him.

"M'lady, sip at this," Jane said as she held out a tankard. " 'Tis an herbal drink that will give you strength."

It took a moment for Saxan to realize that Jane stood by her side and offered her a steaming, aromatic drink. "Botolf."

"Drink it, Saxan," urged Thylda, nodding when Saxan finally obeyed. "Botolf will be fine."

"I think he has been hurt," Saxan said.

"Why do you say that?"

"I felt it. Here. In the chest."

"Oh. Could it be Pitney?" Thylda asked reluctantly. "You two have often had feelings about each other."

"Nay, it was Botolf's name on my lips when the pain struck." Saxan suddenly smiled when she saw the uneasy look on Jane's face. "I practice no sorcery, Jane. I but feel too strongly how those close to my heart are faring."

"As if your hearts are joined?" Jane asked.

"Aye," Saxan agreed. "That describes it well."

"And Botolf now shares that place with Pitney?" Thylda asked.

"It would seem so, Thylda, although I pray to God it is only my own fears that create this feeling. Perhaps I am so afraid Botolf will be hurt that I have simply made myself believe it has happened. I wish I had never seen Cecil."

"How does that matter?"

"Now I know my enemy, the man who means to destroy all that matters to me."

"Is it not best to know your enemy? Most men say so."

"I know, Thylda, and it is the truth in many cases, but I am no warrior. Looking into the eyes of my foe only adds to my fears. Before I saw Cecil, he was a man who resembled Botolf but was bad. Ah, but now," she shook her head, "I have seen the evil in him, the hate and jealousy that twists his soul, and his cunning. I know he has the wit to entrap Botolf and that there is no mercy in him, no brotherly love to stay his sword. If the chance comes, and Cecil has the wit to see and grasp at all chances, Botolf will die at his half-brother's hand as will Botolf's wife and child. And Cecil will know no remorse over his crime."

Thylda put her arm around Saxan's shoulders and hugged her close. "I cannot believe that God would sacrifice such a good man as Botolf to the evil that is Cecil. You believe that, too, Saxan, and still all those fears that can only harm the babe you carry."

Saxan tried to heed Thylda's words. They held some truth. But her traitorous mind proceeded to reveal to her how many times a good man had fallen to the blow of a bad one. Whatever God's reasons, He was not always there to save the good.

"The men return, m'lady," a page cried loudly as he dashed into the great hall only to spin on his heel and dash out again.

Cursing her increasing lack of agility, Saxan got to her feet with Thylda's help. She ignored Jane's soft admonition to go carefully and nearly ran out into the bailey. Even before she reached it, a cold dread began to creep over her. There was a subdued tone to the murmurs of those gathering to greet the returning men that told her her fears had been justified.

Her first sight of Botolf sent her reeling. Thylda and Jane hurried to support her as she swayed. Now that her fears had been realized, however, she found an inner source of strength. Fears were intangible things that tormented a person and could not be wrestled into submission with medicines and worldly goods. Botolf's wound could be treated, the danger of it fought. Straightening her shoulders, she moved to where Little Peter now stood with Botolf in his big arms. She touched Botolf's forehead and his eyes opened. She smiled at him to hide her worry.

"Saxan," he whispered as he fought to see her clearly.

"Only a man like Little Peter could bring you home to me like a babe in arms. Peter, please follow me." She started toward her chambers. "This cold cannot be good for him."

"Nay, m'lady," agreed Peter.

Hunter hurried to fall into step at her side and said, "It was a trap just as we had feared."

"Aye," said Pitney as he moved to her other side. "But we held our own. When Hunter appeared, Cecil's dogs began to scatter."

"And when was Botolf hurt?" she asked in a quiet voice, astonished at how calm she sounded.

"That coward Cecil threw a dagger even as he retreated. There was no defense your husband could make."

"Which is exactly how Cecil likes matters to stand," she said as she led everyone into her bedchamber. "Place Botolf on the bed, Peter, and undress him."

"The wound needs closing, Saxan," Pitney said as he and Hunter moved to help Peter. "We could not do it there."

" 'Tis best that you did not, for it should be well cleaned first."

With Thylda's and Jane's help, Saxan gathered what she would need to tend to Botolf's wound. By the time she was prepared, Botolf was stripped and tucked up into bed. As Saxan approached the bed, Hunter caught her by the arm.

"Mayhap you should not tend to him," Hunter said.

"He is my husband," she replied.

"Aye, but you are heavy with child and this can only upset you. That cannot be good for you at such a time."

" 'Tis not good at any time. I am good at this, Hunter. I do not think it is only vanity which makes me say that I am, mayhap, better than anyone here. I must tend him. It will upset me less than to stand back and let other, less skillful hands care for him." When he let her go, she added, "You will be needed to hold him steady."

To her relief, Botolf quickly succumbed to his pain. She cleaned him and his injury thoroughly before stitching the wound closed. He had lost a lot of blood, but she found some hope in the fact that she was able to stop its flow. After she was done, she cleaned herself up and had Peter place a seat near the bed for her.

"You should rest, Saxan," Hunter said.

"I shall rest here," she said.

"Saxan—"

"Do not fret so, Hunter. I will not endanger the child Botolf has prayed for. Howbeit, I will take care of my husband."

"As you wish. Little Peter will stay here. Let him lift his lordship and do all such heavy work when it is needed."

"Thank you, Hunter. Cecil was unharmed?"

"I fear the cur escaped with but a few small cuts from Botolf's sword."

"I tried to make him stop this," Botolf whispered hoarsely. "I was willing to forgive all if he would but cease this now."

Saxan urged Botolf to drink some of the herbal potion Jane had brought while Little Peter gently raised him up slightly and ordered, "Hush, m'lord. You need to rest. That is the only way to heal."

His brief hold on consciousness slipping away, Botolf muttered, "You need to rest, too, for the baby."

"The babe is fine," she said, but knew he could not hear her. "Hunter, it might be best to send word to Lady Mary. I do not wish to offend by keeping this from her. She may not choose to come, but I feel certain she would wish to be told."

"Aye. I will send word out at dawn's breaking," Hunter promised.

"Go and clean up," she told him. "There is naught you can do here. Mayhap Farold can help Peter in that room." She waved a hand in the general direction of the room Botolf used to dress in.

"I will see to it," Hunter said, "and I will have food sent up. Do not wear yourself out, dearling."

"I will not. Jane," she said as her brothers left, "we shall need a pallet for Peter."

"And for you, m'lady," Jane said firmly as she started to leave.

"I will help you, Jane," Thylda said as she followed the maid.

When Farold arrived and led Peter away, Saxan found herself alone with Botolf at last. She knelt by the bed and fervently prayed for her husband's recovery. It was impossible to ignore the seriousness of his wound, but she fought to cling to her hopes. Hope would be what gave her the strength to get through the ordeal ahead of her.

Jane and Thylda soon returned with two other maids. They set up pallets for her and Little Peter. Despite her own grief, Saxan had to smile at the way Jane could not keep her eyes off Little Peter. She wondered if it were due to a real attraction for the man or a fascination with such a large specimen of manhood. Jane needed a nudge from Thylda to finally leave the room.

Hunter himself brought the food up to her and Peter, saying the moment he entered the room, "I hope you realize what an honor I do you."

"Aye, Brother. I am truly humbled," Saxan murmured.

"So you should be. Now, eat it all. Thylda will come soon to sit with Botolf so that you may get some rest."

Saxan did not argue. She was being allowed to stay near Botolf and that would have to be enough. While Botolf lay ill, Hunter would take his place as the man in her life and she knew he would not tolerate any disobedience in this matter. It was important that she care for the child she carried as well as she cared for Botolf. Both duties required that she take care of herself, too. As she ate the food, which tasted like ashes in her mouth, she sought a more complete report on the battle.

"So you feel you have well trimmed Cecil's followers," she murmured after Hunter told her all he knew.

"Aye." Hunter gathered up the few scraps left of her hearty meal. "If that was Cecil's full strength, it will be a long while ere he reaches it again."

"His attack was nearly successful, however."

"Aye, but a costly one for him and nearly is not good enough, is it?"

"Nay. Cecil is also wise enough to know that such a ploy will not work a second time."

"True enough. We must be wary though. Cecil has shown his great skill in these devious games."

"Until he is dead, we must be most careful whom and what we trust. The man has no sense of honor."

"None," agreed Hunter. "The blow that felled your husband was the strike of a coward."

" 'Tis a shame that such dishonorable strikes can wound as well as the honorable ones."

"By such an act Cecil lost all rights to being treated fairly and honorably."

"That should have been lost when he resorted to an assassin's knife in the dark," she said.

"Ah, well." Hunter shrugged. "We had no real proof he was the one behind those attacks even though everyone felt sure it was him. This loathsome act was done before many witnesses and will soon be widely known. I myself will now feel no qualms about meeting Cecil from behind and slipping a knife between his ribs. His sort deserves no better. Thank you, Peter," he said with a smile when that man growled an agreement.

Thylda entered and Saxan stood up, knowing she would have to lie down now. She bent to place a kiss on Botolf's forehead and what she felt beneath her lips turned her blood to ice. She straightened up, her gaze fixed upon the bright color in Botolf's cheeks. Her hand trembled as she rested it on his forehead only to prove what her lips and eyes had already told her. She felt all her hopes shatter.

"Fever," she whispered, and the looks upon the faces of the others in the room told her she was not alone in her fear.

Fifteen

Weary, but fighting to hide it, Saxan entered her bedchamber only to freeze at the sight that met her eyes. A priest she did not recognize stood by Botolf's bed delivering the last rites. A wild cry of denial escaped her as she raced to the bed where Botolf still fought for his life. She turned a burning gaze upon the affronted priest.

"Get out," she snarled at him.

"Now, Saxan," Hunter began.

"Nay. Botolf is not dead yet. I will not have this man looming over him like some carrion bird."

She knelt and clung to Botolf's hand, keeping her gaze fixed upon the priest. She watched as Hunter tugged the priest away from his deathwatch. The two men conversed in low tones for a moment before Hunter returned to her side.

"Saxan, heed me for a moment," Hunter said.

"Botolf is not dead," she said.

"Nay, and no one here wishes him to be. Howbeit, Saxan, he has been caught in the grip of a fever for four long days. You cannot deny how ill he is."

"I do not deny it, but I do not bring thoughts of death to his ears either."

"Do you wish him to die unshriven?"

"He will not die."

"Then think of this as a foolish caution, but let it

be done, for your husband's sake. Let us be readied for all possibilities, no matter how grim."

"All right," she agreed, reluctance and anger filling her voice.

When the priest returned to Botolf's bedside, Saxan closed her eyes and pressed her forehead against the hand she held. It was not piety that caused her to do so, however. She did not wish to watch. This was a ritual of death, and she wanted nothing to do with it. It was as if she were the only one left who felt that Botolf would live, that he could fight off the fever which had such a firm grip on him and recover.

" 'Tis over, Saxan," Hunter said at length. "The priest is gone."

"You think me foolish," she murmured and peered up at him from beneath her thick lashes.

"Nay." Hunter sat on the edge of the bed and placed a hand on her head. "Howbeit, I needed all my skill with words to convince that priest that you were not a heretic."

Laughing weakly, she asked, "What did you tell him?"

"That the babe causes you to act like a madwoman. That and fear for your man," he added in a gentle voice.

"A madwoman, am I?" She moved to refresh the water and cloth she used to bathe Botolf in a thus-far vain attempt to still his fever. " 'Tis a ritual of death. I wanted no part of it."

"I understand and I think the priest will when he gets over the shock of being called a carrion bird."

She smiled faintly. "I shall do some penance for that. Why did you bring that man and not Father Chesney?"

"Father Chesney is away at his kinsmen's."

"There is no sign of Lady Mary?"

"Nay, but the weather has been very poor."

"He cannot die," she whispered, her gaze fixed upon her husband's face.

Hunter pulled her into his arms. "Everyone prays for him, Saxan. No one from Regenford can leave the castle without being besieged by questions about the earl's health. They all know how fortunate they are to have such a liege lord. One need not look far to see how it could be, how fortunate the people of this demanse are. If prayers count for aught, he will recover."

"I felt it, you know," she said softly as she tried to find some comfort in her brother's hold.

"Felt what, sweeting?" Hunter asked.

"The wound Botolf got. When the dagger pierced his flesh, I felt it. I had prayed that it was just my own fear causing me to feel the pain."

"You have grown that close to him?"

"He is my life."

"You have another life to think on as well," he reminded her as he urged her into her seat.

"I know. The babe."

" 'Tis a part of him, Saxan. 'Tis the future of Regenford. You know in your heart that your husband would not wish you to do anything to put that life at risk. Aye, while he lies so ill and so in need of care, it is easy to forget the importance of what lies in your womb. 'Tis not only his heir but, if anything happens to him—"

"Nay."

"If anything happens to Botolf," he pressed, "you will be hungry for the life he has bred in you, for that part of him that he has nurtured within you."

"Aye, I know."

"And never forget it. You look weary, dearling. I

know you do not tend to yourself as well as you should."

"I do try, Hunter."

"I know, sweeting." He urged her to accept a tankard of wine, smiling his approval when she began to drink.

" 'Tis just that I am so afraid for him. I fear to leave, as if by staying at his side I can hold off death. There is a vanity, eh?"

"Nay. 'Tis a common feeling," Hunter assured her. "E'en though we all know death can steal upon a man when he is surrounded by a hundred or more armed men, we still fear to leave an ailing loved one alone. I think, too, that we do not wish our loved one to face death alone. We feel guilty if we are not there, but that should not plague you, Sister. You know Botolf would want you to think on the child first and foremost. Therein lies the future of Regenford and all who depend upon it."

"You do not think it lies there?" She nodded toward Botolf.

"Nay, not as strongly as it does within your womb. You know this to be the truth."

"Aye," she admitted sadly. "I wish him at my side to help build that future."

"Everyone wishes for that, Saxan. The chapel swells with people praying for Lord Botolf. But, Saxan, do not deceive yourself into believing he will heal, that no other fate could await him. There are two roads he could travel now, and you must be ready for either."

"I know this, Hunter. I have tried to think only of his healing, but I cannot forget that some other fate may await him. My mind will not allow me the comfort of that lie."

"Truly, dearling, that is for the best. I think I am

to lose my squire," he said abruptly in an attempt to distract her.

"Nothing could draw Peter from your side." She struggled to go along with his diversion.

"Then you are to lose Jane."

"Ah, 'tis like that, is it? I had wondered at first, for she could not cease looking at him."

"Many suffer from that affliction."

"Aye, but I felt even then that it was not merely amazement. I had no time to think upon it or watch her more closely."

"Will you miss her?" he asked.

"Aye," Saxan replied. "She is a good, honest girl. She will serve Wolfshead Hall well and loyally. I think only Peter would overrule you, but he would never even try to do that."

"She seemed a trifle bold with you."

"Botolf ordered it. He wished to be sure that I would take good care of myself and the child I carry, but could not always watch over me himself. Jane blushes and sometimes trembles when she stands firm in that, but stand firm she does."

"And that can only be praised."

At that moment Lady Mary burst into the room. One look at the woman's pale face told Saxan that she would have to put her own fears aside to calm Lady Mary's. As she moved to put a comforting arm around the distraught woman, Hunter offered what little he could and left.

"Never has he come so close," Lady Mary murmured in a voice thick with tears as she sat by Botolf's bedside.

Saxan served the woman some wine and said, "It is still not close enough."

"Saxan—" Lady Mary began.

"I can see how poorly he is as well as you can, m'lady. Howbeit, he is not dead yet."

"Nay. Has the priest come?" she whispered as she took her son's limp hand in hers.

"Aye, Hunter brought him." Saxan gave her a faint smile. "I was none too pleased to find the man lurking over Botolf like carrion; but, though I sorely offended the priest, Hunter convinced me to let him perform the last rites."

"I understand. I, too, would have been upset to see it, but I can only be glad that Botolf will not," she took a deep, unsteady breath and continued, "die unshriven."

"He will not die, m'lady," Saxan said firmly and scowled at Botolf, only to frown in confusion when Lady Mary suddenly laughed. "What is funny?"

"Very little. 'Twas the way you spoke and looked at him." Lady Mary shook her head. "You were ordering him about, child."

Saxan smiled. "I have been doing a great deal of that."

"I hope you have not tired yourself too much. You look weary."

"I am weary, but I am not allowed to exhaust myself. There are scores of people who have made it their duty to see that I eat well and rest." She pointed to her pallet. "They have made me a bed right here so that I cannot argue that I will not leave Botolf's side."

Lady Mary looked at the pallet and shook her head again. "I do not believe my son would approve of that arrangement." She held up her hand to halt Saxan's protest. "I understand. 'Tis a fine compromise. Howbeit, when Botolf recovers, I would put myself into a proper bed as soon as possible if I were you. As soft as that pallet looks, it cannot be as good for you as a proper bed."

"True. I do find it difficult to get to my feet." She sighed and sat down on the bed. "I am in the mood to accept some painful truths, m'lady. So, tell me, how does he look to you?" she asked Lady Mary.

"He still lives, and that can only be a good sign. There is no poison in his wound?"

"None. I change his dressings several times each day. The wound itself appears to be healing as it should."

"Another good sign. 'Tis just this fever. He has suffered it for four days?"

"Aye, m'lady. We can occasionally force some hearty broth into his mouth, but not much. I wondered if there were a poison on the dagger which made the wound poison, too; but, as I said, his wound appears clean. Nothing breaks this fever."

"A fever can be difficult to cast off or drive away. Fevers are also frightening. They are too often the harbingers of death. That knowledge may feed our fears. To me, he looks poorly, and I want to weep with fear. The stronger side of me sees only that he is still alive and so there is still hope. Have you brought in a physician?"

"Nay." Saxan realized how sharp her reply was and took a deep breath to calm herself. "They would only bleed him, and he has lost too much blood already. I have little faith in those men."

"To tell the truth, I do not have much myself. I have never felt that they know more than we do. And their readiness to use bloodletting as a cure has always troubled me." She smoothed her hand over Botolf's hot, dry brow and bit her lip to stop its sudden trembling. "I fear I have never learned of a sure way to bring down a fever."

"We bathe him with cool water several times a day. It helps for a little while." Saxan quickly covered her mouth with her hand when she failed to smother a yawn.

"I think it is past time you had some rest." Lady Mary stood up, took Saxan by the hand, and tugged her to her feet.

"But you have only just arrived," Saxan protested, yet she did not fight Lady Mary as the woman led her to the pallet.

"And I shall remain here until Botolf is well, so there is no need to tire yourself for my sake. I will sit with Botolf and tell you if there is any change."

"You do not wish to clean up or rest after your long journey?"

"I can wash right here. After fretting about Botolf throughout my journey, I need to sit with him. And you need to rest." When Saxan had settled down on the pallet, she tucked the light coverlet over her.

"And you will wake me if there is any change?" Saxan asked even as she got comfortable and felt the need to sleep grow overpowering.

"Of a certain. No matter what the change."

"He will not die, Lady Mary."

"If a wife's determination can work a cure, then Botolf will indeed recover."

"Saxan."

The hoarse cry yanked Saxan out of sleep so abruptly her head ached. She started to get to her feet and gasped in surprise when Little Peter suddenly loomed over her. The unsteadiness she felt told her she still needed more sleep, and she frowned up at Peter.

"Is something wrong? Why did you call me?"

"I did not call you, m'lady," Peter replied and he pointed to the bed. "The earl did."

"Saxan."

The voice was definitely coming from the bed, but it was so weak and raspy, Saxan did not recognize it as Botolf's. She wanted to rush to his side, but fear kept her rooted to the spot. Was he better or was he about to bless her with his last words? When she had gone to sleep, Lady Mary had only just arrived and Botolf had been in the same fevered state with no hint of a change. Saxan found that waking after a nap to hear her husband's voice for the first time in four days was not the joyful experience she had anticipated. It terrified her.

"M'lady," Peter said and nudged her toward Botolf. "He calls you."

"I know. I have just panicked, is all." She took a deep breath to steady herself and walked to the bed.

Botolf stared at her and, although the light from the candles was too dim for her to be certain, his eyes looked clear. Her hand shook as she reached out to touch his face. It was slick with sweat. His fever had broken. Saxan swayed, and Peter quickly steadied her.

"His fever has broken," she said, sitting on the edge of the bed as she struggled to calm herself.

"I had a fever?" Botolf asked.

"Aye, for four long days." She smiled her gratitude to Peter, who lifted Botolf up enough to drink some mead. "That should soothe your parched throat, Husband." Botolf tried to reach for her hand, but was too weak. Saxan took his hand between hers. "We shall have to wash you down and change the linen."

"I am as weak as a babe," Botolf complained, briefly closing his eyes. "Have you been taking care of yourself?"

Saxan grinned at the hint of his old arrogance in his voice. "Well enough. Now, we had best tend to you so that you can be comfortable again."

With Peter's help, Saxan washed the sweat from Botolf's body and changed his linen and bandages. Although they tried to be gentle, Botolf was pale and exhausted by the time they were through. She hurried to get some hearty broth into him before he fell asleep. Several times she paused to feel his forehead and reassure herself that his fever was truly gone.

"I should wake your mother, yet I hesitate to do so," she said. "Lady Mary only arrived here this afternoon and she sat with you for a few hours. It seems a shame to wake her when, by the time she can come, you will most likely be asleep again."

"Tell her woman Elizabeth and let her decide," Botolf said, grimacing as he swallowed another spoonful of broth. "God's toenails, I am almost too weak to swallow."

"Your strength will soon return now that it is not exhausted battling a fever." She glanced at Peter. "Would you tell Lady Mary's maid what has happened, Peter?" As the big man started to leave, she added, "Be sure that she understands that Botolf will soon be asleep again."

"You sound very certain of that," Botolf murmured after Peter left.

" 'Tis the way of it," Saxan replied, accepting his refusal to eat any more and setting the nearly empty bowl aside.

"Even after I have been asleep for nearly four days?"

"Aye, for that time was spent in a hard battle against the fever. It has left you exhausted and weak. Now you will sleep so that you can renew your strength. The real trouble will come when you are still not well enough to do much, yet think you are for you are heartily sick of being abed."

He tried to squeeze her hand. "And you shall undoubtedly command me to do as I should."

"Undoubtedly." She moved closer and pressed his hand to her cheek. "I shall be remembering all too well how close we came to losing you. I will probably grow quite shrewish."

"Nay." He sighed then winced at the pain that slight movement drew from his wound. "Cecil nearly won."

"Only if all he wished were your death. He would never have gained Regenford. Nay, not even enough of the land to be buried in. I would cut out his heart myself ere I would allow that."

"Methinks Cecil does not realize the fierceness of the wife I would leave behind."

"He would soon know." She smoothed her hand over his brow. "You must rest."

"I know, and I can feel sleep beckoning me. Yet I feel a need to talk, although I do not have anything to say."

"Mayhap the need to talk comes from being so close to death or being nearly silent for four days."

"You mean I did not rant and rave whilst I was fevered?"

"Nay, m'lord. You said little save for a few profane remarks concerning Cecil." She smiled when he gave a weak laugh, but then grew solemn as some of the fears she had suffered from during his illness returned. "I wish you had raved, cursed, and bellowed, no matter how wild and nonsensical the words. Your silence was chilling. It made it all too clear that death stood at your bedside."

"He obviously got tired of waiting for me. And I

do not intend to invite him for another vigil until I am very old and have seen my child have children."

Saxan knew he jested, but prayed that his words were prophetic. She smiled and placed his hand over her stomach. To her delight the child within her responded vigorously. Botolf's red-rimmed eyes widened as he felt his child kick. Or children, she thought with an inner joy, wondering if he would realize what a prodigious amount of activity there was.

Botolf felt such a wave of emotion it almost swept away his weakness. He had felt the movement in her womb before, but it had never been so strong. That he had nearly died certainly added a poignancy to what he felt. He knew the tiny woman smiling at him, his seed growing in her belly, was one reason he had fought death so hard. Botolf realized that he had never had such a reason to live before.

"There is certainly no doubt that our child is alive," he said.

"No doubt at all. There is definitely strength there."

"A good thing for a son to have." He grinned when she gave him a mock scowl. "Or a daughter."

"Very wise," she murmured, then stood up and made sure he was properly tucked in. "Do you want a drink before you go to sleep?"

"I am going to sleep, am I?"

"Aye, you are. You know you will soon anyway. Your weariness is already reddening your eyes and it begins to slur your speech. If you do not pander to yourself now, your fever could easily return."

"And I am now too weak to endure any more of that." He sighed and closed his eyes. "If my mother decides to visit, wake me. If I can speak to her, it will help ease her worry."

"I will, but I begin to think she has decided to try and wait until the morning."

"You are to rest as well. From the movement I could feel within your womb, you will need to be strong to carry that child."

Saxan nodded. She bent down and gave him one kiss on the mouth. A sudden sharp look in his eyes told her she may have conveyed far more emotion in that small kiss than she had planned to, but she did not care. Botolf had almost died. If he remembered the hint of emotion in her kiss at all, he would probably attribute it to the high drama of the moment. Instinct told her that Botolf would not press her for the answers to any questions her kiss had raised, not when it concerned something emotional. She doubted that his close brush with death would change him that much.

"Good sleep, Botolf," she whispered and moved to her pallet.

"Is that where you are sleeping?" he asked as she settled herself on her meager bed.

"For now. We can argue about it later."

"We will."

She hid a smile as she squeezed her pillow into the right shape. That promised argument would be welcomed. It would prove that at least some of the strength stolen by the fever had returned. As she closed her eyes, she heard Little Peter return. Knowing Botolf would be in good hands, Saxan let the need to sleep conquer her.

"Do you see what she is sleeping on, Mother?"

"Hush, Botolf. It has only been for a few days. She needed to be near at hand to see to your care."

Saxan shook off the last vestiges of sleep. Botolf's

voice was stronger, more easily recognizable as his. That one night of an unfevered sleep could give that added strength to his voice eased her last doubts about his recovery. She stretched and realized that she was really hungry for the first time since Botolf had been carried back to Regenford.

"I know you are awake, Saxan," Botolf said, ignoring his mother's command to be quiet.

"How can anyone sleep with you squealing like a stuck pig?" Saxan winked at Lady Mary, who hurried over to help her stand up. "You have rapidly gone from silent to very loud, my husband."

"You are fortunate that I am still too weak to bellow," he said even as he exchanged a good-morning kiss with her. "I was too groggy last night to fully comprehend the inadequacy of what you have been sleeping on."

"Talking loudly and using such big words, too. A very good sign."

"Saxan," Botolf said, directing a scowl toward his mother when she giggled, "that is not a good place for a woman in your condition to sleep. The cold and damp of the floor cannot be good for you."

"There is the pallet, linen, and a sheepskin between me and that floor." She patted his cheek, savoring its healthy coolness. "I will sleep there one more night and then find a more suitable bed. Now, I must go and have a bath and a very hearty meal."

"Saxan," he called as she started out of the room.

"I will be back in just a little while."

"You enjoy a good, large meal," Lady Mary said. "I will stay with Botolf."

"Mother," Botolf protested after Saxan left, "I wished to talk to my wife."

"Nay, you wished to argue with her." Lady Mary carefully set a tray of food on the bed. "I think it is much more important that she have a relaxing bath and a quiet, filling meal."

"She has not been eating well?" he asked between bites of the hearty broth his mother fed him.

"Saxan has been eating and sleeping well enough. Not as well as you would like, certainly, but she has not neglected herself. She is well aware that everything she does affects her child. Howbeit, she also needed to remain at your bedside." She helped steady him enough so that he could drink some cider.

"Well, she should not have been so determined to do her duty to me. Her duty to her child is far more important."

" 'Tis odd that men, who feel they are able to rule, can be so silly at times," muttered Lady Mary.

Botolf stared at his mother in surprise. "What do you mean?"

"Do you really believe that it was duty which kept that child at your bedside night and day? Duty only required that she insure that you got the best care. It was certainly not duty that had her offending the priest brought to give you last rites by calling him a carrion bird. It was not duty that had her denying the very real possibility that you could die. Nay, I have heard all about what went on here before I arrived yesterday and duty is not the word I would use to describe your wife's behavior."

"And how would you describe it?"

"That child loves you." She watched his face and sighed. "You do not want your wife to love you."

"I want a comfortable, peaceful marriage," he said, fighting the sudden surge of joy he felt at the thought that Saxan loved him. "Love does not often bring comfort and peace. I have dealt with love before—"

"Nay, you have not. You dealt with a mean-spirited whore who would not have recognized love if God

Himself had shown it to her. Oh, Alice quite liked the fact that you loved her, but she had no heart for love. That particular marriage does not allow you to say you have dealt with love."

"It certainly showed me the folly of allowing myself to be entrapped by it."

"Has Saxan given you any indication that she wishes to entrap you or trick you or deceive you in any way?"

"Nay, but she knows she does not have the power to do so. I have not given it to her."

"And you are doing your best to never give it to her," Lady Mary said in a soft, sad voice. "I had not realized how deeply Alice had cut you."

"Do not be ridiculous," he snapped. "She was a lesson, and I had the wit to learn it well."

"Nay, you learned the wrong lesson. You learned that the actions of one heartless whore are the ways of all women. You insult women with that belief, myself included. I had thought that, despite your woeful experience with Alice, you would see through my actions that all women are not like her. Instead, you heed Alice's lessons over mine. You choose to see only the worst."

"There is nothing wrong with being wary." Botolf shifted uncomfortably beneath his mother's angry look.

"You are not being wary; you have closed yourself off. Has Cecil's attempts to murder you made you mistrust every man? Nay, of course not. Aye, you will be more cautious, but you will still trust men. But you allow the betrayal of one stupid girl to make you distrust all women."

" 'Tis not just Alice." Botolf wanted to defend himself, but, suddenly, his usual arguments seemed foolish. "At court one sees many women like Alice."

"And you dare to judge the world by what happens at court? Do you truly see the world filled with sycophants, whores, and intriguers?" Lady Mary shook her head. "Mayhap it is my fault. I know I can be naive, too trusting, and too ready to see only the good in people. Mayhap I did not prepare you well for the place you have had to take in the world. I sent you out into the world with my naivete, and that caused you to feel any hurt inflicted more deeply than another would have."

Botolf winced as he reached for her hand and the action pulled at his wound, but he managed to grasp hold of her. "You have not failed me."

Before Lady Mary could reply, Little Peter and Hunter arrived. Inwardly, Botolf breathed a sigh of relief. The conversation with his mother had begun to get uncomfortable. The look she gave him as she left told him that the discussion had only been delayed, not ended, and he cursed silently. He knew he did not want to hear any more of what she had to say because her words held too much truth.

Saxan slipped into Botolf's room as quietly as she could only to find him watching her. "Good afternoon," she said and sat down on the edge of the bed.

"That was a very long meal you enjoyed," he grumbled, taking her hand in his.

"A long bath, a full meal, and a little nap. The first two made me need the last. Have you been well taken care of whilst I was gone?"

"Aye, I have been fed, turned, bathed, prodded at, my dressings changed, and thoroughly ordered about."

"Well, I am glad you have been so well entertained." She laughed when he glared at her.

"You find my ill humor amusing?"

"Today—aye. As I become more confident of your recovery, I shall probably treat your irritation with the scorn it deserves." She saw his lips twitch as he fought a smile. "Have you rested?" Saxan gave in to the strong temptation to feel his forehead and nodded her approval when she found it was still beautifully cool.

"Aye, I was also strictly ordered to nap, you impertinent wench."

Caressing his hand, she brushed aside a lock of hair that had fallen onto his forehead. "I hope you obeyed that command. Rest is the strongest medicine you can take now. Each time you rest, you gain back some of the strength the fever stole from you. And Regenford needs you strong again."

"And I need to be strong to fight Cecil. Has there been any sign of him?"

"Nay. The man has the ability to disappear like a wisp of smoke in a strong wind. The fact that he must hide is in our favor, though. With such a vigorous search being conducted for the man, he cannot get near to us while you are stuck in this bed and, mayhap, for the weeks it will take you to fully recover. We have a small respite from that trouble. Mayhap we will even be lucky enough to see it all ended before you are strong enough to pick up a sword again."

Botolf smiled faintly. "That would be a blessing. Howbeit, I feel certain that that particular trouble will be waiting for me, that I will still be forced to end it by my own hand."

He watched her nod, a look of fear and sadness clouding her eyes, and found himself wondering if his mother were right about Saxan's feelings. The thought that Saxan loved him was so heady, so exhilarating, he instinctively retreated from it. It was almost painfully tempting to reach out to her, to grasp tightly to all she had to offer, and he fought that temptation.

Since his mother had left, he had been unable to stop thinking about what she had said. There was simply too much truth in her words for him to ignore it, although he had tried. He was willing to admit that he unfairly slandered all women because of the actions of a few. He could not, however, simply cast aside his deep wariness. Saxan beamed at him, and inwardly he sighed. He wanted to reach out to her, to let his emotions run free and savor whatever she gave in return, but he was afraid. If Saxan betrayed him, if she did anything to hurt him, he knew that the pain she could inflict would make the nearly fatal wound Cecil had delivered seem like a pinprick. Botolf hated to admit it, but he did not think he had the courage to risk testing Saxan.

Sixteen

"You are pushing yourself too hard," Saxan complained when she entered Botolf's bedchamber and caught him practicing his swordplay with Wesley.

Although he put his sword aside and allowed Wesley to make a discreet exit, Botolf protested, "I need to rebuild my strength and regain the skill lost to me after three long months as a bedridden invalid."

"You have not been bedridden for the whole three months." Saxan sat on the bed as he washed up and she sighed. "I know you are healed. Even the scar begins to lose its red angry appearance. 'Tis not easy to shake the image of you lying close to death, however, with the priest giving you the last rites. I will admit that it makes me overcautious."

Botolf sat down next to her, tugged her into his arms, and heartily kissed her. "Does that feel like the kiss of a man who is still near death?" he asked, his voice husky with desire.

Saxan grinned and draped her arms around his neck, then teased, "Mayhap swordplay is not all you need to practice." She giggled at his scowl.

"When are you coming back to my bed?" he demanded abruptly.

She blushed and stared at his throat in an attempt to avoid his eyes. This was the first time since he had shaken off his fever that he had asked her outright, but he had been strongly hinting at it for weeks. With the return of his strength had come a return of his desire and, suddenly, Saxan had found herself feeling shy and unattractive. Each time she undressed she saw her well-rounded belly which, due to the vigorous activity within, sometimes moved around. Although she loved what her awkward shape promised, she did not find it very attractive and was certain that Botolf would not either. She did not think she could bear returning to his bed only to have him reveal no desire for her.

"I did not wish to aggravate your wound," she murmured.

"My wound has been healed for weeks, You could not reopen it now unless you used a dagger."

"You need your rest. I would disturb you."

Botolf cupped her chin in his hand and turned her face up to his, studying her closely for a moment before asking, "Does your being with child prompt your reluctance to share my bed again?"

Saxan met his gaze and bit her lip nervously. There was a strange guarded look in his dark eyes. He had already made an assumption about her hesitation, and she had the feeling it was not only the wrong one, but probably unflattering as well. She decided that the wisest thing to do was to put aside her fear of sounding foolish and tell him the truth.

"I am fat," she replied.

"Pardon?" Botolf stared at her in total confusion.

"I am fat. I am ungainly, and my stomach sometimes moves around."

She scowled at him when his lips twitched with a smile, pleased to see him quickly subdue it. Just as she had feared, he found her silly. Saxan began to think it would have been easier to just get back into bed with him and have him turn away. It was possible that she hated to be thought silly as much as she dreaded being seen as undesirable. She tensed when he kissed her.

"You are with child, Saxan," Botolf said.

"I believe I know that."

"You did not think you would remain as slender as you were, did you?"

"I am not quite that stupid."

"Oh, you are not stupid at all. In fact, sometimes, you are far more clever than any man wishes his wife to be." He smoothed his hand over her stomach. "You are lovely."

"That is utter nonsense. I look quite grotesque when I am naked."

He grinned and started to unlace her gown, ignoring her attempts to slap away his hands. "Should a husband not have the right to judge that for himself?"

Saxan struggled for only a moment against his gentle but firm seduction. He kissed her until her senses swam. He was dressed only in his braies and hose, and the feel of his warm, taut skin beneath her hands only added to her desire for him. She forgot her fears, her doubts, and even that she was well rounded with her pregnancy. That pleasant oblivion ended when he tugged off the last of her clothes, tossed them aside, and stared at her. All her insecurities returned in one hot rush of embarrassment. She tried to cover herself, even as she admitted to herself that it was a foolish and useless gesture, but Botolf caught her hands in his.

"Ah, Saxan, you are quite lovely," he murmured.

"Such foolishness." She squirmed then gasped with surprise when he kissed her stomach.

"Not foolish." He pressed his cheek against her abdomen, smiling when he felt the baby kick. "Aye, you are well rounded, Saxan, but 'tis my seed which made you look this way. How could I not see that as lovely?"

"You are a skilled flatterer, Botolf," she said.

He kissed his way up to her mouth. "Nay, I but speak the truth."

When she felt the hard, indisputable proof of his arousal pressed against her leg, Saxan began to feel more at ease. She was not sure she believed his claims that she was beautiful, but she knew he did not find her ugly. His kisses and caresses soon had her passion strongly revived, but one small concern held her back from completely giving into the heady desire he awakened in her.

"Botolf, you may not find this stomach of mine repulsive," she said, her voice hoarse and unsteady as he nibbled at her ear. "Howbeit, you most certainly must find it obstructive."

"I believe we can work around it."

She had no chance to ask him how he planned to do that. His hungry kiss stopped her mouth and soon drove all clear thought from her mind. She clung to him, returning kiss for kiss, stroke for stroke, as their passion swiftly engulfed them. A brief check in her desire came when he moved to arrange their bodies in the spoon position. She was wondering what he was doing when he cocked her leg back over his and slowly joined their bodies. The only reply she could give to his hoarse query about how she felt was a gasp and a shudder of pure pleasure.

Botolf held Saxan in his arms and smoothed his hand over her stomach, his body sated and relaxed. "Are you certain that did not discomfort you?" he asked.

"Did I sound discomforted?" Saxan murmured as she stretched then reached for her scattered clothes.

" 'Tis sometimes hard to tell if a woman's squeals are of pleasure or pain."

She looked at him, seriously considering swatting him, and drawled, "If you are attempting to be amusing, I should keep practicing. That was not it." She ignored his laughter.

"Why are you getting dressed?" he asked as he reached for her.

Saxan neatly avoided his grasp, standing up to tug on her chemise. " 'Tis the middle of the day."

"You are not going to become shy and pious, are you?"

"I am certainly not going to become so bold I wish to sprawl abed naked for anyone to see. The chances of someone coming into the room are high. I am surprised that we have been left alone for so long."

"Ah, of course. I shall have to remember to bar my door," he murmured as he sat up and began to dress, laughing at the sour glance she sent him.

"And I did not come here, well," she blushed and waved her hand toward the tangled bedclothes, "for that. I came to tell you that I am going to look for herbs."

"Going? Going where? We have an herb garden behind the kitchens."

"Aye, and it is a very good one, but it does not have all I need."

"Surely that can wait until after you bear our child. There is plenty of time to add to the herb gardens."

"Nay, there is not. 'Tis the end of March and will be April in but a few days." She smoothed her hand over her stomach. "I will need the herbs and plants I seek very soon."

She watched him closely as she moved to pick up

her brush and tidy her tangled hair. As soon as the weather had improved and spring was in the air, she had known she would have to leave Regenford to search out the herbs and plants she needed for the birth of her child. They were not at Regenford, and none of the women were sure of what she wanted. Saxan had contemplated simply going on her own and not mentioning the expedition to Botolf, but had decided that would have been foolish. He would have found out, and then they would have argued. One look at his scowling face told her she had probably not evaded the argument by being so honest.

" 'Tis not safe outside the walls of Regenford," he said. "Now that winter has faded, the chances of the Scots raiding us have increased. And Cecil is still a threat, curse his eyes."

"Although we will soon be rid of Cecil's threat, the Scots shall always threaten us," she replied. "I cannot live my life entombed in Regenford, no matter how beautiful it is."

"You could certainly do so whilst you carry our child. Aye, especially now, when you are so close to your time."

"The fact that I am close to my time is exactly why I must go search out what I need. I would have liked to have gone sooner, but it was winter. Not only did the poor weather prevent me, but the plants I seek could not be found or would be in a useless condition. 'Tis still a little early in the year, but I think I can find much of what I need."

"Then send one of the women or Thylda."

"I would like to, but they do not know what I need. These are not remedies the women of Regenford are familiar with, and Thylda has not yet learned them. She will come with me and begin her lesson.

Denu taught me, but at that time Thylda was still too young."

Botolf shook his head, paced the room for a moment, then stared at her. "And how do you mean to travel?"

She took a deep breath to strengthen her determination, for she knew that Botolf was not going to like her reply. "I will ride."

"Ride a horse in your condition? Are you mad?"

"I do not mean to go for a gallop, simply ride to the meadows north of here, dismount, search out what I need for my potions and cures, and calmly ride back."

"You could still fall."

"Thylda will share the saddle with me so that I will be well protected."

For almost an hour, Botolf argued with her, even threatening to secure her in her room. Her determination to go did not waver. He knew that if he tried to order her to stay, she would find a way to do what she wanted. She had not been asking his permission, but giving him the courtesy of telling him what she was planning to do. Saxan clearly felt that the plants and mosses she was going to look for were vital to the birthing process.

"Then wait until I can go with you," he compromised. "You know I cannot do so today. I have men coming to meet with me and other business that cannot be rearranged at such late notice."

"And I do not really have the time to wait," Saxan said. "Aye, I could wait a day or two for you, but what if the next day it rains or it is too cold and windy? Today is warm; the sun shines, and I feel well enough to go."

"Have you been ill?"

"Nay, I just feel lazy or uncomfortable at times. I

have to go, Botolf. I need the mosses to stop the bleeding—"

He held up his hand to stop her explanations. "Nay, I do not really wish to hear why you need these things and what dire consequences of childbirth each one can help you overcome. I loathe this, but you may go. Howbeit, you will do so my way."

Saxan bit back a smile and carefully listened to his instructions. They were not as bad as she had thought they would be, although she was annoyed when he said she could not ride her black stallion Midnight. Even pointing out to him that Midnight would be the best horse to have if something went wrong did not change his mind. When he went to pick the six men-at-arms she had to take with her, she hurried to get ready.

"I am surprised Botolf has allowed this," Thylda said as she frowned down at the sturdy, placid mare she and Saxan were riding. "I am also thoroughly disgusted by his choice of mount."

Saxan laughed and patted the mare's thick neck. "He wanted to be certain we could not travel too swiftly or be thrown off."

"This poor beast could not move swiftly even if a pack of hounds began gnawing on her rump."

It was not easy for Saxan to restrain her laughter, especially when the six burly men-at-arms with them did not, but she tried to maintain some air of gravity. "She is a good horse and will take us where we need to go."

"Then collapse from old age and we shall have to walk back," Thylda muttered. "Do you think our brothers will arrive soon? I am to return to Wolfshead Hall for the summer and, although I have had a pleasant time at Regenford and do not wish to be separated from you, I am also eager to go home."

A small twinge of pain touched Saxan's heart. She knew it was caused by pleasant memories of Wolfshead Hall and the thought of her sister's leaving. Although she was content in her new life, she missed her old one. It would be nice if they could somehow be combined so that she could have everyone and everything she loved within easy reach, but she knew that was foolish. Botolf, Regenford, and whatever children she would bear were her life now.

"Our brothers should arrive any day now," she replied. "They promised they would be here when my time was near, and that is now. In truth, my time is so near it is why we are looking for plants and mosses despite the fact that it is still very early in the year."

"Do you think you will find what you need?"

"Some of it. Everything begins to bud and grow greener. They will not be as good as I should like, but I have not the time to wait for them to reach their full growth and strength."

"Saxan, are you afraid?" Thylda asked in a soft voice so that the men with them could not hear.

"Aye, a little bit," Saxan replied in an equally quiet tone. "After all, I have never had a child before. I just keep reminding myself that Denu and Tuesday have had no difficulties. If they came through childbirth unscathed, so can I."

"And Mother is said to have been much like us, and she had nine children."

"So I remind myself from time to time." She stared at the ground they rode over and waved the men to a halt. "I think this is a good place to look."

" 'Tis open," muttered John, the oldest of her six guards, as he dismounted.

"Is that not to your advantage?" Saxan asked.

"It could be to our disadvantage, too." He shrugged his wide shoulders. "Will you be long?"

"Nay, what I search for is not so hidden. 'Tis either easy to see and ready to pick or we must move to another spot." She collected her bag of birthing medicines and, with Thylda in tow, began to search for the medicinal plants she wanted.

Botolf fought to keep his mind on the work that had kept him at Regenford. He had regretted letting Saxan go from the moment she had ridden out of the gates. If she had not been seeking something to help her with her childbearing, he knew he would not have let her go at all. Even reminding himself that there had been no sightings of the Scots or of Cecil did not ease his mind. The Scots and Cecil had slipped dangerously close unseen before.

"There is a good day's work done," Wesley said as he poured himself some wine and looked around the nearly empty great hall. "When did Roger and Talbot wander away?"

"About half the way through Master Taylor's speech on the need to protect the townspeople with more vigor." Botolf took a long drink of wine and wondered if Saxan had finished her work yet.

"It would not have been quite so long if you had not kept asking him to repeat things." When Botolf did not respond to his complaint, Wesley nudged him. "Your thoughts have wandered all afternoon. Your little wife will be fine. She has six of our best men-at-arms with her."

"She is also near her time," Botolf grumbled. "It was madness to let her ride out when she is so far gone with child."

"You said she needed to collect medicines for the birthing."

"I know." He dragged his fingers through his hair. " 'Tis the only reason I let her go. I could not deny her the chance to collect things that might ease that trying time. Aye, and which might make it safer for her." He drummed his fingers on the table as he stared at the heavy doors to the great hall. "I just cannot shake the feeling that she is not safe out there."

"No man has seen hide nor hair of Cecil or the Scots."

"That does not mean they are not near at hand, and well you know it."

"You fret so because she carries your child."

"Mayhap. Howbeit, I will give her but two more hours and then I shall ride out after her."

Saxan straightened up, tossed the lump of moss into her sack, and rubbed her lower back. She had not found everything she wanted, but that did not surprise her. It was too early.

She looked over her shoulder, then cursed. She had been doing that the whole time she had been there. A strange foreboding had settled into her heart, and she could not shake it. Yet every time she looked around, she saw nothing. Sighing over her own skittishness, she looked at Thylda as her sister walked up to her.

"Are these what you seek?" Thylda asked, holding a tiny grouping of newly budding plants in her hands.

"Aye. They may be too young and tender, but toss them into the sack." She shivered and stared hard at the trees just behind Thylda. "This place unsettles me," she murmured.

Thylda looked behind her, shrugged, and looked

back at Saxan. "Mayhap being so far gone with child makes you fretful. There is nothing in those trees. I just came from there."

"I know, but I have not been able to shake my unease since just after we stopped here. There is no more worth gathering; I believe we had better leave." She took her sister's hand, signaled to John, who had stayed close by her side, and started back to where the horses stood. "I want to get away from those trees."

"Did you see someone, m'lady?" John asked, scowling as he looked around.

"Nay. I saw nothing. Mayhap I am just tired."

"Do you feel something?" Thylda whispered.

"I told you—I feel uneasy," Saxan replied, her voice low. "I have not had some vision if that is what you are asking. I just want to leave here." She stopped suddenly and cursed. "And I do not believe I will."

John screamed as an arrow thrust itself through his shoulder. Even as he fought to pull his sword with his uninjured left arm, several men raced out of the wood. Saxan knew at a glance that they were Scots. She looked to where the other five men from Regenford stood and saw that they were overwhelmed by the enemy. Saxan looked for an opening. A clear run to the old mare opened up, and she took it.

"Thylda, hurry to the mare," she ordered her sister, pushing the younger girl ahead of her as it became painfully clear that she could not run too far or too fast.

"I cannot leave you," Thylda protested.

"There is no sense in the both of us being captured. Try to get to the mare."

As Thylda started to run ahead of Saxan, she complained, "That old horse will never help me escape."

"Not if you never reach her because you are too busy complaining."

Saxan clutched at her side as she watched Thylda bolt ahead of her. She dreaded being captured by the Scots, but her pregnancy stole the speed she needed to get away. It made no sense to hold Thylda back as well. The men from Regenford would soon be defeated, and Thylda had to grab what could well be her only chance to escape.

Since she knew she could not run fast enough, Saxan slowed her pace. She did not want to hurt herself or the child she carried. Just as she began to regain her breath, the cramp in her side unknotting, she saw Thylda reach the mare. Saxan felt the first sharp sting of joy, thinking that her sister would slip free, only to cry out in denial and frustration when three burly Scots reached the girl and dragged her out of the saddle.

The Scots threw a cursing, thrashing Thylda onto the ground. Horror and fury gripped Saxan as she watched two of the men pin her sister down while a third fought to yank up her skirts. Those feelings gave Saxan the strength to run again, drawing her knife even as she gained speed. She knew she ought to keep trying to escape, that she should not try to help Thylda but should think only of saving herself and the child weighting her down. Saxan also knew that she could not run away and leave Thylda to be raped.

A cry of pure rage escaped her when she reached the men. She struck at the man who had wedged his way between Thylda's legs and was readying himself to take her. He put up his arm to protect himself, and she slashed at him, cutting the length of his forearm. The man screamed, clutching his bleeding arm as he tumbled off Thylda.

To Saxan's astonishment and delight, the two men holding Thylda down released her. One of them tried to swing at her, but his companion stopped him, berating the cursing man for trying to strike a pregnant woman. Saxan found it puzzling that a man ready to rape a young girl would be so appalled over his friend's attempt to hit her, but she did not take the time to try to understand his twisted morals. Thylda was already on her feet and, since the mare had run off, Saxan pushed her sister toward the wood. If they could reach the trees, they might be able to hide.

Yet again, Saxan fell behind as she and Thylda ran for the forest. The pain returned to her side, but she fought to ignore it. All she could think of was getting Thylda to a safe place before any other Scots tried to take their pleasure of the girl. She hissed a curse when she realized the men from Regenford had been killed or subdued, for there was a chilling hunter's cry as the Scots turned all their attention on her and Thylda. Although they were already in the thick wood, Saxan did not think they would have time to find the secure hiding place they needed.

Thylda crouched behind some tangled bushes, the fat buds on the branches adding to her cover, and caught Saxan as she stumbled up to her. "We need to catch our breath," she said between gasps for air. "Are you all right?"

"Nay, but I can go on." Saxan heard the Scots thrashing through the wood looking for them. "We dare not rest for long."

"I know, but we really need to rest or we shall just collapse at their feet."

Saxan grasped Thylda's hand, noticing that it trembled as badly as her own. "Are *you* all right?"

"Aye, although I suspect I shall have a nightmare or two about how nearly I was raped. That pig had not even realized that I was wearing braies, so I still had a few moments. I just pray that we are not captured."

Saxan nodded and squeezed Thylda's hand. She

could hear the fear and lack of hope in Thylda's voice. The chances of their eluding capture were slim, and now Thylda knew that capture meant rape. The Scots could have simply been caught up in the headiness of the attack, but there was no ignoring the fact that many soldiers considered women prisoners free for the taking. Saxan was terrified for her sister. Her fears for herself did not run as deep since she was the wife of a marcher lord and extremely pregnant.

"If we are captured, we must stress that we are Todds as well as our relationship to the Earl of Regenford," Saxan said.

"Do you think that will help? These men must consider our kinsmen their worst enemies."

"Aye, but they respect them and, most important, it will enhance our worth in ransom."

"Ah, of course, and our worth could fall if we were, er, damaged."

"Exactly. Now, we must move. We want to try and stay just beyond the area they are searching. If we are lucky, we may find an impenetrable hiding place or be able to slip back into one of the areas they have already searched and will not return to."

Saxan secured the hood of her cloak over her hair, indicating that Thylda should do the same. She thanked God that they had both dressed in nearly unrelenting brown, for the hues would now aid them in hiding. Hand in hand, they kept low, scurrying from bush to tree, crouching behind fallen logs, and trying to stay one step ahead of the Scots.

As the dangerous game continued, Saxan began to grow suspicious of the Scots' determination to find them. The longer the Scots stayed in the area, the greater the risk they would be discovered by the English, and Saxan was sure that they did not want that. Although there had been enough of the Scots to overwhelm her guard, there was certainly not enough of a force to survive any larger battle.

The moment the opportunity came, she and Thylda slipped back into the area the Scots had already searched. Her hopes began to rise as they edged closer to where the horses had been left. Judging by the number of men thrashing through the wood, there would be a light guard by the horses and they might be able to steal one. The moment the horses were in sight, she crouched behind a gnarled barrier of thorn bushes and tugged Thylda down beside her. Two Scots stood guard over the disarmed, battered men of Regenford, and one lolled against a tree near the horses.

"Do you think we can get a horse?" asked Thylda.

"Aye, and, oddly, that makes me very suspicious." She shrugged. "Mayhap these men simply cannot believe a woman would have the wit to slip back and try such a thing. I do not know what, but something about this whole attack begins to trouble me."

"It did seem rather lucky on their part to just happen upon us."

"Aye, very lucky. Mayhap too lucky."

"How could they know we would come here?"

"I have not made it a secret that I wished to come this way to search for my herbs and mosses. Nay, or that I needed to do it soon. You must recall how I spoke to every woman in Regenford to see if any of them knew enough to perform the chore for me."

"Do you think these men are after you? That this was all planned?"

"Aye, I begin to. They are risking a great deal by lingering here just to look for us. The Scots rarely dawdle. They rush in, do their cursed worst, and rush away, either home or further into England."

"But who would go to such trouble? Oh, do you think there is still a spy for Cecil in Regenford?"

"I begin to think so. I but pray that I am being foolishly suspicious and not as clever as I think."

"Cease praying, m'lady. Ye are verra clever indeed," drawled a deep voice from behind them, the Scottish burr clear to detect.

Saxan slowly turned around and sat up. She put her arm around Thylda, who huddled closer to her, and stared up at the man standing before them, his sword pointed at them with a deceptive casualness. His black eyes held an odd expression of cold amusement. He wore a loose white shirt and his plaid, the swirl of the skirt just touching his bare knees. Rough deerhide boots were laced around his strong calves. Long, thick black hair hung past his shoulders, framing his lean, almost hawkish face. He looked dark and dangerous. Saxan briefly allowed the traitorous thought into her head that he was somewhat barbarously beautiful.

"My men thought me a madmon when I said ye might circle round us and try to reach the horses," the man said, his mouth slanting ever so slightly into the ghost of a smile. "Ah, but I ken that the Todd lasses are a clever lot."

"You know that we are Todds?" Saxan asked.

"Aye, as ye have guessed, I ken exactly who ye are. Iain, Fraser, help the lasses to their feet," he ordered the two men with him. "I am Sir Bretton Graeme." He made a small bow.

"I am Lady Saxan Lavington," Saxan said. "This is my sister Mistress Thylda Todd."

"He said ye were with child," Bretton murmured, frowning at her stomach. "I dinnae think he kens how big ye are." He shrugged. " 'Tis further proof that ye are the one he seeks."

"Why would a Graeme work for an Englishman?"

Saxan demanded, certain that the man was in Cecil's hire.

"M'lady, ye were born and bred here. Surely ye ken that a Graeme will do most anything for a few coins." Once his men had a firm grip on the women, he sheathed his sword. "Delivering one English lord's pregnant wife to a brother seeking to usurp him is but a petty crime. Who am I to question the right or wrong of Cecil and Botolf Lavington's quarrels?"

There was the hint of bitterness in his voice, and Saxan wondered if it were bred of a reluctance to do what Cecil wanted. If the man had any distaste for what he did or had somehow been forced to do Cecil's bidding, she might find that a weakness to be exploited in her favor. Sir Graeme might not even know what Cecil intended to do to her. It might prove a crime the man wanted no part of.

"And what of the murder of a woman with child?" she asked.

"There has been no talk of that," he replied.

"Then why does he want me?"

"He doesnae confide in me, m'lady."

"Cecil wants Botolf dead. He wants me dead. He wants my child dead. Do you wish all that blood on your hands? If you take me to Cecil, it is the same as cutting my throat."

"Be quiet, woman." He pushed her toward the horses. "Ye will go to Cecil, and your sister and your men will be sold back to Regenford."

"You cannot give me to Cecil."

"Be quiet. I have heard all the English lies I can stomach for now."

Saxan fought back tears of hopelessness as she walked to the horses. She knew she was walking to her death; but worse, she knew she would be used to lead Botolf to his.

Seventeen

Saxan winced as one of Bretton's men helped her dismount. She studied the towerhouse they led her into. It was battered, but still strong enough to withstand an attack, at least long enough to cost the enemy dearly. She was sure her kinsmen and Botolf had closely inspected every property within a few days ride of Regenford, yet somehow Cecil had eluded them. The man's ability to do that made him chillingly dangerous.

Cecil waited in the great hall. Saxan needed a moment to adjust to the darkness of the room. The multitude of tallow candles could not push all the gloom away. She tried to stand straight and act brave when she was brought to stand before Cecil. His look of gleeful triumph made her shiver with cold. When his gaze fell to her stomach, the hatred which twisted his features caused her to take a step back and she came up hard against Sir Bretton's long frame.

As she wrestled her own fears into submission, she became aware of the tension in Bretton's body. Cecil and Sir Graeme were not allies, she was sure of it. Sir Graeme was caught in Cecil's trap as surely as she was, except that he had a chance to leave the trap alive.

"I have what ye sought," Bretton said to Cecil. "Now, return what ye hold."

"So impatient," Cecil murmured and lazily turned to one of the dozen armed men he had close at hand. "Martin, fetch our prisoners. We have no more need of them."

Saxan glanced up at Sir Graeme. His lean face was taut and white with fury. He wanted Cecil dead as badly as she did. She waited to see what Cecil held that would make Sir Graeme bow to his command no matter how distasteful he found it.

When Martin and another man returned with the prisoners, Saxan understood. They shoved two small boys and a girl who looked to be only a little younger than Thylda toward Bretton. The children hurried to him, got one brief hug, and then huddled behind him. That and their looks made her think that they were either his children or very close kin. She had never had a chance of talking Bretton out of bringing her to Cecil.

"And there they are, Graeme. Alive, as I promised," Cecil said.

"Aye, but 'tis clear from the bruises they carry that ye didnae make their stay an easy one," Bretton said, his low voice little more than a snarl. "Has any mon touched the lass?"

"Nay, I told you she would be safe."

Saxan looked at Bretton and said, "I hope you can offer the same assurances this cur gave you. You hold my youngest sister. You may also tell any man who eyes her with lust that, if he values his manhood, he will keep it away from my sister or there will be a veritable horde of my kinsmen seeking to cut it off." To her astonishment, a grin lightened his dark face.

"Aye, and a veritable horde of her kinswomen as weel," he drawled. "I ken the truth of that as weel as any mon. I was outside the walls of Wolfshead Hall with my father when your lady mother held us back until your father arrived to chase us away. She looked glorious upon those cursed walls. My father was much taken with her. Your wee sister will be safe."

"At least I have that small comfort."

"If you two are finished becoming the dearest of friends," Cecil sneered, "you may leave now, Graeme."

"I should watch my back as I leave," warned Saxan, glaring at Cecil. "A man who has sunk so low as to kill his own brother will not hesitate to betray an ally."

"I am weel aware of the mon I was forced to deal with," replied Bretton.

"Get out," snapped Cecil.

Saxan watched Bretton and his small group leave even as she kept an eye on Cecil. She wanted to hate the Scotsman for delivering her into the hands of her killer, but she could not. Watching him shepherd the three terrified children out of the great hall, she could understand why he had done what he had. She suspected that the one who allowed the children to fall into Cecil's hands would pay dearly.

Slowly, she turned to face Cecil and shivered when he smiled at her. "You think you have won."

"I have," he said, briefly tilting his tankard toward her in a mock salute. "I have you, and Botolf will walk into my hands like a lamb in the vain hope that he can save you and that child he has bloated you with."

"And so you will kill him and me and thus our child. What can you win with the blood of three people on your hands?"

"Everything—the lands, the titles, the wealth."

"Mayhap for a little while. A day, a week, a month, at most a year. I doubt you will laud it over anyone for long. In truth, I doubt you will be able to enjoy your ill-gotten gains at all. There will be so many swords pointed at you that, if they all struck at once, you would resemble a hedgehog."

"You are so certain your family will lust for my blood. I will be their liege lord."

"You will never be anything more to them than the murderer of their rightful liege lord and their kinswoman."

"Then I shall have to cull their numbers until they become more dutiful. Take her away, Martin." He held out his dagger. "But first cut a lock of that hair and remove her wedding band."

As calmly as she could, Saxan stood while Martin cut off one thick curl of her hair. She could not completely stop herself from struggling when he took the ring Botolf had given her. One hard glare at the burly man who took her by the arm was enough to make him ease his tight grip, but Saxan made no further attempt to fight his hold. With Cecil and all his men around and the awkwardness of her shape, any bolt for freedom would be utterly useless and would simply get her hurt. There was only one advantage to her weighty pregnancy and that was that none of the men looked at her with the glint of lust in their eyes. She wondered if she could use her condition to convince the men that she did not have to be watched closely either.

When they went up the tower stairs, instead of down into whatever dungeon Cecil had, Saxan breathed a hearty sigh of relief. She did not think she could have tolerated confinement in a dank, dark cell for long, and it would have seriously lessened any hope of escape, the chances of which were very small already.

Martin shoved her into a tiny room on the third

floor and slammed the door behind her. Saxan heard the bar slide into place and fought down a sudden surge of fear. She was simply locked in a room, not dead or facing some horrible torture, she reminded herself sternly. Any chance of escape had been severely limited, but she was still alive and there was some hope to be found in that.

After assuring herself that the small rope-slung bed was not too filthy, she sat down on it and studied her tiny prison. She doubted that even she could lie lengthwise on the floor without banging into the thick, damp walls. There was one arrow-slit for a window, but since she was three floors up, she knew there would be no escape through there. She grimaced as she admitted that she could never squeeze her well-rounded shape through it anyway.

Saxan lay down, wrinkling her nose at the musty smell. She was tired, too tired to make any clever plans for an escape. Whatever agenda Cecil had would need time to be set in motion. She would rest and then study her precarious position with a mind not clouded by exhaustion. As she closed her eyes, she prayed for a miracle. No matter how hard she tried to boost her hopes, she feared only divine intervention could save her now.

"How could you hand my sister over to that murdering cur?" Thylda demanded when Bretton rode into the rough camp his men had established just inside the Scottish border.

Bretton stared at the infuriated young woman as he dismounted. "May I brush the dirt of travel from myself ere ye begin to berate me?"

"You can brush yourself all you wish, you can

never brush away the filth you have splattered upon yourself by dealing with Cecil."

Thylda resisted the urge to take a step back when he glared at her. The moment his men had made camp she had tended to the men of Regenford. It struck her as odd that none of Botolf's men had been killed, although one was dangerously wounded. It was as if the Scots had tried to make the abduction as bloodless as possible. There was also no repeat of the attempt to rape her. She was being treated most courteously.

She began to wonder if Sir Bretton were not really Cecil's hireling, but had in fact been acting under coercion. As the time slipped by, she began to grow anxious for his return. If he had any sense of shame or guilt over what he had done, she was eager to try and take advantage of it. When he arrived and she saw the children, she knew she had been right—he had been forced to act as he had. Now all she had to do was find out just how badly he felt about it or, she glanced at the bruised pale-faced children, how furious he was with Cecil.

"Ye have a verra sharp tongue, wench," he said. "Considering the precarious position ye are in, ye might take better care of whom ye whet it on." He nodded his thanks to one of his men who had brought him a wineskin and taken his horse away. "Has a messenger been sent to Regenford, Iain?" he asked his sergeant-at-arms, who was crouched near the campfire next to Thylda.

"Aye," Iain replied. "We set the ransom as ye asked, though I still think 'tis too low."

"Nay. I have taken enough from the earl this day," he murmured as he sat down on the other side of Thylda and helped himself to some of the rabbit Iain had cooked.

"Aye," snapped Thylda. "You have murdered his

wife and unborn child." She leaned away when he spun around to glare at her.

"She was the price for my dead brother's children. I had no choice."

"There are always choices," she said, but her tone was softer for she did understand.

Before Bretton could say anything, one of his men rushed up and hissed, "Ye were right. That bastard has sent some of his murderers slinking after us. And they have killed our messenger to Regenford, for one of them rides his horse."

Thylda had no chance to ask what was happening. Bretton grabbed her by the arm, pulled her to her feet, and pushed her toward the Regenford men as he snapped out orders to his own men. She and the Regenford men were pushed and dragged a few yards from the camp and hidden amongst the trees and bushes. Two Scotsmen stood guard over them, but she got the feeling they were more for protection than restraint. When the men of Regenford encircled her, Thylda knew that they also sensed the approaching danger, one that threatened them and her as much as it did the Scots. As the first clash of swords echoed through the forest, she wondered where the children had gone.

She covered her ears to block out the sounds of men dying. It was chilling and frightening, for she could not see who was dying—enemy or protector. Thylda huddled closer inside the circle of men from Regenford and closed her eyes, praying that the fighting would end quickly.

" 'Tis done, lass," John said, gently tapping Thylda on the shoulder.

"Who won?" she asked as she opened her eyes.

"We did," replied Bretton as he grasped her by the hand and pulled her to her feet.

"You should leave the child with us," said John, eyeing Bretton with blatant distrust.

"There is no need to become so protective," said Bretton. "I swore to Lady Saxan that naught would happen to her sister. The lass is safe with me."

" 'Twas Cecil who attacked you," Thylda said as Bretton led her back to the campfire.

"Aye."

She looked at the three children huddled by the fire. There was no sign of the battle just fought except for the newly wounded Scots and two blanket-shrouded bodies. Thylda sat down by the fire, smiled at the children, and listened to Bretton order half his men to return home with the children, the dead, and the wounded.

"And what are you going to do?" Thylda asked, ignoring his look of surprise at her impertinence.

"Do ye expect me to discuss my plans with some wee English lass?"

"Aye, as I believe those plans may have something to do with me."

He cursed and combed his fingers through his hair. "I begin to understand why ye Todd women have such a reputation."

"We have a reputation?" she asked, pleased yet not sure she ought to be.

"Oh, aye, on both sides of the border. I am nay sure 'tis something ye should look so pleased about. Most ladies wouldnae like to be thought of as being as strong as a mon or as clever as one."

"True. We Todd women prefer to be thought of as stronger and cleverer." She smiled in surprise when he laughed.

"Ye just may be at that, lass. Aye, either that or too stupid and naive to be let loose upon the world." He met her angry scowl with a faint smile. "Aye, what I now plan does concern you and your men. I am taking ye all back to Regenford."

"I know that. You mean to ransom us."

"Nay, no longer. That cur Cecil thinks I am no longer a problem to him, that his murdering pack of dogs has cut me down. Ere he has time to realize that his betrayal has failed, he will be fighting for his life. If ye want any of that rabbit or a wee drink ere we ride for Regenford, ye had best have it now."

" 'Tis nearly dark," she protested even as she helped herself to the cooled rabbit and a long drink from the wineskin he held out to her.

"Now, lass, ye should ken as weel as anyone that the darkness has ne'er stopped a reiver."

Saxan slowly opened her eyes and tensed when she saw Cecil standing by the bed staring down at her. She could not completely stop herself from glancing at his hand to see if he held a dagger. The cold look in his eyes frightened her, but she fought her fear, refusing to reveal it to him. As calmly as she could, she sat up.

"What are you doing here?" she demanded.

"Admiring my brother's choice of woman. My only complaint is that this time he found one without a whore's heart. It has made things most difficult for me."

"Odella was not all the help you thought she would be?"

"Nay. She was never able to get close enough to Botolf. Merry, the kitchen maid, has been much more use. Of course, when she told me how I could get my hands on you, she became too helpful."

"How can anyone be too helpful?" She leaned

away when he reached out to touch her hair, but he still stroked his hand down the length of her braid.

"Her information was so valuable this time that I dared not risk the chance that she would be forced to reveal what she had told me."

"You killed her."

"Do you know of a surer way to silence someone?" he demanded. "I was hurried, however, and that troubles me. 'Twas not done as neatly as I wished it to be." He shrugged. "It matters not. Even if they find the little whore's body, it will gain them nothing. She cannot tell them who killed her or why, can she?"

He spoke of murder with such calm, Saxan could barely suppress a shudder. "I am surprised you have let Lady Odella and her father remain alive."

"Have I?"

She could not fully hide her shock. "You have killed them, too?"

"Not by my own hand, of course. If they are not dead now, they soon will be. The man I sent after them is very good."

"Your path is fairly choked with bodies. I do not understand how you can still believe you can go unpunished."

"Those I cannot trust, I kill. 'Tis quite simple."

"And you are quite mad." She bit back a cry when he backhanded her across the face.

"I would be careful with my words, m'lady. I have not forgotten that it is your fault my mother has turned from me." He clenched and unclenched his upraised fist, but did not strike her again.

"My fault? You have been trying to kill her son, your own brother. 'Tis only her great love for you that kept her from seeing the truth of that as soon as everyone else did. If you had not attacked me and threatened the life of her grandchild, she might still

be denying it. Even a mother cannot forgive such a crime."

"Do not deny your part in her change toward me," he said, a hint of anger roughening his cold voice. "I know all about the things you said to her after our meeting in the wood."

Saxan shook her head. She did not know how to deal with the man. He was unquestionably mad and saw everything in a twisted way. She knew she had no chance of talking him out of his plan to murder her and her child. He was not a man who could be reasoned with. She could not even begin to guess what words might prompt him to strike her again.

"And because Lady Mary cannot condone your killing her son, you blame me," she said. "And what do you blame Botolf for?"

"Everything." He gave her a cold smile. " 'Tis simply enough that he was born." He glanced toward her stomach, then met her eyes. "His child will not be."

"This child shares a blood kinship with you and has done you no wrong."

"That child can grow up to try and claim what is mine."

"You murdering bastard," she hissed, her fear and anger stealing her calm, and she was not surprised when he struck her again. She straightened up, glared at him, and wiped the blood from her lip.

" 'Ware, m'lady. I want you only to draw Botolf here. Your lifeless body will serve as bait nearly as well as your live one. True, I am eager to make Botolf watch as I end the life of his wife and the child he craves. Howbeit, I will forego that pleasure if you goad me. You may die sooner or later. 'Tis your choice."

"What a choice," she whispered and shuddered when he left.

His words made her want to weep, but she took several deep breaths to still the urge. Crying would gain her nothing and could even weaken her. Yet the images he had left in her mind chilled her to the bone. Her own death and that of her child was hard to face, but the thought of their murders being used to torture Botolf was horrifying. She covered her face with her hands and tried to calm herself enough to push those images away and think only of how to escape.

She walked to the narrow arrow-slit and leaned forward to look out. Even if she could squeeze her body through the opening, it was at least a thirty-foot drop down a sheer wall to rocky ground below. She circled the room, feeling the cool damp walls, but found no secreted door or hatch. As she sat back down on the bed, she stared morosely at the thick door. It was the only way out. She would either have to overpower someone and make a run for freedom, which was probably not possible in her condition, or pray that someone forgot to bar the door after leaving.

By the time she was brought some food and water, Saxan was despondent. She lay on her back on the tiny bed, staring up at the ceiling. It took her a moment to realize it was a young, timid maid who was setting down the tray of food on a battered table near the bed. Saxan could hardly believe her luck when she glanced out the open door and saw no guard. Either Cecil was so arrogant, so certain that he had won, he had grown lax, or his servants were witless fools.

Saxan leapt from the bed and raced for the open door. The maid cried out in alarm as Saxan slammed the door shut and barred it. She prayed no one had heard the maid call out. After a quick glance around to be sure there was no one else in the hall, Saxan began to creep toward the stairs. She knew that, if she failed to break free this time, she would never be given another chance.

She scrambled down the stone steps to the second floor and cursed. It was as devoid of hiding places as the floor she had just left. With her distinctive hair and shape, she could not walk about openly pretending to be one of the servants. The brief flare of heady anticipation that had invigorated her as she fled her room was slipping away fast. She was easy to recognize out in the open, and it was still daylight. Somewhere between the second floor of the towerhouse and the gates she had to meet someone. It began to look as if her recapture were inevitable.

After taking a deep breath to steady herself again, she slipped down the next flight of stairs. Even as she reached the bottom step, she heard voices. A panicked look around revealed no one in the hall, and she bolted for the door.

Her heart pounding so fast it was painful, Saxan clutched her cape around herself, hoping to disguise herself just enough to get across the bailey and out the gates. It was hard to resist the urge to run, but she knew that would draw too much attention to her. The gates were just a few feet away when a cry went up, and her heart jerked down into her stomach. Saxan did not even look to see who or how many were after her, she just ran.

She felt hands clutch at her cloak as she bolted through the gates. Her speed was drastically cut by the added weight of her baby and the awkward shape of her body, however, so she was not surprised when someone finally grabbed her from behind. Although the man's body buffeted her fall somewhat, she still hit the ground hard. Winded and aching, she could only squirm fruitlessly as he yanked her to her feet. Some of her composure had returned by the time she was dragged back to the towerhouse where Cecil waited by the door.

"That was very foolish of you," he said in a calm voice which did not match the painful way he grabbed her arm and pulled her back inside.

Saxan was too weighted with disappointment to fight as he forcefully led her back to her room. " 'Tis just as foolish to sit and wait for you to kill me."

"I should kill you now and save myself any further trouble." He shoved her into her tiny room.

"And lose your chance to torment Botolf?" she asked as she walked to the bed and sat down. "This little annoyance is not enough to make you forego that opportunity." She wanted to ask what had happened to the maid, but quickly decided it was probably better if she did not know.

"I have sent word to Botolf that I hold you. He will be here on the morrow."

"Mayhap he will guess at your treachery and refuse to walk into your trap."

"Nay, not the honorable Botolf. Even though he knows he will be walking to his death, he will come. A man like him can do nothing else, and that has always been his weakness. Good sleep."

She spat at him, but the door was already shut. When the bar was dropped, locking her in, she sagged onto the bed. She fought the urge to cry again, for she knew she would weep herself senseless if she began. It was a hard knot in her throat. That had been her one and only real chance. There was no doubt in her mind or heart. Yet again Cecil had made her feel helpless, and she detested him for that. All she could do now was wait and pray that Botolf would somehow thwart Cecil's deadly plans for them all.

* * *

Botolf was preparing to go and look for Saxan when his oldest man-at-arms, Matthew, hurried into the great hall. It was not only the concerned look on the man's craggy face that told Botolf he was not going to like the message the man brought; a chill of premonition settled in his veins, and he tensed.

"There is a messenger from Cecil, m'lord," Matthew said. "He wishes to talk with you."

Fear was like a hand tightly squeezing his heart. Botolf gripped the edge of the table so hard his hands hurt. He knew Cecil had Saxan. He also knew he would be the ransom his half-brother asked for her. Cecil would then kill him, Saxan, and their unborn child. What Botolf did not know was how, where, and when, and if there were going to be any way he and his newly begun family could escape the trap.

"Send him in," Botolf ordered as he retook his seat at the table.

"This is not promising," muttered Wesley as Matthew left.

"He has Saxan. Cecil holds my wife and my unborn child," Botolf said, the strain of fighting the turmoil inside him making his voice flat, almost lifeless.

"How can you know that? We have not been told anything," protested Wesley.

The cautious way Wesley eyed him made Botolf wonder what he looked like. He had hoped that his tightly strung emotions were well hidden. Then he wondered why he was making himself ill trying to hide those emotions. All he needed to do was keep enough of a rein on them to keep his head clear. If it were the trap he suspected, Botolf did not want to be so caught up in his own fear and anger he missed an opportunity to thwart whatever murderous plan Cecil had devised.

"Cecil has Saxan, Wesley," he replied. "I do not

need to be told—I just know. 'Tis why she has not returned."

"She may have just become very busy collecting plants," suggested Wesley.

"I pray it is something as innocent as that, but then why is Cecil sending a messenger?"

"To make his peace with you?"

"There is too much blood on his hands."

Before Wesley could say any more, Matthew led in Cecil's messenger. Cecil's minion was tall, dark, and narrow of face and form. Botolf thought that the man was a fitting lackey for Cecil.

"What does my half-brother want?" Botolf demanded, not even allowing the man time to introduce himself.

"His lordship—" the man began, his voice reedy and soft.

"Cecil is no lord. He never even got his spurs to be a knight. He is naught but a bastard."

"He holds your lady-wife."

Even though he had expected that, it still hit Botolf hard. He had to take a slow, deep breath simply to stop himself from lunging at the man. Common sense told him that that would gain him nothing, but he ached to strike out at something or someone. Beating Cecil's messenger senseless would certainly not help Saxan, however.

"Why should I believe your claim? What proof do you have?"

"This, m'lord." The man held out a square of cloth.

Botolf signaled Matthew to bring it to him. When his old retainer set the small package before him, Botolf was reluctant to open it. Cecil was a cruel man. He dreaded seeing what his souless brother felt was the proof he needed to support his claim. Noting that his hand shook, Botolf unwrapped the cloth, blindly smoothing it out as he stared at a painfully familiar lock of silver hair curled gently around the ring he had slipped upon Saxan's slender finger on their wedding day. He was not surprised, when he finally looked up, that Cecil's man took a hasty step back. If only part of the rage he felt was reflected in his eyes, Cecil's messenger had good cause to be terrified.

"So you hold my wife," he said. "Where is her sister and my men?"

"The Scots hold them and will soon ransom them."

"What does Cecil want for my wife?"

"You, m'lord."

"When and where?"

"Botolf," Wesley protested, but Botolf silenced him with one slashing movement of his hand.

"Tomorrow afternoon at the gates of Collinburn Tower. If you are not there by the time the sun sets, your lady-wife will die. You are to enter the gates alone, but you are allowed three companions so that you can be assured a safe journey."

"And what happens to my wife if I dutifully walk into Cecil's hands?"

"She will be released."

"Of course. Tell my half-brother I will be in front of his gates before sunset on the morrow."

The moment Matthew escorted Cecil's messenger out of the great hall, Wesley demanded, "You cannot just give yourself up to him. That is madness. His promise to release your wife is useless. You know that."

"Aye, but at the moment, I have no other choice," Botolf replied. "If I do not go, Saxan dies. If I go, I can at least gain more time. She is my wife, and she carries my child. I cannot turn my back on her even if the ransom is my death."

"This is nothing but a trap. The bastard must be convulsed with glee."

"Mayhap. What puzzles me is how did he know where she would be? I thought we had found the traitors in Regenford."

"There had to be someone here telling him where to look. There were no outsiders at Regenford to hear her plans."

"I think I know how he found out, m'lord," said Matthew as he returned and walked to where Botolf and Wesley sat at the head table. "I was coming to tell you of a gruesome discovery when Cecil's messenger arrived." He bowed. "If your lordship would come with me?"

Botolf reluctantly followed Matthew, Wesley keeping pace at his side. They went outside the walls to the banks of the stream which helped fill the moat around Regenford. Three men stood by a blanket-shrouded form. Still holding the lock of Saxan's hair and the ring Cecil's man had brought him, Botolf signaled the men to lift the blanket. He uttered an angry oath when he saw the body of a young woman.

" 'Tis Merry, the kitchen maid, m'lord," said Matthew. "She disappeared nearly three days ago. We thought she had run off with a man. Stephen here," he nodded toward the youngest of the three men, "was looking for peat or anything else to fuel his fire and found poor Merry in a shallow grave."

"Do you think she was giving Cecil information?" Botolf asked.

"Aye, I fear so. One of the other kitchen women had begun to suspect her. Too late to help her ladyship, though."

"And too late to help poor misguided Merry. For her loyalty she gets her throat cut. 'Tis clear that Cecil wished to be sure we could never discover Merry's betrayal or what secrets she told him. He must have been rushed, for this careless burial insured that we would find her, surmise that she had told him something, and know that he had been near at hand again." He laughed harshly. "He squats in Collinburn Tower, only a half-day's ride from here. He has always been near."

" 'Tis hard to find a man who knows every place you mean to go looking for him," Matthew said as he signaled the three men to take Merry's body away. "I am only sorry we did not find the lass sooner. It would have been a warning."

"Warning enough to make me hold Saxan here." Botolf turned to look down the road at the sound of approaching horsemen. "I fear the day is too filled with unpleasant surprises," he murmured when he recognized the riders as Saxan's brothers.

"They can help us save Saxan," Wesley said. "How is that unpleasant?"

"Because I must tell them that one of their sisters is being held by our deadliest enemy and their youngest sister is being held by the Scots." Botolf sighed as he started toward the keep. "Aye, and then I must convince them to wait. 'Twill not be easy to convince them that the best way to help Saxan is to do nothing at all."

Eighteen

"It appears that my brothers have arrived," Thylda said as she stared down at Regenford from her place before Bretton on his horse. "I believe that is Hunter walking toward the keep from the stables."

"That could make this more difficult," murmured Bretton.

"More difficult than telling a man you gave his pregnant wife to a murderer?"

"A night sleeping on the cold ground hasnae made ye any sweeter, I see."

"When you said we were riding at night, I thought we would come directly here. I do not understand why you then stopped to camp half the way here."

"I did *not* wish to remain where Cecil could find me and I didnae wish to spend a full night in a Sassanach's castle," Bretton explained as he nudged his horse into a slow walk. "I also ken that one of Cecil's dogs came here yestereve, so the earl now knows what danger his wife is in. That may make him readier to heed what I have to say."

"Or very eager to kill you."

"Aye, which is why ye shall stay in front of me until the truce is called."

"You would hide behind my skirts?"

"Aye, if it means I can stem the earl's wrath until

he is willing to listen to me. Then we may be able to save your sister."

"You keep hinting that you can help, but you never say how."

"Ye will ken the how of it soon enough. Now, silence. Ye would better spend your time thinking of ways to keep your kinsmen from killing me before I can offer my help."

Botolf sipped his ale and surveyed his solemn companions. They had gathered in the great hall to break their fast before riding to Collinburn Tower, but no one appeared to have much of an appetite. He was sure that last night had been the longest one of his life. Each time he had closed his eyes, he had been tormented by visions of what Saxan might be suffering at Cecil's hands. He had not rested at all, but what frustrated him most was that, after all those hours of waiting and thinking, he still had not devised a way to slip free of Cecil's tight grip.

The dark looks on Saxan's brothers' faces told him they had not thought of anything either. When he had informed them of all that had happened to their sisters, it had been hard to hold them. It had been dark before they had been calmed enough to listen to reason. The news that he could only approach with three companions had almost undone that work. They were loath to wait, but even more so to be left behind.

"You may find it hard to believe what has just ridden into Regenford," Hunter announced as he entered the great hall.

When a tall, dark man followed Hunter in, Thylda held close to his chest and three large well-armed men flanking him, Botolf joined the others in leaping to his feet. There was no doubt in his mind that these were the Scots Cecil's lackey had referred to. Botolf could not believe they would boldly march in to demand the ransom for one sister when they were undoubtedly responsible for handing the other sister over to a murderer.

"I should cut you down where you stand," Botolf hissed, drawing his sword.

"Ye would have to go through the lass first," said Bretton.

"So, you would cower behind a girl's skirts to save your cursed neck."

"Nay, just to keep my head on my shoulders until the bloodlust clears your eyes and you are ready to listen to what I have to say."

"Tell me what ransom you want and leave."

"The ransom I ask for this lass and your six men is that you allow me to aid you in defeating that bastard Cecil."

"All six of my men live?" Botolf asked, surprise briefly dimming his fury.

"Aye, although one is poorly. He hasnae died of his wounds yet, however, so there may still be hope."

"Am I wrong to think that you are the one who handed my wife over to Cecil?"

Bretton grimaced, then shrugged. "Cecil held my dead brother's three children." He eased his grip on Thylda when the men slowly began to resheath their swords. "Your wife was their ransom. He would take nothing else, not even my life in trade. So, I did his filthy work."

"Would you have me believe you did not know he intended to kill my wife?"

"Nay, I had guessed that. He made it clear enough."

Botolf slowly resheathed his sword and sat down, the others following his lead. "You cannot have come here just to explain yourself. No Scot would care what an Englishman thought of him. Certainly no Graeme would; and if I guess your badge and plaid correctly, you are a Graeme."

"Sir Bretton Graeme, m'lord." He gave Botolf a small bow.

"I still do not quite understand why you are here. 'Tis not the custom to bring the prisoners with you when you talk o'er the ransom."

"I am not ransoming them. I told ye that. I but wish to help ye get your wife back and kill that traitorous bastard." He released Thylda, who immediately hurried to her brothers' sides.

"You could not get those children back without giving Cecil my wife, so how can you help me? I cannot ride up to Collinburn gates with an army at my heels. Cecil would not hesitate to kill Saxan then."

"I ken how to get into the castle unseen," Bretton announced.

"Then why did you not rescue the children that way instead of bartering with my wife?"

"Because it was the children who told me."

For a long moment Botolf stared at the man, not sure he should trust him, yet knowing that he had little choice. If there were even the faintest chance that the Scotsman could help, he had to take it. Everything could be as simple as it appeared—Sir Graeme regretted doing what he had been forced to do by Cecil and now tried to make amends.

"Sit," he ordered in a curt voice, not fully ready to trust Graeme, but willing to listen to what he had to say. "I have not got much time, however, so you had best convince me quickly. I must get to Collinburn by sunset."

"I will begin by saying that ye must not get to Collinburn until as near to sunset as ye dare," Bretton said as he sat down opposite Thylda and her brothers and helped himself to some wine.

"I cannot dawdle. It could mean Saxan's life," Botolf protested.

"And I canna slip inside the towerhouse in the stark light of day."

"How do I know this is not just another of Cecil's tricks?"

"Ye dinnae and there isna anything I can do to make ye believe me. There is one thing to consider—ye have no plan now except to go to Cecil and die right alongside your wee wife and the bairn she carries. Even if I am playing some game, how much worse can your fate be?"

"No worse. Tell us your plan."

Saxan held her cloak tightly around herself to ward off the damp chill of Collinburn as she watched Cecil pace the great hall. As the time for Botolf's arrival drew near, he had released her from her room; but with a burly guard standing on either side of the chair she sat in, there was no chance of escape. What troubled her most at the moment was that she would probably have no chance to defend herself when Cecil finally struck. And neither would Botolf. If they had to die, she heartily wished they could meet their ends with a sword in their hands. Waiting to be butchered like an animal destined for the stew pot was no way to die.

She glanced out the narrow defensive window and was surprised at how late it was. If Botolf were coming, he would be arriving just as the sun finished disappearing over the horizon. She was emotionally torn over the possibility of his arrival. Part of her wanted him to care enough to offer his life for hers, but another larger part of her wanted him to be smart and stay away, not to join her and their child in death. It served no purpose except to satisfy honor, duty, and Cecil's greed. As much as she did not want to die, she wanted Botolf to live.

"Mayhap I misjudged him and your value," Cecil said, standing in front of her. He grabbed her roughly by the chin and forced her to look up at him. "You are pretty, but mayhap not enough to inspire love."

"Love?" She laughed even though she knew what she was about to say would hurt her. "Botolf does not love."

"My brother is a man of strong emotion."

"He may be, but your foolish whoring with his wife Alice taught him to control such weakening emotions as love and affection." She smiled when he frowned. "That was not part of your plan, was it?"

"And mayhap you make excuses to soothe your own vanity, badly bruised when you were unable to make your husband love you."

That stung, even though she knew it was not true, but she fought to hide her reaction. She did not want to let Cecil see that his words could affect her. If he thought he could reach her and hurt her with words, her last hours would be a worse torment than they already were.

"My vanity does not need some man's love and pretty words to nurse it. One would have to be a fool to build one's hopes upon such fleeting things."

"So you build your hopes upon that child. And now that, too, has proven to be a fleeting thing."

"Mayhap." She shrugged, astounded at her outward pose of calm, for inside she was a tight cold tangle of fear and fury. "When you first threatened this child, I was upset. Howbeit, the only other choice you have beside killing him is to raise him as your own child. I would prefer him to die than to be raised by a twisted, stinking killer like you."

She bit back a cry when he struck her, resisting the urge to touch her throbbing cheek as she glared at him. "What? No reminder that you can kill me sooner as well as later?"

"Botolf may well leave you to my mercy so that he may be free of that sharp tongue." He strode to the window and slapped the wall surrounding it. "He should be here. If not for you," he glanced back at Saxan, "then because duty and honor demand it."

"He is not witless. He may well have devised a plan that allows him to keep his honor, satisfies the call of duty, and yet does not require that he walk into your trap." Her eyes widened when he cursed, paced the great hall for a moment, then whirled to face her again. "You did not plan on his being able to think either, did you?"

"I begin to think that I shall no longer see your death as a necessity but as a pleasure."

"M'lord," called one of his men, waving Cecil over to a window. "I think he comes."

Saxan started to get up, intending to see if Botolf were entering the bailey of Collinburn, but Cecil pushed her roughly back into her chair. "I do not think you need to fear my giving him a warning," she said. "Botolf is fully aware of the fate he walks to. I doubt he even believes your promise of releasing me in trade for him."

"Yet he comes," Cecil murmured.

"You gave him little choice. I wish it were not so, but honor demands he do this. Whoever wrote the rules of honor obviously did not anticipate that good men would have to deal with traitorous, murdering filth like you." She ducked as he swung, and his fist just grazed her cheek. "If you spend too much time trying to beat the insults out of me, you will miss Botolf's arrival," she said as he prepared to hit her again.

"Watch her," Cecil commanded his men. "I do not want her and her husband to get close together. I do not know what one fool and one woman could do, but I do not intend to find out."

"Unlike your brother, 'tis clear that you are afraid to die," Saxan taunted.

Saxan did not flinch from his glare, but watched him coldly as he sat at the head of the hall facing the doors. It just did not seem possible that Botolf was going to walk in, surrender to his half-brother, and then Cecil would kill them both. She prayed everything was not as black as it looked and that Botolf had some plan.

"Has he gone into the towerhouse?" Hunter asked Bretton as they crouched in the tangled shrubs that rimmed the clearing encircling Collinburn.

"Aye. His three knights are being held in the bailey," Bretton answered after watching one of his men signal from a higher vantage point.

Hunter glanced back at the man Bretton had stationed high in a tree. "You can tell all that from a few waves of his hands?"

"We have a number of signals we all ken weel and a few we add as needed." Bretton looked up at the sky. "I think we can begin to creep to that hidden entrance now. 'Tis gloomy enough if we move cautiously."

" 'Tis hard to believe Cecil would make such an error as to let those children see this secret entrance," said Pitney, eyeing Bretton warily as he secured his scabbard more firmly against his body.

"Many a mon doesnae practice caution around women and children," replied Bretton. "They are simply too arrogant in their manhood to think that anyone other than another mon could do anything they needed to worry about. Aye, and those who have little to do with children never ken how much a child can see and understand the value of. When my nephew saw Cecil let that slut Merry in through a hidden doorway, he knew that was something he should remember."

"That may be another reason Cecil killed Merry," Hunter mused, following Bretton as the Scot began to creep through the undergrowth. " 'Twas not only her knowledge of his plans for Saxan he feared she would reveal."

"Aye, could be," agreed Bretton. "Or it could be that he is one of those men who just likes to kill people." He muttered an oath as a thorny branch skimmed sharply across his cheek. "The lass may have just decided that killing a woman big with child was not something she wanted any part of and Cecil realized he could no longer trust her. Here we be."

Pitney swore as Hunter and Bretton stopped so abruptly he bumped into them. "Where is it?"

"Just inside that thicket," Bretton replied, pointing to a gnarled clump of thorny bushes.

"They certainly did not need to fear that someone would stumble across it, or even wish to look in there if they were searching for it. I am fair surprised that our kitchen maid would dare it."

"A lass in love would fight most anything to get to her mon." Bretton signaled to one of his men who awkwardly crept forward, his arms full of thick blankets. "Toss them o'er the far side, laddie."

"Those children may have told you there was a secret way in, but how could they have known where it came out or what was around it, for I see that you came prepared for it."

"So suspicious for one so young," Bretton murmured. "My nephew heard your traitorous kitchen maid complain about the thorns and Cecil made a few comments on them as weel, such as how they nicely encircled and hid the opening. I sent a few men here to find it."

"But—"

"Leave it be, Pitney," Hunter ordered.

"I will not apologize for being cautious," Pitney said. "Even if I could ignore the fact that he is a Scot, one of a breed the Todds have fought since the first hearthstone was set down at Wolfshead Hall, there is all the rest to consider. He kidnapped our sisters and gave Saxan to Cecil. Now I am to just accept that he has had a change of heart?"

"You have no choice. From what Thylda herself told us, neither did he. Now, I think you will be the first man into that hole."

"Aye, so that I am the first one to get my throat cut."

"It might serve to still your clattering, impudent tongue."

"I do not suppose it has occurred to you that he could end the Todds right here by killing all the brothers," grumbled Pitney as he crept toward the now-open hatch door into the hidden passageway.

"Nay, I couldnae for one of you is missing," Bretton said and grinned when all four Todds stared at him. " 'Tis no great secret that the lord of Wolfshead Hall had five sons. Since I have not heard that any of you has died, I must assume that one of your number was left behind somewhere."

"Why should we do that?" asked Hunter.

"So that all the Todds dinnae die here. 'Tis a ploy

I used, doing all I could to insure my brother was safe if I had to face the sword." He shrugged. " 'Tis wise to try and insure that one of your blood breeds a few sons ere he joins the fray. Now, I think we should move, dinnae ye? I cannae be sure the earl can keep his brother talking too long."

"What awaits us at the end of this?" asked Hunter, nudging Pitney who slipped into the opening.

"A door into the dungeons and one, mayhap two guards." Bretton moved to follow Pitney. "If no one is being held in the dungeons, there may not be anyone there to greet us."

Hunter moved to follow him. "That would be a fine piece of luck, and I think we are past due for a bit of good fortune."

Saxan turned as the doors to the great hall opened and Botolf was led in by two of Cecil's men. She managed a smile for him when he looked her way. The tight angry expression that crossed his face told her better than any mirror how Cecil's blows had marked her. Botolf attempted to step toward her only to be stopped by his guards. When she saw that Botolf's scabbard was empty, her heart sank. Even if a chance came for them to attempt an escape, he could not fight his way out.

"You should not have come," she said.

"I could not leave you here," Botolf replied.

"Do you really think he will release me?"

"Nay, I knew long ago that his promises are empty, worthless things. Still, I could not leave you here."

" 'Tis no real comfort to know that you will die with me."

"We are not dead yet, sweeting."

She smiled, but inside her tension mounted. *We are*

not dead yet. They were simple words, possibly empty words of hope, yet something in the way he had said them put her on her guard. Instinct told her he had a plan. Saxan did not know what he could possibly do when they were both weaponless in a room with seven armed men, two by her, two by him, and two by Cecil. Nevertheless, she remained alert for some signal from Botolf. If he did have a plan, she did not want her inattention to complicate it. She kept her gaze fixed upon Botolf, waiting and hoping.

Botolf stood before Cecil and tried to control the fury and hate he felt for the man. He needed to be clearheaded. Although it was an advantage that Saxan was close at hand, the fact that two armed men guarded her could be a dangerous complication. Her brothers had insisted that she would be alert for any signal or action and respond accordingly, but Botolf had his doubts. She was a tiny, very pregnant woman, who, if the bruises on her face were any indication, had been through a terrifying ordeal. He was not able to tell her what was planned or even hint at it for fear Cecil would also catch the hint. All he could do was try to convey some message through his eyes and tone of voice. It was so tenuous it made him nervous. He tried to calm his apprehension by reminding himself that at least there was a chance for them and he would be foolish to allow any timidity to ruin it.

"You may release my wife now, Cecil," Botolf said. "My knights will return her to Regenford."

"Ah, well, I have changed my mind," Cecil replied and idly sipped his wine. "It would be unwise to let her go. I would just have to hunt her down later, her and whatever brat she spawns for you."

"Did you expect me to be surprised by that?"

"A little shocked perhaps, your high sense of honor offended."

"My honor is but a small part of what you offend." He watched Cecil reach for his sword and hesitate. Cecil did not want to make a quick end to it, and Botolf knew he could use that to his advantage. "Release Saxan, Cecil. She can gain you nothing."

"She carries your heir and she herself could impede me in gaining what is mine."

"Nothing is yours and if you harm her—"

Cecil interrupted him with a harsh laugh. "Will you rise from the dead to strike at me?"

"Nay, not I. The worst I could do is haunt you and, if it be possible, I will. Howbeit, if but one hair on her head be harmed, her kinsmen will swarm after you. You will not even have time to sip a tankard of wine at the head table of Regenford ere they come for you. S'truth, I doubt you will live long enough for her blood to dry on your sword." Botolf could tell by the slight narrowing of Cecil's eyes and the tightening of his jawline that the man knew it was no idle threat.

"I will have my men to fight them."

"You can never have enough men to fight all the Healdons, Todds, and Jagers who will ache to cut out your heart. You know this land and its people better than I. You know you can never win against them. They will make your death their crusade, and each of their sons and daughters will seek you out as soon as they come of age. Let her go, Cecil, and you may buy yourself a little time to savor your victory. Her kinsmen have sworn to avenge my murder, but they would not suffer the bloodlust they will if you kill her."

"You think to afright me, but it will not work." Cecil leaned forward. "Ye attribute too much loyalty and determination to too many people. Her kinsmen are as corruptible as anyone else. I will worry on them as they confront me. I will also be the earl, and they will be my vassals. They may speak of honor and vengeance now, but their song will change quickly enough when I rule them."

Botolf shook his head, quite certain that Cecil was mad. There was no other explanation for his blind singlemindedness, his refusal to see matters as they really were. The man had no rightful claims to anything their father had left and, in his greed to have it all, had tossed away the generous gifts the late earl had given him. It was also clear that Cecil did not believe he would suffer any retribution for his crimes. He thought a murderous usurper would be accepted and those who did not accept could be killed or coerced into silence. Only a moment's clear thought would show the man how wrong he was, but Cecil no longer had the ability to see reason.

He tried to think of something else to say, something that would inspire Cecil to argue with him, but not enrage the man into striking him or Saxan. If the Scotsman did not reveal himself as yet another of Cecil's hirelings, their rescuers would soon arrive; but Botolf knew he needed a few more moments. He decided to try and plead some more for the life of Saxan and their child. It would be the sort of thing Cecil would take great pleasure in.

"Instead of killing Saxan, why not take her as your wife?" he suggested. "She is beautiful, and you could claim the child as your own."

"And why should I do that?" Cecil asked as he slowly stood up. "Why should I want your leavings?"

"My leavings have graced your bed before. In truth, I begin to wonder if you can lure any other woman to your bed. 'Tis clear you must either pretend to be me or promise to murder me ere you can stir any woman's desire."

"Beat him," ordered Cecil, banging his fist upon the wooden planks so hard his tankard fell, staining the table.

Botolf heard Saxan scream out a protest even as he was grabbed from behind. He caught a glimpse of her being forced back into her seat as the first blow struck. Although he tried to break free and twisted his body to avoid the worst of the blows, his head was clouded with pain by the time Cecil called a halt to it. As he tried to clear his head and regain the breath knocked out of him, Botolf sank to his knees.

"Not so arrogant now, are we, brother of mine? Not so full of power and vanity, are you?" Cecil said, his voice a cold snarl of gloating. "I do not intend to kill you swiftly, you know. Nay, I mean to savor your death. You have been a thorn in my side for far too long, and I will make you suffer for that. Aye, and you will not die first," he hissed. "I mean to make you watch the death of the child you so badly wanted and your pretty little wife. I mean to make you grovel, to make you weak. I mean to make you see just how completely you have lost."

It did not surprise Botolf to see the taint of blood when he spat at Cecil. He was sure his lip was split, and he had cuts inside his mouth. "You could threaten to put my mother to the sword before my eyes, and I would still fight you."

"Fool, you have lost," Cecil screamed. "Admit it! Say it! You will die here."

"Nay, Cecil," he drawled even as he heard the doors to the great hall being kicked open. "You will die here."

Saxan did not even look to see who had burst into the hall. Botolf's brief hard look her way had been warning enough. She hurled herself to the floor and rolled out of the immediate reach of her guards. They decided quickly that the armed men racing into the room were more important than she was. Pitney was at her side a moment later, dragging her to a safe corner and staying at her side.

"Is that Sir Bretton Graeme?" she asked as she caught sight of the tall Scot.

"Aye," replied Pitney, never taking his eyes off the battle. "He led us in here."

" 'Tis a small force," she murmured, watching Botolf and Cecil circle each other.

"The rest have gone into the bailey to fight."

She winced then cursed as a distinct pain encircled her belly. Absently she touched the bag of medicines still secured to her skirts. If her labor had begun, perhaps prompted by all she had endured, she intended to hide it for as long as she could. Saxan did not intend to bear her child in Collinburn, the place that had nearly become her and Botolf's grave. Subtly taking deep, slow breaths to ease her discomfort, she fixed her attention on Botolf.

Botolf had grabbed the sword of one of his guards before they could stop him and had been armed and ready when Cecil attacked. The two men were equally matched; but, suddenly, Saxan knew Botolf would win. There would be no victory or escape for Cecil this time. She was heartily sorry that Botolf had to be the one to kill Cecil, but hoped that he would do so quickly. It was dark and there had been the promise of poor weather in the air. That would slow their journey back to Regenford. Saxan silently apologized for her heartlessness, but she wanted Cecil to meet his well-deserved end swiftly so that she could leave. She needed to leave soon so that she had time to get to her own bed and the women she knew could skillfully help her through the birth of her child.

"It ends here, Saxan," Pitney said.

"I know," she replied and exchanged a brief smile with him. His expression told her that he felt the same certainty she did.

Botolf swore when Cecil's sword point grazed his left arm. As he and Cecil circled each other, lunging and parrying, Botolf caught sight of Saxan, safe and guarded by Pitney. There was a calm, expectant look on her face; and he knew that she waited for him to defeat Cecil, that she was sure of his victory. Her confidence enhanced his own.

"Surrender, Cecil," he said in one last attempt to avoid killing the man.

"Why? To embrace the hangman's noose?" Cecil's voice was hoarse with fury. "Nay, I win or I die here."

"You cannot win. My men have already defeated yours. Even you can hear that that battle has been lost. 'Tis just you and me. All your men are dead, captured, or have fled to the hills. Even if you kill me, you will be cut down before I hit the floor."

"I will not swing from any scaffold or tree branch."

"Mayhap we can come to some agreement—exile or the Crusades."

"A crusade is exile. Nay, I live or die here. If it troubles you so much to kill me, then let me go." He laughed, breathless from the effort to hold his own against Botolf.

"If you force me, I will kill you. Surrender."

"And deny myself the chance of staining your hands with my blood, a brother's blood? If I must lose, I mean to force you to cut me down. Then at least I may savor the thought of how the pure, so honorable Botolf will be forever tormented by the crime of fratricide."

"You are no brother of mine," Botolf said in a cold voice and saw Cecil pale. "You cut all ties when you first threatened the lives of my wife and unborn child. Now you are no more to me than a murdering bastard who must pay for all his crimes with his own blood. If I must be the one to spill it, then so be it."

Botolf could tell by the look upon Cecil's face that he had somehow cut at the man's confidence. He was ready for the wild attack that followed, but not for how quickly it ended. He was not even sure how his sword was plunged into Cecil's body. Suddenly, he was staring into his half-brother's eyes, watching the film of death coat them. He yanked his sword free and watched Cecil fall. It was over and, although he was grieved, the strongest emotion he felt was relief.

"Botolf," called Saxan as she moved toward him.

He met her partway across the great hall and held her close. "Are you all right?"

"Aye. I am so sorry," she whispered and stretched up to kiss his cheek.

"So am I. Are you sure you are unhurt?"

"Only a bruise or two. I wish to return to Regenford now."

"But, 'tis night and the scent of rain is strong. It would be wiser to stay here until the morning."

"Nay," she said sharply. "I must leave this place."

He tried to argue with her, but she was adamant. Botolf knew he was bowing to her condition, loath to add to the upset she was already feeling. He thanked the Scots and gave them leave to rest at Collinburn, leaving unspoken yet clear the invitation to take what they pleased when they left. Although

Saxan's brothers made a few attempts to change her mind as well, nothing worked and they, too, prepared to leave for Regenford. Botolf prayed he was not making a mistake in pandering to her because of her pregnancy or allowing his own need to flee the dark memory of Collinburn to force him into taking an unwise step.

Nineteen

Saxan grimaced, tugging her cloak more tightly around herself, but it did little to ward off the chill of the rain. No one complained, but their displeasure reached out through the rain and the dark to touch her. She sat on Midnight in front of Botolf, but he had not yet noticed that she was already in labor. Saxan suspected it was another one of those things a man would not notice simply because he was so ignorant of the whole process.

In fact, she thought with a touch of humor, she could not have chosen a more unsuitable group of people to attend her on her childbed. A contraction tore through her that nearly caused her to cry out. She was not going to reach Regenford in time. The contractions were too strong and too close together. Ahead was a crofter's hut, and she knew she was going to have to stop there. She also knew that Botolf would be furious.

Botolf arranged his cloak around her, trying to shelter her from the cold and the wind. "The weather worsens. Are you all right?"

"Nay," she said between gritted teeth as another contraction rolled over her. "We must stop."

"You were hurt," he said, slowing the pace of his horse as he tried fruitlessly to see her in the dark.

"Nay, I fear our child does not wish to wait until

we reach Regenford." There was a long silence, and Botolf felt rigid behind her. "Botolf?"

"You are having the baby? Now?" he asked, his voice a hoarse whisper.

"Well, not right here in this saddle, although I might well do so if I do not find somewhere else soon."

"We should have stayed at Collinburn."

"Nay, I could not have my child in that place of death. 'Tis bad enough that we must carry the man with us, but I can accept that for Lady Mary's sake." She could not fully suppress a low moan as the next contraction wracked her body. "I believe an old crofter's hut lies just ahead. It will be shelter enough."

"Are you certain you cannot reach Regenford?"

"Very certain."

"I did not know this could happen with such swiftness."

"It may not be that quick. I could have begun my labor while I was still a captive. I was too upset to notice the contractions until they grew too strong to ignore."

The next few moments were hectic. Botolf sent three of his men ahead to do whatever they could to prepare the crofter's hut for Saxan. Despite her pain, Saxan found the men's horror at this turn of events somewhat amusing. Childbirth was not something they knew much about, and they definitely wanted no part of it.

When they reached the crofter's battered cottage, the light shining from it was welcoming. Botolf carried her inside, and she could see that his men had tried hard to make the deteriorating place comfortable, finding a dry corner and preparing a soft pallet for her near a fire. Once she was settled on the pallet, she looked up to see Botolf, his three knights, and four of her five brothers staring down at her in ill-disguised horror. They were going to be useless. She was not only the mother-to-be, but she would have to be her own midwife as well.

"I will need hot water," she said and almost laughed as her four brothers scrambled to get it.

"I think we should help them," mumbled Roger as he, Wesley, and Talbot hurried after the Todds.

" 'Tis raining. It will not be that difficult to find water," Botolf called after them, then looked at Saxan in astonishment when she giggled. "How can you laugh?"

" 'Tis funny." She tried to relax and not fight the contraction rippling through her. "Now, I fear you must listen closely, Botolf. 'Tis painfully clear that not one of you men knows much about childbirth."

"It is something best left to the women," he murmured as he crouched by her side and took her hand in his, wincing when she tightened her grip as she suffered through another contraction. "I do not feel at ease doing this."

"Mayhap one of my brothers will help. First, take the bag I have tied to the girdle of my skirts."

Botolf was not surprised to see his hands tremble as he fumbled to untie her bag. When Hunter entered with the others and began to heat some water, he ordered him to come and help. Since the storm had worsened and he could not force all the men to wait outside, Botolf had his men string a rope across the room and hang blankets from it so that Saxan could have some privacy. He then helped her undress to her chemise.

Saxan told Botolf and Hunter everything she could think of about the birthing process and what she would require them to do. She found it amusing that men who thought nothing of wading into the bloodshed of battle, sword in hand, should look so squeamish about this. Her contractions were growing so strong and continuous, however, she feared she might soon lose the ability to direct them step by step. She had Hunter mix her a hot drink of basil, honey, and nutmeg to ease the birth. He bathed her face with a cloth soaked in cool water and gently scented with lavender even as he helped her sip her drink.

"Is there anything you think I have not told you?" she asked, still panting from the strength of her last contraction.

"Aye. Where can we find a woman round here so that we may hand this duty o'er to her?" asked Hunter, smiling at her.

She laughed weakly. "Men—so quick to put the babe in there and so reluctant to help get it out."

"I do not like to see you suffer so," said Botolf.

" 'Tis a pain that will soon be gone and which brings great rewards. I hope you two men have paid close attention to all I said, for I think I am going to be too busy to help you."

A blindingly painful contraction swept over Saxan, but she struggled to hold back a scream. She gulped the herbal honied brew Hunter served her and savored the feel of the cool lavender-scented cloth, but doubted that any of her potions had the strength to ease the pain rippling through her almost constantly now. Despite her blurred vision she looked up at her husband and brother, wishing she could ease the fear they so clearly felt. Then the need to bring her child into the world stole all thought from her mind.

Through the fog of pain enfolding her, Saxan was faintly aware of Hunter's and Botolf's words of encouragement. Soon the pain blended into one all-encompassing need to push, the strain of it on her body frightening her. Through a haze she heard a scream and realized it was hers. She started to give into a tempting blackness, but a sharp cry pulled her back to consciousness.

"My baby is alive?" she asked.

"Aye, sweeting," Botolf replied, his voice hoarse with emotion. "We have a son."

Saxan turned her head to look at the squawling child Botolf held warily. She only caught a brief look, however, before her body demanded her full attention. Although she had suspected it for months, she was caught off guard when fierce contractions ripped through her body. She heard herself curse and caught a fleeting glimpse of both Botolf and Hunter going white.

"Saxan? What is wrong?" Botolf cried.

"Nothing is *wrong,*" she said through gritted teeth. "Best to put your first child down, Botolf."

Hunter laughed. "She has not finished. Surely you must have considered this possibility?"

"What possibility?" Botolf snapped, terrified for Saxan.

"Twins, you fool. Our family is rife with them. Pitney," Hunter cried.

Botolf had suspected Pitney had been lurking on the other side of the blanket wall, and his suspicion was proven by the speed with which the youth stuck his head in when Hunter called. Still stunned from the news that he would be the father of twins, Botolf watched blindly as, following Hunter's orders, Pitney took his firstborn from the earl's arms.

"Bathe him, swaddle him, and try to mark him as the firstborn," Hunter told Pitney.

"Mark him?" Botolf asked, struggling to shake free of his stunned immobility because Saxan was going to need him.

"Just a bit of cloth about his wrist for now," Hunter

said. "Your next child may be a girl or look nothing like his brother, so any other marking may be unnecessary."

"Just a tiny cut meant to leave a small scar, Botolf," Saxan said, hoping she could ease Botolf's confusion and worry before she lost the ability to do so. "We speak from experience when we tell you that if the children are too much alike, even the parents can grow confused at first. Long ago our family learned that, for all it pains the parents to do so, 'tis best to mark the firstborn so that all doubt can be eased by one quick look."

Botolf grimaced when, as another contraction tore through her, she tightened her grip on his hand. He suspected it would be a few days before his hand recovered from the birth of his children. Out of the corner of his eye he saw Pitney slip away with the baby and looked at Hunter.

"Does he know how to tend to it?" he asked.

"There are very few in our large family who are *not* familiar with babies."

Reassured, Botolf turned all his attention back to the heavily laboring Saxan. Nothing appeared to have gone wrong, yet his fear for her was still strong. She was so tiny, so delicately built; he did not understand how she could endure. Although she seemed oblivious to him as she fought to bring their second child into the world, he continued to offer words of encouragement.

His second son was smaller, but the strength of his first cry eased Botolf's concerns. He worked to clean Saxan, change her bedding, and even used the moss as padding to absorb the blood as she had instructed him to. Hunter and Pitney took care of the babies, marking the firstborn, bathing and swaddling them.

Saxan barely stirred as each child was put to her breast for the first time, and that frightened him.

Saxan fought to push aside the heavy exhaustion she felt. Her whole body ached. Slowly, she opened her eyes to look at her babies, Hunter holding one out for her to see and then Botolf showing her the other. For months she had seriously considered the possibility that she carried twins, but seeing them was still a shock. She mustered enough strength to kiss each baby before Hunter and Pitney took them away.

Despite Botolf's efforts to make her, Saxan could not eat. She did not have the strength or appetite. The smile she gave Botolf as he crawled beneath the blanket with her was not enough to smooth the worry lines from his face. He took her into his arms, his hold so gentle and tender she was prompted to look at him. The expression on his face as he brushed a few wisps of hair from her cheeks made her heart beat faster.

"I am fine, Botolf," she said and felt his arms tighten around her.

"Are you certain?" he asked, his voice soft and hoarse.

"Aye, very certain. I am just very, very tired." She frowned when he gave a shaky laugh. Botolf was clearly emotional, and she wished she were not too exhausted to try to judge exactly what he was feeling.

"I am not surprised. You are so small," he whispered and touched a kiss to her forehead. "Thank you for my sons."

"You are very welcome, m'lord."

"Although I was deeply moved to share in their birth, I think I prefer leaving such things to the women." He smoothed his hand down her thick braid. "I cannot abide watching you suffer, knowing I can do nothing for you."

"You proved to be very skilled."

"And you proved to be far stronger than anyone would expect. I do not think you can ever understand how grateful I am that you would endure that for me when I can give you so little."

"You give me a lot," she said and knew she was losing the battle against the need to sleep, for her words were faintly slurred.

"Nay, I deny you a lot and for no other reason than I am a complete coward."

"You are no coward, Botolf."

"Aye, sweeting, I am a very great coward, but now is not the time to discuss that. You need to rest."

Saxan did not want to sleep now when he was speaking so openly, but she had no choice. Sleep was pulling at her so strongly she could not fight it any longer, no matter how desperately she wanted to hear Botolf say more. Men picked the worst times to be open and reveal their emotions! She vowed not to let him forget the heart-to-heart talk he had vaguely promised her.

Botolf entered the bedchamber, and Saxan watched as he washed up for bed. It had been almost three months since the twins had entered the world in the dark crofter's hut. She was bathed, strong, and ready to renew the more intimate side of their married life.

It was also time to have that long, intimate talk Botolf had tentatively begun after their birth. He had never been cold or too distant; but since that night, he had definitely been more affectionate, more open, and there was a much more tender expression in his eyes when he looked at her. Something had changed and she was tired of trying to guess what that was. She took a sip of cider from the lovely silver tankard

Sir Bretton Graeme had sent her and eyed Botolf closely as he shed the last of his clothes and slid into bed beside her.

"I am still not sure we ought to be accepting gifts from that Scotsman," Botolf murmured as he frowned at her tankard before taking a drink from it.

" 'Tis just the one," she said, retrieving the tankard, finishing her drink and setting it on the bedside table. "A small gift in the way of an apology, although none was really needed, and a thank you for naming our son Bretton."

"Naming a marcher lord's son after a Scot must be a sign of madness."

"We needed a second name. We had only the one and could not name both boys Leofric after your father. And, Sir Bretton did not have to help us, but he did." She settled herself into his arms, smiling crookedly when he gave her a chaste kiss on the forehead. "What troubles me about it all is that he insisted Thylda be the one to meet him and that she was a little too eager to do so. Now, I do not wish to talk about them."

"Oh? And what do you wish to talk about?"

"I do not wish to talk at all," she murmured, sliding her hand down his stomach.

When her small hand inched lower and she curled her long, soft fingers around his manhood, Botolf groaned as his barely controlled passion immediately flared to life. He had been fighting to subdue his desire for her since only days after the birth. That whole sequence of events, from her capture to the birth of the twins, had made him face how much she meant to him. Despite this efforts to fight it, the need for her had grown and deepened within him. He had faced those emotions, freed them, and they had made his desire even harder to control. He ached to make love to her and try to convey all the emotions he was too afraid to speak of.

"Is this wise so soon after a hard birth?" he asked, but gave in to the temptation to stroke her sides, lingering over the curve of her hip.

"It was no harder than many another birth, just a little more exhausting. I am fine."

"Are you sure?"

"More than sure," she whispered as she traced the shape of his ear with her tongue.

Botolf growled softly as he rolled so that she was sprawled beneath him. "When you tempt a man so, you had best be prepared to pay the consequences, m'lady."

"I am quite eager to pay a few of those particular consequences, my lord." She rubbed her feet up and down his calves.

"They could be fierce and exacted several times during the night." He unlaced her thin night rail and tossed it aside.

"Mayhap it is your strength we should worry about."

"Oh—ho! A dare, is it? You have thrown down a gauntlet I must pick up. What man could resist such a challenge?"

"None, I should think." She grinned as he kissed the tip of her nose. "Howbeit, I begin to think there are one or two who would keep talking about meeting the challenge until the one who made it falls asleep."

Botolf laughed and kissed her, his amusement immediately swept away by desire. He struggled to rein in his passion enough to enjoy the reuniting of their bodies. It had only been a few months, but it felt like it had been years. He stroked and kissed her, trying to leave no place on her slim frame untouched before he lost all control. The fierce passion Saxan was openly displaying was quickly severing his restraints. When she dragged her nails lightly up the backs of his thighs as she rubbed her body invitingly against him, he could wait no longer.

Saxan met his fierce possession with an equal greed. Botolf cupped her face in his hands, kissing her hungrily, matching the thrust of his body with the strokes of his tongue. When he felt her crest nearing, he grasped her by her slim hips and held her tightly against him. Their cries of release blended perfectly as they reached passion's heights as one. For a long time after he collapsed in her arms, he held her close, dotting her neck with kisses. When he finally moved, it was only to roll onto his back; Saxan still held close to him.

"I have missed that," he murmured, combing his fingers through her hair.

"A high price to pay for a child?" she asked as she lifted her head to look at him.

He laughed when he saw the glint of mischief in her beautiful eyes. "That is a difficult question to answer." He frowned as if considering it, then chuckled when she struck him playfully on the chest. "Nay, nay. Have mercy, woman."

"Your sons are going to look like you," she said, smoothing his tousled black hair off his face.

"With your eyes. 'Tis actually a striking combination."

"A handsome one."

"Aye, of course." He exchanged a grin with her.

He stared up at her, suddenly serious, and Saxan saw that tender look in his eyes again. She knew that now was the time to have the talk they had almost begun three months ago. An attack of cowardice grabbed her by the throat, choking back the words she had planned to say. What if she were misreading his expressions, seeing more in a slight change than there actually was? What if he really had not wanted to say anything about his feelings that night in the crofter's hut? She knew she would feel dreadful if she exposed her feelings and asked things of him he was not ready to give, only to discover that he had just wanted to discuss their children that night. Or that the tender looks were no more than a natural softening of a man toward the mother of his children.

"You are looking very solemn, dearling," Botolf murmured.

"Am I?"

"Aye, you are. Do you have something you need to tell me? There is nothing wrong with our sons, is there?"

Saxan sighed and rolled off him. It was embarrassing to admit it, but she was jealous of her own children and the blatant affection and interest they received from Botolf. When he turned on his side to look at her, she glanced up and knew she would have to say something. He looked worried and confused.

"There is nothing wrong with Leofric and Bretton. They are strong, healthy, and getting bigger each and every day. But you know that," she muttered, "since you spend so much time with them."

"Why do you sound displeased by that?"

"Do I? I did not mean to. 'Tis good that you care for them and see them a lot. Too many fathers do not. The boys are fostered out, and the father only notices them when they are old enough to pick up a sword."

"Are you already worrying about fostering? If you do not want it done, you may just say so. I was not fostered. My father saw no need to send me away to learn things I could learn at Merewood and Regenford. In truth, my father was not sure he trusted the custom. I am not sure I do either. What do I gain if I give my son to another man to raise? Nothing that I can see."

"Very few of my kinsmen are fostered out. They stay a short while with other kinsmen if it is felt to be needed." Saxan was briefly distracted from her plan for a heart-to-heart talk by this welcome revelation. It had not become a real concern yet, but she had already found herself looking at her infant sons and wondering if she would be forced to bear the pain of having them fostered out, sent away to be raised and trained by other people. "I am more than pleased I will be allowed to follow my family's way."

He smoothed his hand up and down her arm as he studied her. "And I am pleased I can ease that worry for you. Howbeit, 'tis still not what has you looking so solemn." He frowned. "Aye, and uncertain. Come, am I to keep guessing and talking aimlessly in the hope of striking upon the matter which truly troubles you?"

"Nay." She smiled faintly. "Although I must say 'tis very tempting to let you try."

"Just tell me what has made you so serious, so contemplative."

"Do you recall that night in the crofter's shed?"

"I shall never forget it. I do not believe I will ever be so terrified *and* so enthralled at the same time again."

"Well, you said a few things I found very interesting, but I was too weary to pursue the discussion. You told me to rest and that we would talk about it later. It has been three months. I believe I am well rested now."

Botolf stared at her and lightly traced the delicate shape of her face with his fingertips. He had wondered when she would remind him of that vague promise to talk. Several times in the past three months he had caught her staring at him, an expectant, almost-hopeful look on her face. It was past time to set his own fears aside. He had had plenty of time to adjust to the realization of his own feelings, to finally accept that, even though they could cause him great pain, they could also give him great joy. He also owed it to Saxan, who could well return his feelings, to take a chance and be honest with her.

"Do you have any idea of how frightened I was when Cecil captured you?" he asked, threading his fingers through her hair.

"As much as I was?" she asked softly.

"Aye, mayhap. I cannot say I have never tasted fear before, but I know I have never suffered such a gut-wrenching terror, one that threatened to steal all my wits and skill as a knight."

"I should not have insisted on going outside Regenford. I put us all in danger."

"That did occur to me," he drawled and exchanged a grin with her. "But you cannot hide behind these walls every day, fearing what might lurk out there. That is no life. We did everything correctly. I begin to think that final confrontation with Cecil was fated, that we could have done nothing to change that."

"Nay, mayhap not." She turned and moved into his arms. "I am not sure I like things to be fated."

"Oh? I think you and I were fated." He kissed her on the nose when she looked up at him. "For you to reach my side, dagger in hand, required a somewhat astonishing and complicated sequence of events."

"It only required my cousins to be their usual lack-witted selves."

Botolf laughed and kissed her forehead. "From the moment I wrestled you to the floor and realized you were a woman, my life began to change." He sighed and hugged her close. "I had locked myself away, Saxan. My mother tried to talk to me about how wrong and foolish that was after I recovered from my fever, but I did not really listen. I did not want to. In truth, I did my best to insure that she did not continue that particular discussion because what she was saying was all too true. I ran from it, and I am not proud of that."

"People often run from the truth, especially when it may force them to change."

"Aye, and I ran from you."

She leaned back to look at him in confusion. "You ran from me?"

"I tried to. Each time you touched something I tried to keep buried inside of me, I tried all the harder to close it away. I wanted peace and comfort in our marriage, Saxan. I truly believed I could not have that if I allowed emotion to clutter our relationship. Passion was enough, but I was determined that there would be nothing deeper than that."

"Because of Alice."

"Aye, and other women I was acquainted with, especially at court."

"And you just assumed *I* would be like *them?"* Saxan sat up, outrage roughening her voice.

Botolf eyed her warily. She looked as if she wanted to thrash him or find someone big enough to do it for her. It was not going to be easy to confess his feelings and, perhaps, gain some declaration of the same from her, if she were furious.

"It was unfair. I know that. I think I have always known it, but it took my mother's saying so in very plain language for me to really look at what I was doing. I would not judge all men because of the actions of a few, so why was I doing it to women? I also found it hard to judge you that way. Whenever

I found myself softening, I never thought *beware, she is like Alice.* Nay, I always feared that you could hurt me far more than Alice ever could or did." He looked at her in slight surprise when she returned to his arms.

Saxan smiled at him, amused by his surprise, and kissed him on the mouth. She doubted he would ever realize how much he had revealed with that last sentence or how much it meant to her. She had also realized that, no matter how infuriating and insulting his opinion was, it was not the time to get angry. That would stop what appeared to be a full confession of his feelings and that was the last thing she wanted to do.

"I am glad to see that you came to your senses," she murmured.

"Oh, aye, I did, but it was still slow. As a result I have denied you and myself for a year."

"You have been a good husband, Botolf. You have given me a lot."

"But nothing of myself save for my passion. Well, 'tis past time for cowering behind my pride and fear of pain." He cupped her face in his hands. "I love you." He touched a kiss to her mouth then frowned when he realized she had gone rigid and was staring at him. "I realize you may not return my feelings, especially since I have done nothing to win your heart—" He stopped talking immediately when she placed her unsteady fingers over his mouth.

"I had not expected you to just blurt it out," she said, her voice soft and trembling with emotion. "I love you, too." She laughed shakily as he kissed her with a fierce hunger that swiftly ignited her passion. He held her tightly. "I think I have loved you from the start," she continued, smoothing her hand over his broad chest. "I was just too uncertain about what love was, so I hesitated to call my feelings by that name."

"And I fought every indication that I was falling in love with you. I think it was there almost from the start as well, but I did not want to recognize it."

She murmured her pleasure when he ran his hands down her back. "And when did you finally stop fighting?"

"When Cecil took you. I could no longer deny it to myself." He turned so that she was sprawled beneath him and he could look directly into her eyes. "It was when I was confronted with the very real possibility of losing you forever. The mere thought of that caused me such pain, I realized I was accomplishing nothing by fighting and hiding my emotions. It was easy enough to walk into Cecil's hold because I had no fear of dying with you, but a great fear, a wrenching terror, of living without you."

Saxan curled her arms around his neck and kissed him, trying to convey the depth of the emotion she felt in her embrace. Here was everything she could ever want. Happiness welled up in her so strongly it brought tears to her eyes. She smiled when Botolf looked at her, gently brushing a stray tear from her cheek.

"This makes you cry?" he asked, tentatively.

"Since I first understood that, aye, I did love you, I have feared that you would never love me back."

"I am sorry I put you through that torment. I suffered the same fear for only a little while, and I would not wish that torture upon anyone. From the beginning you have given me so much and I have treated you most unkindly."

"Nay. You never asked me to love you, never tried to force me to give you any more than duty, passion, and children. 'Tis best that you fought your demons before you freed your heart or those old wounds could dim this joy. Now you can give me a heart that is whole and unshadowed. That can only be good. Now we need not fear that every word or action could weaken what we can share. Our love can only grow stronger."

"Aye, and last, enriching the rest of our lives."

"And longer. Even death cannot still the love I have for you, my fine, dark knight."

Saxan welcomed his hungry kiss. She had been right. Botolf Lavington was indeed a man of strong emotion, and she would joyfully revel in that for years to come.

Please turn the page for an
exciting sneak preview of
Hannah Howell's
next captivating historical romance
MY VALIANT KNIGHT
coming in January 1996
from Zebra Books

Scottish Highlands—1210

Ainslee tensed, abruptly yanked from her dark memories of the past. She heard nothing, yet every muscle in her body was taut with a sense of danger. Her eyes widened and her heartbeat increased to a painful speed when she saw the men step out of the disguising shadows of the deep wood into the clearing. There was no time to use her bow. She might lose one arrow, but then they would be on her. Slowly, she rose to her feet and took a protective stance over Ronald, her sword held securely and threateningly in her small hands.

Gabel stared at the girl and, realizing he was gaping, quickly closed his mouth. She was taut and prepared to do battle, her thick red hair sweeping around her slim shoulders, stirred to life by the increasing wind. Like some wild thing cornered, she faced them with the bravado of desperation.

He looked slowly over every slender, well-shaped inch of her. Her tunic was of a light-grey hue and fit snugly over her strong slim arms. The bliand was of a bright woolen plaid and the three-quarter-length overtunic was slit up both sides and laced tightly onto her shapely form. He expected that beneath that feminine attire she wore long loose trousers of a heavy linen and hose of an equally thick cloth. That and the soft leather boots which reached to her knees and were held in place by cross gaitering were why, when he had seen her riding, he had thought that she was a he. Gabel wondered briefly if she wore a man's braies as well. Since she wore such heavy clothes beneath her gown, he suspected that she was also more slender than she looked.

His attention was drawn back to her hair, and he understood why she had worn a snug hood. No braids held the thick, dark-red hair in check, the fading light picking out the golden highlights in its depths. Her hair was like some glorious beacon, hanging beyond her waist in heavy waves, and he was not surprised when the sight stirred his blood. He doubted that any man could view such beauty and remain cold. As his desire quickly surged to a crippling height, Gabel looked at his men. They clearly felt as stunned and as moved as he did. The situation needed to be smoothed over and swiftly.

"M'lady," Gabel called to the girl in a light, friendly voice as he stepped to the fore of his men. "You cannot believe that you can take us all."

"Nay, my fine knight, I am not such a fool," she replied as she crouched into a fighting stance. "Howbeit, I shall leave ye sorely aware that ye have faced a MacNairn."

"Sweet heaven," murmured Justice as he edged closer to Gabel. "That bastard MacNairn breeds some very fine women."

"So, you believe she is that laird's spawn?" Gabel did not even glance at his cousin, his gaze fixed unwaveringly on the girl.

"Aye, Gabel. She wears the MacNairn brooch at her shoulder. You could see that for yourself if you would but tear your eyes from her hair."

"Glorious, is it not? I have a craving to wrap myself in its thick waves. I will see if I can hold her gaze upon me whilst you edge up to her from the left. Tread warily, cousin. She may well be able to wield that sword with some skill. It looks to have been made specifically to fit her small hands." Gabel smiled at the girl as Justice inched away. "There is no need for bloodshed, m'lady. We do not seek to harm you."

"Oh?" Ainslee glanced at his men. "Ye brought a score or more fighting men with you so that we might exchange court gossip? Stay back," she hissed when she saw him edge toward her, Ugly's low growl of warning a confirmation of her suspicion that the man tried to sneak up on her. "Watch Ronald," she ordered the dog, and the animal adopted an unmovable stance by the unconscious Scot.

"Do not urge your beast to the attack, m'lady, for my men will quickly cut him down." Gabel knew he had judged her right when her eyes widened; she glanced nervously at the dog and then glared at him. The animal was trained to command and eager to protect her and the man. It meant she had spent time and affection on the grotesque beast. "Give over, m'lady, and you will come to no harm."

Ainslee studied him closely and realized that she wanted to believe him, but she suddenly did not trust her own instincts. The man was too handsome, and she was far too aware of that despite the tense confrontation they were engaged in. He was taller than most of his men, his long body lean and muscular. Since he wore only his braies and boots, she could see that his complexion was naturally dark, not browned by the sun. His somewhat angular features could not really be called handsome, but they intrigued the eye and demanded respect. An aquiline nose was framed by well-defined high cheekbones and led to a firm, slightly thin-lipped mouth. Straight dark brows crowned rich, deep-brown eyes so heavily lashed Ainslee was certain they had caused some women to suffer sharp pangs of envy. His jaw was firm, implying a strength she had no doubt he possessed in full measure. His broad chest was smooth and hairless, a hint of dark curls finally appearing just below his navel and lightly dusting what little showed of his long, well-shaped legs. Both her mind and her body found the man far too intriguing, and she fought hard against that ill-timed interest.

She made a sharp, scornful noise in response to his claim that she would come to no harm. "Do ye mean to escort me home then, Norman?"

"I mean to hold you to ransom," Gabel replied.

There was such a strong tone of honesty in his voice that Ainslee almost submitted, but she suddenly espied one of the Normans stealthily approaching her from the side. Swiftly, not allowing herself time to consider what she was doing, she pulled her dagger from beneath the wide girdle at her waist and hurled it at the man. Confident that her weapon had found its mark, she fixed all her attention on the man facing her, for she knew there would be swift and lethal retribution.

"Justice," cried Gabel when his cousin yelped in pain. "Are you harmed?"

"Aye, but 'tis only a small wound in my shoulder," Justice replied.

Gabel scowled at the slim girl who stood before him, her sword at the ready. "You try me sorely, woman."

"Aye, but not enough, I am thinking," Ainslee replied, "for ye still cower out of reach of my sword, me frail, trembling knight."

He grit his teeth against the sting caused by the

sneer in her melodious voice. "I will fight no woman."

"Then ye shall be a lot easier for me to kill," she said with a chilling sweetness even as she attacked him.

Gabel barely dodged the blade of her sword in time. His eyes widened as he raised his own sword in defense. Her swing had been well practiced, not merely a blind thrust. The girl did possess some skill. His men fell silent and edged closer as he faced her, and Gabel knew they were intrigued by a battle between such an ill-matched pair. Gabel cursed as he realized he had been forced into a corner. He had to fight to protect himself and could only hope that he could disarm the girl without hurting her.

The clang of steel against steel echoed loudly in the small clearing. The dog, caught between the command to guard the wounded man and his urge to protect his mistress, began to howl mournfully. The horses, infected by the dog's loud agitation, also grew noisily restless. Gabel was amazed by the girl's strength and skill. It took far longer than he had anticipated for her to begin to weaken, thus giving him the advantage he sought.

When he was finally able to knock the sword from her hands, she lunged to retrieve it. He kicked it out of her reach, and she threw herself at his legs, knocking them out from beneath him. She fell upon him, yet another dagger in her hand. Gabel caught her by the wrist as she tried to thrust the point of her knife into his chest. He cursed as they rolled over the rough ground and he struggled to disarm her. The knife finally dropped from her hand, and he quickly pinned her firmly beneath his body. He could see that she was panting as heavily as he was.

"Now, mistress, be that all of your weapons?" he

asked, eager to pull away, for he was becoming all too aware of the tempting softness of her.

"Aye," she snapped, her angry tone weakened somewhat by her breathlessness. "So, ye can remove your hulking great weight."

He got to his feet, watching her closely and keeping a firm grip on her slender wrist as he pulled her up. "Answer me true, mistress. Are ye the daughter of the laird MacNairn?"

Ainslee nodded. "I am Ainslee of Kengarvey, the youngest daughter of Duggan MacNairn."

"Who is the man?"

"Ronald MacNairn, a cousin."

"Call off your dog," he ordered and almost grinned when she did, for he found the animal's name humorously fitting. "Pascal," he called to a short, balding, and stoutly built man. "Search the man and their horses for weapons. Gather whatever is at hand." He dragged Ainslee over to where one of his men was dressing Justice's wound. "Shall we survey your handiwork, Mistress MacNairn?"

Ainslee fought to hide all hint of emotion as she looked at the handsome young man's wounded shoulder. Her aim had been high, her knife piercing his smooth, brown skin high on his left shoulder. Although it was not a mortal wound, it was clearly painful. Justice's features were taut and his face lacked color. She met Justice's dark gaze with a look of complete unconcern, contrary to the turmoil she felt. It upset her to cause anyone pain, although she never hesitated to strike if the need arose.

"Feeling remorse, m'lady?" pressed Gabel, frustrated by the lack of expression on her delicate face.

"Aye. Twas not one of my better throws," she replied in a too-sweet tone. "May I see to my companion Ronald? His wound needs tending far more than this boy's pinprick." Just as she tried to pull away from the stern-faced man who held her, the man tending Justice began to cover the open wound with a piece of filthy cloth, neither washing nor dressing the wound first. Ainslee knew she could not idly stand silent and allow that. "Ye great fool," she snapped, wrenching the dirty scrap from the startled man's hand. "Do ye wish to turn a minor wound into a fatal one? This cloth is not fit to wipe a dripping nose. Get me some water."

When the man looked at him, Gabel nodded, indicating that he should obey that sharp command. He cautiously released Ainslee's wrist when she tugged at it again, allowing her to fetch a small bag next to her cousin Ronald. He found it strangely reassuring to discover that she was not as unmoved by a man's pain as she tried to pretend. When, after washing Justice's wound, she poured a dark liquid over it that clearly pained his cousin, Gabel knelt by her side and snatched the flask she held.

"What is this?" he demanded, grimacing slightly as he sniffed it.

"*Uisge-beatha*—the water of life. A strong drink we brew. How long have ye been in Scotland?"

"Long enough, but I have wit enough to abstain from tasting any of the local poisons. Why pour it o'er his wound?"

"Tis said that it will aid the healing, and it appears to do so."

"Now what do you put on him?" he asked as she smeared a gruesome-looking paste over the wound.

Ainslee sat back on her heels, rinsing clean her hands before applying a bandage, and cast the man a look of pure annoyance. " 'Tis an herbal salve to aid his healing. When ye slither back into whate'er hole ye crawled out of, ye can wash it clean and stitch the wound, then apply some more."

As she wrapped a clean strip of cloth over Justice's injury, Gabel grinned at his cousin. "An ill-tempered wench, eh?"

"A prisoner canna be expected to be all that is courteous and cheerful," Ainslee said.

"You are no prisoner, mistress, but a hostage," Gabel replied.

"There is some difference?" The man nodded as she rose to her feet, and she added, "Weel, I fear it eludes me. I will tend to Ronald now."

Gabel watched her walk away, then ordered a man to fetch their horses and the other men before looking at Justice. "The lady has a sharp tongue. How fares your shoulder?"

"Whatever the girl did has served to ease the pain," Justice replied. " 'Tis naught to concern yourself with. I have had far worse than this, although it grieves me to have suffered it at the hands of such a tiny lady." He weakly returned Gabel's grin.

"A storm still brews," Gabel murmured aloud, scowling at the sky. "We must find some shelter soon."

"We must tell them where shelter lies," Ronald said as Ainslee helped him sit up.

"I care little if the Normans suffer a true battering by the weather," Ainslee muttered.

"Nor do I, but we are now in their grasp and we shall suffer with them. We both ken that a Highland storm can be both fierce and dangerous. I dinna want us to sit out in it."

Ainslee sat beside Ronald as he called to the leader of the men and told the Norman where they could all find some shelter. She suffered from an uncomfortable mixture of anger and sadness. It puzzled her that she felt no fear. A twinge of self-disgust rippled over her as she wondered if that lack were because she found the Norman knight far too handsome for her own good.

She quickly shook aside that thought. He could easily have killed her, yet had clearly made an effort not to hurt her. She also could have been well used by him and his men by now, yet not one man had made a lustful advance toward her. Ainslee was not fool enough to think that meant that her virtue was safe, but she was growing confident that she would not be used as some communal whore. That bone-chilling fear was rapidly fading. Somehow she had realized that from the start. When she recalled her decision to take her own life if she were threatened by rape, she grimaced in self-mockery. When the Norman stepped up to her she could tell by his dark expression that she had not succeeded in hiding all her thoughts.

"Why do you look so forlorn, mistress?" he asked.

" 'Tis merely that I have had to confront my own cowardice," she replied as she stood up and walked to her horse.

Gabel kept pace with her and shook his head. "You are no coward, mistress. No man here would question your bravery. You faced me with all the courage any man could hope to show."

She knew he was speaking the highest flattery, but it did little to raise her spirits. "I am alive."

"It would have been more courageous to die?"

"Mayhap. At least in death my honor would remain untouched. I made a vow, ye see. If dishonor threatened, I would take my own life. Instead, I but talk myself out of feeling threatened. I dinna have the courage to honor my own vow."

"Dishonor does not threaten."

"Nay? And whose word am I to put my trust in? I ken ye not."

Gabel flushed as he realized he had neglected to introduce himself. "I am Sir Gabel de Amalville, and the man you skewered is my cousin and sergeant-at-arms, Sir Justice Luten. And I should not need to remind you that suicide is a mortal sin. You would be denied a resting place in consecrated ground."

"The MacNairns have been excommunicated. I dinna think I can rest in consecrated ground anyway."

"If your father would cease his lawless ways, that would quickly change."

"My father was born into a lawless land and a lawless man seeded him. I dinna think some French guest of our king will cause Duggan MacNairn to change his ways."

"I am no guest, but an anointed knight of the king and will soon hold my own lands."

Before Ainslee could reply, a low rumble rolled across the sky. " 'Tis a pleasant conversation, m'laird, but I fear it must end or we shall never find shelter ere that storm begins."

She swung up into her saddle, scowling down at him when he grasped the reins as she reached for them. A quick glance toward the others revealed Ronald and Justice being settled on hastily prepared litters despite their protests that they did not need such coddling. Ronald could not escape now, and she could not leave him behind. He was a poor man and her father would never ransom him. Ronald could be in grave danger once the Normans discovered how worthless a hostage he was. She looked back at Gabel and knew he did not really trust her to stay with them once he released the reins.

"Mayhap you should ride with me," Gabel said, his tone indicating that was an order not a request.

"I willna try to escape. Ye hold my dearest friend," she replied.

"Who would undoubtedly cheer if you should manage to slip my grasp."

"Undoubtedly. Howbeit, I didna heed his urgings to flee ere ye stumbled upon us and I willna leave him now. Aye, especially not now that I have seen how poorly ye tend the wounded." He opened his mouth to protest, but she halted his words by adding, "So, if ye willna allow me to ride alone, then I think ye should ride with me."

"Nay, I *willna* allow you to ride about alone," he drawled.

She ignored his mocking of her speech despite how it irritated her. "Then ride with me. I ken the way we must go, and my mount is verra surefooted."

"Your companion told me how to find the place."

"Then ye will be able to see if I try to lead you in the wrong direction." When he swung up behind her, she glanced at the brown arms encircling her waist, then at the strong, bare thigh touching hers. "I pray ye havena lost your clothes, Sir de Amalville, for ye will be in sore need of them when the rain starts."

He chuckled, then called to his men to follow and Ainslee immediately decided that riding two in the saddle with this man had not been a good idea. His warm breath stroked her hair and the feel of it stirred something to life deep inside her. As they rode, his legs brushed against hers, increasing that newborn feeling until she recognized it for what it was—lust.

Her body was responding to the proximity of his with alarming haste, greed, and ill-judgment.

She cursed inwardly. It was a poor time for her womanly desires to spring to life. Gabel de Amalville now held her prisoner. He had said she would not be dishonored, but they had been speaking of rape. He had not sworn not to seduce her and, if he sensed her interest, he could well try and lure her to his bed. The feelings now running through her body told her that he could probably succeed. It would not taint his honor if she went to his bed willingly. Since she had never felt attracted to a man before, she did not know how to control the wanting she now suffered, and now was a very poor time to try and learn such lessons.

A moment later, she scolded herself for being vain. She had not spent many moments of her life fighting off the unwanted attentions of men. There was no reason this man should crave what no other man had. The cajoling voice in her head gently reminding her that she had had little contact with men aside from family did not ease her self-castigation by much.

The chill touch of rain on her face yanked her from her musings, and she frowned up at the sky. "I dinna believe the rain will be kind and wait until we reach the shelter we seek."

Gabel also scowled up at the sky. "Ye are not far from it, if your companion spoke the truth."

"He did. Ronald has no desire to weather a Highland storm in the open." She glanced down at his leg and smiled when she noticed the bumps raised on his skin by the increasingly cold wind and the damp. "Ye will soon sorely regret your lack of covering."

"You are most concerned about my state of undress, mistress. Does it trouble you?"

"Only in that I have no wish to nurse even more Normans."

"A little wetting will not cause me to fall ill. It will but wash away the dust."

"A warm, French rain may weel be so refreshing, Sir Gabel. Howbeit, this is a Highland rain and 'tis late in the year. This rain will push the cold through your flesh to your verra bones."

"Then nudge your mount to a greater speed. The hill we plan to hide in is but a short trot from here."

"My horse shouldna be made to endure such a trial. He is unused to carrying such weight."

"This huge beast could carry two fully armed knights upon his strong back and little notice it." Gabel patted the animal's side.

"Aye, when he hasna already been ridden for hours and forced to flee a pack of French reivers."

"I am no reiver. Once we are in our shelter, sitting round a warm fire, we will talk. You will learn that I am no reiver once you come to know me."

That was the very last thing Ainslee wished to do. It was proving difficult to ignore the allure of his body and handsome face. He was dangerously attractive. She dreaded thinking of how much that attraction could deepen if she began to know the man, to respect or even like him. As she reined in by the mouth of the cave they sought, Ainslee prepared herself to face an ordeal—fending off Sir Gabel's attempts to charm her, to make her forget that she was a prisoner and lead her to falsely believe that she could ever be anything more.

RECEIVE

$1.00 REBATE

WITH PURCHASE OF

ONLY FOR YOU

To receive your rebate, enclose:

★ Proof of purchase symbol cut from below
★ Original cash register receipt with book price circled
★ Print information below and mail to:

ZEBRA REACH FOR THE STARS REBATE
Post Office Box 1052-F, Grand Rapids, MN 55745-1052

Name____

Address______________________________________

City____

State__________________**Zip**__________________

Store name____________________________________

State__________________**Zip**__________________

This certificate must accompany your request. No duplicates accepted. Void where prohibited, taxed or restricted. Offer available to U.S. & Canadian residents only. Allow 6 weeks for mailing of your refund payable in U.S. funds. OFFER EXPIRES 9/30/95.

PROOF OF PURCHASE
0-8217-4993-5